CRIMSON SHADOW:
FORBIDDEN DANCE

NATHAN SQUIERS

Copyright © 2013 by Nathan Squiers

Cover art by ShinyShadows (DeviantArt)

Design by Eden Crane Designs

Published by

Tiger Dynasty Publishing, LLC

This is a work of fiction. Names, characters, places, and incidents either are the product of the author's imagination or are used fictitiously. Any resemblance to actual persons living or dead, events, or locales is entirely coincidental.

If you purchased this book without a cover you should be aware that this book is stolen property. It was reported as "unsold and destroyed" to the publisher and neither the author nor the publisher has received any payment for this "stripped book."

All rights reserved. No part of this book may be reproduced or transmitted in any form or by any means, electronic or mechanical, including photocopying, recording, or by any information storage and retrieval system, without the written permission of the Publisher, except where permitted by law.

ISBN: 978-1-940634-10-4

*Dawn,
The plot thickens!*

DEDICATION

Dedicated to all those out there on the brink of a choice...

*Stay gnarly!
Nathan*

PRAISE FOR NATHAN SQUIERS

"[Nathan Squiers] can write the most brutal, horrific, and, incredibly enough, moving material. His depth of knowledge on the English language and its use for crafting emotional responses is just mind blowing. He can take you out of your comfort zone and into a hellishly elaborate nighPraise fortmare quicker and with more power than most A-listed authors."

~Zack Long (author of *The Stranger and The Man Who Will Always Be*)

"Nathan is a wordsmith of the highest caliber. I highly recommend any of his works, but be warned: come with an open mind and some plastic sheeting. It is going to get messy."

~J.H. Glaze (author of *The John Hazard* Series and *RUNE* series)

"Nathan is the hardest working man in the darkest shadows of oblivion. Yet, though his tales of evil and soul-ravaging make our spines bristle and bend, we sense the struggles of the heart in its effort to overcome self - immolation. Check him out!"

~Jon Palzer (SUNY professor of English & Literature)

ACKNOWLEDGEMENTS

The Crimson Shadow series strives ever forward, and, like Xander's legacy, the players and contributors that have allowed these books to become what they are, while still being so early in the series, are nothing short of inspiring and heartwarming.

It is to those who have been there at any point in the developmentof the series, be it the earliest stages over ten years ago or be it the most recent supporters to emerge, that the spotlight now shines on...

And—oh!—but what a grand spotlight that it is!

To even begin to try to list every cherished comrade and colleague and conspirer would demand far more words and sub-plots than this series and many others to follow will have in total.

But there still remains one specific contributor to whom I owe a great debt of gratitude:

You.

These words, this work of fiction, and, yes, all pieces of mine would not be complete without the beloved reader to channel the words, and for that most crucial of generosities I thank you.

Rock out, read on, and, as always, The Literary Dark Emperor and

The Legion love you! Nathan Squiers

(The Literary Dark Emperor).

"Perhaps an individual must consider his own death to be the final phenomenon of nature."

-Stephen Crane (1871-1900)

PROLOGUE
A BITTER HEART

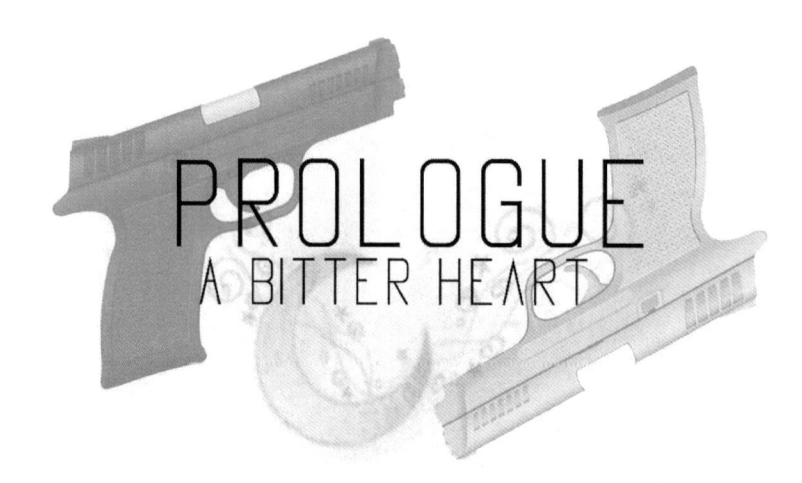

They hurt.
Merciful Earth Mother, the accursed fangs hurt ap so much!
Estella knew that they were her body's reaction to the hunger. She knew that the fangs extending like this meant they wanted her to pierce the flesh of something alive; to steal the life energy from something—goddam *anything!*—and make it a part of her.
But she simply couldn't do it!
She *wouldn't!*
Not again!
She shook her head—taking the moon pendant around her neck tightly into her hand—and clenched her teeth, hoping that if she pressed hard enough she'd break off the damned things. Instead they dug into the bottom of her gums and tore them. She ignored the pain, but relaxed her jaw.
It wouldn't work anyway.
It never did.

The band continued to play, and though she'd sat as far from the stage as possible in the darkest, most hidden corner table she could hope to hide in the sound was still unbearable. The singer—a boy wearing far too much eye makeup and wearing his pitch-black hair down one side of his face—was like a banshee; his voice ringing in her skull with every one of his so-called musical shrieks. She clenched her eyes against it and envied the humans around her who probably only heard it as though it were nothing more than soft, raspy whisper. The source of the howls strummed his electric guitar, cuing the rest of the band to pick up on the set.

Suddenly the voice didn't seem so bad anymore.

A hard *TWANG* from the bass—a deep and vibrant sound that shook like an earthquake through Estella's core— accompanied the guitars, which now coated and clung to her like a syrup of pain and made her body itch from the vibrations and body heat surrounding her. The drummer hit the cymbals and she nearly started crying.

That was it!

She had to get out of there!

Her superhuman hearing was going to kill her if she stayed any longer!

Shooting from her seat she headed for the exit, gritting her teeth and cursing the café's open mic night. A barista, delivering two steaming cups of coffee to a couple at a nearby table, tried to side-step out of her path but wound up bumping her hip with her own. Estella stumbled, hearing the girl's heartbeat hasten and sending excited torrents of life through her veins.

The roar of the music faded.

There was no sound at all...

Nothing but the rhythmic thumping of the barista's pounding heart—the only song her body cared to hear at that moment—and the blood coursing like a river just under her skin.

Her fangs extended further and it felt as though they would finally tear through her mouth in an effort to escape her starvation...

Her gums were on fire!

The barista backed up, nervously. "Oh, I'm sorry. I—"

"IT'S FINE!" Estella screamed to hear herself over the girl's heartbeat. Everybody turned to stare. She blushed and stepped back; away from the girl, whose blood was still calling to her. Her eyes darted about, seeing that everyone was staring at her and she felt a deep, gravel-thick growl crawl up her throat. "WHAT?" she roared at the staring crowd.

The band stopped in mid chorus and any who weren't staring before were now.

And all their heartbeats beat like the damn bass-drum in her head.

She covered her ears and ran, knocking the barista over on her way to the exit. Tears formed in her eyes—burning hot and blurring her vision—and she wished she could cast a spell, any kind of spell, to make it all go away.

But she didn't have the materials.

Or the focus.

The door crashed outward before she'd even reached it— reacting to her chaotic magical energies—and began to tear it from the hinges, sending the small bell fastened over the frame into a rattling frenzy that sounded like a series of gongs in her head. Behind her the crowd gasped and cried out in surprise.

So many heartbeats...

So much blood...

What was just one bite going to hurt?

"NO!" Estella slapped her palms against her temples, trying to jar the temptation from her thoughts.

The hinges finally lost their battle with Estella's wayward spell, throwing the door from its twisted frame and into the street where it crashed into a passing cab and lodged itself in the passenger-side door. Estella found enough control of her new abilities to jump into what Xander had referred to in the past as "overdrive", the sangsuigan ability that allowed them to move faster than the human eye could register. She moved down the road in a powerful-yet-energy-draining sprint, ducking and weaving between the seemingly time-frozen crowds. Her effort to distance herself from them, however, took its toll on her starved body. Unable to fuel the process any further, her exhaustion grew more intense, and though she fought to stay in overdrive—fought to get as far away as possible—the people around her appeared to move more quickly as her speed began to wane.

With her body drained, she fell out of overdrive and crashed to the sidewalk in the middle of a crowd. Startled by the spectacle of a young lady falling out of *nowhere*, the onlookers gawked while several who proved more kind than astonished closed in around her to help her up.

"Oh my god! Are you alright?"

"Did you break anything?"

"I think she's bleeding!"

"Should we call an ambulance?"

Estella's mind reeled as she scrambled away from one person only to collide with another; her fangs throbbing with the promise of blood. Her mind roared as the hunger pushed her to cross the unspeakable threshold. They were all around her! Potential prey! They were coming to her! There was no need to even hunt!

Take it.

Take it!

TAKE IT!!

"NO!"

Estella thrashed to try and clear her mind as well as the people around her. Still dizzy, she pulled herself up and looked for a gap in the crowd to break through, holding her murderous instincts at bay despite every fiber of her being pushing her to remedy her pain and exhaustion.

She sensed somebody approaching her from behind and she spun, pushing them away. Miscalculating the act and her superhuman strength, the large man was thrown off his feet and sailed into the street. An SUV leaned on its horn and screeched to a stop a short distance from him. The shocked onlookers let out a collective sigh of relief when they saw that their fellow Samaritan hadn't been run over, but his survival was not yet insured.

He'd scraped his palms...

The scent!

Estella groaned and keeled over, throwing up all over the pavement before turning and scampering off, away from the gasping and yelling crowd.

"What the hell's the matter with her?"

"She almost killed him!"

"Hey! Get back—"

But she didn't go back, didn't even look back. Instead she ran, clutching her burning stomach and pushing through anything that was in her way. By some strange miracle she made it to the bridge and the dank crate beneath it where she'd been sleeping in for the past few nights.

Nobody ever came there; it was swampy and cold and dark.

The perfect place for a monster.

The perfect place for her.

She'd been there for barely half a minute before a passing rat fell victim to her hunger and she tore into its heaving belly, ignoring the sharp little teeth that felt like a minor itch as they bore into her hand. The bites stopped quickly as she drained the creature, and as it uttered its final, pained squeaks she heaved forward, dropping it and coughing what little blood remained in her mouth all over the ground. The rodent's small body still twitched with lingering spasms, and Estella felt the first wells of scalding tears grow in her eyes at the sight of its suffering.

"Sorry..." she sobbed, "I'm so sorry..."

The display of pain and death was soon over, but the memory carried on in her mind. Over and over she saw it and all others like it that her monstrous desires had destroyed. So much pain and suffering and death. All at her own hands. All to keep herself alive.

Just to have another day and another chance to ruin another life.

But, for the time being, the pain was gone, and her fangs receded back into the hollow shafts in her gums where her canines had once been.

Waiting for when they could torture her next.

Finally able to rest, she crawled—unable to get to her feet—to the entrance of the wooden shipping crate and wrapped the ripped and dirty blanket that she had found in nearby motel's dumpster around her to keep the rising sun from touching her. Once protected from the outside world, she clenched her eyes and tried to block out the roar of the growing morning traffic overhead. Behind her eyelids, the welling tears that had blurred the blood-filled world continued to spill and she wrapped her arm around her face to stifle herself.

"Xander..." she sobbed, choking on the name as she took the moon pendant around her neck tightly into her hand "... how could you let this happen?" Her body shook with her growing rage, "GOD DAMN YOU, XANDER!"

Her vampiric strength coupled with her magic took its toll on the crate, which finally burst into fragments and left her exposed. She lay there for a long moment, trying to decide if it was worth it to finally let the sun take her. However, as tempting as the notion of freedom was, the fear of what lay beyond was too powerful to humor it for long, and she rose to her feet, pulling the blanket over her head like a shawl.

With no destination in mind, she cast her sights towards the West—away from the source of the impending morning light—and started off for her next shelter.

Wherever that may be...

Journal entry: October 31st

Estella,

I guess I should be happy that it's my birthday, but it's hard not to feel like it's just like every other day.

But that's what I get for leaving civilization, I guess.

It's been a couple of weeks now since ~~you left~~ I lost you, and while I'm sure you're long gone and will never read a word I've written here I can't stop writing and I can't stop looking.

I can't even tell you how many times I've covered the city from skyline to sewer trying to find you...

And you're probably in another ~~goddam~~ country!

I still can't believe I'm doing this. Osehr says this is my own, personal way of punishing myself. I told him it's like a journal, but he's probably right (he usually is).

~~Least I'm not trying to blow my brains out anymore...~~

So, anyway, the pack found out that it was my birthday (I blame Trepis and his big mouth) and they got all excited and tried to throw me a party. It was fun, I guess, though I would have preferred the typical chocolate cake over the wide-eyed deer's head they plopped in front of me.

I suppose it could've been worse. They could have been hanging snakes from the trees like streamers.

~~Oh shit~~... what a visual, huh?

It was alright, all in all, I suppose. I would have liked to have you here, though... but, then again, I'd like to have you with me all the time.

~~Fuck...~~

Sometimes I wake up in the middle of the day because I think I can smell you...

God! That sounds so corny, right?

Doesn't matter anyway...

I love you, Estella.
X

CHAPTER ONE
KRISS-MAS

"TELL ME OF THIS *KRISS-mas* again," Osehr barked as he leaned forward in the carved stump that served as his throne.

Xander sighed and cupped his face in his hands. Much like the fat, frigid flakes that had begun to sink the barren branches of the forest, Christmas and its heavy memories were growing harder and harder to ignore. And while Xander was not only content but outright determined to ignore the encroaching holiday, it was becoming painfully evident that neither his memories nor the company he kept would allow such a callous indulgence.

Not that he *needed* reminding.

Even if he'd been hardened enough to ignore the sprouting seeds of excitement in his comrades, the occasional supply-run out of the therion camp and into the city—with its bright, invasive lights and eager, consumer-driven bustle—served as enough of a reminder. On those outings, as he watched the chaotic and stressful scurrying of his former species, Xander was all the more thankful that he was no longer bound to their ways.

Though this Christmas would mark his second since becoming a vampire, the holiday, like all others, had long since lost its meaning. As a child, the greatest gift Xander could have been granted was a day free from the tortures of his misery-hungry-and-insatiable auric vampire of a stepfather; a gift that, holiday or not, was a rarity. Later, after his mother had been murdered at the hands of his abuser and he'd been sent to live with his grandmother, Christmas became a shadowed mockery of what he was certain it was supposed to have been. No matter how much his widowed grandmother tried, every gift he was given felt like a failed attempt to patch the shattered remains of his childhood. And, though that previous year's Christmas—spent in the company of his late-father's white tiger companion, Trepis, and his vampire mentor, Marcus, who, while sporting a Santa-style hat, had given him the gift of a shattered collarbone during a training session—had brought with it an awkward comfort, Marcus' death several months earlier had put a sour tone on the memory.

However, as he'd learned the previous year when he'd finally put a bullet in the brain of the bastard responsible for destroying his childhood, vengeance did nothing to squelch the pain of loss. And, though this lesson had been well-kept in Xander's heart, killing Marcus' murderer, Lenix, had reawakened his understanding of just how futile his efforts had been.

And at what cost?

Aside from Marcus and his pride, Lenix had robbed him of his home and his purpose.

Robbed him of his motivation.

His legacy.

And, as if that had not been enough, Lenix had robbed him of *her*.

Estella.

Her name had become a constant fixture in the back of his mind, keeping him ever-mindful of how he'd allowed his closest, dearest friend and lover to come to harm; to be taken and subjected to the diabolical plot of the scornful Lenix and, finally, to be bitten—to be *turned*—and left to fester on the undeniable fact that Xander had failed to protect her and, in doing so, condemned her to a life that demanded the pain and death of others. Day-after-day Xander dreamed of her, and, day-after-agonizing-day, he saw the pain and anguish on her face when she'd awoken to discover the fate that had befallen her.

"*I can never forgive you for this.*"

If there had been any hint of holiday cheer in him before, there was no doubt in his mind that those seven words would have eradicated them over and over again.

Xander scowled and looked down.

"*I can never forgive you for this.*"

Hearing the ghostly vow resound in his mind, Xander felt a tear well in his right eye—a blood-stained orb courtesy of Lenix—and moved to wipe away the moisture before it had a chance to spring free and roll down his cheek.

He shook his head and let out a misty sigh.

"Fucking Christmas..."

Osehr cocked his head in confusion and leaned forward expectantly.

"*Kriss-mas*," he pressed, "Will you tell me more of this custom?"

Dragging his focus from the past, Xander shifted his gaze to the therion pack's leader. Being a solitary and isolated pack, the therions that he was staying with had no notion of the human holiday. To them, the concept of a *scheduled* festivity was unheard of—their focus being on a successful hunt or a won battle over their territory—and they approached all celebrations, no matter the occasion, with vast amounts of meat, guttural songs and clumsy dances.

It was no surprise that they had caught on to Thanksgiving with relative ease.

Xander didn't mind, however, and even appreciated the escape from the old ways. The therions had accepted him when he'd had no other place to go—nobody else to rely on—and that meant a lot to him.

Especially since it was more in their nature to shift into hulking beasts at the slightest sign of trouble and eviscerate the problem.

And even more so since it was because of him that their leader was missing an arm.

Though the wound that Osehr had suffered during a battle against Lenix and an army of mind-enslaved mythos creatures—the *same* battle that had marked Marcus' last—seemed to bother the beaming therion. Even then his worn and weathered face was as bright and cheery the holiday décor as it had been the first time the young vampire had mentioned it in passing. Though the eager and child-like expression was an awkward sight when plastered on the face of the aged shapeshifter—a face that normally wore the stern appearance of what Xander imagined a war-hardened grandfather might look like—Xander was unable to appreciate the humor. Sighing, he looked away from Osehr and watched as Trepis and a few of the younger therions darted about in the snow a short distance away, trying to think of yet another way to describe the holiday to the impatient elder.

Finally, finding himself at a total loss and tired of trying to fake it, he shook his head, "It's just another stupid human tradition."

"Nothing worth celebrating is stupid," Osehr bared his teeth as he chuckled, and Xander couldn't be certain if it was a threatening gesture or not.

Xander rolled his eyes. "If you say so," he watched his white tiger let out an excited growl as it rolled in the snow.

"So why do they celebrate this day?"

Xander shrugged his left shoulder absently, "It's... well, it happens around this time of year, in the month of December—"

"Dee-sem-ber," the therion played with the word.

Xander nodded, "Yea, December. Fun word, right?"—he couldn't help but smirk—"So, anyway, every year they have this one day near the end of the month when they get together with friends and family and give each other gifts."

The therion frowned, "Why?"

Xander shrugged. "Because they're greedy bastards who either want more shit or want credit for giving the best shit."

The two laughed.

"But you were once human; once just as greedy as the rest of them, yes? Why do you not like this *Kriss-mas* now?" Osehr asked, "Was the shit you were given not to your liking?"

Xander shook his head, "No, nothing like that. If there was anything my life never fell short on it was an abundance of shit, it was just..." he sighed, "It's complicated."

"It does not sound complicated. Family. Friends. Gifts." Osehr laughed and clapped his hand against the side of his stump-throne, "Quite simple!"

Xander laughed, "This is a *human* celebration, Osehr! They're not happy unless everything is as complicated as possible; the more misery they can burden themselves with the more they can blame for *staying* miserable." Xander glanced over at the therion leader, "Even something as simple as Christmas has its rules and restrictions. It's all about this... well, a lot of beliefs; beliefs that I just stopped believing in."

Osehr nodded, though Xander was sure he didn't understand what he'd said. Finally he smiled, "I believe that this *Kriss-mas* sounds fun!"

Xander smirked, "Maybe you're just a greedy bastard too."

They laughed again, Osehr bellowing harder while Xander's chuckles went unnoticed by even himself. The therion elder sat forward in his throne, still barking out his cackles, and slapped Xander's shoulder.

Even with only arm, Osehr had enough strength to nearly throw Xander from his seat.

Osehr nodded, "Yes, I think I'd like to try this custom of gathering with friends and family."

"Gathering with... *really*?" Xander scoffed, looking up at his friend, "You gather with the pack every night! Hell, you even celebrate with them *at least* four times a week!"

"Ah, we do. We do," Osehr nodded as a wide curl stretched the corner of his lips, "but we don't give gifts, do we?"

Xander rolled his eyes, "Yea. Great custom," he chuckled and shook his head, "Good luck wrapping your deer antlers!"

Another wave of bark-cackles issued from Osehr and, with them, another series of sledgehammer-like slaps to Xander's shoulder. "Oh Xander! Your wit is most welcome in our pack"— Xander, though no longer facing the therion, could sense the playful roll of his aura and knew that he was grinning again—"were it not for your humor, we'd have probably eaten you by now!"

Despite the playful tone and matching auric signals, Xander didn't doubt his words.

"Not much on me to eat, Osehr," Xander cocked his head in his direction and smirked, "or is that why you have me gorge myself on deer blood every night?"

"Perhaps," Osehr's grin widened until he could no longer hold in his laughter and let it erupt from his chest once again. As his most recent bout of full-body cackles died down, Xander watched him suck in a deep breath—the old therion's face now blood-red—and restore his excited smile to his calming expression. "So," he began, his voice still sounding forced from his heavy breaths, "what would *you* want for *Kriss-mas*?"

Before Xander could even hope to stop it, Estella's face rolled to the top of his boiling mind; her bright blue eyes and exuberant face framed by her short-cut, raven-black hair. The vision was relentless in Xander's mind, and even without the benefit of her physical form he could feel her passion and intensity—could feel her *magic*—rolling through him as though she was seated beside him. He remembered the love she'd shown him, giving him her body and soul...

And then he remembered what he'd told her.

I promise that everything will be alright.

He felt his jaw tighten as he clenched his teeth; his fists following suit. From deep within his core, he could feel his aura beginning to whip and writhe with the urge to destroy. As he fought to suppress an outburst, the energies started to turn inward and made him feel like he was being cooked from the inside-out.

What did he want for Christmas?

The question seemed to mock him, and Osehr's impatient gaze grew too demanding to ignore. Xander closed his eyes and let out a long exhale, forcing his body to relax before he did something he knew he'd regret later.

"Nothing," he lied, "I got used to not getting anything a long time ago."

The night drew on, and though the therion leader said nothing more of the human holiday that intrigued him so much Xander knew that he was cooking something up. He didn't fight it; knowing full well that Osehr was a stubborn and aggressive arguer who would ultimately have his *Kriss-mas* if he wanted it. Plus, the silence allowed him to dwell more on his memories of Estella, and once again left him asking the same questions he did every night.

Where was she?

Was she alright?

And—by far the most persistent question in his mind—was there a chance he could make things right? Despite her last words to him, could she ever forgive him for not being there when she needed him most?

For allowing Lenix to turn her into a vampire...

He sighed again and excused himself from Osehr's side, preferring to be alone with his thoughts. Shuffling out of the clearing and under the canopy of snow-covered treetops, he headed for his tent on the outskirts of the pack's territory, where the trees' overlapping branches blocked out most of the sunlight. Trepis, seeing him start off, quickly followed after, tracing Xander's steps and replacing his smaller tracks with those of the tiger's massive paw prints. He smiled at this and rubbed the tiger's head as it took its place beside him and matched his pace.

Though Lenix was long-since gone—Xander having snapped his neck before burying him under the rubble of a collapsed parking garage—he'd left his mark. Just like the year before that when he'd caught Xander off guard and left him with a blood-red right eye, there was an unmistakable stain on his life. With both his mentor and his lover out of the picture, he had nobody to turn to, no place worth calling home...

And no purpose.

With the lingering hope that he might still be able to find Estella, he'd stayed. Though every part of him wanted to escape—either to someplace far from the memories or simply to reacquaint himself with the receiving end of his gun in the hopes of finally dying—he still felt compelled to drive on; still felt compelled to stay.

"There is *always* one more thing to live for," he grumbled his own mantra to himself, feeling trapped behind its meaning.

Having nowhere else to turn, he'd sought the hospitality of the therions who'd helped him to fight Lenix several months earlier. Despite the nearly unlimited funds at his disposal—both from the now-destroyed Odin Clan's private accounts as well as his and Marcus' sizable earnings as bounty hunters—he'd seen no reason to indulge in anything resembling a luxury. It was with this mindset that he'd established his "home". For the first few weeks he'd spent his days huddled in a small cave, which grew unpleasant enough to convince him to stock up on whatever would make his new lifestyle as a vampire hermit a less miserable one. The tent he'd gotten included several compartments—what the salesperson had referred to as "rooms"—which allowed Xander to organize his belongings. The smallest section housed several coolers that he kept constantly stocked with "super sang juice"; a magically-charged synthetic blood that his weapons expert had concocted. Despite its name, the stuff was potent enough to keep Xander's needs sated. The next dome-like compartment was bigger, and was filled with several trunks that he kept stocked with clothes and supplies. The largest dome, where the simple flap that served as the tent's only entrance and exit, was his sleeping area and "living room" where he'd set up an air mattress, a sleeping bag, and a few pillows. Also inside this were a radio—a device that a majority of the therions enjoyed listening to and had even helped the pups begin to learn English—as well as a small space heater.

And then there was the notebook.

With all of the things that Xander had bought it was the notebook that he cherished the most. Had the heater blown and set the entire tent on fire, it was this that he would have run in after to save.

Since moving into the woods he'd taken to writing letters to his old friend. He wasn't sure why he did it; they were, after all, undeliverable. Despite this and the many other reasons that existed to not bother with the heart wrenching task, he wrote in the notebook each morning as the sun was rising. Most of the time they were nothing more than random thoughts that he wished to share, but, occasionally—in the midst of his written rants—apologies and pleas for forgiveness bled through. It was when this happened that he found himself hurting the most.

Reaching his tent just as the first rays of the sun peaked over the barren tree branches and through the scattered pines, Xander fought to ignore the itchy warmth as the UV struck the side of his face. Though there was no denying that it *was* an irritating sensation, it was not nearly as dramatic and fatal—at least in small doses—as the legends led on. Still, while he could find solace in the knowledge that he wouldn't soon be bursting into a pile of ashes, it was enough to urge him to hasten his already purposeful stride. He sighed at the sensation, still petting Trepis on the head, and allowed himself to rub his cheek with his free hand as he finished his trek to the tent. Daring a glance at the sunrise, he watched the golden orb's emergence from the purple sky as he finished scratching the tiger behind his ear, just next to the knick he'd gotten from trying to protect his father during the attack that had taken his life.

With the burning itch spreading further across his exposed flesh and the urge to punt newborns growing, he turned his attentions away from the spectacle and opened the zipper to the tent. Beautiful or not, sunlight brought out the worst in his kind. Trepis let out a small noise—not quite a growl or a roar, but an attention-getter nonetheless—and Xander looked at his friend with a smile.

"You want to play some more, don't you?" he asked, not expecting an answer. Trepis sat back and raised a hind leg and scratched at an itch. Xander smirked and nodded his head back towards the therions' camp, "Go on then. I'm sure the pups are missing you already." He knelt down and rubbed the big cat's chin with his palm, "Thanks for walking with me."

Trepis panted happily as Xander reached gently out with his aura and "spoke" with him; sharing mental images and basic emotions with the tiger. Soon after, his friend made another noise—happier this time—and loped back towards his therion friends.

He lingered a moment longer outside the tent as he watched the white tiger head deeper into the thickness of the trees and smiled. Though things had been hard—hell, downright shitty—there was something in Trepis' excitement that made him believe that the chaos of his life might finally be over. He smirked as he thought about Osehr and the idea of a therion Christmas.

"*Kriss-mas...*" he mused to himself.

Finally, with the inherent irritation of the sun's poisonous effects beginning to sink in, he pushed himself through the opening in the tent and headed towards the "back" of his tent for some synthetic blood before starting to write in the notebook.

Journal Entry: November 1st

Estella,

The snow is starting to come down hard now. I'm getting more and more glad I got the supplies like Osehr suggested. I feel embarrassed that I didn't think of it myself, but I was never the thinking type...

That was always your thing, wasn't it?

I dreamt about you again last night, though it wasn't the same one as usual. You and I were fighting Lenix, but you didn't run away this time... and I remember feeling so happy that you'd stayed. There was this part where you'd pinned him down and I was about to take the shot, but then I began to realize that it wasn't the way it had really happened, and Lenix pulled free and killed you...

... took you away from me even though you'd decided to finally stay.

And when ~~that motherfucker~~ he finally turned around to face me again, he had my face and my guns.

And then I realized that it had been me all along...

Even after I woke up I couldn't shake the feeling that everything that's happened has been my fault. If only I'd been there when he came for you!

Instead of out trying to figure out what I already should have known to be true.

Everything I needed was right there!

And I handed it all over.

~~Fuck!~~

I feel like such a ~~fucking~~ IDIOT!!

~~I mean, I had you! I finally got a taste of what I'd always dreamed of having and I turned my back on it because I was too fucked up to know better!~~

~~Sometimes I wonder what I'm still doing he~~

~~I tell myself to imagine the good like everyone else does when shitty thoughts like these come to haunt them, but all it does is make it hurt more. It's like twisting the damn knife after it's been stuck in you!~~

~~And then all I can imagine is that whoever this "imagine the good" asshole is needs to be stabbed in the fucking ribs and have the blade twisted just as a reminder.~~

~~"Imagine the good"??~~

~~Yea fucking right!~~

~~Maybe I'll find some fucking sunshine remembering about when I was human and I'd torture myself with the thoughts of my mother and what that sick bastard did to her.~~

But who can I blame for all of that?

I mean, I know that what happened to you was my fault (believe me, I know! I haven't forgotten). But how far back can I go before I finally find who's responsible for ALL of it? Was it Lenix for killing my father? Was it Depok for making Lenix what he became? Or could it have been my mother and grandma...?

CRIMSON SHADOW: FORBIDDEN DANCE

I mean, I loved them both, and I HATE to think that they could have done anything wrong... but they're the ones who kept me from the truth for so goddam long!

But if I'd have been a vampire all this time I'd have never met you at all...

...

The whole thing makes you wonder if fate does exist.

Was I fated to hurt like this?

~~Was losing you a part of some grand asshole's shitty plan?~~

...

Philosophy sucks, doesn't it?

I know! We'll just blame me for all of it and say "to hell" with all this fate crap!

Works for me.

Love you always,
X

CHAPTER TWO
SANCTUARY

DESPITE THEIR BEST efforts to blend in, the small mythos group could feel the analytical gazes of the surrounding humans, who turned and stared at the bizarre spectacle as it passed. While they would have preferred to remain unnoticed, it was not at all surprising that onlookers would take notice. Though they *were*, for the most part, dressed just like everyone else occupying the city streets that night, even they understood that, as a group, they were undeniably out of place.

Zeek sighed as another passing group paused to study them and whispered amongst themselves. He considered taking a swing at them with his staff, but knew that that would solve nothing and, in the end, land them in even more hot water than they were already treading.

Besides, he couldn't *really* blame them.

At nearly six-and-a-half feet tall and standing at the head of the group, Zeek wore an outfit of neutral-yet-mismatched colors underneath a long, tan duster, which only helped to call attention to his too-pale skin and intense emerald eyes. His light brown hair, splaying out from under a too-large, bright-red baseball cap that he wore to hide his long, pointy ears, fell halfway down his back and whipped about with every long stride he took. However, despite the stoic anapriek's attire, it was the seven-foot wooden staff—which he made a poor attempt at passing off as some sort of walking support—that drew the most attention to him.

 Just behind him and walking side-by-side to each other were the therion sisters Karen and Sasha. Where there were some similarities that allowed them to pass as the siblings they were, the traits that made each unique made for a very obvious night-and-day comparison between the two. This effect was made all the more noticeable as they seemed to mirror the other's stride without the slightest effort. Both had dark skin that was the color of honey at night and the same dark brown hair and fierce and predatory yellow-green eyes of their wolf-cousins, and they both had strong, lean bodies that stretched and coiled with every movement they made like a tightened spring. Karen, who had always prided herself on formality, was more reserved and casual than her sister and dressed mostly in blue—her favorite color—and kept her hair short and simple to manage. Sasha, however, who'd always preferred to attract attention where her sister seemed to dodge it, had allowed her hair to grow long and wild like an exotic plant and opted to wear fiery-bright ensembles of tight-fitting and skimpy clothes that showed off her ample feminine assets.

 At the very back of their haphazard convoy, as usual, was Satoru. Always the shy and silent type, the nejin always hid his cat-like features and small assortment of bladed weapons under thick layers and anything with a hood. While effective in hiding his clearly inhuman form, the excessive layers made him look like a walking laundry hamper and only served to call further attention to him.

 All in all, however, it was little Timothy, a ten year old vampire with a short, black ponytail, scuffed sneakers, and wearing a pair of faded jeans and an Adventure Time tee-shirt—a perfectly average-looking child without a single oddity working against him—who was the most out of place within the group.

So, while the staring and muttering of the human onlookers was not only unsettling, but downright unwanted, Zeek didn't resent it and couldn't bring himself to act against it.

Besides, they had more pressing matters to worry about.

Timothy was hungry...

And tired...

And growing more-and-more cranky.

And with the threat of the ten year-old sangsuiga's temper-tantrum drawing nearer, it was no surprise that the others, suffering just the same, were becoming tense.

There were only five of them left, and though what remained of their unconventional "family" had finally made it into the city there was a no denying the heavy losses they'd suffered. Ever since the hunters' attack on their home—a home that Timothy's parents had worked long and hard on turning into a safe haven for all breeds and creeds of mythos wanderer—they'd been running and suffering the loss of more and more of their comrades at the merciless hands of their pursuers. No matter how hard they tried, they couldn't seem to shake the hunters, who had continued to pick off their numbers one-by-one until they were all that was left.

And there was not a single mind among them that believed the hunters were finished or that they had given up the chase.

They were still being hunted.

They all knew it.

Especially Zeek.

"Come on," he urged the group, pausing long enough to herd all of them across the street, using his left arm to gently nudge each one to continue moving as they past while checking to be sure his ears were still tucked under his hat with his right. "Just a little further. Then we'll be able to rest."

Timothy whimpered as Zeek's hand met the small of his back and an extended fang poked past his lower lip, "B-but I'm so *hungry!*" he wailed, the force of his resistance forcing Zeek to finally pick him up and step out of the street.

Zeek was doing his best to keep them strong; doing everything he could to keep those that had become his family from falling victim to the hunters' wrath. The others were strong in their own right, but none of them had the training or fortitude to deal with what was happening to them. Despite this, however, Zeek had made a note of telling everyone in their small group that he was proud of each and every one of them.

Especially Timothy.

Who had begun to kick and pitch within his arms.

"HUNGRY!"

Sighing, Zeek returned the thrashing vampire child to his feet when they were safely at the sidewalk, "I know, Tim. I know," he sighed and instinctively checked his ears again before scanning their surroundings for some hint as to where they should go, "And I'm working on finding food, but you've got to be—"

The gentle plea was drowned out by the first shrill wail and the others tensed.

Strong and able as he was, Zeek couldn't help but flinch as well. He was in a foreign land with a ragtag crew of untrained mythos, and he was feeling increasingly out of his element.

Normally, an anapriek was only as strong as its best hiding place, and in that regard Zeek was beginning to feel they wouldn't survive the night.

But before anything else, he'd need to find some blood for Timothy...

Zeek sighed and straightened himself, knowing that there was nothing he could say that would help to calm the little vampire. With the others watching him with expectant eyes, he turned his gaze towards Satoru. Because he'd been the last one to join the group before the attack, Satoru had put all the blame of the attack on their home and the murder of Timothy's parents on himself and, in an ongoing effort to uphold his personal sense of honor, very rarely missed an opportunity to try and redeem himself to the little vampire. Giving a slight nod, Zeek could see the whiskered lips of the nejin shift as he nodded his understanding to the silent plea and stepped away from the group; a thin, short knife falling free from the sleeve of his hoodie and coming to rest in his palm. The fluidity of the gesture would have looked like a magic trick to an unfamiliar eye, and, though they knew that there was nothing magical about it, Zeek and the others knew better than to take Satoru and his skills with a blade lightly. Slipping into a nearby alley with the stealth and mystery of a shadow their comrade vanished from sight, and even Timothy—still whimpering and sniffling from hunger—was forced to fall into a stunned hush at the spectacle of the nejin's skill.

Barely five seconds had lapsed before the first—and last—sound echoed past the concrete confines, and though the shrill wail of the alley cat was not something to be ignored, it was short lived and, as a result, easily forgotten by any late-night passersby. A moment later Satoru's shadowed outline appeared at the mouth of the alley and Zeek guided Timothy to his waiting meal.

While Timothy satiated his thirst on the stray, Zeek offered a sympathetic nod to Satoru, whose eyes reflected the sadness at what he'd had to do, before turning towards the others as they made their way to his side.

Several minutes later Timothy had finished, and Sasha went about helping to clean the trace amounts of blood from his chin, playfully scolding him as he wrestled to dodge her attempts. Finally, once he was presentable, she nodded her approval and reminded him to mind his manners and gestured towards Satoru.

Blushing, the little vampire looked up at Satoru with a broad smile. "T-ank 'ou," he struggled to speak around his still unsheathed fangs.

Satoru's features shifted slightly from under the hood and he dipped his head in a gesture that was part nod and part bow.

"We should keep moving; try to find him tonight," Karen offered as she joined Zeek at his side.

Zeek scowled but nodded and motioned for the group to follow him as he lead them from the alley. "He'd better be there," he muttered, "I don't want all of this all to have been for nothing."

His lover gave his hand a slight squeeze, and though he knew it was for reassurance he couldn't help but feel that she, too, was worried.

With nothing more to delay their journey, the group started

down the sidewalk and towards the east, where the trees began to outnumber the buildings. For several miles they walked, Timothy skipping up ahead—energized by his recent meal—while the others kept a steady pace behind him.

"He'd better be there," Zeek repeated to himself.

⸻⸻

The sun was just setting as Xander stepped out of his tent.

While the final rays of UV that caressed his skin were irritating and rage-inducing, he had, for the past few months at least, taught himself to bear the sensation so that he could take in the last few moments of daylight. After losing Estella—with her warm smile and bright-orange aura—and the sliver of humanity that she represented, trying to recapture those traits while simultaneously punishing himself seemed a fitting way of honoring her memory. That, and living with the therions had taught him to appreciate nature, and he could think of no greater moment than one that turned the entire sky purple and orange...

... and red.

To hell with rainbows, the best colors in nature were in the bleeding skies of dusk and dawn!

Trepis was already there when he stepped out, the big cat's head rising as he heard the sound of the tent's zipper and a big, audible yawn emerged from his gaping maw. The tiger sat up beside him, watching the sky as well and letting the event bathe its beauty across his white-and-black fur. Xander smiled at his friend and laid a hand on his head, not petting, but simply letting it rest there. The contact sparked a loud, rumbling purr, and, feeling less burdened by the dwindling UV, he returned his eyes to the darkening sky.

Before nightfall was completely upon them, however, the last few moments were interrupted by a crashing in the brush a short distance away, and Xander sighed as he realized that one, if not more, of the youngsters was probably coming to retrieve Trepis for more of their games. He looked away from the sky and waited for their company to emerge. When it finally did he was surprised to see Tarlin—one of the pack's older therions—break through the shrubbery and approaching on all fours. Xander could see that he was in a hurry, and, as Tarlin was rarely one to seek amusement, he knew it wasn't to play with the Trepis or ask Xander for one of his stories like some of the other therions did so often. Realizing that something must have been wrong and eager to know what it could be, he began to close the distance between them.

Tarlin was panting when they finally came face-to-face, and it took a moment for him to catch his breath after he transformed back to his human form. Though Xander was more than aware of the pain that the transformation put them through, the old therion was too proud to show it as his body twitched and snapped—the excess bulk withering away like a deflating balloon—back into its human form.

Xander frowned, not wanting to rush the therion but eager to know what was so important, "I hope whatever's going on is important enough to have an asthma attack over," he joked. Tarlin looked at him, confused. Xander rolled his eyes; of course he didn't know what asthma was. "So...?" he pressed.

Tarlin took another deep breath and straightened his posture to something more human-like before pointing back at their clearing, "Outsiders!" his voice was a deep growl, "Not human! Close to throne!"

Narrowing his eyes, Xander studied his friend, "Not human? You mean mythos?" he shook his head, "And the pack didn't just kill them?"

"Wanted to," Tarlin nodded, "Many ready to kill, but no kill. Osehr say 'no kill', so we no kill. Osehr say find you; say 'send fastest' to find you—sent Tarlin," he beamed and offered a toothy smile before pointing back once again, "Outsiders close! Not human! Osehr say 'no kill; find Stryker'! Many want outsiders dead now! Stryker come!"

Xander frowned and shook his head. He knew Osehr and his code against allowing outsiders into their territory. Hell, he'd nearly killed Xander *twice* when they'd first met just for entering the area without permission, and they'd at least known him by that point. To have the therion leader hold his pack at bay meant something. "Do you know why Osehr is letting them live?"

Tarlin shook his head quickly, his long brown hair shifting

like a lion's mane. "No say. Just tell us 'no kill'. Said get you."

Xander nodded and followed the therion away from his camp and towards the clearing with Trepis keeping up behind them. As he pushed through the dividing foliage, he dared another question, "Did you get a look at the outsiders?"

"Yes," Tarlin sounded proud for that fact, "They mixed up."

Xander ducked under a tree branch and kept on, looking at his friend with a curious eye. "'Mixed up'?"

Tarlin nodded, "Yes. Like can of nuts you bring Tarlin two moons ago," he frowned as he realized his explanation wasn't helping and illustrated by pressing his fingertips together and just as quickly dividing them, "Not same. Two therions"—he grinned—"*girl* therions."

Xander rolled his eyes, "And?"

"They travel with a cat-man, a little vampire," he suddenly growled, interrupting himself, "and anapriek."

"An *anapriek*?" Xander stopped and studied the therion with a skeptical eye. It was rare for therions to travel outside of their own kind, and it was even rarer for them to travel with an anapriek. The fairy-slash-elf beings were known within the mythos community as "the *other* other white meat" due to their potent blood and, from what Xander had been told, irresistible meat. Though The Council had laws against killing, let alone *eating*, fellow non-humans, it was not uncommon for an anapriek carcass to be found either eaten or drained of blood. Or worse. Xander shook his head again and pinched the bridge of his nose. This was just getting more and more bizarre. Letting out a deep sigh, he moved his hand away from his face and looked at Tarlin, "You're sure about that."

The therion nodded, "Tarlin sure," his voice sounded insulted that Xander would even question it. "Tarlin *very* sure," he tapped his index finger against the side of his nose, "Tarlin know anapriek smell."

Xander nodded, showing his friend that, as unbelievable as his story was, his trust was unwavering, and the two continued towards the clearing. Before they'd come into view of the pack and the newcomers, Xander reached out with his aura and allowed his mind's eye to explore the newcomers:

An exhausted-looking young sangsuiga, barely out of his baby fangs, huddled beside a stoic nejin who was hiding more than a dozen blades under his baggy hoody. Several paces away were the two female therions and, sure enough, a bold-looking anapriek who stood at the front of the group gripping a long wooden staff as he looked Osehr straight in the eye. While Osehr's aura gave away that he wasn't happy about the newcomer's brashness, he remained seated at his throne and made subtle gestures to any in the pack who started to show any sign of agitation.

Xander shook his head as he "saw" all of this in his auric sweep. Anapriek or not, a newcomer on the pack's turf who decided to lock gazes with the therion leader would not last long.

He turned to Tarlin and motioned for him to leave, knowing better than to add another irritated packmate to the equation. "I'll take care of this," he promised. The therion nodded, though he was clearly disgruntled by the situation, and ran off, leaping into the trees and soon disappearing in the distance. When he was gone, Xander looked down at Trepis and touched his aura to the tiger's head to convey the message he wanted.

Stay.

It was a simple enough command, but one that weighed heavy in the tiger, whose aura whipped and writhed in response to the growing tension. Xander knew that Trepis didn't want to let him step into that clearing on his own, but he couldn't risk his friend's life if these newcomers *did* turn out to be a threat. Huffing his protest, Trepis walked in a tight circle before plopping himself on the ground.

Confident that his companion wouldn't get in the way, Xander ran ahead and into the clearing, stopping between Osehr and the pack's unwelcome visitors. Though his weapons were back in the tent he was confident that he could take them all out on his own if the occasion called for it, especially with only two of them actually armed.

The anapriek took a cautious step back at his emergence, though neither his features nor his aura gave away any sign of fear, and his gaze shifted from the therion leader to his own.

Xander sneered, ignoring the sweet and alluring scent of the mythos' blood—it would appear that the rumors *had* been true—and peeked over his shoulder at Osehr. Using his aura to establish a psychic connection with the pack leader, he asked the burning question.

What's this about?

Though it was rare for a therion to have any auric control, Osehr had proven himself an exception to the "rule", having taught himself how to psychically connect with others, a trick that, while not impossible, was impressive nonetheless. It had been with this skill that he'd first tracked Xander down several months ago to explain that his life was in danger, and it was how he now responded outside of the visitors' awareness.

They've come asking for you.

Xander frowned, eyeing them again and looking back at Osehr, *Well I don't know them.*

I know, Osehr replied, *But they were insistent, and I decided I'd leave it up to you whether or not they die.*

After a moment of watching the two stare in silence the anapriek cleared his throat to remind them that they were still there.

Xander turned his attention to the newcomers and sighed, not wanting to deal with whatever it was they were bringing into his life. "You have five minutes to explain yourselves before I let my friends turn you all into tonight's feast." As he said this the little sangsuigan shuddered and clung to the nejin, who tensed and reached for his knife.

The anapriek, though his gaze was still locked with Xander's, held up his hand to calm the growing tension behind him. When the two had settled down once again, he opened his mouth to speak, "You are the son of Joseph Stryker?"

Xander frowned at the question and studied the small group, "I suppose that all depends on who's asking?"

The anapriek stared at him with cold, emotionless eyes—not at all the exuberant and magic-filled ones that were attributed to his kind—before finally deciding that Xander was, in fact, who they were looking for. He offered a slight nod as he dropped to one knee, the others in the group following the gesture, and extended his staff hand towards him, "We require your aid,

Stryker."

The woods hushed as the collective tension from the entire pack suddenly shifted from agitation to confusion.

Xander's eyes widened at the group that knelt before him and, for the first time since he'd become a vampire, he retreated. Though he'd only taken two steps before regaining his composure, the long strides away from the group were an undeniable act that he already felt haunted by. Clearing his throat, he forced himself to take the first step towards them once again, "Aid with what, exactly?"

"We are being hunted; my family and I," the anapriek explained, "Many of us have already been killed"—the little vampire whimpered and buried his face into the nejin's side— "and I know that they will not stop until we are all dead."

"Hunted?" Xander frowned. He'd heard of mythos hunters— humans who had trained and studied to take out their kind—but had never directly dealt with any. For the most part, their efforts were directed towards mythos that posed as a blatant threat to humans, and those types of mythos were usually already being tracked by Council-appointed warriors for extermination. If nothing else, human hunters were doing them a favor. However, as he looked over the visitors and scanned their minds he saw that they were not dangerous or law-breaking rogues that would need to be dispatched; nothing that should have caught the eye of *anybody*—mythos or human alike—as something worth terminating. Which could only mean one thing...

The hunters were killing for sport.

He sighed and shook his head. "Are they tracking you?" he asked, already knowing the answer.

The anapriek nodded.

He growled angrily and took a heavy step forward, "Then you've already led them here!"

The threatening advance was met with a sudden combat stance from the anapriek, who was off his knee and prepared to defend himself in the blink of an eye, the staff held in front of him in preparation. The anapriek's stance and resolve were strong, but Xander could already count four key weak points that were left unguarded. Xander sneered and, using his vampire speed, took the end of the staff in his hand and whipped it away from him. As the anapriek's eyes went wide with realization of his folly, the opposite end of the staff swung behind him and caught the back of his knee, dropping him to the forest floor with Xander standing over him with the staff still clutched in his hand. "You've led them here," Xander repeated as he bared his fangs and crouched down, closing the distance between himself and the fallen anapriek, "You've led them to *my* family!"

"They're not close," he promised, "Not yet, anyway. But they *will* find us, and we are not equipped or prepared to defend ourselves," he locked his gaze with Xander's, "Not like you."

Xander shook his head in disbelief, "You've come *here* looking for protection?" he made a show of looking around him, illustrating their surroundings, "Does this look like a fucking stronghold to you?" he allowed his sweeping arm to point towards a small pod of therions waiting for the signal to rip them apart, "And do they look like your fucking bodyguards?"

The short-haired therion growled and stepped forward, "Watch your language in front of the boy!"

Xander frowned, narrowing his eyes at the strange therion before looking at the little vampire, who tightened his grip on the nejin's hip. Something in the boy shone with familiarity; something pained...

Shaking his head, Xander looked away from the boy and snarled, "You come *here* asking *me* for help and then tell me how I'm supposed to *act*?" he threw out his aura and made a note of ruffling the earth around them to illustrate his power. "*You're* the ones that jumped into the fire to avoid the frying pan!"—he jabbed a finger towards them—"*You're* the ones that brought the boy here!"—he took a step towards her—"And *you're* the ones who have endangered these innocents just so you might— MIGHT!—have a chance at survival! Now, tell me again why I should watch my *fucking* mouth in front of an issue that *you* **chose** to bring here!"

The therion yelped at the display and clung to the risen anapriek's arm for protection. Seeing this, a collective gasp rose from the entire pack, echoing down from the trees. Though the bizarre union was nothing short of a taboo to the therions,

Xander wasn't swayed by the idea of an anapriek-therion union. He had better things to worry about.

"Our apologies," the anapriek said, making a show to the other therions of sliding his arm free from his lover's grasp, "Both our losses and our travels have taken a toll on us and our manners. We've become very close with the boy and only wish to raise him as his parents would have wanted."

Xander frowned at that and took another look at the little vampire. He was afraid—outright terrified, in fact—and his aura told of the sort of pain and loss that Xander knew all too well. Taking another sweeping glance over the group, he could see that they were all just as scared and pained, though their efforts to appear strong for the boy weren't easy to see past.

But there was no denying the desperation they all wore on their auras.

Whatever had happened to them, they were convinced that he was their only hope.

Xander sighed and nodded, "Osehr, our guests are going to need something to eat," he looked at the little vampire again, "be sure that they bring plenty of deer blood." Already missing the serenity of the sunset, he wiped the excess sleep from his eyes and looked back at the anapriek.

"Now... tell me everything."

CHAPTER THREE
WELCOME TO CHAOS

DEREK AND MARY HAD stowed away a great deal of wealth during the course of their mutually prosperous lives, and while success and money certainly made for comfortable living, it did not provide them with a sense of accomplishment. More than anything else, however, they found the tedious lifestyle of the rich to be a lonely one, and, less than a year after deciding to settle down and start a family, Timothy was born.

Several months after their son's birth, they happened across an injured anapriek deep in the woods that served as their hunting grounds. Though his seeping blood was an alluring temptation to the sangsuiga couple, they fought their baser instincts and agreed that it was better to nurse the poor mythos back to health and brought him back to their home. As it turned out, a small gang of rogue vampires had stumbled across the anapriek camp and gone on a killing spree that only Zeneik—or "Zeek" as he preferred to be called—had survived. Alone and without a home, Derek and Mary agreed to take him in and it wasn't long after that he'd become as much a part of the family as their son.

It was then that the two decided that their home and desire for a family could serve a greater purpose, and they soon began taking in any and all mythos that, like Zeek, needed a home. Very quickly, their house, which had, at first, seemed too large for just the four of them, grew too small to house all of their new "family", and the renovations began.

As more and more wayward and needy mythos came to join their household, bonds were formed; bonds that, outside of their peaceful home, may never have been, and the happy couple enjoyed the unity that they had sparked between the different races.

For years their numbers grew and prospered, and all seemed well and perfect.

Then, in one swift move, the hunter twins invaded the estate that the two vampires had put together and destroyed it all.

Nobody was quite sure how they'd gotten in, but it was a teenage auric named Luke who'd first sensed them in the master bedroom. Calling on their newest member, Satoru, Zeek was quick to start up the stairs while the nejin leapt to the wall and began to ascend to the balcony on the second floor where, side-by-side, the two worked their way to the third floor. By the time they'd reached the master bedroom, however, Derek and Mary were already dead, and the two hunters were sprinting down the hall after Timothy.

Seeing the danger that the little vampire was in, Satoru quickly vaulted the railing and cut the hunters off from their prey, and, letting out an angry roar, the nejin slashed at the pair with his claws. The hunters reeled back to dodge the attack, the male drawing two swords from a pair of sheaths at his back and lunging forward while the female drew a gun and leveled it in their direction. Seeing this, Zeek had charged the female hunter and tackled her to the ground.

Before long, Karen and Sasha—already transformed into their bestial therion forms and looking like a pair of sleek, seven-foot tall foxes—crashed through their bedroom door on the second floor and started up the stairs. Though the two therion sisters were untrained and had never before seen battle, Zeek was surprised when Sasha threw the hunter off of him and across the hall. Catching himself on the railing, however, the hunter was quick to bring himself back into the fray.

It was awkward and clumsy; what few fighters there were doing their best to hold the swift and agile hunters back. The fight was made all the more complicated in the narrow hall. Meanwhile, the hunters, who attacked with gunshots and stabs, gained more and more ground, effectively bringing down Dante, a therion and close friend of Sasha's, as well as Cheryl, Derek's younger sister.

As the hall filled with dead mythos, Satoru, cradling a deep gash in his shoulder, ran into Timothy's room and yanked the little vampire from the corner where he was hiding. The chaos spread, approaching the entrance to Timothy's bedroom, and in one swift move the nejin threw a chair through the window and leapt free of the oncoming assault with the screaming vampire youngster in his arms. The landing had been rough, but, like all cats, Satoru was able to stay on his feet.

Zeek was pleased to see that the boy was safe from the two hunters, and as he ducked under an oncoming blade he kicked out, knocking the male hunter into his female companion and giving the others a chance to get to the lower levels. Seeing the opening, Karen and Sasha jumped down the flight of stairs.

Seeing their prey escaping, the male hunter screamed in rage and Zeek watched in horror as the network of tribal tattoos the two hunters wore began glowing. Knowing that no good could come from this, Zeek had hurled himself over the railing as a wave of energy tore the stairwell from the wall and began shredding it in midair, sending the debris down on the others below. Still falling, Zeek cried out as a jagged length of the banister was driven into the back of his shoulder. Seeing that Zeek was injured, Karen and Sasha had worked together to catch and pull Zeek to safety as another wave of power was forced throughout the house and the three were thrown back.

As the two hunters leapt down to the second floor, Luke, using his aura to propel him, shot up the stairs like a bullet. As he came around the bend, the male hunter turned his efforts on the auric and threw out his arm. Before the auric could understand what was coming, the walls on either side of him ripped free in jagged chunks and closed in on him. As Zeek watched, the hunter's raised hand clenched into a fist and the mass that sandwiched the young auric burst into flames. Before the others could come to the poor vampire's aid, his life was swallowed by the fire and cast aside; the flames beginning to spread across the bits of debris and up the woodwork of the nearby railing.

All three jumped from the overpass of the second floor, Zeek pausing at the sight of the charred remains of his friend before finally following after Karen and Sasha. Behind them, the male hunter bellowed again and the fire rose and spread. Caught off guard by the sudden wave of energy, Zeek faltered in his landing and toppled through the glass coffee table, landing hard on his side. Ignoring the pain, the anapriek looked up as the still-glowing hunter directed the magic-controlled flames into each room as he casually navigated the halls and started for the staircase. Though most of the survivors had already made it out, Zeek grimaced as he heard the pained shrieks of those who had sought safety within their rooms as they were burned alive.

Knowing that nothing more could be done to save the house or the poor mythos occupying it, Zeek yanked the length of wood from meat of his shoulder and scrambled to his feet, snatching Derek's keys from the shattered remains of the coffee table and calling for the others to run.

The next few minutes went by in a haze. As the screams and cries of his allies faded in and out of his focus, Zeek struggled to keep himself conscious despite the pain he was in as he herded the survivors to cram into Derek's SUV.

Finally, with everybody crammed in the SUV—the two therion sisters back in their human forms and hid their naked bodies from the little vampire under a blanket they'd found in the back—they peeled away from the house as it collapsed under the weight of its own structure.

They drove as far as they could before finally stopping the next day for food and clothes; the only one fit to go out being Zeek. Though his ears were an attention-getter, most passed if off as a costume prop as he went through the Salvation Army store, finally paying, with a pained heart, with the house's emergency credit card that was kept in the SUV's glove-box.

As he carried the clothes back to his friends, he kept his eyes down, feeling the pain and sorrow of what had occurred hit him with the full force of a bullet between the eyes. Just then, in the middle of his thoughts, he heard Karen cry out his name and looked up in time to see the two hunters racing down the street towards them on a set of motorcycles that he recognized as their neighbors'. Glaring at the two, he was surprised as they both leveled their guns—despite the public setting—in his direction and opened fire on the parking lot.

Seeing the trail of automatic gunfire coming at him, Zeek threw himself into the bed of a nearby pickup truck. As the bullets began to pepper the pristine blue paint, Zeek called out to the others to hide, hiccupping on his words as the tires were blown out and the vehicle dropped several inches. The cries of pedestrians sounded as the motorcycle engines grew louder with the hunters' approach before suddenly dying down. Curious, Zeek dared a peek over the top of the perforated truck bed and watched as a human, stammering and begging for the two to stop their attack on the store and its shoppers, was backhanded into the tail-end of a nearby convertible. Seeing an opportunity in all of the confusion, Satoru took the driver's seat pushed the accelerator to the floor, aiming for the truck.

Zeek, catching on to his comrade's intent, leapt from the truck just as they collided with it and landed on the roof of the SUV. Seeing their quarry once again getting away, the hunters began shooting after them. Satoru, trying to navigate the parking lot without putting Zeek directly in the hunter's range, jerked the wheel to avoid a Smart Car that pulled out in front of them in an effort to escape the scene. As Zeek's grip on the roof waned, he was forced to roll over the edge and into the arms of Karen, who'd momentarily set aside her modesty and fear of exposing Timothy to the female form to save his life.

With the three bags of clothes miraculously still in his white-knuckle grip, Zeek passed his purchases off to the therion sisters to make themselves decent as he took the wheel from the panicked nejin and maneuvered out of the parking lot with the hunters closing in on their stolen motorcycles.

"The highway!" Sasha pointed to a sign announcing the onramp, "We might be able to lose them!"

Zeek frowned at the idea but, not having a better one, jerked the wheel to the right and steered onto the shoulder as he accelerated past a beige Cadillac that honked at them as they shot past. Behind them, he could see the hunters as they forked in either direction to pass the car and begin to close in on them once again.

Steering the SUV to the far-right lane, Zeek kept his eyes darting between the road ahead of him and the mirrors. With each sweep of his eyes, the hunters were that much closer, and it wasn't long before they'd pulled up on either side of the vehicle and took aim at the driver's and passenger's side doors. Unable to get the bulky vehicle to go any faster, Zeek called out a warning just before he slammed on the brakes. The SUV screeched—leaving a reeking black vapor in its wake from the tortured tires—and hunters shot forward, the wave of gunfire meant for Zeek raking across the hood and threatening to hit their companion on the other side. Unfortunately, they were too skilled to fall victim to friendly fire, and both screeched to a halt several yards ahead. The group, flustered from the sudden stop, worked to gather themselves amidst the blaring horns of cars swerving around them. Blinking against the ringing in his hears, Zeek's eyes rolled about in his head until they fell on his rearview mirror.

"INCOMING!"

The collision shook the SUV and pitched it forward. Before Zeek could call out to the others he found himself buried in a synthetic cloud that wrapped around his face and suffocated his efforts and blinded him. Behind him, the sound of the therion sisters yelping in surprise and Timothy's shrieks of terror echoed.

"What's happening?" Zeek demanded, trying to pull the airbag free from his face.

Beside him, Zeek heard the sound of the passenger-side door open and felt the car shift as Satoru stepped out of the vehicle, followed shortly after by the twin roars of the hunter's motorcycle engines as they went after the fleeing nejin. Finally freeing himself from the deflated mass Zeek tore himself free of his seatbelt and rolled back into the second row of seats to join the others. The gunfire sounded again, and the windshield burst inward as the driver's and passenger's seats were pummeled with bullets.

"Out! Get out!" Zeek instructed as he leaned over the second row of seats to get Timothy free of his seatbelt.

"We're pinned!" Sasha growled, fighting to open her door against the guardrail that the SUV had been pushed into during the collision.

"And this door's jammed!" Karen announced, yanking futilely at the handle.

"Kick it out!" Zeek called, "Transform if you have to!"

Karen frowned, "But what about the humans?"

"To hell with the huummaAAA*AAARRGGH—*" Sasha's voice warped into a snarl as her face twisted and warped into her therion form.

Zeek offered Karen a single nod of approval before pulling Timothy to his side. "Close your eyes! Cover your face!" he instructed. Despite his instructions, he couldn't help but dare a glance as a sudden wave of heat flared up from the therion sisters' boosted metabolisms.

Though terrified Timothy did as he was told, and the sisters began driving their inhuman feet into the jammed door before it finally—with a shriek of strained metal and ripped wires—was ripped free.

While Karen and Sasha began to transform back to their human forms and wrestle into their clothes, Zeek pulled Timothy and himself free of the SUV.

"Got you now, monster!"

Zeek turned towards the voice in time to see his attacker's enraged face as he was tackled to the street. The hunter, spitting in Zeek's face, reached behind him to retrieve one of his swords.

"Timothy! Run!" Zeek called out to the little vampire.

Sobbing, Timothy stumbled back and turned away to run and spotted the car that had crashed into them. A puddle of fluid grew from beneath the passenger-side tire, and Timothy could see that the hood had folded in on itself like an accordion, the contents of the hood having found escape through the dash board and into the chest and face of the driver. Timothy's eyes went wide at the sight of the eviscerated human just as Satoru sprinted by and scooped him up before starting towards the opposite side of the highway.

"SIS! GET THAT UGLY FUCKER AND HIS SNIVELING RAGDOLL BEFORE HE GETS AWAY!" Zeek's attacker bellowed over his shoulder, "I can handle these cunts on my own," he smirked at Zeek and tapped his blade against the side of his head, "When this is over, I'm gonna turn your ears into a necklace!"

"You'll need some teeth to go with it!" Sasha growled as she drove her naked foot into the hunter's jaw. Zeek gasped as the weight was removed from his chest and he looked up at the therion sisters, who had only managed to dress themselves in some ratty tee-shirts and boxer-briefs.

"Filthy... fucking monster," the hunter groaned past his tortured jaw, "You're all going to suffer fo—"

"SHUT UP!" Zeek roared as he drove a fist into the back of the hunter's head and reveling in the sight of his eyes rolling back in his skull as he lost consciousness.

"Damn," Sasha muttered under her breath, turning towards her sister, "Remind me never to piss off your boyfriend."

Zeek turned towards them, rubbing his knuckles as he nodded his thanks. "We need to get out of here!" He struggled to speak as his voice scorched his throat on the way out, "I don't care how you do it, but you need to get us a car!"

He started off in a full sprint towards Timothy and Satoru, who had managed to separate the female hunter from her gun and was struggling to bury two of his blades into her flesh.

But she was too damn quick.

Realizing that he'd be of little help to the nejin unarmed, Zeek paused to scan his surroundings for anything that would work as a weapon.

Several yards away, traffic on the highway had come to a standstill as drivers spotted the chaos ahead of them and became locked in by the cars behind them. Frowning at the growing scene, Zeek spotted a mass of wooden dowels that protruded from one of the closest car's rear window. As he ran towards the car, the driver, growing ever more afraid with every step he took towards them, finally leapt from their car and ran off into the sea of parked cars behind him.

Rolling his eyes, Zeek called the sisters to the abandoned car as he retrieved one of the seven foot long dowels and charged towards Satoru and the female hunter.

As the sisters went about moving their limited supplies to the new car, Zeek closed in behind the hunter with all the stealth and agility that had come to define his kind. When he reached Timothy, he held his index finger to his lips and gestured towards the sisters, who began to urge Timothy to go to them. Though he was still shivering from fear, Timothy nodded and pursed his lips to keep from making a sound as he started towards the car.

Confident that the boy would be safe, Zeek started towards the female hunter's back—moving like a shadow across the asphalt—and raised the dowel to attack. Before he could strike, however, Satoru's eyes widened as something behind them caught his attention and Zeek pivoted in time to dodge a downward swipe from the male hunter. With his cover blown and Satoru distracted, the female threw out her left leg and right arm and took down the two with a spinning maneuver. Groaning, Zeek clutched his hip and cursed the hunter's steel-toed boots under his breath; Satoru, writhing a short distance away, trying to breathe despite having just been punched in the windpipe. With the two incapacitated, the female hunter retrieved her gun while the male—her brother, it appeared—drew his second sword.

"Bet you think that those cheap shots were clever, eh motherfucker?" The male spoke through clenched teeth, "But you'll come to regret them when I make you watch me shred your fellow maggots!" His eyes shifted to Satoru and a malicious grin tugged at his cheeks, "Starting with your *hideous* pet!"

Taking a single step back he nodded to his sister, who leveled the gun at Satoru's head. The nejin's ears flattened against its skull as a deep, angry growl rumbled from his throat; the hair on the back of his neck beginning to stand as his shoulders tensed. Before either of the hunters could figure out what he was doing, Satoru palmed a pair of throwing blades in his left hand.

"SHOOT HI—"

The male hunter's command was cut short as the first blade buried itself in his hip and he dropped to his knees, spitting and hissing around his own rage as he struggled to get enough of a grip on the smooth, blood-covered metal to yank it free. Momentarily distracted by her brother's situation the female hunter cried out as the nejin dipped his head and spun out of range of her gun and put the other blade between the ribs on her left side.

Zeek whimpered in pain as he pulled himself to his feet, his breaths coming out in short, jagged bursts. "Kill them!"

Nodding, Satoru reached into his hoodie and produced a short sword from under his left arm and positioned himself to kill the male. A ways away—on the other side of the traffic jam—the sound of approaching sirens made itself known. Satoru paused, his ears rotating towards the sound as his eyes shifted towards Zeek. Behind him, the sisters pulled up in their stolen car.

"Come on," Karen called to them from the passenger seat, "They won't catch us anytime soon, and I know somebody who can help us!"

Zeek growled, "You mean we should just *leave* them here?"

Karen nodded, "If you kill them, there's going to be an investigation. Either the humans or The Council will be looking for those responsible for their deaths," she reached out the window and took his hand in hers, "There's no way either of those situations end well for us."

"What if they tell the cops?" Zeek didn't take his eyes off the hunters.

Sasha scoffed, "Do you *really* think that they'd believe them? If they start spouting about mythos then they'll be put in a loony bin and The Council will send an undercover warrior to deal with them!"

Growling at the idea of letting them live, Zeek glared back at the two—each one still fighting to pull the serrated blades from their bodies—and shook his head, "Let today be the day you see what *real* monsters look like!"

The female hunter's eyes widened at his words as her brother let loose a stream of threats.

Even as the two climbed into the car and they peeled away from the scene, the male hunter's echoed promises to find them resounded.

"You know they're going to find us eventually," Zeek growled.

Karen nodded, "I know, but if the rumors are true then we could have a powerful ally on our side; one with direct connections to The Council."

Zeek leaned forward, "So who is this mystery savior?"

CHAPTER FOUR
THE DEAL

XANDER SHOOK HIS head as the anapriek, Zeek, finished telling their story.

These hunters, whoever they were, didn't care about being subtle or discreet about their hunt. They didn't even care about the humans that might get caught in the crossfire! All they cared about was adding another mythos head to their score charts, and, from what Zeek had told him, they'd keep hunting them until they were all dead.

He growled and looked down, "I really don't know what to tell you…" he looked at each of them before locking eyes on the little vampire—Timothy, as it turned out—who looked up at him with desperate and expecting eyes. "I mean, *this* is all I've got now," he explained, "I'm not a warrior anymore."

Five pairs of eyes suddenly grew sad and desperate. He could tell they'd come a long way and gone through a great deal to have him help them and protect them.

But that wasn't who he was!

Wasn't who he wanted to be!

All it did was lead to pain and loss.

His mother. His grandmother. The Odin Clan. Then Marcus, and even Estella…

All had paid the price for being close to him.

And all because he had chosen to take up arms as a mythos warrior.

But he was no hero.

Everything he'd done, every battle he'd thrown himself into with complete disregard to his wellbeing, he'd done for himself. Tracking down and slaying everyone responsible for the death of his mother and father, fighting whoever Marcus pointed him towards in some effort to shape him into something he wasn't…

All of it had been for him; for the sake of seeing something other than himself bleed and suffer just so he could justify not turning all that hatred back in on himself.

He was no hero.

And knowing that Estella was out there somewhere struggling with her new vampire body and instincts drove that fact into his mind like a rusted nail being hammered into his skull.

Every time he fought, something else was taken away.

And he'd lost too much already.

He finally had a family with the therions who had given him a home in his hour of need, and after all his losses throughout his life—both human *and* vampire—he was not about to risk them so that a small group of misfits might be able to live to see one extra day.

He shook his head again, "I can't help you."

Osehr, still seated in his throne behind him, had been listening intently. Always a fan of a good story, the therion elder had been horrified by the tale and the struggles depicted therein. Finally, he used his one remaining arm to push himself up from his throne and stepped down to join Xander at his side. "You said that these hunters had glowing tattoos?" he asked.

Everybody looked at the elder, wondering where he was going with this.

Xander frowned, "Does that mean something to you?"

"Maybe," Osehr looked at the anapriek expectantly, "These tattoos, describe them to me."

The anapriek shrugged and began tracing a serpentine and intricate design in the thawed dirt surrounding their campfire, "It was all interconnected with several symbols—glyphs—filling in the empty spaces. When we first saw them on the male we believed them to be just what they appeared: human tattoos, but as they continued to raid our home the designs began to glow."

Xander frowned, "And you say that both of the hunters had these tattoos?"

The anapriek nodded.

Osehr sighed and returned to his throne, grunting as he let himself drop back into his seat. "They must be using taroe ink," He muttered.

"Huh?" Xander turned towards his old friend, "Taroe? Like the cards?"

The therion barked out a laugh, "Not *tarot*; taroe," he corrected, though Xander still didn't hear the difference, "They *are* humans, no different from the ones on the street, but they are born and raised within tribal systems that pride themselves on secrecy and obscurity. They are very religious, believing that there are many gods who can harness and control magic through will and desire alone, but rather than worshipping these gods, they work to *become* like them. They learn the art of magic—training almost from the day they are born—until the day finally comes that they are initiated."

Xander frowned, "And what's the initiation?"

Osehr nodded towards the designs etched into the dirt, "They are tattooed."

Xander narrowed his eyes at the design, hoping to decipher something in the markings. When nothing presented itself, he looked back towards Osehr, "So?"

"So..." Osehr closed his eyes for a moment and Xander wondered if he might actually fall asleep in the middle of the explanation, "... the ink is enchanted. It is prepared for several days and by the eldest of the tribe and carefully applied with the thorns of a rare flower that they cultivate. The entire process takes days, even weeks, depending on the size of the tattoo and the skill of the initiate."

"Magic tattoos?" Xander raised an eyebrow.

Osehr nodded, "They allow those with them to channel their powers; to strengthen them. When the energies are focused, they can do nearly anything with them,"

Xander frowned, "How do you know all of this anyway?"

"Because I have studied the magical arts," Osehr gave him an absent stare, "I'd have imagined you'd known this, as well."

Xander heard Zeek chuckle behind him and swiveled to shoot a death-stare at the anapriek. Though his enraged expression did little to sway the newcomer, Xander emphasized his point by using his aura to drag the still-smirking Zeek across the dirt to rest only a few feet from him.

"I've learned all I know by *killing* whatever needed to be killed in the field," Xander growled, glaring down at the anapriek, "You should remember that!"

Osehr cleared his throat then, drawing Xander's gaze and relieving some of the tension. As Zeek moved back to join the others, Xander relaxed and nodded to his friend. Osehr smirked knowingly at him before turning back towards the newcomers, "However, it's rare for a taroe to leave their tribe and enter the human world."

Xander frowned, "Unless they have a *reason* to come out!" He turned to the group, "Don't suppose you'd know why there'd be a few members of this tribe eager to leave home and make your lives a living hell?"

Osehr shook his head, "I do not believe that these hunters are true taroe," he explained, "The taroe are a peaceful people, and there's only been one known documented case of them using their magic in hate, and The Council put a swift end to that particular tribe when they learned of what they'd done."

Xander glanced over his shoulder, "The Council destroyed an entire tribe of *humans*?"

Osehr nodded, "You know full well the shaky truce they hold with magic-trained humans. A while back some very stupid mythos stumbled into this particular tribe's camp and murdered the chief's daughter. When they were discovered, the chief ordered that the two be bound by an ancient taroe curse—what they called the *Maledictus* curse; some sort of walking plague of destruction—and cast into the world to rip it apart."

"Jesus!" Xander shook his head, "They have *that* much power?"

"Under the right circumstances, yes," Osehr nodded, "After The Council was finished with that tribe, they sent out a message to all other taroe that any caught using the *Maledictus* curse would meet the same fate."

"Well that's a pretty big fucking 'if', don't you think?" Xander scoffed, "Only one *documented* case of violence, but that *one* can easily trump the multiple crimes that certain rogues have earned the death penalty committing! Killing those dumb fucks—hell, even torturing them—would have *maybe* earned them a slap on the wrist since they *had* killed one of their own, but to cast on them and send them—"

"Only one of them was ever seen again," Osehr interjected.

Xander threw up his arms, "For fuck's sake, Osehr! Do those sound like a peaceful people to you?"

Osehr sighed, "If you understood their beliefs and knew what The Council's actions did to all the other tribes around the world, you wouldn't think them capable of casting a hateful eye onto another living being, let alone casting any sort of curse. No, these hunters are not of any taroe tribe, though there isn't a doubt in my mind that they wear their markings," he sighed, "I can already feel their magic; I can smell the taroe ink in the air."

Xander frowned, "They're already in the city?"

The therion nodded, "See for yourself."

Xander scowled and cast his aura out, stretching it out of the woods and into the city limits where he instantly locked on to a surprisingly strong energy. Though he couldn't "see" them through all the power, the tribal designs of their tattoos shined through the black fog of power; cutting through like lightning. As he dug deeper he could see them storming the taroe tribe and massacring their people. When the hunters had killed all but several of the elders, they'd forced them, through torture, to tattoo them with their enchanted ink.

Once their stolen initiation was done, they'd used their new magic to kill the last of the tribe.

"I 'see' them," Xander growled.

Osehr nodded, "You need to do something."

Xander bit his lip, "But... the pack! If they find this place, you could all be in—"

"My pack is more than capable of defending themselves," Osehr interrupted. Finally, he turned to the outsiders, "We will allow you to stay with us for the next five days. In that time you will be treated as our guests," he narrowed his eyes at the anapriek, "Take advantage of this and you will be killed! Disrespect Stryker, and I'll leave you to his devices! Is this understood?"

Four heads bobbed in unison while the little vampire pushed his face into the nejin's side, letting out a nervous whimper.

Xander watched this for a moment before shaking his head, "Not the boy."

Osehr, and the others, stared at him for a moment.

"What do you mean?" The short-haired therion outsider asked, stepping protectively in front of Timothy.

"He'll be safe either way," Xander assured them, "If one of you slips up, you'll all pay with their lives for it, but the boy will stay with me."

The anapriek lightly tapped his staff against the dirt, calling Xander's attention to him. "What do you want with him?" He demanded.

Xander bit his lip as he studied Timothy for a long moment, trying to figure out exactly what he had in mind. For a long moment he thought about what a terrible tragedy the little vampire had been dealt, the same sort of tragedy that he, himself, had faced years ago. As he reflected on this, he thought of what he would have wanted—what he would have *needed*— and, as he did, it all became clear to him.

Maybe he wasn't the hero everyone who had sacrificed themselves on his behalf had believed him to be...

But that didn't mean he couldn't give the world the *true* hero.

After a long moment of silence he locked eyes with Zeek, "I'm going to train him."

Journal entry: November 11th

Estella,

I'm not sure how differences in mythos is supposed to work.

I mean, I KNOW that there's a difference (a whole ~~fuckload~~ bunch of them) between those like us and therions and whatnot, but what does that mean for us?

Would it really be so wrong for a vampire to be with a therion? Is that like getting it on with a pet? Or is it just like a biracial human couple?

Biologically it seems to work. I've heard of (and even dealt with my fair share) ~~of~~ hybrids, but something about it just seems so... I don't know...

One of the therion females made a pass at me earlier tonight, at least I think it was a pass (it was hard to tell, honestly). Her name's Yaltera, but I'm not sure if that's the right spelling (or if spelling even matters to them).

Not like they're signing their name on anything.

Anyway, she was nearly naked (though that doesn't mean much within the pack) and kept getting in REAL close to me as we sat around the fire. Now, I could just be misunderstanding or misinterpreting, but the way she was looking at me and the way she was smiling, but it all just seemed to have a real "take me" sort of tone.

I could be wrong, of course (it sure as hell wouldn't be the first time I've been wrong) but the entire thing got me to thinking about what a relationship (or even a fling) with a therion would mean for those like us...

~~Man... that's a mind-fuck if ever there was one.~~

I won't lie and say that I didn't at least consider it. Between all the lonely days and the cold it was definitely a tempting thought, but I think what made me linger on it the longest was the hope that I might be able to go a day without blaming myself. Every day when I'm trying to get myself to sleep, I see you and those last few seconds that we had together, and I hate myself more and more for it.

Part of me just wanted to not feel that pain... if only for one ~~goddam~~ day.

~~FUCK~~

But then I remembered whose fault this is, and I realized that I have no right to escape that pain.

~~Whatever that escape might be...~~

I turned her down as nicely as I could.

She didn't seem to mind, and as I was leaving I even saw her approaching another male in the pack.

Who knows? Maybe she just wanted some company and I was being a total douche about it.

Still, now I can't stop thinking about you...

~~I remember your warmth and I~~

~~Not that you're like them (not that there'd be anything wrong with~~

~~Anyway, I was thinking about you and that one time we had together and it made me miss you all the more. That's not to~~

say that that moment is the only reason I miss you, of course, but it was just something that

It hurts so fucking much! I'm sorry...

You know what? This one just isn't working...

I miss you and wish you were here.

I love you, Estella.
X

CHAPTER FIVE
STARVING

ESTELLA STUMBLED FROM what remained of her broken crate and cast aside the blanket that had served as her only protection from the sun that day. She stood as best she could for as long as she could before keeling over; the cramping in her stomach too much for her to stand. The rat's blood from the night before hadn't been enough to sate her thirst, and while she'd been able to get a few labored hours of sleep in, she'd been kept awake by the growing pain in her stomach; the gnawing drive to finally feed her vampire body what it needed growing evermore intolerable.

A need that was spreading to and corrupting her mind.

Even her own resolve was being twisted by her body's demands, and she was having a harder and harder time coming up with reasons why it was wrong.

The tantalizing promise of nourishment lingering just behind the soft flesh of a—

She cried out and sucked in a tormented breath before

heaving it out just as painfully. Just the thought of taking another life threw her into a nauseated fit, and she doubled over again as she sobbed.

Anything that wasn't blood was just as quickly refused.

Even the act of breathing seemed to be killing her from the inside.

Her fangs once again stretched to their limit and threatened to tear the roof of her mouth apart.

It was all too much!

While she knew nothing of her kind or their anatomy she was positive that her vampire body was beginning to feed on itself. As her guts continued to churn, she wondered if her body had given itself an ulcer just to get some blood into her stomach. Either way, she could sense that she wouldn't last much longer.

Not like this, anyway.

She knew that it was necessary—imperative!—to her survival that she find a source of blood and feed. It was a painful knowledge that boiled in her gut and bubbled in her mind...

She couldn't just take it like that; couldn't just steal a life to keep her own!

Could she?

She shook her head.

The rat the night before had been an accident. Every time her body's urges and needs drove her to kill—to feed—had been an accident, but she'd never fully given in to her body's demands, and each time it was becoming harder to not give in entirely. She'd been happy—if happiness was really an emotion she was capable of at that point—that she had been strong enough to hold back and not feed from a human during her first few weeks as a vampire. Now, however, it appeared that this accomplishment had only culminated in a growing bloodlust that she knew she wouldn't be able to resist. Her greatest strength had made her too weak to maintain it, and even her magic was suffering.

She was dying...

And when death was imminent, all beings resorted to desperate means to survive. Estella shivered at the thought; when her vampire instincts took over, there would be no stopping the carnage.

Whimpering at this realization, she struggled to stand up once again and looked up at the bridge overhead. Her thoughts led her down dark paths until she finally thought of a solution...

An awful, horrid solution.

But a solution nonetheless.

With a goal in mind and the promise of blood on the horizon her body's pain numbed and allowed her to move forward with her plan. Taking the moon pendant around her neck tightly into her hand, she forced herself to take the first step.

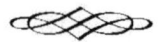

A short distance out, only an eighth of a mile down the rancid-smelling swamp to the stream that fed it, was a plot of land squared away behind a long wooden fence. Beyond this lay the barn, an old-fashioned structure that had been kept standing through constant care and maintenance of the family that owned the land. Though it was still a short distance away, her eager senses caught the sound of heartbeats, thundering in her head and rolling through every fiber of her body like the drums from the night before. With the promise of sustenance that much closer, Estella's body lurched and fed her the final dose of its energy reserves so she could finish the journey.

She found the door to the barn locked, held shut with a thick, rusted padlock that looped through an equally rusted iron latch. Part of her—the part that was still coherent and mindful of her actions and *not* driven by vampire urges—started to take this as a sign that it had been a bad idea. As she started to turn away, however, her body refused and, no longer her own to control, ripped the lock from the wooden doors as though she were peeling a Post-It Note and casting it aside with a loud and heavy THUNK.

A short, panicked whinny sounded from inside as the doors slid open, and one of the nearest horses stomped its hooves several times as it craned its neck around to see who had come to visit at such a late hour. Estella inhaled sharply, taking in the smell of the interior and the beasts dwelling within; taking in the smell of their blood. She wouldn't be hurting anybody if she fed from just one.

Not in the long run, at least.

She started towards the closest, leaping easily over the barricade and landing beside the creature as it lurched and shifted uncomfortably. Though she wasn't afraid that it could hurt her, Estella held back in the hopes that it would tire itself soon enough. However, as the horse's fit continued, the others that were scattered about the barn in their own pens started to panic, as well, until the entire barn was roaring with the sounds of their terror.

It wasn't long after that the sound of footsteps outside gave away the approach of the owner who, no doubt, had been raised by the calamity. Estella frowned, and jumped up onto one of the rafters, using what little agility she'd learned to control from her several months as a vampire to momentarily perch on the beam before jumping the several yard stretch into the hayloft that served as the second floor to the structure. Just at that moment the farmhand—a young boy, no older than fifteen—kicked the sliding doors the rest of the way to allow more of the moonlight through. Crossing the threshold, the young man swung a shotgun to his left and then again to his right, checking the inside corners of the barn, before bringing the double barrels to aim forward and began to make his way deeper into the barn.

The horses, recognizing the scent of the farmhand, began to settle down, and the growing silence allowed Estella to listen to the teenager's irritated grumbles about a demanding father and his "damned animals". His anger made his pulse quicken as he finished scouring the barn for the intruder, obviously eager to have an excuse to release some of his pent-up aggression, before he reluctantly lowered the shotgun. Disappointed, he stepped towards the stable directly below Estella's perch and the horse—a marbled stallion whose heart still roared with panic—that occupied it.

"What's wrong, boy?" He asked, running his palm over the side of its neck to calm it. "What's got you all so spooked?"

The already deafening chorus of heartbeats and the addition of the farmhand's coursing pulse echoed in Estella's head and, unable to control herself, groaned as the pain in her stomach flared up again.

"Who's there?" The boy demanded as he lifted the shotgun once again and swung the barrels back-and-forth, "I don't know how y'all did what ya did to our lock, but ya owe us a new set of doors! Now come on out! We've a'ready called the cops, so it'd be better for y'all's health if ya didn't force me to come lookin' for ya!"

Shifting slightly to duck down further behind the piles of hay, a loose floorboard squealed and Estella cringed at the sound of the gun cocking. Before she had a chance to react the barn was filled with the thunder of gunfire and a bale of hay beside her exploded.

As the strands of straw continued to rain down her, Estella jumped for the closest rafter, hoping to make her way to the exit before the boy could get off another shot. In her hunger-induced weakness, though, she undershot the maneuver and crashed chest-first into the wooden beam before falling; the middle of her back crashing to the edge of a stall door before she slammed to the dusty floor on her side, whimpering and cringing at her injuries.

The boy wasted no time with asking questions or even looking at who'd just crashed down several feet ahead of him before pumping a pair of fresh shells into the chamber and firing the weapon.

"AAHHHHG!" Estella cried out in agony as the buckshot filled her stomach and chest, the force of the shot rolling her onto her opposite side where she curled up in an attempt to fight the pain.

Something in the boy's vengeful resolve wavered as he closed the distance between them and caught his first sight of Estella, and his once furious and determined posture went weak as he leaned the shotgun against the nearby wall and knelt down over her. "Oh God! Oh my god I'm... I'm so sorry! I panicked and I... I..." he shook his head, "What in the hell are ya doin' in here? Are ya in trouble?"

As he reached down to try and help her, Estella could see the veins in his wrists throbbing. Practically begging to be torn into...

"NO!" She shrieked, pushing the boy away and pulling herself to her feet, still hugging her torso where the multiple pellets had torn into her, "STAY AWAY! STAY THE HELL AWAY FROM ME!"

The boy's eyes were wide in surprise, "Miss, I didn't mean nothin'! I just…"

Before he had a chance to finish, however, Estella was already stumbling out of the barn and heading for the fence at the other side. With the last of her energy tapped out, she didn't have it in her to jump or even climb over the divider, and instead threw herself against the top rail and allowed her body to spill over and fall to the ground on the opposite side. The ground, though still unforgiving, was soft with overgrown grass, and for a moment she felt that she could just lie there forever. However, with the approaching sound of sirens—the boy *wasn't* lying about the cops—she was forced to get to her feet and stumble further into the darkness.

A night in a brightly-lit and confining jail cell with other prisoners was the last place she felt she'd be able to stay in control.

Her starved body was enraged, and as she headed further and further away from what had seemed like sure chance for a decent meal she felt the gnawing sensation return in her gut. This, on top of the buckshot, caused her to stumble and collapse. With nothing left in her to move forward, she struggled to reach up to her chest, taking the moon pendant around her neck tightly into her hand, and started to sob.

The pain was too much!

She was starving to death!

Journal entry: November 14th

Estella,

I've been worrying about you a lot more than usual lately.

While I know that you're smart and already know all about most of The Council's laws, I'm afraid of what your new life without anybody there to help you might result in.

There's so much that could happen...

So much that could go wrong...

I mean, you haven't even gone through the training!

I can't imagine what it must be like.

~~I don't even know if you're still alive or~~

Dammit! I can't let myself think like that! If you're gone, really gone, then I just don't have anything left...

~~Do I?~~

Everybody has something to define themselves by... something to call their own.

A legacy.

I was supposed to be this big deal fucking vampire messiah and instead I'm a bloodsucking bum living in the forest with a bunch of werewolves!

My father and Depok had the Odin Clan...

Marcus had his duties as a warrior and my mentor...

And I was supposed to protect you...

And now I have nothing!

Nothing left but my hope that you're still alive out there somewhere and that I might find you someday.

~~If you're gone... I mean REALLY gone... what does that leave for me?~~

Part of me still wants to do the warrior thing. To be some big-deal fighter like I was and to uphold what's right for my kind (for OUR kind) like my father was.

I'm sure that that part IS my father, what's left of him, I mean. He's somewhere inside my head still... I can still feel his strength and eagerness like a manic drive that pushes me to pick up my guns again. And I KNOW that I'm letting that part of me down (letting what's left of him down...)

But the truth is I just don't want to do anything anymore!

I've finally found a family I can call my own and the rest of the world seems to be doing just fine without me running around on rooftops and blowing the heads off of rogues. I know that the option of living a normal human life is out of the question at this point... but is it too much to ask that I don't have to live the hero's life?

I just...

I just wish you were with me.

That would make everything better.

And I feel like, if you WERE here, then I'd know what I was supposed to do...

Until then...

Love you always,
X

CHAPTER SIX
BRING ON THE HUNT

RICHARD AND DIANNA had come a long way.

It had taken a lot of effort to track the few straggling mythos, and though Dianna thought that their time could be better spent continuing their efforts back at home it wasn't worth the effort— or the beating—to question her brother's motives.

Anything, even wasting time pursuing mythos that had done *nothing* wrong, was better than enduring the beatings. There had been times in the past when her brother's savagery had been so bad that they'd had to put their hunts on hold while she healed. It was times like those that had taught her not to question or meddle. It was really quite simple, if Richard said "shoot", she shot; if he said "kill", she killed.

And when he said they'd track down and kill the survivors of their last outing then she'd follow them to the ends of the earth and kill them.

Eluding the authorities and patching up their injuries had been hard enough—especially when the hundreds of witnesses on the highway could identify which way they'd gone—but, with a little creativity and a lot of luck, they'd managed. Granted, without their stolen Harley Davidsons the process of tracking the creatures had been a long and tedious one, but after hotwiring a Chevy at a diner fifteen miles from the highway in a small hick town they'd been able to make up for lost time. They'd ditched the ride a mile or two out from the city and continued on foot from there; stuffing their weapons into a series of totes and instrument cases that they'd stopped to purchase along the way. Before leaving, Richard had made a note of syphoning the remaining fuel from the car's tank and using it to torch the interior, claiming that it would destroy any evidence they might be leaving behind. While Dianna had been tempted to remind him that he'd burned both of their fingerprints off nearly three years earlier, she knew better and watched as her brother set the blaze. Still holding her tongue during their trek, Richard discussed—or rather ranted without a chance for an outside word—the matter of them needing a tracker.

"We were lucky to trail the monsters this far," he'd pointed out, "but finding them in this shithole isn't going to be easy!" He shook his head and glared at Dianna then, and she knew he was looking for a way to blame her despite her being the one who had caught on to the residual magic trail of the anapriek. "What we need... is a dog," he boasted.

Dianna looked at him questioningly but didn't open her mouth. Instead she took a deep breath through her nose and simply nodded. She knew better than to answer; no matter what she said Richard would have found fault with it.

And fault warranted a beating.

She knew better.

"Pick up the pace, will ya!" Her brother called over his shoulder, "I don't want to have to wait all fucking night for your lagging ass!"

She bit her lip and nodded, doing her best, despite having the burden of carrying most of the load, to catch up. As she did there was a slight rattle in a bass guitar case that they'd picked up.

Richard stopped and turned, "Be careful with that! My

swords are in there, and I don't want you nicking the blades!"

Dianna flinched and averted her eyes as she forced herself to nod again, "S-sorry."

"You sure are," he spat as he turned and continued, "Sorriest sack of shit I know." He sighed, looking around at the buildings that were beginning to grow taller and taller around them as they went deeper and deeper into the city, "Now's the perfect time!"

Dianna looked up, "The perfect time?" She spoke before she could think to stop herself.

Stupid! She *knew* better!

Richard shot a look over his shoulder that told her that she was in for a beating when they got somewhere private, "Weren't you listening, bitch? We're getting a dog!"

"B-but it's the middle of the night," while she knew it was a danger to question whatever motives her brother had, she could not help but feel confused.

He stopped then and turned, his hand rising as if he may strike her then and there. Several pedestrians stopped and gasped, sure they were about to witness an act of abuse. Still shaking with rage, however, Richard caught himself at the last minute and made a show instead of reaching back with his hand and rubbing the back of his neck. He narrowed his eyes at his sister and, through gritted teeth, spoke under his breath.

"I'm aware of what time it is," he turned away, shaking his head and saw a couple still staring at him; both with looks of shock and disgust painted all over their faces, "What the fuck are you looking at?"

The man narrowed his eyes and started to step forward, ready to take Richard up on the fight he was trying to start but his significant other grabbed his arm and pulled him away. As they walked off the man turned his head and smirked at him, "Consider yourself lucky."

Before Dianna could put their bags and cases down to stop him, Richard was on the man. His attack was strong and swift, far more than it should have been considering his opponent was only human. In the blink of an eye he had darted forward and brought his elbow up and into the back of the man's head. As the stranger stumbled and cried out in pain, Richard gripped his left arm and twisted, popping the joint from the socket while, at the same time, spinning the man around to face him. When he was nose-to-nose with the unsuspecting man, he slammed him against the wall of the nearby building and pinched his fingers tightly around the man's throat, ready to cut off his air supply.

"I consider myself *very* lucky," he growled in the man's face, "But I don't think it's me that needs the luck right now, eh shit-eater?"

As the woman shrieked at Richard to let go of her boyfriend, more and more people began to take notice and circle around the scene. As the crowd grew, their mutters grew to enraged threats and a series of flashes began as cell phones were drawn to capture the moment.

Dianna looked around, getting nervous; this was not a good way to make an entrance into the city.

"Richard!" She called out, more worried—for the moment, at least—about the potential of oncoming authorities than about the threat of what her brother would do to her.

Her brother shot her an angry look and then glared back at the man, whose face was beginning to turn blue. Before any permanent damage was inflicted, however, he released the man's windpipe and took a step back, wiping the sweat from his palms and motioning for his sister to follow.

"Come on," he instructed, giving the gasping man one final glance, "Keep this in mind for the next time you want to measure dicks, pal, 'cuz King-Kong ain't got shit on me!"

As they started off, members of the crowd tried to keep them pinned in, hoping to keep them there until the police arrived. Both of them, having no desire to answer for what had just happened, took their own paths around the barricade, Richard shoving and fighting his way through while Dianna ran up the side of the nearby wall and flipped over the awestruck group.

They ran for several blocks, darting and weaving through the checkerboard network until they were certain they'd lost any potential followers. Finally Richard stopped—giving Dianna the opportunity to do the same and catch her breath—beside an old payphone booth.

"Holy shit," he chortled, "I can't believe one of these things still exists! Still...", he struggled to slide the old door open and stepped into the booth.

Dianna sighed, looking around for an uncertain moment while her brother dug out the dusty phone book and began flipping through it before finally taking several of the pages in his grip and tearing them from the binding and stepping out again. They walked on aimlessly for a short while, stopping now and again to observe a street sign and compare them to the addresses on the stolen pages, until they finally found themselves standing in front of a small shop that was simply labeled "Pets".

Richard, sporting a wide and unsettling grin, pressed his face against the glass and scanned the interior like an excited child outside a toy store. When he finally found what he was looking for, he turned to his sister.

"Gun," he demanded.

Dianna frowned but handed him a pistol nonetheless.

Holding the weapon like a hammer, Richard wrapped his opposite arm around his face to cover it and smashed in the window. Instantly the sound of an alarm filled the streets as well as a flood of startled animal calls.

Leaping through the opening he'd just made, Richard hurried towards the sound of the barks, using the gun once again to smash in the lock on the cage belonging to the animal of his choice. Dianna watched nervously from the sidewalk as he came back into view with a golden retriever close behind. As he made his way back towards his make-shift entrance, he grabbed a collar and a leash from the shelves, quickly fastening both around the dog's neck. Before leaving, he hoisted a fifty-pound bag of kibble over his shoulder and stepped through the window and into the street.

"Great! Now we us got a huntin' dog."

Journal entry: November 21st

Estella,

I couldn't sleep, so I went out looking for you again.

It was a cloudy day (for the most part at least). There WERE some sunny spots where the clouds gapped and the beams cut through like in all those artsy-fartsy pictures you see in college photography and cheesy family flicks, but I barely noticed them until my skin started to blister. I just couldn't stop thinking about you. Still, after a while the sunlight became too much and I ended up yelling at a passing mother whose baby wouldn't stop crying.

Scared the ~~shit out o~~ ~~crap~~ mom, but the kid started laughing.

Still not sure if that was funny or a blow to my ego.

I checked around the local bookstores and at the library you used to work at. I knew you wouldn't be at either, but I knew I wouldn't be able to forgive myself if I at least didn't check at your normal hangouts. While I was there I saw a few historical romances like the ones that were on your bookshelf and picked a few out that I thought you might like.

The cashier gave me a funny look. Not sure if it was because of the way I looked or if it was my selection. I didn't bother to read his mind to find out.

I also checked a couple of cafés. Had a cup of tea at one of them. I wasn't really thirsty, but I needed to think, and I always did my best thinking over tea…

…or a cigarette… or a bottle of booze (not that any of those

do me any good anymore).

Anyway, over my tea it occurred to me that I never really went out with you much when you were human. I mean, we hung out a lot at your place, but it's not the same as what other couples do.

Though I guess we weren't like other couples...

It was really discouraging.

So yea... I spent the better part of fifteen hours scouring the city, trying to pick up on your auric signature only to finally remember that it wouldn't be the same as it was when you were human.

God damn, did I feel stupid!

That was when I yelled at the mother and kid...

What can I say? I was sunburned and pissed!

I mean, it just suddenly occurred to me that, even if you HAVEN'T left town there's no way for me to find you...

It was a REAL downer.

So you can't really blame me when the screaming kid set me off.

With nothing left to do in the city I bought a couple of cases of beer (the liquor store clerk was a real easy mind to tweak) and brought them back to the therions.

Most of them liked it just fine, and I'll tell you right now that a drunk werewolf is just about the funniest thing you've ever seen... until they start fighting.

Osehr said it smelled like piss and refused to try it.

Kinda made me miss drinking with Marcus...

Anyway, brought a six-pack back to my tent hoping that maybe it'd help me forget about today's epic failure even though I KNOW it won't. I sorta miss being able to get drunk...

Dammit! Where are you?

I miss you so much...

CHAPTER SEVEN
SWEETNESS

THE LACK OF BLOOD was making Estella woozy.

After her failed attempt at feeding from the farm she tried to return to her "home" under the bridge, only to find it occupied by a bunch of teenagers trying to get high. Upon seeing her, the group was quick to close in on her as they threw out their cat calls.

"Hey, baby!"

"Oh yummy!"

"C'mere, sweetness!"

Estella whimpered, taking the moon pendant around her neck tightly into her hand, and struggled to back away despite her growing dizziness. She knew better than to get any closer to them, but this meant little with them approaching her. As they drew nearer, their heartbeats turned into an unbearable temptation. She tried to block out the sound by covering her ears and closing her eyes, but even without sight or sound her body—even her goddam skin!—seemed to pick up on the warmth of the fresh blood that was approaching her and urge her to feed on them.

The first of the group tried to force Estella to the ground. Estella was stronger.

In her effort to both get him off of her as well as free herself from the burden of the temptation she moved to push him away and stumbled into him—something that was greatly appreciated at first—before she regained her balance and tossed him several feet to the side where he landed in the swamp. As he emerged, gasping and cursing from the murky, muddy waters, his friends laughed and jeered.

The next attempt was the last.

As another started to approach—muttering "my turn" in between throaty chuckles—Estella felt her fangs extend to a painful length and she hissed at him and bared her assets, hoping to scare them away.

"Oh, isn't that cute?" The boy taunted, "This bitch thinks she's a vampire!" They all laughed again, "Hey, honey, why don't you take those cheap-ass things out and try sucking a dick? I got something for you that's a hell-of-a-lot sweeter than blood!" He took another step and grabbed her arm, squeezing her tightly and trying to push her to her knees.

The contact proved to be more than her system could handle, and her stomach lurched. As she heaved once, then again—her body pitching forward with each violent wretch—the boy took a step back and his friends all laughed harder.

"Hey, Mack, what's it tell ya when you be makin' a hoe sick!" one of them taunted.

"P-please! Get... get away! Stay back!" Estella pleaded.

Suddenly the dry spell of her heaves ended and a wave of bloody vomit erupted from her mouth. The boys all took a cautious step back, but watched in morbid fascination as it continued for nearly half-a-minute. When, at last, it ended, Estella was too dizzy to remain upright and collapsed in a heap.

"Oh, shit! What the fuck was that all about?"

"Guess ya really did make da bitch sick!"

"Fuck you, man! Stupid twat's prolly jus' wasted or some shit."

"Fuck me? You betta' check who you mouthin' off to, muthafucka!"

"Damn, dudes, this whore looks drugged out of her mind!"

"Ain't stopped me b'fore! You guys still want a piece?"

"And have her spew on my cock? No-fuckin'-thanks! 'Sides, if *that's* what's spewin' from her ho-mouth than I ain't pokin' 'round her fuckin' pussy! My buddy porked a bitch like this once and they had to cut his cock off!"

Estella's guts churned like an angry sea as the boys all joked and laughed at her expense. Several more times her stomach found hold of something—though she wasn't sure what—to expel and another bloody expulsion ensued.

"God! It fuckin' stinks!"

"That's sayin' something considering we're in a damn swamp!"

More laughter.

Nobody made a move to help her, though she didn't want them to come any closer in fear of what her body might do. She was scared; more scared than usual. Her hunger had never driven her to this much pain. Tears welled in her eyes and she closed them tightly, clenching her teeth as best she could before throwing up again; the force so powerful that it came up through her nostrils as well. A sob escaped her lips once this was over and a heavy coughing fit started.

Her body had waited long enough for her to get the message. She'd teased it for months, giving it small doses of what it needed and promises of larger meals to come that never did. Now she was paying for it. The immense pain; the growing nausea... she was getting sick; her starved body was shutting down. If there was any doubt in her mind before there was none remaining that she was dying.

Whimpering in agony, she took the moon pendant around her neck tightly into her hand and prayed for an end.

And still the boys stood there and laughed.

Journal entry: November 28th

Estella,

I'm not the poetic type, but I keep trying, over and over again, to write something beautiful for you. Ultimately I just end up tearing the page out of the notebook and setting it aside to get burned in tomorrow's fire.

In the books and movies, when people are in love, they're able to say such wonderful things to the person they care for that make everything all better in the end.

If only life were that simple...

~~I'm sure as shit not an action hero, and nobody would~~

I don't think there are any words for making everything better. And, though I don't want to believe it, you don't seem to be coming back.

... no matter what I think or say.

It makes me realize that all those magical storybook endings are ~~all a load of bullshit~~

You would not believe the pile of unfinished poems I've got sitting beside me!

I'm beginning to feel more and more at home in this forest with the therions, and I can't begin to tell you how much that scares me. While we have our differences and I still feel like an outsider from time to time, I've stopped missing the world out there as much (it's a lot quieter for one. You'd get a lot of reading done). But what does that mean? Part of me wants to be out there in the city, and the more I find comfort in these woods the more that part of me crumbles.

~~Maybe I'll wind up like Tarzan~~

I passed by your old house the other day on an outing. It looks like somebody's finally gotten around to fixing the place up, there's even a "FOR SALE" sign posted in the yard.

~~I doubt anybody's going to want to buy it, though.~~

~~Not if they know what happened there, and I think the realtors are required to release that information.~~

~~At least I hope they are... it'd be fucked up if they didn't.~~

Anyway, as I was standing out there, just staring at the place, I was wondering if you ever stopped by there. It's kind of a mixed-up notion. On the one hand, you'd probably like to visit the old place to remember, but on the other, if you DO go there to remember, you're forced to remember what happened...

I know... it took me forever to finally visit my mom's grave.

I still haven't visited Dad's... but what's the point when a part of him is still "alive" inside of my head.

It's still creepy to say it out loud... or to write it in this case.

Anyway, I still love the hell out of you (how's that for poetic?)
X

CHAPTER EIGHT
WAKE-UP CALL

XANDER STILL WASN'T sure why he'd taken on the little sangsuiga boy as an apprentice, but he was content in chalking it up to good, old-fashioned boredom.

Despite this, he knew there was something more to it.

With nowhere else for the little one to stay during the daytime, Xander had made room in his tent. Though they were initially skeptical, those he'd traveled with were happy that he was finally getting the attention that he'd needed from the start.

That first night, Xander had brought him a thermos of his magically-charged synthetic blood, which he'd spit out at the first sip. After he was done laughing at the boy's response to the repulsive concoction, he'd explained that, while the stuff might taste wretched, it would more than do the trick when it came to sating their bodies' needs.

After several deep breaths, Timothy drank the whole thermos in several gulps.

For some time after that the boy was too energized by the elixir to get a solid, meaningful moment of training with him, and Xander, seeing no chance in getting any time with the boy while he was bouncing off the walls, introduced him to the younger therions in the pack. Between Timothy's hyperactivity and the therion cubs' excitement at having a new playmate, they were instantly bonded and sprinting about the woods like wild animals.

While Timothy worked off the excess energy, Xander sat by Osehr to watch.

"Where are the outsiders?" he asked after noting that they weren't in the clearing with them.

Osehr motioned towards the woods to his left, "They went to explore the area."

Xander nodded, appreciating the newcomers' absence while he started with the boy.

The less distractions the better.

"It was a nice thing you did, taking on the challenge of training him," Osehr went on.

"It was nothing. I was just bored," Xander recited the lie to his friend just as he had recited it to himself earlier.

Osehr smirked and Xander sighed, knowing that the old therion didn't believe him.

One of the boys cackled in the distance as their play continued and Osehr looked up to watch them chase one another around the network of trees. "You miss them, don't you?" he finally asked without looking away.

Xander frowned and looked up, "Who? The kids? Why would I—"

"Your father," Osehr answered in a scolding tone, "And your own trainer." He sighed and leaned forward in his throne, not taking his eyes off the youngsters, "What was his name again? Marcus, right?"

Xander looked away and shook his head, "What do they have to do with anything?"

"A great deal, actually," Osehr finally broke his gaze and looked at him, "More than you can imagine."

"Name *one*," Xander scoffed.

Osehr returned the scoff with one of his own, "I'll give you *three*!"

Xander frowned at that and looked up at him.

"There are *three* dangerous ways to approach a situation when you miss someone," Osehr explained, "You can ignore their absence and anything that reminds you of them altogether and hope that the pain will go away, or you can try to fill the void by being more like them and forever weigh your life against theirs." Osehr nodded to himself, "You miss your father, but cannot bring yourself to be like he was out of fear of failure. However, you are *also* ashamed that you're here doing nothing with your life, and so you've taken on the boy in an attempt to be more like Marcus."

Xander scowled, "Or maybe I'm just fucking bored with doing nothing because there's nothing to do and I've decided to occupy that time with training the boy because he needs to learn from someone!" He rose from his seat and started to walk towards the still-playing children.

"Wouldn't you like to know the third method?" Osehr called out behind him. Xander cringed and, though he didn't turn, he knew that Osehr was confident that he had his attention. "The third way a person can cope with loss: self-destruction."

Xander looked down, not sure what to say.

Osehr sighed and Xander heard him grunt as he adjusted himself in his throne, "You lost your father—"

"Look," Xander turned to face his friend, "I don't want—"

"No, Xander! Now is your time to listen! This is still *my* territory—you are of *my* pack—and, as leader, I am *telling* you to shut up!"

Xander narrowed his eyes at the old therion as a growl worked up his throat. Before it emerged, however, he opted to hold it, not wanting to create more of an incident out of it.

Osehr nodded, seeing Xander's silent struggle and offering his approval at the decision he'd made, "As I was saying: you lost your father before you were born and you feel that you should be like him because it's what is expected, but because you don't know *where* to begin you've simply decided to not even try. You lost Marcus to a monster who was after you and now you feel guilty that he's gone and are now taking on your own apprentice to make up for that void. But you're too busy—too damn *stubborn* and *ignorant*—trying to do what they *did* that you've completely ignored *why* they died in the first place! Instead you've chosen to go nowhere with your life and—"

The growing rage in Xander reached its peak and he growled and his red-and-black aura slithered from his chest like an angry serpent. As he glared at the therion elder, his body tensed and shaking, the bolt of energy turned inward and began to coil around him. Through all the resentment and pain that fueled his anger, he fought to keep control of his aura and, through clenched teeth, urged Osehr to finish, "A-and what?"

"And," the therion leader went on, pointing to the snake-like auric tendril that only the two of them could see, "you are destroying yourself from the inside-out because you blame yourself for what happened to Estella."

Xander roared at the mention of her name, baring his fangs and hissing at his friend. He didn't want to remember—didn't want to think about all those he'd failed and all those he'd lost; all those he'd let down—and hearing the words that mirrored the phantom taunts that echoed in his own head every time he was alone was too much to bear. Like a tidal wave, an entire life's worth of pain crashed over him and drowned him in every truth he'd struggled to ignore.

The clearing went silent then, the children frozen in their tracks and staring as the other therions in the pack snarled at Xander's tone to their leader and began to close in on him. "Stay out of my head!" he snarled, ignoring the others around them.

Above him he could hear the rustle of branches and a chorus of growls as his packmates closed in to defend their leader.

He knew that if the old mythos commanded it, he would be killed instantly, and he couldn't bring himself to care. His eyes narrowed and locked on Osehr's own calm gaze, and he felt another wave of shudder-inducing rage creep up his spine and forcing his aura to writhe and whip around him. A twig snapped a short distance behind him and he whipped his head around, positive that one of the therions was about to attack, and spotted Timothy as he slowly approached.

"Is sumting wrong, Mister Xander?" the little vampire asked as he took his place at his mentor's side.

And just like that the pain was gone.

Buried in a truth he'd been forced to come to grips with several years earlier:

"Always one more thing…" he whispered to himself.

"Mister Xander?"

He looked back at Timothy, his own aura—a small, golden wave that swirled around the boy like water in a stream—rolling excitedly. As he looked up at Xander, he reached up and took his hand within his tiny grip.

"C'mon, Mister-Xander! I'm ready to start," the little vampire's voice was soft but eager.

Xander stared down at his new apprentice. "Are you sure? It won't be easy, y'know," he stammered, "And you won't get it all on the first try."

The boy nodded, still smiling widely, "I know, but that's what makes it fun. Daddy always said 'if it's worth doing, it's worth failing at in the beginning'."

Awestruck, Xander stood, repeating the little vampire's words in his mind for a short while, before finally nodding, "Your father was a wise vampire, Timothy, and you're going to make him proud."

Journal entry: December 4th

Estella,

Trying not to imagine the worse, but it's real, REAL hard not to...

There's just so much that can go wrong when you're somebody in your situation.

Anyway...

Osehr is really intrigued with the idea of Christmas (even though he can't even SAY it right) and ever since I explained it to him he's been talking about how the pack should do it. I'm not entirely sure how it would all go down (probably just a lot of deer meat, a big fire, and the exchanging of... ~~shit,~~ I don't know... antlers...?)

He's pushing me to do it as soon as possible... wants me to be the king of "Kriss-mas" or ~~some shit~~ something like that (like I'm really the one to be going to for things like that).

Oh but he seems so happy at the idea of it.

Just like a damn kid at... well... Christmas

He keeps asking each night if we can celebrate it, but I keep telling him we have to wait.

That's sort of the point, isn't it? All that excitement and anticipation? That always seemed to be the best part of it when it still meant something...

Anyway, hope you're safe.

Love you,
X

Journal entry: December 6th

Estella,

I'd ask how life was in the city, but I'm not even sure if you're still in the city.

Plus there's the little nagging fact that you'll never read this and I won't get an answer.

I had a scary thought earlier that you're doing TOO well (boy that sounds stupid). Not that you're happy and safe and all that, of course I wish the best, but I was worried that you might be out there slaughtering people by the dozens and draining them... maybe even leaving them and allowing them to change into freaks...

I know I told you all about The Council and their laws when you were still human, and I just hope that you're not out there making yourself a target for extermination.

I guess what I'm just trying to say is don't make yourself noticed.

But you'll never read this...

Dammit! I just hope you're being safe and smart.

Or, if nothing else, I hope you're staying well hidden

I trust your judgment though. You always were the smart one.

And the pretty one.

And the nice one.

TOO damn nice, if you ask me. Always putting others before yourself. Willing to take any pain necessary to not hurt or upset others...

Oh god...

Please let you not be that nice...

~~Shit!~~

I love you too damn much to think about this
X

CHAPTER NINE
TRAINING

XANDER KNEW THAT TIMOTHY was ready for whatever obstacles that were put in front of him. From what he'd heard of his recent past nothing had been easy, and at least now he would be getting stronger. Xander regarded the little vampire with a smile before he looked up and gave Osehr a passive nod, and though his rage had subsided he still felt an apprehension towards the elder therion for having read him so easily.

Finally, he turned away from his friend and began to walk away with the boy as his aura recessed back into his body.

"So what *did* your father teach you?" he asked the boy.

Timothy looked down, blushing, his aura sagging with his shame. "Daddy didn't want me fighting," he confessed.

Xander nodded and gave him a reassuring pat on the shoulder, "That's what I thought," he smirked down at him, "But what do *you* think?"

Timothy looked up at him for a moment, startled that his opinion was being brought into question. "I think," he finally spoke up, "that Mommy and Daddy would be upset with me."

Xander frowned at his apprentice's response, "Upset? How come?"

"Because they said that hate is a bad thing and that I should never hate anyone."

Xander nodded, "I see. And you feel bad because you hate the hunters?"

Timothy nodded, his face showing shame but his aura flaring angrily.

"Listen, Tim—do you mind if I call you 'Tim'?"—he shook his head and Xander smiled down at him—"Tim, there's a lot of hate in the world; an unbearable shit-load of it."

Timothy's eyes widened and he gasped in surprise.

Xander offered a coy smirk and shrugged, "Don't worry, that sort of talk is okay while you're with me. It'll be our 'training talk'. Just don't tell Zeek, he strikes me as the sort of person whose head would explode if he ever heard a bad word," he reflected the word "explode" by gesturing over his head with both hands and Timothy giggled.

"Anyway," Xander continued, "there's so much hate in the world that it's damn near impossible to avoid it all, and your parents *were* right: hate breeds more hate; kind of like a spreading fire. Those hunters that killed your parents; they hated them—they hate all mythos for some reason or another—and their hateful act has made you hate them. Now what's important to remember is that hate is dangerous, it's like…" he smiled, remembering what a good man had once told him, "It's like eating rat poison and expecting the rats to die. Do you understand?"

Timothy shook his head.

Xander laughed, "Don't worry, you will. The important thing to take from all my babbling is that it's alright to be prepared to fight against those who hate you, but you can't let hate turn *you* into what *they* are." A moment was spent in silence as they continued to walk and Xander sucked lightly on his lower lip, not sure what to say next.

"Do you hate Ose'r?" Timothy asked suddenly.

It took Xander a moment to link "Ose'r" to "Osehr" and he

finally shook his head, smirking, "No, I don't hate him. He just made me a little angry."

Timothy thought for a moment before finally looking up at his mentor again, "Daddy used to say that 'angry' is bad too."

Xander sighed and nodded, "So I've heard."

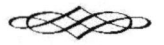

It took a moment of explaining before Timothy understood what Xander meant when he said "overdrive". This didn't surprise him, though; it *was* a term that, as far as he could tell, Marcus had made up. He was sure that, while it was a great way of describing the next stage in sangsuigan movement that allowed them to move faster than the human eye could even see, not many others used that word for it, and he was even surer that, somewhere out there, there was an *actual* word for the act. When the description finally caught on, Timothy's eyes went wide with excitement and he nodded, telling of how his father and he used to play tag like that.

Xander smiled, explaining that this was a very useful tool in both hunting as well as fighting. With that he told his young apprentice that they would spend that night, like he'd suggested, playing tag. The little vampire was excited by this and quickly disappeared from sight before Xander could go on, and, for a brief moment, he was left bewildered as to where the little sang had gone before he felt the sudden and hard slap on his hip where he had been supernaturally tagged into play.

"You're it!" Timothy chided happily a short distance away before disappearing again.

Xander smirked at his apprentice's unrealized skill and jumped into overdrive as well. He spotted his "opponent" in the distance, running back and forth in an effort to keep himself both invisible from sight as well as making himself a more difficult target to reach. He smiled wider as he saw this and began to charge forward, sprinting at superhuman speeds towards his apprentice. Timothy was smiling as well, the first real smile Xander had seen on the boy since he and the others had arrived. As he lunged for the boy and missed, he saw his smile grow wider and he felt his own face tighten with a wide grin. As their mutual enjoyment at the training-slash-playing grew, he found it was enough to allow him to forget all about his outside problems.

For the first time in a long time he, too, was smiling for real.

Timothy ran to one side then faked left before darting to the right. Xander, missing the move, skidded to a hard stop and tore the earth under his supercharged feet. They continued this way for what felt like several minutes until they were forced to drop out of overdrive due to exhaustion.

Xander was first to return to normal speed, taking in a deep breath before looking around for his apprentice, who remained "invisible" for several more seconds. In that time, Xander was "tagged" forcefully several more times, the impact of which was finally enough to force him to his knees.

As Xander held up his hands in surrender, Timothy appeared in front of him, the huge smile still plastered to his face as his breathing came in deep, ragged breaths. "Wow," he exclaimed, "You're *much* faster than Daddy was!"

Xander smirked and nodded, still out of breath. "Thanks."

The boy's training, he realized, would not be as difficult as he'd originally thought. If he'd learned to control all of his vampiric abilities through playing then it was only a matter of shaping his techniques and forming strategy out of the randomness. On top of this, Xander realized, Timothy, being a pure-born, was better equipped to last longer in overdrive as well as reserving energy more efficiently. He just had to make sure that his pupil didn't become too cocky about this fact...

Xander frowned as he thought of young Timothy growing up to become another Lenix.

He shuddered and shook the thought away.

"Alright," he smiled, rubbing his hands together, "Let's make the game even *more* fun, huh?"

Timothy nodded excitedly.

Xander smiled at his enthusiasm, "This time, we're going to play tag in the trees," he pointed towards the canopy of nearby branches, "If you touch the ground, you lose. So you've gotta stay in overdrive *and* focus on jumping, got it?"

Another nod.

With that, Xander leapt thirty feet into the air and landed, crouching, on one of the branches to a nearby tree. Timothy was right behind him.

Journal entry: December 8th

Estella,

Some newcomers came today asking for my help.

The strange thing is that they're all different races. They were even once part of a greater "family" unit that lived under one roof. I guess this vampire couple started bringing them in when they had nowhere else to go, but then these bastard hunters got to them and mowed down the entire household to just the five of them.

But it gets even weirder: two of them, an anapriek (those elfy/fairy-like things I told you about) and a therion, are together. Like TOGETHER-together! I look at them and I swear it's like looking at Trepis cuddle lovingly with a marinated rabbit.

It really makes no sense to me.

Bugs the hell out of the pack too.

You should have seen it! One of the therions in the pack was aching for a snack and thought he might try to take a bite out of this newcomer, and the damn anapriek beats ~~the shit out of~~ him with this stick he carries around!

As if that's not enough, when a few more members of the pack started to get in on it to avenge their kin, the anapriek's girlfriend, a therion, takes on the rest of them! Really wrecked them too!

Never thought I'd see the day.

Then there's Sasha, the other therion's sister, and she's

"friendly".

VERY friendly.

Too damn friendly if you ask me...

Anyway, then there's this nejin (one of those cat-like creatures... I haven't seen too many so far but they're something to look at; guess this one knows it because he's always wearing a hood). I can't remember his name, but he's really quiet. Haven't heard him utter a word since he's gotten here.

Something tells me he's a sight in battle, though. He certainly totes enough knives and swords to make me think he'd know how to use them.

And then there's this kid, Timothy. He's really young, I think they said he's like ten... maybe eleven. Anyway, this poor kid's a sang, and I can tell just by looking at him that he's got no idea how to defend himself, and it's not like this mismatched bunch of stooges knows step one of teaching him anything.

And every time I look at this kid I can't help but think of what happened to me at that age, and I just feel like I HAVE to help him.

So yea...

They tell me that the hunters that did this to them are still tailing them (this really pisses me off, because they might as well just paint a sign on the ~~pack's ass~~ pack saying "shoot here") and I can't decide whether or not I should get involved. Osehr certainly seems to think so, but I'm still on the fence...

So Osehr's letting them all stay and I'm taking on the kid as an apprentice.

I have this feeling that he's really going to need it, and soon.

Here's hoping you're staying safe.

I'll always love you,
X

CHAPTER TEN
MISSION

"FUCKING DISGUSTING!" RICHARD sneered at a spray of blood as he jammed his sword through the therion's heart to the hilt, making a point of twisting the blade before yanking free.

Dianna stayed quiet and holstered her still-smoking pistol as her own kill toppled over with a portion of its skull missing.

There was still one therion left alive; a younger one who had been, early on in the fray, crippled with three throwing knives buried in his left leg. One of them had nicked an artery and the creature was quickly losing blood...

And consciousness.

He'd be dead soon, there was no doubt about that, but Dianna knew that her brother wanted it alive long enough to answer his question.

According to Richard, the monsters knew everything about others of their kind, all of it being a part of some mythos conspiracy—something that Dianna was a bit skeptical to believe. With this thought driving him and her fear driving her, they'd tracked down the small gang of theriomorphs and lured them away from the city.

As usual, they stuck to Richard's "fool-proof" plan of using Dianna as bait.

"These things aren't geniuses," he'd pointed out in the beginning, "They're either going to want to eat you or fuck you. That or both."

It had taken all of Dianna's control to suppress a nervous shudder then.

Despite this, she had gone through with the plan, and, surprisingly enough, succeeded in getting them to follow her out of the city without getting, as her brother had pointed out, eaten or raped.

Now, however, she was almost wishing that they *had* killed her...

Richard was rough with the retrieval of his blades, and when the therion made an attempt to swipe at him with its claws it was rewarded with the loss of its hand. The creature, whose blood loss had already left it disoriented, didn't seem to notice the injury outside of realizing that it was no longer able to attack, and whimpered as it looked up at Richard.

Dianna sighed and approached as well, not wanting to seem out of place to her brother as he crouched down beside the creature and began demanding answers.

"Where are the others?" He growled.

Dianna knew that while the creature was in its bestial form it wouldn't be able to speak, but she didn't want to tell her brother and risk angering him further.

The therion's eyes continued to roll about in its skull as it whimpered and shivered, its body already going into shock.

"Richard, he—"

The flat side of Richard's sword was swung back and slapped her against the thigh, stopping her in mid-sentence. He didn't like being corrected, and the smack was a reminder of that and a promise of far greater punishment later that night for getting in the way. Silently enduring the sting, Dianna took a deep breath and stepped back to let her brother work.

But the therion was too far gone...

Richard heaved an angry sigh and rose to his feet, whipping his sword once to rid it of excess blood and sheathing it at his back before wiping his knives clean and putting them in the holsters at his hip, "Pathetic," he muttered as he turned away, though Dianna couldn't tell if he was referring to her or the therion.

Dianna frowned, looking at the suffering therion, "What about him?"

Richard frowned, eyeing the creature for a moment, and shrugged, "It's dying, stupid. We can't use it. We're done here. Now, are you coming?"

She didn't bother to plead her case but simply nodded and stood up, securing her own weapons, "I'll be right there. I just dropped something—"

"'Something'?"

Dianna nodded, "Yea. My... uh, my bowie knife."

Richard glared at her suspiciously for a moment before shrugging and shaking his head. "Well hurry up," he turned away and started to head out, "Swear to God you can't keep track of anything!" He turned suddenly, "Don't forget to—"

"I won't," she assured him, not waiting for him to finish.

Her brother scowled at being interrupted, but nonetheless turned and left, disappearing into the darkness.

Dianna let out a relieved breath and knelt back down beside the dying mythos. Its eyes were still darting, terrified, back and forth in its head, and its brow was soaked in a cold sweat.

She couldn't bear to see it suffer like that.

She felt the network of tattoos under her vest warm up as she harnessed their power. It wasn't an unpleasant sensation, quite the opposite in fact. She breathed in as the powers swelled within her and she pushed them down her arm and into her right hand. Once there, the powers swirled and jolted like electricity as she applied the proper spell to them. Finally, when they were ready, she pressed her palm to the therion's forehead and sent the magic into his skull.

As the spell worked into the therion's brain, his terrified eyes calmed and glassed over as the magic numbed his pain and allowed the pleasant memories of its life lull it off into a peaceful death.

Satisfied that it hadn't died in a moment of suffering, she forced herself to regain her composure. She knew that if Richard saw her crying there would be hell to pay for it, and, after a few deep breaths, she pulled herself to her feet and started towards the far wall of the boathouse. The winter season had made the lake-front area the perfect place to lure the therions—being both vacant *and* far enough away from civilization to lure any possible onlookers—and the boathouse came equipped with an easy means of disposing of the evidence.

The gasoline pumps were locked, and it took another spell to open the deadbolts. When, at last, she had access to them, she locked the levers and began to flood the structure in fuel. Once done, she hurried out of the boathouse and joined with her brother; his own tattoos already beginning to glow under his shirt.

Dianna frowned slightly as she glanced back; the entire structure was now a towering inferno.

Richard laughed and smiled at their handiwork, "Just like the bonfires back home, huh sis?" He gave her a sharp slap on the back.

Oliver—Richard had named the dog after their father—had been asleep in their stolen van. Now, however, with the ruckus of the explosions not far off in the distance, he was up and eager. As the vehicle bounced along the uneven surface of the unpaved road that led from the boathouse, their new pet ran up beside him and panted. Richard smiled at the animal and gave him a quick pat on the head and used his free hand to turn onto the main road, the keychain that boasted "World's Greatest Grandma" clanging against the other keys in the set. Dianna eyed the plastic charm a moment before forcing herself to turn away from the memory of her brother holding up the old couple at gunpoint for their van. Hotwiring, according to him, was a lazy way of getting a car when you could just as easily persuade somebody to give you the keys.

"Filthy creatures," he growled, pulling the neck of his vest to his nostrils and inhaling, "I can still smell them on me!"

Dianna stayed quiet.

Richard looked over, noticing his sister's silence and sneering, "Don't tell me that you actually *pity* those disgusting things? Those... those fucking monsters! Don't you remember what they did to Mom and Dad?"

"I remember," Dianna nodded, biting her lip.

"And for what?" He roared, pounding the steering wheel with his fist, "What did they ever do to anybody?"

Dianna kept her mouth shut, not wanting to anger him by pointing out that their parents had been hunters who had chalked up a large number of kills, as well. It wouldn't have surprised her if the mythos that had killed their parents were avenging those killed on one of their previous missions, but Richard, apparently, chose to see it a different way.

He shook his head and scoffed, "You know, it's a good thing that we came here. Back at home we were lucky to pick off a few of those monsters in a month, but around here they're walking the streets like they own the goddam city!" He rolled his eyes, "I even heard that there's a couple of vampire *nests* around here! You remember that story about that one nest? The... uh—Od-Odin? Yea!—the Odin nest?"

"I remember," Dianna repeated, nodding again.

"Yea, well, they were around here apparently," he laughed, "Before they went and got themselves butchered and torched. Man! Would I *love* to shake the hand of the guy responsible for that!"

Oliver barked excitedly in response to his new master's excited tone.

Richard smirked as he rubbed the dog behind his ear. "You know, I've been doing some thinking"—Dianna suppressed a shudder—"while the magic tats are cool and all, they might not be enough."

Dianna frowned and looked over at her brother, "Oh?"

Richard nodded, "Fuck yea! I think we should try out Mom and Dad's formula again."

Dianna's eyes widened, "But she never got around to testing it!"

"Then we'll 'get around' to it," he growled at her, "This asscrack of a city is *crawling* in fucking mythos dingleberries—they're practically falling out of the goddam sky here!—and we're gonna be the ones to wipe 'em out," he laughed at his own joke and slapped the steering wheel with the flat of his palm. "Rid this town—and then the fucking *world*—of those filthy monsters once and for all! We'll be heroes! HEROES!" He barked the word to Dianna as though he'd expected her to argue, "Goddam heroes! Just like Mom and Dad!"

Dianna shook her head, unable to wrap her mind around what her brother was saying.

The formula?

There was no way!

"But it might kill us!" She pointed out.

Richard rolled his eyes and gave their new dog another pat on the head, "That's why we test it on Oliver first."

The dog panted and looked up at him lovingly.

Dianna's eyes widened, "Test it... on the dog? You can't be serious!"

"Serious as a knife in your fucking chest," his tone was getting angry and Dianna tensed and shut her mouth. Her brother shook his head, "What's the big deal anyway? If he doesn't live through it we can always get another one."

There was no arguing with him; no getting through to him that what he was planning was wrong. Any attempts that were made at this point would just call down his wrath.

Poor Oliver...

There was nothing Dianna could do.

Journal entry: December 11th

Estella,

Timothy is doing incredibly!

When I first saw him I thought that I was going to have a difficult time training him to be a fighter, but I'll be damned if he doesn't already know all the tricks of our kind!

Turns out his old man taught him all the stuff but told him that it was all for fun. GAMES!

I've been going with that for the past few nights, continuing his "training" by playing tag and hide-and-go-seek.

His control and stamina is unbelievable!

I'd like to think that what I'm doing would make Marcus proud (but don't tell Osehr I said that... nevermind).

Zeek, the anapriek (HA! never realized that it rhymed before. Suddenly the name seems fitting) is being a real pain ~~in the balls~~. I think he's jealous that somebody else has taken the spotlight in the boy's world, but that's just tough ~~shit~~ for him, I guess.

His therion lover, Karen, is much more tolerable. For the most part she stays out of the way, and keeps her lesser half out of our business as well (which has got to be the biggest favor she's done for me).

Her sister is less helpful in that regard. She always pokes her head in while we're training, making more-than-noticeable advances. She even went so far as to poke her head into my tent the other day when Timothy was asleep! Even started to invite herself in before I told her to beat it.

Come to find that that was the wrong choice of words.

After finally clarifying to the too-grabby therion that I wanted her out she reluctantly left.

Then there's Satoru (yes I finally remembered his name, though it took some reminding). He still hasn't spoken a word since he got here, and mostly just follows Trepis around and watches while he plays with the youngsters. He finally took that hood off (guess being around a bunch of nearly-naked werewolves finally loosened him up).

Imagine a six-foot tall cat standing on its hind legs and you've got a nejin.

It was eerie.

I guess I shouldn't be too surprised by looks by now considering my "family"... I mean, there's plenty of therions in the pack that look cat-LIKE, but I swear it's so bizarre seeing something that looks like a human-pet hybrid.

He's quite the hunter, though. He's constantly showing up in the middle of training with a squirrel or badger or something for Tim to feed on. I've told him several times now that there's no need, since I got the synthetic stuff (which is at least ten times more potent... though there's nothing nice to say about the taste).

So he brings a snack for the boy and then just sits and watches with a strange cat-like smile at the sight of what the kid can do.

Osehr seems happy with the way things are going, though he's getting more and more impatient about "Kriss-mas".

I keep telling him that it's not time yet and I swear he looks more and more agitated each time I say it.

I think I'll be lucky if I live to see the damn holiday.

Oh well, least I'll be leaving a spectacular little soldier as my legacy.

My legacy...

Damn...

When will that stop coming back to haunt me.

Anyway, the kid's asking for another story about his mentor as the hero, so I think I'll wrap this up.

Think I might head into town and see if I can find any trace of you after he's asleep... though I'm sure my luck with that will be about as good as it has been for the past couple of months.

Anyway... love ya lots.
X

CHAPTER ELEVEN
CHASING STARS

TIMOTHY, AS IT TURNED out, was a better apprentice than Xander had expected. In only a couple of days they'd gone over almost everything he could think of and the boy already knew it all. It seemed that the only thing that his father hadn't taught him to do through their "games" was to fight.

Something that Xander, too, was hesitant to jump into.

For the first time, though he didn't have much experience with kids—he'd never had a sibling and the neighbors sure as hell never wanted to have him over to babysit—he couldn't help but feel a connection with Timothy. The little vampire had most certainly grown on him, a fact that surprised him to no end and one that Osehr had far too much fun pointing out as often as possible.

It had always been a mission of Xander's to seem as tough as possible. He'd learned early on in his human life that a hard exterior could hide even the biggest pains and fears that lurked within, and, furthermore, that those who wanted to hurt him knew to target any visible signs of weakness. Determined to never appear weak or afraid, he'd simply grown accustomed to not showing his soft side—a side of him that he'd only ever let Estella see.

And look where that had gotten him...

So, while the connection was enough of a shock to him, the fact that it was *evident* was an unnerving realization.

But he couldn't bring himself to fight it.

At sunrise, when their training was over, he'd take his apprentice back to the tent where he'd given him a thermos of synthetic blood to recover from the night's work and tell him stories. He kept the stories of Kyle and Lenix to himself, not wanting to have to explain his own parents' death, though that was more for Timothy's benefit then his own.

It was on the third night, after another story about one of his adventures with a particularly difficult-to-dispose-of ghoul that his apprentice asked to see his now-famed revolvers, Yin and Yang. This caught him off guard, as he'd not had to use the "twins"—though after Yin's destruction during the battle with Lenix Yang had found itself an only child—for several months. Seeing no real problem with it, Xander went into the other compartment where his foot lockers were kept and unlocked the one containing his old weapons.

He started with the revolver, checking the chambers to make sure it wasn't loaded before handing the gun to the little vampire. His apprentice took it like a treasure in both hands, staring wide-eyed at the solid white revolver with awe. After a moment he looked up and asked about Yin.

Xander shook his head, "It was destroyed in a battle." He explained.

Timothy frowned and handed Yin back to him, "Destroyed?" His voice was shocked and pained.

Xander nodded. He, too, was heartbroken at the loss of the other revolver—a solid black copy of its twin—that was just as much an heirloom as it was a weapon. "I'm afraid so," he smiled, "But a close friend of mine made me these:"—he reached back into the case and pulled out a set of custom-made pistols that had been built in an attempt to mimic the originals. Though smaller and more modern, the two were still an impressive pair. Xander held them for a moment, admiring them, before he ejected the magazines and checked the chambers once again for any stray rounds before handing them to Timothy as well.

The boy looked at the guns for a moment before gripping them clumsily at the handles and aiming them out in front of him. Rocking his hands back and forth—mimicking their recoil—he made "bang-bang" noises and smiled up at Xander after several of his play-shots had been fired.

Xander couldn't help but smile back.

"So why don't you fight anymore?" Timothy asked as he handed the guns back to his mentor.

Xander sighed and shrugged, shaking his head, "Because I don't *need* to fight anymore."

"But aren't there still bad people out there?" Timothy tilted his head.

"I suppose so," Xander nodded, taking the pistols and putting them away in the footlocker, "But there are lots of other warriors out there who can take care of them." He smiled and shrugged, "Besides, I like how my life is going right now."

Timothy frowned skeptically for a moment and looked down.

"What is it?" Xander asked.

"You say you're happy..." Timothy looked up, "... but you seem so sad."

Xander frowned, "You think I'm sad?"

Timothy nodded.

"Why do you think that?"

The little vampire blushed and shrugged, "Sometimes..."

Xander raised an eyebrow, "Yea...?"

"Sometimes..." he looked up at him, "... you cry when you're asleep."

Xander frowned and chewed his lip. He wasn't sure what to say to that. After a moment he realized that Timothy was still looking at him and he smiled lightly. "It's alright," he assured the little vampire, "Sometimes I just dream of sad times."

Timothy frowned at this, but didn't press the issue.

Xander appreciated it.

"Hey," Xander gave Timothy a gentle shove, "I gotta go out for a little bit. You think you can hold the fort for me until I get back?" He moved away from the footlocker and grabbed a hair tie, pulling his long, shaggy black hair back tightly into a ponytail so that he was at least somewhat presentable to the outside world.

Timothy frowned and sat up, "But it's daytime!"

Xander nodded, "I know, but I'll be extra careful."

"Promise?" Timothy's face was serious.

Xander smirked and nodded, "Yea. I Promise. Can you stay in here and get some rest while I run a couple of errands?"

Timothy nodded.

"Good man," Xander patted his shoulder, "Trepis will be just outside the tent so you won't be lonely, and I'll make sure Zeek or Karen are nearby if you need anything."

As if the two had been reading his thoughts the anapriek and his therion lover were approaching the tent as he stepped out. Trepis looked up, lifting his head and sniffing at Zeek questioningly before turning his attentions to Karen, who happily knelt down and began to rub and pat the tiger's head.

"Who's a good boy?" She cooed. "Yes you are!"

Xander frowned, not really approving of the baby-talk with his animal friend but not protesting it either. It wouldn't be worth it to go through the conflict if he did say something.

Zeek was less interested in the tiger and stood over Xander with all the confidence and pride of a warrior. It was a dangerous combination, being both the mythos equivalent of a double cheeseburger as well as a cocky asshole, especially on the therions' turf, where his fighting skills would only get him so far once he found himself under the metaphorical—and, Xander supposed, literal—dog-pile. Frowning, Xander noticed the condescending stare and overconfident swirl of the anapriek's aura as he looked down at him. Like the others he traveled with, save for Timothy, he was a nature-based mythos, and his energy signature shone in a honey-like earth tone. It was one of the few things that anaprieks and therions had in common.

Not that a therion would be happy to hear it or even admit it, of course.

"Is there a problem?" Xander asked quietly enough to not catch Timothy's attention.

"You tell me." Zeek fired back, not extending the courtesy of keeping his voice down. There was a rustle in the tent, but it soon stopped. The boy had heard the conflicting tone in his friend's voice, and he was smart enough to lay low and not get in the middle of it.

Xander took a step away from the tent and towards the anapriek, letting his hand come to rest on his shoulder. Though he didn't hurt him, Xander gave a slight squeeze to show that he could, at any given moment, change that fact, "Not if there doesn't have to be." Getting tired of the anapriek and his attitude, Xander turned to Karen. "I need to head out into the city. The boy—"

"He has a name!" Zeek spat.

Xander turned his stare to him, making sure to narrow his blood-stained right eye at him to emphasize just how important it was that he *not* open his mouth again. Finally, when the anapriek's aura receded nervously and he was sure that there'd be no more outbursts, he turned back to the therion woman, "He's resting off last night's training. I told him to stay out of the sun and that you'd be here for him in case he needed anything. I trust that was alright?"

Karen smiled warmly and nodded, "Of course," Zeek frowned and curled his lip at Xander before she took a hold of his hand and gave it a gentle squeeze. "Don't mind him," she said to Xander, "He's just not the trusting type."

Xander smirked and nodded, walking past them, "Trust me, I can relate."

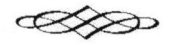

⋘⋙

Osehr smiled when he saw Xander enter the clearing and rose to his feet, "You're going into the city?"

Xander grinned, "You reading my mind?"

"Nope," Osehr shrugged, "You just never come out during the day unless you're going into the city."

Xander rolled his eyes, "Astute as ever, eh?" He nodded,

"Yea. I'm going to go get some supplies and see if I can get a hint of Estella anywhere in the area."

Osehr nodded, "Do not give up hope," he reminded him. Though he, like Xander, had no way of knowing Estella's fate, he remained confident that she was still in the area and, moreover, safe, "I'm sure you'll find her soon."

"Here's hoping," Xander sighed.

"Hey, sugar, you heading out?" Xander turned and found himself face-to-face with Sasha, her wild hair catching the breeze and shifting slightly before falling across her face. With a toss of her head, she cleared the mass out of her vision and smiled warmly. "Want some company?"

He frowned, catching quickly on to the therion's advances—something that he'd already gotten used to from other females in Osehr's pack, though they'd never been so forward. He took a step back, freeing himself of the musky aroma of the new therion and shook his head, trying to keep his response polite, "I'd rather be alone, thanks."

"Aw. Don't make me beg," she pouted her lips and pushed her chest out in a display.

Xander rubbed his face in his palm before pinching the bridge of his nose. He shook his head again, "I'll be fine. Thanks anyway," he turned back to Osehr, rolling his eyes slightly. *What's with her?* he psychically asked his friend.

Osehr smirked and chuckled, *I think she likes you.*

Really? Thanks for clearing that up! I would never have guessed! Xander's sarcasm rang heavy even without the use of tone, *Her sister's with an anapriek and she's aiming her sights on a vampire? Don't the males of your pack still have dicks?*

The therion leader barked loudly with laughter as Xander started off in the direction of civilization. As he passed, Sasha studied him, looking over at the still-cackling Osehr before turning back and narrowing her eyes knowingly at him and winking. Xander shook his head and turned back to his friend, who was beginning to settle down from his laughing fit.

"You want anything? More beer, perhaps?" He laughed, remembering Osehr's distaste for alcohol.

The therion made a disgusted face but shrugged, "None for

me, my friend, but maybe the pack would appreciate it."

Xander laughed and nodded, turning away and heading out.

⁂

It was cloudy, and the dark skies held the threat of rain. Xander appreciated the cover.

He decided that he'd make the liquor store his last stop, not wanting to burden himself with the task of toting around three or four cases of beer all day. While he knew that, though the indulgences could be left to wait, he should have focused the bulk of his outing on restocking his camp's supplies, but, having been isolated in the woods for so long, he had a hard time focusing on such demands. Instead, he spent the majority of the morning walking around the city and people-watching. While there was nothing inherently interesting about the pedestrians that he passed, it was fun to let his aura graze on the thoughts that bobbed in their heads.

... wonder if he'll call me. He said to wait a couple...

... hope it doesn't start to stink before I can move it. Don't need the kids finding out that their mother...

...food! Cat food! Mister Whiskers will KILL me if I forget! Can NOT forget the—Hey, a sale on...

... bitch thinks she can treat me like that? Show her! I'll fuck the first thing with tits that I see! Ew! Not her... not her... not...

Xander shook his head and chuckled, the grumbling man shooting him an enraged glare as he stepped between him and a buxom redhead a short distance away. Smirking knowingly, Xander lifted an eyebrow at the man, who opened his mouth to say something before he caught sight of his blood-red eye and decided that his mission for infidelity could wait.

Continuing on, Xander found himself trekking further and further from the shopping district as the nature of the shops and passersby alike shifted towards the unconventional. Not letting this sway him, he J-walked past a parked police car—the on-duty officer succumbing to an auric tweak and never seeing him—and turned onto a new street marked with a towering sculpture made of spray-painted sheet metal and car parts. Here, in the heart of the art district—where the bulk of the local university's aspiring

Picassos and Rembrandts and, more than any other, Warhols gathered and gabbed—Xander knew that his appearance would mean little. With the likes of Twilight and Vampire Diaries making his kind something far more glamorous than they truly were, the sight of a vampire "wannabe" strolling about wasn't about to arouse any suspicion.

Though that seemed to be all that wasn't aroused in the area.

As the majority of the thoughts funneled towards sex and the abstract—several of the more "creative" minds horrifically combining the two in their warped heads—Xander felt an overwhelming increase in the number of eyes on him. Getting a glimpse at a nearby Latino boy's growing fantasy of seeing Xander dressed in a rabbit suit and rolling in a puddle of honey, he shuddered, deciding to stop reading thoughts for the day, and hurried across the street and towards a small café.

He was more than ready for the silence and a cup of tea.

As he went to push through the door he noticed some damage around the aged and cracked frame, which contrasted with the brand new and freshly painted door occupying the space. Shaking his head, he reached out and picked at a chunk of the frame where it appeared to have been torn out and shook his head.

College kids were crazy; art students were crazier.

Maybe seeking peace in this place was expecting too much.

As he made his way in he was greeted by an older woman who, wiping a nearby table, seemed to be responding more to the tolling bell over the door than the presence of a new customer. Without breaking her stride or even looking up, she robotically called out "good morning" and scooped up the meager tip she'd been left. As he made his way across the room to the counter, he was surprised at how many people there were and worried that finding a seat might be a problem.

"Can I help you?" A peppy, teenage boy wearing a blue apron asked from behind the counter.

Xander nodded and ignored the grimace as their eyes met, "Large black tea with milk."

The boy nodded, unable to look away from Xander's eye as he punched in the order, "Anything else?"

Xander smirked, "Uh, yea. Can I get a glass of cow's blood?"

The boy looked up, startled, "Wh-what?"

"Relax. I'm joking," Xander said flatly as he handed him the debit card to the account with the untold fortune he and Marcus had accumulated over their time as supernatural bounty hunters. "Maybe time to lay off the dark roast, huh? You're a little high-strung."

"Oh... right. That's... uh, that's pretty funny," he laughed nervously and went about filling a cup with hot water.

Xander shook his head and looked behind him towards the seats where a couple of kids were beginning to pack up their laptops. Glancing around the room, he made a note of keeping his aura inside of him so that he wouldn't be tempted to read any more minds.

If the boy behind the counter was any hint, he was doing himself a favor.

"Large tea with milk."

Xander turned at the call and watched as the barista set the drink on the counter in front of him.

Xander scooped up the cup and hurried to the table to stake his claim to it as the last student scurried away. He sat and sighed, blowing absent-mindedly at his drink as he let his mind wander. He was in no hurry to guzzle the beverage. Though his vampiric system allowed him to consume human food and drink there was no real nutrition behind it. His body needed blood or psychic energy and the magic that lay therein; anything else was just filler that allowed him to appear human to those who didn't know any better.

He remembered when Estella...

"Anybody sitting here?" A meek voice called his attentions away from his thoughts and back to the moment.

"Huh," he looked up and saw a girl about his age with long black hair and brown eyes looking down at him expectantly. She held a steaming cup in one hand and with the other was holding the chair across from him that was still empty, "Oh... no. Go ahead."

Though he thought the girl just needed an empty chair to drag off to whatever table her friends were at she instead pulled it out just enough to plop down at the table in front of him. He stared, confused, as she let out a deep sigh and took a sip of her drink. She was quiet for a moment and appeared lost in the relaxation of a hot drink. Xander tried his best not to look at her, trying not to call attention to his confusion as to why she'd sat down beside him, and instead looked over at a small stage set up in the corner with a microphone and a few amps that had been pushed against the back wall.

"That's a neat contact lens," the girl chimed.

Xander turned his attention to her, "Hmm? What?"

"Your contact lens, I like it," she blushed at her own compliment, "Doesn't it hurt, though, having it cover your entire eye like that?"

"Oh, uh... no. I've just gotten used to it, I guess," Xander reached up absently to touch his right temple beside his eye.

"Oh," she looked back down at her drink and nodded slowly, "well that's good."

Xander returned the gesture, not happy that he'd been dragged into an awkward conversation when all he'd wanted was a drink and a place to relax. He swore to himself that if she handed him a pamphlet for *anything* he'd lose it. "So..." he cleared his throat, "You... uh, come here often?"

"Oh, no. I'm actually not from here," she confessed before taking another sip of her drink, "My brother and I just moved into the area."

Xander nodded again, slower this time, "Do you two go to the university?"

She shook her head, "No. We're only here on business."

"I see," Xander frowned, knowing that he had to follow the natural course of the conversation and doing his best to play the role, "What do you do?"

"Hmm?" The girl looked up, apparently getting lost in her own thoughts.

Xander frowned, "You said you're here on business. What do you do?"

"Oh... um... we're exterminators."

Xander laughed, "Kinda young to be an exterminator, aren't you?"

The girl giggled nervously, "I guess. It's a family business. My parents taught us about it and when they died my brother and I took over."

"Oh," Xander looked down and swirled his tea a little before taking another sip, "I'm sorry... about your parents I mean. I lost mine too."

"I'm sorry too," the girl frowned and looked down at her drink, "So are you a student then?"

Xander shook his head, "I'm..." he thought for a moment, "a teacher."

The girl looked at him skeptically, "You teach at the university?"

He laughed and shook his head, "No no. Nothing that boring. I'm really more of a tutor, I guess."

"Oh? What subject?" She cocked her head.

"Anthropology," Xander looked away as a nearby table erupted into laughter.

"Oh," she smiled, "Sounds interesting."

Glad that the answer satisfied her curiosity and she hadn't gone any further on the topic Xander smiled and took another sip of his tea, "Yea, it's a total thrill," he looked over at her, "Since when do exterminators travel?"

"We don't. Well, *they* don't, I meant. But... um... business was slow back at home and my brother decided we'd make a better living here in the city."

Xander nodded and smirked, "Probably true. Lots of pests roaming around that need to be dealt with."

"Yea. That's what my brother says, too," she frowned for a moment, "So what's your name?"

Xander sighed, seeing that the conversation wasn't about to come to a clunky end anytime soon, "Xander."

"Hmm... Short for 'Alexander', right?"

"So I've heard, but it's always just been 'Xander'. Maybe my mom was just lazy."

She giggled, "So do you know what it means?"

"What *what* means?"

"Your name."

Xander frowned and shook his head, "Guess I never cared

enough to find out."

"Well, 'Alexander' means 'a protector of men'," she smiled wide, "Like Alexander the Great."

He stared at her a moment, stunned. "I see. So how do you know that? You got a Xander in the family or something?"

"No, nothing like that," she shrugged, "Just a hobby, I guess. I like to study the meanings behind things, and I guess names aren't any different."

Xander nodded, "I see. So what's yours?"

The girl looked up, confused, "Hmm?"

Xander raised an eyebrow, "Your name?"

"Oh. Right... doy," she made a note of tapping her forehead, "I'm Dianna."

"And what does that mean?"

She sighed, as if tired of hearing the question or not happy with the answer, "It means 'divine'. It was also an ancient goddess of the moon and..." she sighed again, "And hunting."

Xander nodded, "Well, it's nice to meet you, Dianna the 'divine' exterminator-goddess."

Dianna giggled, "And it's nice to meet you, Xander the 'protective' tutor." They laughed, though it was more awkward than friendly. Finally she sighed and looked down, "There really aren't enough protectors out there."

"Oh?" Xander frowned, not sure what to make of the new turn this conversation was taking.

She nodded and took a sip of her drink. "Yea. There are a lot of people out there paid to kill and destroy, but you so rarely hear anybody offering to protect. It's too bad that you're just a tutor, you seem like you might make a good protector."

"Uh huh..." Xander stared down into his nearly empty cup and finally drank the last of his tea and started to get up, "Well. It was nice talking to you."

Dianna bit her lip and nodded, "It was nice talking to you too, Xander."

He stopped suddenly, a thought coming to him, and turned back to the girl, "Oh, just out of curiosity, do you know the meaning behind the name 'Estella'?"

Dianna smirked, "Sweetheart of yours?"

"Something like that," Xander felt himself blush and looked away.

She tilted her head quizzically, but smiled nonetheless, "It's another form of 'Estelle', meaning 'star'. Also a goddess of love."

Xander nodded slowly, considering this for a moment, "Seems appropriate. Thanks."

As he left the café, he found himself frowning and deeply disappointed in himself. Here he'd just met a complete stranger, and even she thought he should be the so-called "protector" that everyone felt he was born to be. He sighed, setting aside his thoughts and going about the rest of the day.

After all, he had a missing star to find.

CHAPTER TWELVE
AIMLESS QUEST

ESTELLA WASN'T SURE when she'd finally fallen asleep, but she was, despite the agonizing pain she woke up to, glad to find the gang of boys gone and all of her clothes still on.

It was early morning, something like seven or eight, and while the sun's damage to her skin was severe, it hadn't killed her. She knew, however, that it would only be a matter of time. Her crate had been smashed and the blanket was in shreds and soaked in urine; it seemed that while the boys hadn't taken advantage of her sleeping body, they *had* left her with no means of protection.

Bastards!

With her options limited to moving on or dying right there on the ground from skin cancer, she dragged herself to her feet and started moving. She didn't know where she was going, or if she'd even make it somewhere safe before dropping one final time of either sun-poisoning or starvation, but she forced herself to keep on trudging forward into a hiking trail that shot off from the park. Several times she collapsed and, unable to immediately pull herself back up, began crawling on her hands and knees until she found something sturdy enough pull her back to her feet.

Though the denser forest lay several miles off, a small canopy of trees were available to provide just enough shade to keep her at least somewhat protected. Struggling to stay on the winding and narrow path that was, thankfully, free of any dog-walkers and joggers that might present her with more temptation, Estella found that her eyesight was beginning to fade in-and-out of focus. Though the violent gash in the otherwise lush grass and shrubbery should have been simple to navigate through, her waning vision made it a clumsy and time-consuming trek.

After what felt like hours of pushing and stumbling forward, the trees and greenery opened up and she found herself in an old train yard. Tracks jutted out in random directions and the gravel-ridden ground crunched under her dragging feet. All around her were empty and waiting train-cars, their large metal gates hanging open like hungry mouths eager for their next big cargo. Staring at them and trying to force her mind to make sense of her surroundings, Estella felt the sun's rays begin to seep through the skin on the back of her neck and she whimpered and stumbled towards the nearest train car, the pitch-black interior offering greater shelter than she'd had in months.

Though it was only a few steps away, Estella's eyesight finally abandoned her and she tripped and hit the ground—unable to muster the breath to cry out as she felt a few of the more unforgiving stones cut into her palms—and dragged herself across the remaining distance. As she reached the car, she pulled herself up, gripping the opening with all the strength she had left and pulling her useless body into the cool shade; finally taking the moon pendant around her neck tightly into her hand.

As her eyes rolled back in her skull and her eyelids dragged shut over them, she accepted the fact that they may never open again.

CHAPTER THIRTEEN
FOUND

XANDER WAS TAKING a long way home.

At least he thought it was a way home; quite frankly he didn't care too much where it took him. He wanted to do some thinking and that's what the path he'd found himself on allowed him to do. All around him were the sounds of nature, except the rumble of a passing train in the distance. He didn't let this bother him too much, though; his thoughts wandering from him letting his own namesake down to shooting stars that could never be seen...

Damn was he out of it.

He wasn't sure if maybe too much UV had gotten to him or if he was just tired, but something was bogging him down.

Refusing to let him focus and head back to the therion pack.

The day was nearly spent, the late afternoon sun hanging in the horizon and waiting for night to swallow it away. An entire day of sleep lost, and no beer to show for it.

Xander sighed; Osehr had no-doubt told them that he'd be coming back with booze, and they'd be pissed to see him show up empty handed.

More than anything, though, he was disappointed—though, ultimately, not surprised—that another day had been spent futilely looking for his lost lover. Sighing and shaking his head he kicked a rock that occupied the corner of the path, letting it roll into the bushes off to the side.

Why did he keep doing this to himself?

Maybe Osehr was wrong; maybe she *was* gone—left town, or worse...

He chewed his lip and shook his head again.

"Estella..."

The path opened up then into a clearing. All around him were spare cars for the nearby train station, all lined up and waiting for their chance to be a part of the next big caravan. Somewhere up ahead—on the other side of one of the cars—were several auric signatures. They were close; too close to be anything but a couple of thrill-seeking lovers who wanted to have some fun in a secluded-yet-public location. He smirked and shook his head.

Humans...

He started on, heading off to the side so that the love-birds could have their moment alone before stopping again and scanning the auras once more.

One was vibrant; alive and vigorous with sexual anticipation just as he'd expect.

But the other...

Motionless.

Dim.

Fading fast.

It was barely even alive!

Plus something else in it; something inhuman.

Something magical.

Xander frowned and glanced back towards the source.

A human was about to rape a dying mythos...

He frowned, staring off for a long moment as he chewed his lip. Was it really any of his business? Was it really something that he needed to involve himself with? Renegade mythos took advantage of humans all the time! Was it really his concern if the tides were turned every once in a while?

Besides, no matter what his legacy was—no matter what his name meant—he wasn't a protector!

Shaking his head, he took another step in the opposite direction.

Let one of the clans' warriors deal with it however they saw fit.

Besides, if he started stopping for every mythos that needed help, he might as well give up on finding Estella right then and there!

A chuckle sounded followed by a meek whimper and carried over to Xander's sensitive ears.

Rape...

He shook his head, unable to take another step away. In the back of his mind he was assaulted with the memory of his mother's rape; remembering the torture she'd gone through at the hands of Kyle and his gang before she'd been stabbed to death.

What if somebody had had the chance to stop that from happening?

Like he had the chance now...

Could he live with the knowledge that he'd let such an awful, heinous act be committed when he was standing right there.

He shook his head violently.

No!

He was across the path and on top of the boxcar before the rapist would have had the chance to blink. He perched on the edge, staring down at the startled man who was in the middle of pulling the pants off the dying mythos inside. Xander's rage ran through his body, burning him from the inside and making his fangs rocket from the sheaths in his gums. He bared them, his mouth opened in a venomous and threatening hiss that had the man stepping back, stammering.

He was afraid.

Good!

He should be!

The vampire jumped down, landing between the human and his would-be victim; his eyes narrowed and locked on the human. He didn't care that there was plenty of the synthetic blood back at his tent in the forest.

It tasted like shit anyway!

And he was suddenly aching for a taste of the real thing!

He stretched out his aura without looking and scanned behind him to decipher the nature of the dying mythos.

Sangsuiga; nearly starved to death.

He smirked.

Fitting!

He'd feed the attacker to them. Maybe it'd be enough to save them, or at the very least let them go with a decent meal.

Jumping into overdrive, he closed the distance between him and the would-be rapist before he even knew that he'd moved. Xander needed to keep him alive; keep the heart beating; keep the blood flowing. He went for the knees; bringing his foot down and shattering both kneecaps. Dropping out of overdrive then, he wrapped his aura around him and drank in the human's pain; savoring in the attacker's agony.

Hey! Why not get a little meal in for himself while he could?

As Xander's attack caught up with the man and he started to collapse, Xander drove his hand into his stomach for good measure and dragged him—dirt and gravel dragging at the exposed bones in his legs—to the boxcar and...

Dropped him.

Xander could do nothing but stare in shock at the would-be vampire victim. Her hair was longer and dirty from not being washed in who-knew how long. Her skin was red and beginning to blister slightly from too much time in the sun. She was dirty and dying...

And every bit as beautiful as in his dreams!

Every bit as perfect!

Every bit as his!

He'd found her!

His Estella!

And he'd nearly let the worst happen to her...

She lay there, her breathing labored and uneven. Her shirt—a tattered and torn tank top—had been pulled up to expose one reddened breast. Her jeans—just as dirtied and destroyed—rested just beyond her thighs, though her panties remained untouched.

He'd made it just in time!

Snarling angrily, he turned on the man.

"You stupid asshole," he growled, stepping towards him, "Your dick just signed your death warrant!"

"Wh-wha—" the man groaned, clutching at his legs and crying out in pain, "What the *fuck* is this?"

Xander's lip curled and he bared his fangs to him again, "This is hell! The *worst* kind of hell! And I'm your personal devil!"

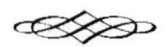

⋖⋙⋗

Enough time was spent to cover the areas of exposed flesh that Estella wouldn't have wanted shared to the world before Xander went on to torturing her attacker. He wasn't sure how much time passed, but by the time he had satisfied the bulk of his brutal urges the sun had set and very little of the man's body wasn't covered in bruises or missing chunks of skin. Though he didn't have a knife, the rocks that littered the train yard—though somewhat dull—served well enough for his purposes. The man's left eye now mirrored Xander's right where he had repeatedly stomped on his head. Through he would have loved to give him a matching set, Xander had left his right eye untouched so he'd be able to watch as both his legs were broken again and again.

And by keeping a secure auric hold on him, Xander was able to keep the man from going into shock and rob him of the pleasure of torturing him.

Finally, he dragged the man towards the boxcar that held Estella and used one of the blood-soaked rocks to cut a fresh wound into his forearm. Estella had remained stable the entire time—her body even beginning to heal itself as he'd funneled some of the syphoned psychic energy into her unconscious form—and, using a blood-drenched fingertip, he gently worked her mouth open.

The taste of the blood sent the unconscious vampire into a frenzy, and she grabbed Xander's hand and began to gnaw at his fingers for more. Ignoring the pain, he worked to withdraw his hand and led Estella's mouth to the human's wound. As the first few drops filled her mouth, she bit down, forcing her fangs through the skin again and again for more of the blood that Xander realized she must have been denying herself the whole time. With her starved body absorbing the stolen life-force, her body rapidly began to heal. A healthy pale-pink hue replaced the sickly bluish-green tint of her skin and her muscles swelled with new strength.

"That's it! Drink! Take all you need!" Xander urged her.

Estella groaned and sat up, pulling the would-be rapist's neck to her mouth and tearing into his throat. The sound of her gulps echoed in the metal box and Xander smiled at the entire scene.

He'd found her!

He'd saved her!

Everything was going to be alright!

Then her eyes opened; snapping to awareness like a switch had been flipped, and they locked onto the still-quivering body that she now drank from. As recognition set in, her eyes went wide in shock and disgust and she threw the man away from her, sending him from the boxcar and back to the ground outside. Her eyes darted back and forth, taking in her blood-covered hands. Sobbing at the sight, she wiped her lips with her quivering fingertips and cried out when they came back bloody.

And then she saw Xander.

"You..."

CHAPTER FOURTEEN
LOST

"WHAT DID YOU DO?" Estella's voice was filled with shock and hate.

Xander frowned and shook his head, "N-no... he tried to... you were dying!"

"THEN YOU SHOULD HAVE LET ME DIE!" She roared. Her aura swelled—fueled by her revitalized magic and rage—and the metal surrounding them squealed and groaned under the pressure.

"Estella! Please!" Xander tried to approach her.

"NO!" she screamed. Her magic slammed into him and he was thrown from the car and sent careening into a neighboring boxcar.

The world flashed red behind Xander's eyes as he slammed into the metal siding and he felt his mind spin as the boxcar tipped from the force. As the boxcar came to rest on its side, Xander cast his weary gaze towards the opening—now facing skyward and offering him a partial view of the waning moon—and fought to regain his senses and free himself from the dented metal box.

"Shit!" He groaned, pulling himself from the wreckage and looking around the train yard, "Estella?"

"XANDER!"

Casting his gaze upward, he saw his long-lost lover's form linger in the sky momentarily like a warrior-angel as gravity began to take hold of her supernatural leap.

And then she dropped.

Xander's eyes widened as he threw himself back, flipping free of her trajectory as she crashed down and left a gaping dent in the spot he'd been standing. Gawking at the spectacle, Xander forced himself to focus as Estella hissed angrily at him and charged at him. Despite having never been trained, it appeared that her rage was enough to carry her forward in a whirlwind of powerful—though ultimately sloppy—attacks.

Xander dodged and parried each advance, refusing to throw a single punch. He wrapped himself in his aura to block another vampire-fueled punch only to have her mutter a spell and have the ground tear out from under him. Landing hard in the magic-born hole, he rolled and leapt out just in time to avoid the avalanche of rock that crashed down where he'd fallen.

"Estella! Please just liste—"

"Stop saying my name, you monster!" She swung her arm wide for a punch, only to have it caught in Xander's grip. She tried with the other arm; same result.

The two vampires stared at one another; Estella struggling to free herself from the unbreakable grasp.

"LET ME GO!" She screamed, her face a twisted mask of rage and sorrow; tears streaming down her reddened face.

"It's going to be okay," Xander assured her, as he started to drain some of her excess energy through his right hand—one of the first auric tricks he'd learned—to calm her down. Her struggling slowed and finally stopped as her growls turned to sobs.

"Please... Let me go..." she pleaded.

"I can't," Xander admitted to her, "Not again."

Her tears poured down her cheeks as she allowed her face to fall into Xander's still-heaving chest. Slowly, still uncertain if there was any fight left in her, Xander released her arms, which fell to her sides before wrapping, with a great deal of struggle and uncertainty, around his waist in a weak embrace.

He held her tighter, "It's okay now, Estella."

Whimpering, she shook her head and moved her tear-stained face up to meet his gaze, "No... it's not," she stepped away from him and turned to look back at the mangled body behind them, "I killed him. *I* killed him!"

Xander shook his head, "No, you don't understand! You didn't do anything wrong!" As he watched her small body continue to tremble under the weight of her own guilt, he saw her right hand rise towards her chest, where she took a small, familiar moon pendant around her neck tightly into her hand.

The pendant that he'd given her before...

His eyes widening, Xander reached out to her, "You... you kept it? After all that's happened you still—"

"Don't you understand?" She demanded, "I *killed* a man! I took a life! Another person's *life!*"

"N-no! Estella, it's not like that! You were starving; dying," Xander struggled to find the right sequence of words to calm her, "And he was trying to..." he frowned and shook his head, unable to speak the words, "He was going to hurt you, Estella! What you did was justified!" He assured her. "And besides, it doesn't need to happen again. I have this synthetic—"

But then she was gone.

Disappearing into overdrive and leaving him...

Again.

Leaving nothing but the lingering memory of her warmth and his tear-soaked shirt.

CHAPTER FIFTEEN
TOUGH LOVE

Journal entry: December 13th

To whoever finds this,

I've decided that it's not worth it to try and keep fooling myself into thinking that this life is worth living anymore. As a human I was an emo bitch-boy, and as a vampire I'm a failure, and as a friend and a lover I'm a letdown. I've heard from so many different sources (including complete strangers) that the path I've chosen is the wrong one, but I don't have the strength or even the drive to do what it is that is expected of me.

Timothy is a promising boy. Give him the attention and training that he needs, and with any luck he may grow up to be the next Joseph Stryker that everybody expected me to become.

Enclosed are several dozen blank checks from my account.

It should be enough to last a good long while. Be responsible with the money and make sure that it goes towards the wellbeing of the pack (don't just spend it all on beer).

I would like the pack, Osehr especially, to get a chance to enjoy Christmas the way it should be. Put Timothy in charge of making sure it all works out (I promise there's no better spokesperson for the holiday than a child).

Osehr: Thank you for being my best friend and damn good therapist when I needed one the most. Believe me when I say that all the things you said were true. You are truly wise beyond all others.

I'd like to think that I could get a message out to Estella, though I doubt that's possible, but if there truly is a miracle this year and she comes within earshot, please tell her that I'm sorry and that I love her more than I ever thought I could love anybody else.

I'm sorry I wasn't better.
X

PS- take good care of Trepis for me. I know I can trust the pack to show the big lug a good life.

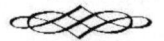

※

    He was used to doing this with Yin, but, with the black revolver long-since lost and likely destroyed, he was forced to settle with its albino twin. When he'd been human it had been a ritual that was performed each night before bed: one bullet in the chamber and one pull of the trigger. Each night, for eight grueling years, the hammer had fallen on an empty chamber. He later found out that it had been his own subconscious controlling his aura—knowing that there was still work to be done—holding back the life-ending shot.
    He wouldn't make that mistake again.
    He wouldn't let it!

All the chambers were filled now, and the only surprise would be whether it was an enchanted hollow point or an explosive round that would break through his skull. He hadn't been picky about what he stuffed in the chambers as he pulled whatever bullets he could out of the bottom of the footlocker.

Timothy was out playing. He'd made sure to send the little vampire away, telling him he had the night off from training.

He had the tent all to himself.

Opening his mouth wide to accommodate the barrel of the revolver as he slipped it in, Xander grimaced at the old-yet-familiar metallic taste. There was a strange nostalgia to the moment as he slipped back into the morbid anticipation and impending terror he'd felt for so many years. Though it was a defeating notion that it would all come back to this, it seemed fitting that it end the same way it had begun. He thumbed back the hammer, bracing himself for the rattle against his teeth as it locked into place, and teased the trigger with his thumb. When at last he was ready, he began to tighten his grip and prepared for the end...

And then it happened!

His world shook and rattled and before he could come to grips with the loss of control he was spinning. The night appeared—he was suddenly outside—and he could feel the winter wind slashing at his bare skin. His jeans, his only protection against the elements, were dragged through the snow-covered grass and he yelped as the denim soaked up the freezing moisture and held it against his legs.

Through it all, sailing and tumbling across the clearing, he was surrounded by a growling and slashing whirlwind.

A furious and renegade storm of muscle and rage that pummeled and beat him.

And, as he felt strike-after-merciless-strike land upon him, his gun was suddenly gone...

Soon the assault ended and he found himself on his back, staring up at the star-filled sky. His nose was bleeding—probably broken—and he had claw marks and bruises littered across his chest and face.

"Fuck..." Xander groaned, trying to come to grips with what

had just happened.

Osehr stood over him, panting and bearing down on him in his bestial form, and clumsily worked Yang in his single-yet-massive hand until he got the cylinder open and dumped the rounds out onto the hillside.

"Hey," Xander groaned, starting to sit up, "those are expensive!"

Osehr snarled at him and began to change back to his human form. Xander frowned and looked away as the massive, hulking creature shriveled to a chorus of unsettling pops and squishes. When at last the therion had the use of his vocal cords again he held up the shredded suicide note and the attached blank checks and cleared his throat.

"Bill me," he scoffed, "I'm sure I can afford them now that your wealth is mine."

Xander frowned and sat up as Yang was dropped in front of him, "You really know how to ruin a guy's plans."

"I didn't like what you had planned," Osehr said with a shrug.

"Yea? Well I liked it just fine, asshole!" The vampire sighed as he felt around his still-tender nose before deciding it was, in fact, broken. He shook his head, "Why in the hell did you stop me?"

"That's a stupid question," Osehr pushed his hand away from his nose and, gripping it tightly between his thumb and forefinger, set it with a harsh twist.

"Ah! Fucker!" Xander cringed and cried out, jumping back and growling, "Dammit, Osehr! Stop! Just stop! It wasn't your decision to make," he spat, "You just don't understand!"

The therion snarled, "I understand that you're being an idiot! What made you think this was what you should make of your life?"

"Make something of my...?" Xander shook his head, "You're the one who said I was *wasting* my life!" He looked away, trying to hide the tears that had begun to well in his eyes, "That I was ignoring of all those I've ever lost..."

"And *this* is how you honor their memory?" The disgust in Osehr's voice made Xander flinch, "Everyone that you mourn—

all those that you use as another excuse to perpetuate this misery you wallow in—*died* because they believed strongly enough in something to make that sacrifice for," he shook his head, "And rather than respecting their beliefs, you *shit* all over them because you're too damn stubborn to find something that you believe in that strongly! So far the only thing you've ever believed strongly enough in to die for *is* death; you seem to think it's *easier* than facing your problems!" He sighed and looked over, giving Xander a few too-hard pats on his shoulder, "If you don't believe strongly enough in something to *die* for it, then you'll never be willing to put your all into anything; you'll never know just how strong you can be! And you, Xander Stryker, are too strong to take the weakling's way out."

Xander stared at his friend for a long while and finally shook his head. "Shred my tent, bust up my shit, ruin my plans and throw out my enchanted bullets..." he scoffed, "You're a real bastard, Osehr."

"And you're an emo bitch-boy," the therion countered with a smirk.

Xander looked up at that, his eyes widening, "You can't pronounce 'Christmas', but you suddenly know what 'emo' means?" He frowned, remembering the letter, "Dammit! You were in my head again, weren't you?"

Osehr nodded, "You were acting strangely when you got back."

Xander sighed and nodded, "Yea. I... I actually found Estella earlier today."

"Then where is she?" Osehr frowned.

Xander rubbed the back of his neck, "Don't know," he sighed, "She bailed after I made her feed off some creep."

"You killed a human?"

Xander rolled his eyes, "I'd hardly call him that."

Osehr leaned forward, finally looking at the note for a long moment before tossing it over his shoulder, "So all of this is because Estella ran away again?"

Xander frowned and shrugged, "It wasn't just that. I think it just—y'know—put me in a dark place. I guess I felt like I'd been holding on to the hope of finding her only to have her kick my ass and leave once I did."

"She kicked your ass?" Osehr raised an eyebrow.

Xander rolled his eyes, "It wasn't like I was fighting back."

Osehr nodded, "So you felt your life had no more meaning; that you had nothing left to live for?" He shook his head, "What about the pack? And have you forgotten about your promise to Timothy?" He looked up at the sky, taking in the stars, "And I don't think you should give up on Estella just yet."

"And why's that?" Xander looked over, "I just told you she kicked my ass and ran *away* from me! What part of that makes you think there's still a shot that I'll get her back?"

"Because she's still here. Doesn't the fact that she hasn't left this place mean that she's staying *for* something?"

"Or maybe she just doesn't have anywhere to go," Xander shook his head and groaned, burying his face in his hands, "God damn... you couldn't have just let me die?"

"It's not your life to take when so many people rely on you," Osehr said, "Very selfish to think only of yourself in these times."

Xander scoffed, "Yea right. Thanks for showing me the ways of The Force, Master Yoda."

Osehr tilted his head, "Yoda?"

"Don't worry about it," Xander chuckled.

Osehr nodded slowly, "Then I won't," he pulled himself to his feet. "But you have to promise that you won't try this again?"

"You gonna beat the shit out of me again if I do?" Xander raised an eyebrow.

Osehr stared at him, "Do you really have to ask?"

"Then I guess I promise," Xander chuckled.

CHAPTER SIXTEEN
COFFEE

THE NEXT NIGHT Xander put Timothy in Zeek and Karen's hands, telling them that the boy needed to begin his combat training. Though the anapriek was confused by the handoff, he didn't seem upset at the idea of spending time with the little vampire. When everything had been squared away and he had assured Osehr for the fifth time that night that he wasn't going to try the previous night's activity all over again, Xander headed into town.

With the exception of a few truckers and late-night stragglers the 24-hour diner wasn't too busy, and Xander was quick to take a seat in the furthest corner after asking the hostess to let him use their phone. The voice on the other end had been both shocked and delighted, and, after a quick back-and-forth, agreed to meet him for coffee.

Half-an-hour later, Father Tennesen stepped through the diner doors and took his seat across from him.

"Long time, no see," Xander smiled, offering his hand for the priest to shake.

Tennesen stared at it for a moment, confused by the gesture—or, moreover, the individual extending it—before finally taking it and smiling, "I must say, Xander, I was surprised to hear from you after all this time."

Xander shrugged, "I was just as surprised to see that you're still in town."

"Oh there is still much work to be done here," he assured him, "It would seem that the Harper-demon was only the tip of the iceberg."

"Yea... well, I wouldn't know anything about that."

Tennesen cocked an eyebrow, "So it's true? You *have* retired?"

Xander scowled at the word choice, but finally offered a slight nod, "I guess you could call it that."

"Seems a bit early to be giving up, doesn't it?"

Xander frowned, "It's not 'giving up'! I've just found a happier life than fighting and having people I care about die!"

"And yet—despite this 'happier life'—you're here with me drinking coffee that you clearly *still* don't like."

Xander looked down at the untouched contents of his cup and clucked his tongue. He still had no desire to drink it.

Finally, knowing that he'd been caught, he shrugged, "I just thought I'd catch up."

The priest rolled his eyes, "Bullshit!"—Xander looked up, startled by his usually reserved friend's language—"You didn't call me at this hour for a simple chat, so don't waste both of our time trying to convince either of us of that rubbish! Now... what is this *really* about?" Tennesen pressed, pulling the lid off of a small plastic cup of creamer and dumping it into his coffee before taking a sip.

Xander sighed and shook his head, smirking at the priest's change in attitude since he'd last seen him. "Alright," he leaned forward, "I tried to kill myself last night."

Tennesen stared for a moment and sighed, shaking his head and taking another sip, "I see. So what stopped you?"

"A werewolf beat me up and told me to stop being a pussy," Xander laughed.

Tennesen stared at him for a moment before laughing as

well, "Well, *that'd* certainly change one's perspective on life."

"You have no idea," Xander replied as he swirled the coffee in his cup.

"Learn anything important from it?" The priest asked.

Xander sighed and nodded, "Yea. He told me that I was being selfish. That it wasn't my life to take since I had so many people out there relying on me."

Tennesen smiled, "Sounds like a smart werewolf."

Xander smiled back and nodded, "He's definitely got his gems."

The priest leaned forward, curiosity painted all over his face, "So why come to me? Not that I'm complaining, I just can't imagine that, after all you've been through, this has suddenly changed your—"

"No no," Xander waved a hand in front of him, "I'm not about to sign up for your bible-thumper newsletter. I don't know... I guess I just wanted your opinion on a few things. You helped me out a lot a while back, and I figured I was overdue for some of your wisdom," he smirked, "In a strictly *non*-religious way, of course."

Tennesen laughed, "Of course. God forbid the dark-spirited Xander Stryker adopt a little bit of faith."

Narrowing his eyes, Xander fell back in his seat and crossed his arms, "I could leave now, you know."

Tennesen shook his head, "And then all this would have been for nothing, and you'd have failed yourself again." He took a sip of his coffee and sighed, "Everyone needs faith," he went on, "not just the religious, God-fearing kind—though believe me when I say that I'll shave my head and do back flips from the altar if you ever came into *that* sort of faith—but also the kind that's necessary to keep us all from trying to kill ourselves each and every day."

Xander stared at him, waiting.

Tennesen sighed and held up his cup, "It's kind of like coffee," he explained. "People wake up every morning, and most of them just *need* that first cup to feel ready to face the day. Without it they're sluggish and unhappy and antisocial and unproductive. Now picture a world without that morning ritual;

that faith in the almighty brew! It'd be hell on Earth!" Tennesen smirked and made a note of taking another sip from his cup before setting it down, "Faith is the same way, Xander. It comes in different forms—some like it black while others want it with cream and sugar and others like to pour in the contents of their flasks—but it all comes down to *one* thing: making it through the day! It's a reason to go on, and we all have our own, personal reasons. For me it's not just God, but the teaching and protecting of my flock," he scowled as he caught Xander rolling his eyes, "For you, however, it might be something much different, but still it's a *reason*."

"So what if I think I've lost my reason?" Xander asked.

"Then *that's* when you need to have faith that it *isn't* lost. Just because the clouds hide the sun doesn't mean you suddenly start fearing that it's forever cast from the sky, but just as much as the sun will break through those clouds you need to have faith enough in its warmth and light to guide and comfort yourself *without* the benefit of seeing it," Tennesen smiled, "Faith is not about hoping that we'll be handed what we want; it's about knowing that we have the strength to find what we need. You can't always just put all your eggs in one basket, son."

Xander scoffed, "I thought we were talking about coffee here."

"Sometimes faith is the whole breakfast table," Tennesen chuckled.

Xander smirked and shook his head. "You're really stretching this one, you know that, right?"

"But something tells me you've still gotten the message."

Xander slowly nodded and took his first sip of coffee. After several moments of mutual sipping in complete silence, he got up and started for the front to pay for his and the priest's drinks. He stopped as he passed the old man, smiling down at him warmly.

"You're still a good man, Tennesen. Thanks again."

CHAPTER SEVENTEEN
"GODS AMONG MONSTERS"

DIANNA HADN'T EVEN noticed that the man they'd passed wasn't really a man. Richard, however, hadn't been fooled by the hunched-over figure in the heavy winter jacket and wool cap, and he'd wasted no time in drawing one of his swords from under his coat and turning after it. As the other people on the streets caught sight of Richard's blade, a series of panicked screams and startled shouts were issued and the crowds began to disperse around them. Though she knew that making a public scene wasn't in their best interest, she'd saved her breath and followed after him. Knowing that the only place she belonged was by her brother's side—after all, where else did she have to go?—she'd made just as much of a scene in brandishing her gun as she followed after.

As their newest target ran from them, it threw its coat to the ground and ripped off its dirty sweater and yellow tee-shirt and exposed a light-gray torso to the world before dropping to all fours and scurrying away like an insect.

Though neither was sure what it was at first, they were both certain that it wasn't human!

Turning its head for a moment, the mythos creature's neck extended and craned around to look behind it. Seeing that the twins were still following, it opened its mouth—its lower jaw jutting out in a tremendous under-bite—and let loose a high-pitched screech. All at once, the hunters were on the ground; the sound echoing in their heads and turning the world on its side.

"It's a goddam gerlin," Richard called out over the racket, identifying the mythos' race.

Dianna nodded in agreement.

They'd never encountered one of the bat-like creatures before, but there was only one type of mythos that could make a sound like that.

"We need to get to it before it finds higher ground," he shouted over the racket, finally shooting an enraged glare at the source before disappearing from Dianna's sight.

The testing of their parents' serum had been more than effective on Oliver, who had become... something more than just an ordinary dog. After the animal testing was completed, Richard had moved on to a human subject.

His sister.

Dianna had never known a worse pain.

When she had lived through the process, Richard excitedly "volunteered" to be the next subject out of the three of them and quickly injected himself. Since that night, every mythos they encountered—and Richard had been sure to seek out as many as possible—had fallen one way or the other and added to the collective pot of genetic material they were using in the elixir. Everything they came across had something that Richard wanted; every species having a trait or ability that he was eager to make his own.

And just as they'd taken the Taroes' magical ink, Richard was set on making himself a walking weapon in the war against all mythos creatures.

The gerlin didn't know about Richard's plans, however, and when it saw one of the humans perusing it suddenly appear only an arm's length away it let out a startled bark and leapt away. Once it was in the air, it threw open its arms and unfolded its wings then, the leathery appendages springing out of hiding from under the creatures arms like the blade of a Swiss-army knife. Struggling to flap free of the unnaturally empowered human, it soon gave up on trying to gain any new height and allowed itself to glide towards a nearby apartment building with Richard chasing after. When it was close enough to the wall that Dianna was certain it would crash, it relaxed its wings and began to drop a short distance before clinging to the wall with its long, thin fingers. A set of talons burst out from its cheap sneakers as soon as its feet struck the brick and stabbed into the wall, allowing it to begin to climb up the side of the building with surprising swiftness.

Not wanting to lose the gerlin or allow it to reach the rooftop where it would have the benefit of height and range, Richard jumped from the street and continued his superhuman sprint straight up the wall. As his vertical run started to wane and gravity began to steal his momentum, he grabbed the closest balcony and flung himself straight up—using his sangsuiga-empowered muscles—to the next balcony where he repeated the process again and again, each time closing the distance between him and the startled gerlin.

The mythos tried to swipe the hunter away as he closed in, but as its long arm came around Richard caught it and finally let the laws of physics pull at him. A surprised squawk escaped the gerlin, which was dragged down with him and began to flap its wings in a hopeless effort to slow its fall. Eager to prove himself, the hunter pulled himself up and grabbed a patch of the creature's leathery wings and yanked the wing back, tearing the extension from its left arm.

The gerlin let out a pained shriek.

Richard yanked out its tongue.

It tried to bite him.

Richard tore off its jaw.

In only a matter of seconds Richard had left his sister's side, cleared half the city block, and dragged the gerlin—kicking and screaming—to the ground. Awestruck by her brother's abilities, Dianna watched in astonishment and horror as the two thrashed about on the sidewalk.

"Shoot it!" Richard demanded as the gerlin pushed him back and jumped to its feet, gurgling and whining in an effort to use its crippling shrieks against its enemy.

Without its tongue, however, its strongest defense had been stolen.

Dianna stammered and stared at the creature and the extent of its injuries, unable to bring herself to raise her weapon to it.

"B-but..."

"Useless!" Richard growled and turned away, crouching down suddenly and grabbing the creature by the ankle. With a solid grip on its leg, he swung with all the unnatural strength he had in him and brought the flailing gerlin around and into the side of the building.

The gerlin's head ruptured like a rotting fruit; the hot stink of its blood saturating the chilled air and casting a reeking fog over the street.

Narrowing his eyes at the dying creature, Richard took in a deep breath and watched as its leg jerked several more times before going still. Offering his victim one final disgusted sneer, he turned away from the mass and stormed towards his already cowering sister and brought the back of his hand across her face with enough force to drop her to one knee.

"Don't you *EVER* disobey me again," he growled down at her, "If I give you an order, you fucking *obey* it! Are we clear, bitch?"

Dianna whimpered and nodded quickly, "Yes! I'm... I'm sorry! I was... you were just... I thought..."

"*Think*?" he hissed between clenched teeth, "You don't think; that's *my* job! You just worry about acting on my thoughts when I tell them to you!"

Diana bit her lip and nodded.

Richard shook his head and walked past. "Let's go," he ordered, "The night's still young."

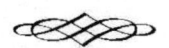

※

The boathouse from the other night had impressed Richard so much that he'd decided to set up their "headquarters"—as he'd insisted on calling it—at one just like it only several miles away.

Though the idea of squatting on somebody's summer home was an unsettling one for Dianna, she couldn't help but be glad that her brother had chosen a location that was, if only for the season, deserted.

"Not many boaters too eager to ride on a frozen lake," Richard had boasted when they'd first come across the place, "And all the free gas we could ever need!"

Returning to the boathouse now, Dianna was less eager to enter and get out of the cold.

She knew what was waiting inside.

Oliver—now nearly twice his original size and several hundred pounds heavier and sporting a monstrous gleam in his eye from the serum testing—was standing guard, as Richard had "told" him with his newly acquired telepathic control from an auric kill the previous night, over a beaten and bound watsuke. The creature—an aquatic mythos with gills along its cheeks and neck and covered in light blue and green scales—was still struggling as they walked in, the hum of the electric current that surged through its body filling the room. In the water this ability—not unlike that of eels', Dianna thought—was no doubt an impressive and effective defense. Tied and cuffed to a chair on dry land, however, the ability meant little for the mermaid-like creature.

"Good," Richard smirked as he approached the mythos, slipping on a pair of rubber gloves, "It's not dead yet."

"Richard..." Dianna pleaded, "This isn't—"

Her brother glared over his shoulder at her, "Go take Oliver for a walk if you're going to be a pest."

Dianna sighed, "But—"

"Go... walk... Oliver!"

It was no longer just an idea.

Dianna chewed her lip and nodded, taking their beast-dog and leaving the boathouse and her psycho-brother alone with the poor, helpless creature. As she wandered about the stretch of snow-coated beach she kept a close eye on Oliver. He'd gotten so large that they'd had to start using a garden hose as a leash and collar. As she studied the monster she'd had a direct hand in creating she couldn't help but think of a shaggy yellow bear.

"What the hell are we going to do with you?" She whispered to the abomination, running her palm over its side.

The watsuke's shrieks started up behind her and she hurried to distance herself from the sound with a brisk jog that Oliver was quick to outmatch. Though fast and strong, their creation didn't have the knowledge to control the abilities it had been infused with. Though it was freakishly large and strong, it could not—or at least didn't know how to—jump to the next stage of sangsuigan movement. Dianna was thankful for this, though; a bear-sized dog that could move faster than a bullet was the last thing she wanted leading her on the makeshift leash.

Oliver's speed was already too much for her to reign in easily, and the idea of it reaching the next level was terrifying.

Though she was sure that Richard would have been delighted by it.

That poor watsuke...

Dianna couldn't get her mind off the mythos that was being tortured by her brother. The creature had been covered from head to toe in multiple layers to hide its inhuman features and begging for change on the streets. She knew that it must have been uncomfortable for it outside of the water and in the cold— though she was sure that being frozen in the lake wasn't a pleasant alternative—and would have been content just walking by and leaving the poor thing alone. After all, it hadn't been hurting anybody. Richard, however, had been able to see that the creature wasn't a human and lured it after him with the promise of a warm meal.

She scoffed and shook her head; he probably didn't even know what they ate!

She sure as hell didn't.

His motives, however, were all too clear. He wanted its gills. There was very little use that either of them would have with the power to create an electric current when they already had the Taroe tattoos, but the ability to breath underwater...

That was just the kind of thing that Richard would want to add to his growing list of abilities.

Even she couldn't deny that it would be a powerful tool for a hunter.

But his methods—his drive—had become more and more psychotic, and she was finding it that much more difficult to define who the true monsters were in the world.

The two of them had gotten into hunting as a means of avenging their parents, who had taught them the tricks of the trade and urged them to make the world safe for humans.

Killing monsters.

It seemed so simple.

But Richard's empathy for mankind had burned out long ago, and it was a painful realization to Dianna that nobody—no human or innocent creature or even herself—was safe from his fury. He'd gone out of his way to separate himself from everything, including the motives that had driven them to take up arms against non-humans in the first place. Those trespasses, however, had paled in comparison to his most recent mission; a mission that had him transforming them into what they'd dedicated their lives to hunting...

Monsters.

The worst kind.

She sighed and shook her head. It didn't make a difference if she saw their actions as wrong. It wasn't her call; wasn't her job to think. She was the little sister—younger by a full ten minutes—and she had to do what her big brother told her. Not just because it was what was expected, not just because it was the sisterly thing to do...

She rolled her eyes.

No! She had to do what he said because she knew that he'd kill her if she didn't.

There wasn't a single doubt in her mind that he'd kill her if he felt she'd outlived her purpose; with more speed and savagery than *any* mythos, and with *far* more enthusiasm, no less. A shudder crept up her spine as the screams behind her rose and suddenly went silent. Biting her lip, she peeked over her shoulder.

It didn't matter who or what he'd been before all of this.

Richard was a monster now.

And if their parents had taught them nothing else, it was that there was always somebody out there willing and able to hunt down and destroy monsters.

"It's only a matter of time now, Mom and Dad..." she muttered to herself. Oliver let out a thunderous bark and turned his head towards her, letting his massive tongue loll out as Richard's energy spiked in the distance. Groaning, Dianna nodded to the beast-dog, "I know, buddy, we might as well head back. He'll have my head if I don't get to work on the newest batch."

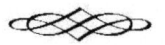

⋘⋙

The blood was watery and orange.

Whether this was normal for the species or if the watsuke they'd taken had been sick—possibly a side-effect from being out of water for so long—was a mystery. Bringing the fluid to her makeshift workstation, however, Dianna was certain that she felt comfortable letting it *stay* a mystery.

The sooner this was over the better!

After setting her equipment to keep the sample at seventy-six degrees Fahrenheit—the last recorded body temperature of the creature before Richard had begun his experiments on it—she began to collect the necessary materials. While their parents' comrades had condemned them for their claims that mythos traits could be harnessed for their purposes, Richard and Dianna had never given up on picking up where they had left off. Though their parents had never perfected the serum, Dianna's continued research after their deaths had, for the most part, proven that their efforts had not been in vain. Opening their late mother's notebook and spreading a set of loose pages across the surface of a nearby table, Dianna offered a silent apology to both their parents and any god that might be watching as she began to infuse her magic to the contents of a beaker until it began to turn purple and shimmer. Setting this aside, she stepped over to a wooden salad bowl that she'd modified for her purposes and began to grind several of the dead watsuke's scales and a portion of a heart valve with a stone she'd taken from the beach several days earlier.

Creating the serum was a delicate process that had to be done in five parts. A delicate balance of magic and science, it required the genetic material—flesh, blood, and heart—to be infused with three separate enchanted elixirs before being individually boiled down, bonded through yet another set of spells, and then filtered to remove any imperfections.

So many processes and so much magic...

Maybe their parents *had* been wrong.

Maybe this *was* wrong.

As she finally extracted the finished product—a small vial filled halfway with the glowing serum—she bit down on her tongue to keep from saying anything, opting to stay silent as she started towards her brother.

She knew that Richard would go ballistic if she told him what she really thought, and a supernaturally-charged psychopath was not something she wanted to deal with.

Even if she *was* just as unnaturally empowered.

With their newest batch ready to be shot up, she approached Richard, who was already tying off a piece of elastic tubing around his left arm.

Dianna tried not to sneer in disgust at all the track-marks that now littered his arm. Her brother had lost his mind for power and now looked like a junkie. It didn't help that her arm didn't look any different, though her punctures were accompanied by a series of bruises where Richard had held her too tightly and forced her to inject the serum. She sighed as she handed her brother his needle. He took it quickly and stared at her expectantly, waiting for her to inject herself first.

She did so without any hesitation.

There was nothing to hesitate for.

Her body wasn't even her own anymore.

The intense burning rocketed through the veins of her arm slowly, creeping like a monster to her heart before it was rocketed to every part of her body. She dropped to her knees as her toes and then her whole foot began to tingle and burn; she had no desire to stand anyway. The watsuke slowly became a part of her, and she felt a dry itch begin at the sides of her neck where the gills would no doubt form in several days.

Whether or not Richard liked it they'd have to wait for the mutation to occur.

Richard let out a groan that was borderline orgasmic as he injected himself. As the serum flooded his system his eyes glazed and started to roll back in his head; his body beginning to sway back and forth on his heels.

Dianna couldn't believe it.

He was actually getting *high* off the magic!

What a sick bastard.

What have we become? She thought to herself.

Richard slowly stabilized and blinked his eyes several times until his pupils were focused on his sister. With the haze in his eyes melting away, he grinned—the sight far scarier than any of the monsters that Dianna had ever faced—and took a step towards her.

"My dear, dear sister," he spoke softly, still riding the high, "what we've become is nothing short of gods! Gods"—he repeated, smiling as Dianna's eyes widened at the realization that he could see into her mind—"among monsters."

CHAPTER EIGHTEEN
THE VISITOR

AS XANDER RETURNED to the pack's territory he was surprised to hear the therions in the distance in an uproar. Their snarls and growls—audible from nearly a quarter-of-a-mile away—were intense and ravenous, and he recognized the sound of his comrades as they readied themselves for a kill. Picking up the pace and hurrying the rest of the way, positive that Zeek's attitude had finally started a riot, Xander began planning how to defuse the situation. As he closed the distance, he could see that, while the sounds were ferocious and intimidating, nobody had been maimed.

Yet.

Instead, the entire pack *and* the newcomers stood in a circular pattern around a lone visitor who stood just a little too close to Osehr's throne for his own good. He and the therion leader said nothing to each other—Xander figured that whatever needed to be said already had been—and instead shared a mutual sneer towards one another. As soon as he was inside the clearing,

Xander jumped up and over the dense crowd of therions and landed inside the circle, placing himself between the two.

"What is your business here, warrior?" He demanded. Though the vampire had not made himself known, his weapons—a standard issue Beretta at his hip and a sword sheathed at his back—gave him away.

The vampire turned, his light-red aura swirling slightly as he recognized the newcomer. "It's about time, Stryker."

Xander, realizing the warrior was there for him, scowled and waved the therions away with the promise that he'd deal with the intruder.

Slowly, hesitantly, they dispersed, though not without offering their final snarls. The newcomers left as well. Though Timothy refused to budge at first, Satoru was quick to lift and carry him off. Soon it was just the two of them and Osehr. The warrior turned to the therion leader and sneered.

"You, too, can leave us to our business."

Osehr shook his head calmly. "You've come to address a member of my pack," he informed the vampire, "And that means that I am a part of whatever 'business' you bring."

The warrior snarled and bared his fangs at this, turning his back to Xander and challenging the therion leader. Osehr clenched his left hand tightly into a fist and began to swell with the beginnings of transformation. Xander quickly lurched forward and snatched the warrior's gun from its holster and pressed the barrel against its owner's temple.

"I would suggest that you don't challenge *either* of us," Xander advised him, switching off the safety with a flick of his thumb, "I think you'll find that neither of us will go down easy, and it'd be a shame to return to your clan missing pieces of yourself."

The warrior's snarl faded and, keeping his movements slow, turned away from Osehr and held out his hand for the gun.

Xander narrowed his eyes, "You gonna keep it peaceful?"

"Peaceful," the vampire spat the word out as if it hurt to say it.

Xander spun the gun in his hand and ejected the magazine, catching it in his opposite hand and tossing it over his shoulder into the woods, before offering it back to the visitor. "Now," Xander narrowed his eyes, "You've only got one round in the chamber. If you decide you want to use it I would *highly* suggest it be on yourself, 'cuz you sure-as-shit won't be leaving these woods alive if you turn it on me or my packmates."

The warrior frowned as he retrieved his weapon and holstered it, "That won't be necessary."

Xander raised an eyebrow at that. He'd been sure that the visitor was there to terminate him for killing the human at the train station, but, judging from his calmness at having only one bullet to his name, that didn't appear to be the case. "So why are you here?" He finally asked.

The warrior frowned, "To ask for your help."

Xander blinked several times. "My help? Between the two of us I'd hardly say I'm the one in a position to offer *anybody* any sort of help! What exactly do you need my help *for*?"

The warrior frowned at the question, "It's hard to say, exactly. We received word a short while ago that a band of hunters were taking out mythos in the area. Naturally we were sent to investigate the occurrences with the intent of neutralizing the threat," he sighed and shook his head, "These hunters were different than others we'd encountered. Usually they're no different than us: gunning for rogues who have become a danger to innocents; if nothing else they're doing us a favor in taking out the stragglers. Certainly saves us the time in tracking them. But these hunters..." He shook his head again, "They're not just taking out the dangerous mythos in the area—near as we could tell they haven't killed a single rogue, in fact—but slaughtering *any* mythos they come across. And every kill they make is just left in the streets for *anybody* to come across! They're becoming a threat to not only our people, but our secrecy, as well!"

"I've heard of these assholes," Xander nodded, "Why don't you guys just execute them and be done with it?"

The warrior sighed and shook his head again, "Unfortunately, almost all operatives sent out have never returned, and those who did were severely injured and didn't survive more than a few hours. From what we were told, these hunters are well versed in the magical arts—"

Xander nodded, "Taroe tattoos, I know. We"—he nodded towards Osehr—"sensed them when they first entered the city. They seem to have been tracking a small group that we've since taken in."

The warrior peeked over at the therion leader, confused, then continued his explanation, "Yes, well, it turns out that they've also begun to develop a formula—some kind of enchanted elixir—that is comprised of mythos blood. With this, they're able to gain the abilities and traits of whatever species they're able to acquire."

"A formula?" Xander frowned, "Where are you getting your facts?"

The warrior sighed and shook his head, "One of those that survived long enough to return home was an auric who'd been lucky enough to 'see' their plans."

Xander lifted a quizzical eyebrow, "And those would be...?"

"They intend to 'cleanse' the world by creating an army of others like them," he shook his head, "Just *imagine* it: there's only *two* of them, and they're creating *this* much chaos!" The warrior took a bold step towards Xander then, "Just imagine what a global army could accomplish!"

Xander sighed. A world of mythos hunters with the powers of anything they killed; not a pleasant thought. Even worse, they were looking for the refugees that the pack—*his* pack—was hiding. And who knew what they had planned after slaughtering them and the others in the city! Finally, Xander nodded slowly, letting out a slow, heavy sigh, "If it gets to the point where there are hunters like this all over the world..."

"Mythos Armageddon," The warrior finished for him.

"I understand," Xander nodded and locked eyes with the warrior, "Well, I suggest you and your boys get your asses in gear and deal with this situation then."

The warrior stared, "You won't help us?"

"What? And lead those supercharged hunters here? This was a big enough problem for us before they started stealing mythos blood for their sick experiments, but now I have to focus my efforts to keeping the pack safe."

"You can protect them by helping us!" The vampire growled.

Xander scowled and looked away. Estella was out there somewhere; lost and scared and confused. He'd found her once already—seen enough of her new auric signature to track her down—and he had every intention of doing it again. Then there was Osehr and Timothy and all the others to watch out for. Noticing that the warrior was still staring him down, he shook his head. "I've got my own problems to deal with, and just like you're not going to help me with my problems I can't help you with yours. Plus, I'm not a warrior anymore."

The warrior growled at that, "Not a warrior? You're the son of *the* Joseph Stryker! What, if not a warrior intent on defending what your father *died* to build, are you?"

Xander shrugged and gestured to his surroundings, "I guess I'm a therion."

"You're insane!" The warrior spat, "You can't possibly think that these... these *dogs* are more important than the entire world!"

Xander smirked, "That's *exactly* what I think, actually. I've seen what happens when I get involved with shit like this! If I step in, you've already doomed th—"

"Xander!" Osehr's voice was heavy and thoughtful, "You should—"

Xander growled, cutting off the therion elder, and turned towards his friend, "Go tell the others that we might need to travel. I need to try to find Estella while there's still time." He turned his gaze back to the shocked warrior, "I think you should go now. You have a lot of work to do."

CHAPTER NINETEEN
FORGIVENESS

XANDER...

She loved him so much.

So damn much that it hurt to hate him.

And Estella was so very, very tired of hurting.

She wasn't sure where she was going, all she had to lead her was the spell she'd cast earlier. With it she'd been able to see through Xander's eyes as he'd written the suicide note; feel the tears welling in his eyes as if they were her own. She'd seen the gun—a different one than what he'd used more than a year earlier for the same horrible act—and felt it in his mouth as though it were her own.

He was so prepared to do the unthinkable.

And then a blur; lots of pain; and then the caring words of a friendly therion.

He was somewhere in the forest. This much she knew.

Treading through the darkness with her new, supercharged vampire eyes, she was surprised to see that, when properly fed, she could see everything clear as day. Regardless, she was completely blind as to *where* she was going, but she couldn't bring herself to turn away and return to the unforgiving city. She'd seen the truth, realized after her encounter with him what he'd saved her from, and what he'd done for her; the risk he'd taken.

A tear rolled down her cheek as she thought of him and everything he'd done; everything he'd gone through.

All of it for her.

How could she possibly hate him?

Then there was the pain in his eyes...

She *had* to find him!

And so she navigated through the forest, clueless to where she was heading but refusing to care. She was ready to show him how much he really meant to her; ready to show that, despite what she'd been through, she couldn't blame him.

Not anymore.

She'd seen how hard and unforgiving the world and the life of a vampire really was, and, despite that, Xander had fought to protect and love her.

And she loved him.

So damn much!

But Xander had faced so much worse in the end.

He'd lived a life of such excruciating pain and agony as a human that the choice between living that life and being turned had been a simple one. He had accepted his path then; chosen to be an inhuman fighter like his father. He'd always been meant to do great things, and it was that moment—that choice—that had given him that chance. The choice had been the right one, of course, and everyone could see that.

Except him...

But she could show him the truth!

Show him what he meant to the world.

Show him what he meant to her.

She could ignore the truth no longer; the inevitable fact that, though she hated to admit it, her being what she had become wasn't something he'd allowed to happen. Xander had worked so hard to protect her—to keep her from the fate that had befallen her—but Lenix's vendetta against him had spilled over into her world because *she* had refused to let him go.

He had tried so hard, and, even after all that had happened, he was *still* trying!

She could no longer deny that fact.

Nor could she deny how badly she needed him; now more than ever.

And right now, he needed her, too.

"Don't worry, Xander," she huffed as she ran through the woods, hoping that it would take her to him, "I'm coming."

Chapter Twenty
Defense

Journal entry: December 15th
Estella,

After some thought and a severe, supernatural ass-kicking, I've decided that what I did was justified. I understand that you're hesitant to accept what you are now, but you need to come to grips with it before it gets you killed.

There's some bad, dangerous humans (if they can be called that anymore) out there killing lots of innocent mythos, and I need to make sure that you don't become one of their victims.

Now that I have seen your aura and I know what I'm looking for, I WILL find you, and I will bring you back with me.

Nothing will stop me from saving you and showing you how sorry I am for what happened and how much I love you!

Xander

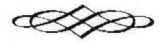

Xander closed the notebook and set down the pen. He wasn't sure why he'd felt compelled to write that one last letter before going out to make things right, but after months and months of writing letters to Estella that he was positive would never be read it just seemed like the right thing to do.

Timothy, who had patiently sat nearby with a toy gun that Xander had bought him and exterminating imaginary enemies, glanced up at him with eager eyes as his mentor rose to his feet; excited to know what was in store for him. Xander smiled at his apprentice and ruffled his hair before patting his shoulder.

"I want you to train with Zeek again tonight."

Timothy frowned, "You're leaving again?"

Xander nodded, "It's important; very important. But I promise that when I get back everything will be alright."

"What about the hunters?" Timothy's voice cracked.

"Don't worry about them," Xander smirked, "You're already tough enough to take both of them on one-handed."

Timothy laughed nervously, "I don't know..."

Xander shrugged, "Maybe you're right. But soon," his smile widened. "You're doing really well."

Timothy blushed at the compliment, but quickly looked away and frowned, "What if they come tonight while you're gone?"

"They won't."

"But what if they do?" The little vampire demanded.

Xander frowned, "Then I want you to run—run faster than you've ever run before—and find the best hiding place you can; let the others fight."

"But if they fight then they'll die!" Timothy's eyes were beginning to water.

"They may," Xander saw no reason to lie, not about this, "But they'd all proudly die to make sure you lived, so you can't let them down. Understand?"

Timothy wiped his eyes and nodded.

"Good," Xander stepped out of the tent, "I won't be long."

Zeek was already waiting outside for them as they emerged. Timothy smiled at the sight and stepped from Xander's side to join the anapriek, and Xander couldn't help but smile at the little vampire's strength and eagerness.

Xander silently promised himself that he wouldn't let anything happen to him.

"Be sure to kick his ass," Xander chuckled.

Zeek glared at him but said nothing in protest as he took Timothy's hand and turned away, leading him off.

⋘⋙

Estella was close—at least she hoped she was. She'd been walking for several hours now, her trek into the forest starting in the late afternoon, when the sun was still hanging in the sky. She'd been up all day anyway, wandering and thinking life-changing thoughts.

Her mind was still a jumbled mess that she was slowly working to organize when she first heard the growling. Like an audible bear-trap, it picked up as her foot touched down on the frost-bitten forest floor; ensnaring her in a fearful tremor. Her first instinct was to step back away, hoping that reversing the step she'd taken would appease the creature.

It didn't.

Instead it grew louder as whatever was making the sound came closer.

Xander had told her about therions. The description had been slightly biased at the time, the explanation coming shortly after he'd almost been killed by one of the creatures, but somehow it still came out sounding strangely beautiful. Unlike the legends of werewolves, therions didn't simply come in the one shape. Like humans, there were all different sizes and shapes to them.

As Estella stood there, watching the creature charge at her now, however, it wasn't as easily labeled as Xander had made it sound. Large, broad shoulders like a gorilla pumped as it loped forward, its body the color of burnt toast and speckled with spots like a leopard. A large, brownish-red mane of hair flurried about its head as it came, and the jaws that snapped were broad, the muzzle jutting out like a bear's.

It was massive.

And it was angry.

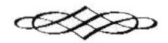

<hr />

Xander was nearby when he first heard the snarls; unmistakably Inarin's. The therion was probably one of the biggest he'd ever seen, and by far one of the pack's most loyal members. Xander had seen him fight only once several months earlier when they all tried to hunt down and kill Lenix. Though they'd failed, most of his mind-controlled army had been destroyed, and Inarin had brought down more than his share.

But what had him so worked up now?

Had the warrior from the other night come back to try and convince him once again to join their efforts against the hunters?

Whatever it was, it was about to get ripped apart.

And then Xander sensed it.

The familiar auric signature…

Estella!

He was in overdrive and rocketing in the direction of the sounds before he'd fully registered what he was doing. Her aura, a darker shade of orange than it had been before, shone in the distance like a beacon. He pushed himself to go faster than he'd ever moved before. Inarin's golden-brown aura was nearly on top of Estella's own! Though time was practically frozen for the world around him he knew it wouldn't be long before…

NO!

He couldn't allow it!

He knew that the moment he jumped off the ground he'd be thrown back into normal time, and he fought to gain enough momentum to combat the unforgiving force of nature.

He had to time it perfectly!

When he was practically right under his pack-mate he threw himself upward with every bit of strength and speed he had. Shifting Inarin's course would not be simple. As he crashed into the therion's massive form he saw the world around him suddenly spring back to life as the two slammed into ground with enough force to tear the earth beneath them.

Xander was the first to his feet, breathing heavily and making sure he was between his snarling packmate and Estella. Inarin pulled himself up, standing at his full height as his lips peeled back and displayed his teeth. Xander countered with an angry hiss, baring his own fangs and flaring his aura so that the forest pushed and swayed away from him and the broken ground cratered even further beneath his feet.

He *would not* let anything take Estella away!

Not again!

And if that meant killing Inarin—killing a razor-sharp, nine-foot monster—then so be it!

"Xander..." Estella gasped.

Her voice was all the proof Xander needed to know she was still alright, "Stay behind me."

Inarin roared, once again announcing his disapproval in the only audible way his bestial form would allow. Xander didn't need words or his psychic abilities to know what he was thinking, though. Estella was another trespasser among many; yet another outsider. This was the third time that their territory had been made infringed upon, and the majority of the pack had grown bloodthirsty after the first night when Zeek and the others had shown up.

This one last visitor had been the last straw, and Inarin was eager to vent his pent-up rage by spilling blood.

But it wouldn't be Estella's.

Not if Xander had anything to say about it.

Xander pointed back at Estella, never taking his scorching gaze off of the therion, "She lives," he growled, "She *LIVES*! You can have anybody else but her. Go into the city and rip apart all the humans it takes to calm your ass—put yourself on The Council's list of rogues to be executed—but you *will not* hurt her!" He hissed and took another step towards him, kicking up his aura once again, "Or I *will* kill you!"

The therion glanced over his shoulder at the trespasser, roaring and pounding his chest.

"You don't want it to happen this way," Xander assured him, already clenching his fists.

Inarin didn't listen.

He charged—running on all fours as he usually did when prepared for battle—before throwing himself into the air, ready to use his bulk to crush Xander in an attempt to get past him and to Estella. Seeing this intention—both reading his mind and having seen the tactic before—Xander leapt up to intercept the therion and brought his knee up, driving it into the underside of his comrade's snapping jaw hard enough to send the therion reeling backwards.

As Inarin crashed to the ground, Xander threw out his aura and held himself in midair for a moment before floating down, softening the landing for himself and his now-sore knee. Inarin was up in a flash, grabbing a young sapling and ripping it from the ground—its tortured roots snapping and raining clumps of soil—and brandishing it like a baseball bat. Xander bared his fangs again. The tree was swung with tremendous force, its branches whistling as they cut through the air. Just before impact, Xander wrapped his aura around himself like a shell and Inarin's weapon splintered and shattered around him.

The sound was like thunder.

OSEHR! Xander sent out a telepathic message, *GET OVER HERE, NOW!*

Inarin was in the air again, coming down like a wrecking ball. Xander, relying on his instinct, executed a back handspring that landed him several feet away from the spot that he'd been occupying; the spot that Inarin then crashed down upon. Though there was no way to know for sure, Xander was positive that it would have been enough force to shatter even a vampire's bones.

This was no longer about getting past him.

Inarin's fury had taken over, and he saw Xander as an enemy now.

Enraged by Xander's agility and the difficult time he was having in his attempts at breaking him, Inarin roared again and pounded the ground before he charged once again. Dodging this, Xander pivoted to keep his position between his packmate and Estella and wrapped the ballistic therion in his aura, lifting him off the ground and throwing him several yards away. He was up and storming back towards them in seconds.

"YOU CAN'T TAKE HER!" Xander roared, sending out an auric blast.

Unable to see the crimson energy wave, Inarin continued onward until it collided with him and tore him off his feet and sent him into a pine tree. His aura pulsed erratically, telling Xander that he was dazed, and as he slid down the tree and onto the ground he rolled to his knees and whined—a loud and angry whimper.

"Stay down," Xander muttered, more a wish than a command.

The therion stood and started to approach, his body swaying as he struggled to stay upright on clumsy legs. When he was close enough he pulled back his arm, ready to punch Xander in the face with a fist the size of a football.

Osehr caught the powerful arm in his hand and instantly stilled him.

"Stand down!" The therion leader's voice was hard and intimidating, his left arm bulging as he partially transformed.

Xander gaped, never knowing his friend had that kind of control.

Inarin's aura spiked once in surprise and just as quickly withdrew as his senses returned to him. Seeing the seriousness in the pack leader's eyes, he whimpered and looked back at Xander and Estella, issuing a soft growl, and dropped his arm before he began to transform back to his human form—still an intimidating creature, Xander thought—and glared.

"She is *not* one of us," he spat, "No outsiders! That was our rule!"

"I wasn't one of you either," Xander replied, backing up to join Estella at her side. "She stays!" He looked over at his long-lost lover and realized that she was blushing and turned back to Inarin and frowned. "Now will you go put some pants on?"

Inarin narrowed his eyes and looked to Osehr, who nodded.

"Do as he says," he calmly commanded, "Make yourself decent. And see to it that the others do the same." He gave Estella a warm smile, "We have a very special guest joining us."

This brought a smile to Estella's face; the familiar, warm smile that Xander remembered from when she was human.

He couldn't help but smile as well.

CHAPTER TWENTY-ONE
TOGETHER

WHILE OSEHR AND INARIN headed off—the therion leader trying to explain the concept of manners as they went—the vampire lovers took their time, opting to share a moment of mutual awe at finally having reached that moment. Estella's eyes, though glowing with the unnatural iridescence of their kind, still shone with the same warmth that Xander had felt drawn to before she'd been turned. Finding himself once again lost in those eyes, Xander was in no real hurry to get back. All he could think of was making that moment last a bit longer; a coveted moment that he never thought would come.

A moment...

"A-are... are you sure you're alright," he asked for probably the tenth time in just as many minutes.

Estella smiled and nodded, pressing herself more against him. "Yea," her voice was just like he remembered it, "You showed up just in time."

Xander frowned and looked away, "I guess that was kind of

overdue."

Estella's small hand squeezed his and he looked back at her. She was still smiling. Her eyes were warm and caring again.

She really had forgiven him!

"So what made you decide to come back?" He asked, hoping the question wouldn't make her suddenly change her mind.

Estella shrugged, "I finally opened my eyes to everything and saw some truths that I'd been keeping from myself." She stopped then as a thought suddenly came to her and she scowled at Xander and swatted him hard across the back of the head.

"Hey, ow!" He rubbed the sore spot and looked at her questioningly, "What was that for?"

"If you ever put that gun in your mouth—or any gun for that matter—I'm going to melt it and replace it with my foot!" She glared at him.

Xander stared at her a moment and then smirked, "You cast that spell again, didn't you?"

She was still glaring when her chin started to quiver and her eyes started to water. Finally she broke down altogether and fell into him, "I... I couldn't stand the thought of losing you again! After seeing you at the train station... I just knew that this was where I belonged!"

Xander held her close and took in her scent, which, though still sweet and flowery, was laced with a vampiric musk.

She smelled like autumn.

"I can relate," he offered before kissing the top of her head. "Believe me, I can relate."

She looked up at him then, a smile blossoming on her face as she stood on her toes to give him a quick kiss on the cheek.

Xander frowned and rubbed the spot, "I've been looking for you for months, waiting and hoping everything was alright... and all I get is a peck on the cheek?"

Estella smirked and started walking again, adding a deliberate swagger to her hips. "Don't forget that I've been waiting, too. Just consider that a warm-up," she giggled and continued on ahead.

Xander watched for a moment, his blood running hot and his fangs beginning to poke at the inside of his lip. After all this time

she had more magic in her then she ever knew.
He was totally under her spell.
And it was exactly where he wanted to be.

By the time Xander and Estella got to the clearing overlooking Osehr's throne the therions had already put together a large fire to celebrate. Xander smiled at the gesture, nodding his thanks to Osehr while Estella marveled at the festivities.

"Everything alright?" Xander frowned as the words once again slipped past his lips, sure she was getting sick of the question.

Estella nodded and looked up at him, "It's just been a while since I've been warm."

Xander smiled, "Get used to it."

Shortly after a few of the other therions returned to camp, dragging three deer behind them—one of the largest feasts that Xander had seen. They were quick and clean with extracting the meat and made sure to save the blood in several large thermoses that Xander had bought for just that purpose. Once they were done, these were presented to the vampires before they turned their attentions to the meat and the feasting began. Xander watched as Estella hesitated only slightly—giving him a nervous glance—before finally taking the first sip. Watching her eyes light up from the rejuvenating effects, Xander smiled and pulled her to him before taking a long chug from his own thermos as well.

Karen, Sasha, and Satoru feasted on the meat with the therions while another thermos of blood was given to Timothy, who enthusiastically mimicked Xander's long, hard gulps. For Zeek, a sharpened stick was provided so that his own portion of meat could be cooked over the fire—something that the packmates were quick to laugh at the anapriek about—and, after his first bite of the venison, his scowl faded as he too got into the spirit of things.

Estella was treated to her first ever show of therion song and dance; the chaotic-yet-beautiful sounds and movements mesmerizing and captivating her. After a short while of watching she stood and pulled Xander into the pile of moving bodies, mimicking the motions as best she could while applying her own style and grace. It wasn't long until everybody, Timothy included, was stomping and moving to the percussion and howls.

As the night drew to a close and the fire died down the partiers began to disperse and the vampires began to head towards Xander's tent. He had—since Osehr's violent prevention of his suicide—patched up the tattered portions of his living-space with several large tarps, some home-made stakes, several rolls of duct tape, and a great deal of help from a few of the more handy therions.

The outcome, though not very pretty to look at, was decent enough to sleep in, and even made the living quarters slightly larger.

This, however, worked out in their favor since they had a third to add to the space.

Timothy, clearly worn out from the party, was quick to curl up and fall asleep, leaving Xander and Estella to talk as the sun began to rise.

"I still can't believe you kept it for all this time," Xander whispered.

Estella cocked her head, "Hmm? Kept what?"

Xander motioned to the pendant around her neck, "The necklace."

Estella blushed, taking the moon pendant around her neck tightly into her hand. "I... I couldn't bring myself to take it off."

Xander smiled at that and gave the jewelry another glance as she moved her hand. The pendant sported a sapphire held, as if by magic, in the middle of a diamond-encrusted crescent moon. It had seemed as magical as the girl he'd bought it for with the same deep, bottomless blue gem as her eyes.

Timothy let out a soft snore and rolled over in his sleep, and the two shifted their focus on him to make sure they hadn't awoken him.

"He's so cute!" Estella cooed.

Xander smirked and shrugged, "Yea, I guess." He smiled proudly, "He's a fast learner. I thought I'd be teaching him all the basics, but he already knew more than he thought."

Estella bit her lip, "Would you mind..."

"Hmm...? Mind what?" Xander pressed.

"Would you mind teaching me too?" She finally asked.

"Why should I mind?" Xander chuckled.

Estella shrugged and blushed, "I don't know... it's just..." She looked back down at Timothy, "Even *he* knows more about being a vampire than I do!"

"Yea. He really does," Xander nodded and laughed as Estella playfully slapped him on the arm. "But"—his voice turned serious—"he was *born* a vampire; had the time and nurturing to learn all of it. But you... you've been on your own all this time. Everything you know at this point is purely instinct."

"Or accidental..." Estella moped.

Xander shook his head, "You've done nothing wrong!"

Estella nodded slowly, though she didn't seem convinced.

"Estella, nobody could blame you for what's happened. Lenix was the one who turned you, which is already a violation against The Council's laws about siring new vampires."

Estella frowned, "Then how was the Odin Clan able to turn you?"

"Special circumstances," Xander shrugged, "Plus: I was already part vampire anyway. I just hadn't known it."

"So I really haven't done anything wrong? All the displays I've made, and that poor man—"

Xander growled, "That 'poor man' was more of a monster than we could ever hope to be!" He sighed and shook his head, "And, no, you have done *nothing* wrong. Your mistakes all root back to Lenix breaking the rules, and he's already been killed. I'm just glad that a warrior on patrol didn't catch you."

"Why?" Estella's eyes went wide, "I thought you said I did nothing wrong!"

Xander shook his head, "You haven't! But that's because of past circumstance and the way you were turned. A warrior wouldn't have known any of that. All they would've seen was a clear violation."

Estella nodded and thought for a moment. "But what about you?" She asked, "Your involvement means that you could be blamed for what happened, right?"

Xander smirked and shrugged, "We just won't tell anybody about that."

Estella rolled her eyes and sighed.

"Don't worry," Xander assured her, "Nobody's going to get hurt anytime soon."

CHAPTER TWENTY-TWO
HE WHO MAKES A BEAST OF HIMSELF...

RICHARD'S GILLS WERE JUST beginning to come in; the skin around his neck peeling away like the aftermath of a bad sunburn. Though they still had a little while to go before they would be of any use—a week or two at the most—they were more-than effective at disturbing Dianna to no end. What made matters worse was knowing that her own neck was beginning to go through the same process, and most likely looked just as grotesque.

It didn't matter, anyway. She'd stopped looking in the mirror long before; no longer able to stomach what she saw in it anymore.

Her brother, on the other hand, proudly inspected the emerging slits on the side of his throat. Though they'd only been awake for an hour, more than half of that time had been spent staring at his reflection.

"Just look at that," he mused, tilting his head slightly to get a better look, "Fucking beautiful!"

Dianna didn't answer. Though he seemed content and healthy, her reaction to the changes was less pleasant. A better part of the day had been spent out on the beach, where she'd decorated the frosted shore with the contents of her stomach. She would have liked to have vomited in at least the moderate comfort of the slightly warmer boathouse, but Richard, having been woken up by her initial heaving, had ordered her to take it outside.

Now, after having completely purged her system, she was left with nothing left to throw up and wrapped herself in her jacket to try and fight the wave of chills. Throughout all of this, she'd been forced to not only be careful of what she'd said, but also what she *thought*, as Richard was now keeping constant psychic tabs on her. Though she was able to shield some of her more private thoughts through a conscious effort—courtesy of her new and still-sloppy auric abilities—she could not completely hide everything from her brother, whose control, for some reason or another, was far superior to her own.

This was the biggest mystery of all. Though they had been taking the same serum since day one, it appeared that Richard was reaping more of their benefit than she was. This fact, while confusing for her, only served to irritate Richard, who felt that she was simply being lazy and not committing to the mission.

The "mission".

That's what he'd started calling it.

Like somebody had sent them to be murderers and freaks of nature. Though she was sure that's not how he saw it, she couldn't imagine that this had been what their parents wanted.

"You're thinking about Mom and Dad," Richard raised an eyebrow.

Dianna looked up and shivered, more from nervousness than the fever. "J-just h-hoping they'd be p-pr-proud," she wasn't lying; not really. Though she was distorting the truth, she wasn't positive if he'd be able to see past the psychic shields.

He narrowed his eyes at her for a moment before sneering. "Course they would be," he chided her, "We've perfected their formula! Made it all possible! And, in the process, we've turned ourselves into the ultimate-fucking-killing machines."

Dianna shivered again and nodded, returning her gaze to the floor.

Oliver lay nearby, taking up a great deal of space. All the animal's teeth had fallen out and since been replaced by horrible, monstrous fangs that extended to ungodly lengths when he got hungry. On top of that his spine had begun to mutate, the vertebrae extending from his back in the form of sharpened barbs.

Richard had truly created a monster.

And all in the name of tracking down a few innocent mythos that had been lucky enough to escape their slaughtering rampage through their home.

"He'll be ready to sniff those beasts out soon," he promised her, reading her thoughts again.

She nodded. "How will he be able to find them?" She asked, hoping to discourage him and sway him from "the mission" altogether.

Instead he smiled and got up, going to his bag. After a moment of rummaging he pulled out a red blanket that had faded to a pinkish shade. He waved it triumphantly and chuckled, "I snatched that little baby blood-sucker's blanky. In just a day or two, we give Oliver the little fuck's scent and have him to sniff it out," his smile was wider than it should have been and Dianna wondered if he knew that he'd changed that much. "Then that loose end will be tied off for good and we can move on to bigger, better things."

Dianna looked at him for a moment, unable to even think. Her body shook again and her stomach, despite her previous beliefs, found something to expel.

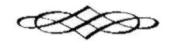

<hr />

Richard was nice enough to give his sister a half-hour to get herself fit to go out to hunt.

Knowing what "half an hour" really meant to her brother, she was ready in ten minutes.

She had covered herself in an obscene number of layers to counteract the cold, but shortly after the fever shifted and her body began to boil under all the clothes.

"Jesus-fuck-me-Christ, bitch! Will you make up your damn mind?" Richard screamed as she began to peel off three sweaters and an extra pair of pants.

She blushed and frowned, finally putting their equipment in the van that they'd stolen the other night and settling into her seat.

Once again Oliver was left behind, though this was more for appearances' sake than the security of their base. The monster their stolen dog had become wouldn't pass for anything but what it truly was out on the streets. As they pulled out and headed up the path, Dianna, forcing herself to suppress a coughing fit, looked in the rearview mirror and frowned at the sight of their experimental canine standing by the entrance and watching them leave.

She forced herself to suppress her pity for the animal, not wanting Richard to pick up on it.

They were halfway to the city—about ten minutes on the road—when Richard looked in the rearview mirror and frowned, "We're being tailed."

"Huh?" Dianna looked over at him.

"Tailed? You know? Pursued! Chased! We're being *followed*," he smacked her across the face, "Deal with it!"

Dianna rubbed her cheek and nodded, unbuckling her seatbelt and stepping into the back of the van. Snatching up one of their automatic rifles, she slapped a magazine into the weapon, cocked it, and threw open the rear hatch. Sure enough, there was a black BMW tailgating them so close that the swinging door scraped its hood. The windows of the sedan were mirrored, hiding the driver and any potential passengers behind a reflection of the night.

"What the fuck are you waiting for, idiot? Shoot there goddam tires out!" Richard looked over his shoulder at his sister and the motion jerked the wheel, swerving the van.

Dianna stumbled and nearly fell onto the hood of the pursuing car, but grabbed the frame in time to keep herself inside. Once sure she wouldn't end up a smear on the BMW's windshield, she raised the weapon. Lining up a clean shot on the front tires proved nearly impossible, however, and as she tried again and again to get a shot she could sense her brother's anger rising.

"JUST SHOOT THE FUCKER!" He roared.

Knowing better than to hesitate she pulled the trigger and let loose a spray of automatic fire all over the trunk and rear window. What she expected to crack and shatter instead dimpled only slightly. She frowned and turned to her brother.

"It's armored," She informed him.

"What?" He demanded.

She bit her lip, "I-it's bullet-proof..."

"Shit!" Richard paused, then, "I'll show this son of a bitch!"

With no warning he slammed on the brakes and allowed the black car to ram into their rear bumper. Jostled by the impact, Dianna lost her grip and spilled from the van, hitting the hood and nearly rolling over the edge.

Laughing, Richard hit the gas and peeled away before throwing the vehicle into a fishtail that spun it back around. As Dianna watched, their stolen van's nose came to face her and the enemy's car she was lying on top of and began to accelerate. Her eyes widened, seeing her brother coming towards her at breakneck speed, and quickly leapt from the hood and out of the way as Richard smashed into the BMW, flipping it onto its roof.

As Dianna pulled herself to unsteady legs, Richard stepped out of the van and drew his two swords in both hands, rubbing the sides of the blades together and creating an eerie harmony as he approached. The door to the flipped car flew open and, before either of the hunters could respond, a sang was standing behind Richard and pushing the barrel of a gun to the back of his head. Richard froze for a moment and held his arms out, looking like he might surrender, before he disappeared from sight just as the gun went off, sending a bullet meant for his skull down the road.

Soon after jumping into the inhuman speed the vampire did the same, and Dianna was forced to follow suit just to see what was happening. With the benefit of her new perspective, she could see her brother and their attacker circling each other. Richard still had his swords drawn and the vampire had a pair of forked daggers in either hand. As he spun the blades in both hands, the vampire noticeably took in Richard as the two measured each other up and soon they lunged forward.

Richard struck again and again, each blow being caught and

pushed away by the expertly wielded weapons. The hunter spun around and swiped, intending to behead the vampire, who deflected the blade with his own weapon and got in close, bringing a dagger around and spinning it in his palm, hitting Richard in the forehead with the end of the handle and knocking him down and back to a human speed. Still able to see their enemy's movements, Dianna watched the vampire grip his weapons in both hands and prepare to bring them down for a killing blow.

Time froze as Dianna found herself wondering if she should allow the attack to land; to let her brother be killed.

But then where would she be?

Who was she if not Richard's partner?

And what if the warrior failed and Richard survived to punish her for not acting?

"NO!" Dianna dove in and tackled the vampire from the side, saving her brother.

Both hit the ground a short distance from Richard. Able to see the vampire now, Richard jumped to his feet and thrust one of his swords through his shoulder, pinning him to the street as he brought his other sword's point to his throat.

"You're a warrior," he growled down to the mythos. The vampire groaned and hissed, struggling to get free but unable to fight Richard's superior strength. The hunter twisted the blade slightly, winning a pained growl in the process. "You will bring us to your clan's headquarters now."

The vampire narrowed his eyes and stifled his pained grunts, "N-never!"

Richard chuckled and knelt down close to his victim, "I have the means to make the remainder of your already short life very, *very* painful if you don't do as I say."

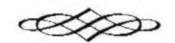

⋘⋙

Dianna, as per her brother's instruction, began casting the spell on the shackles that they'd put the warrior in. The vampire snarled and thrashed, several times getting his fangs dangerously close to the hunter's face and throat. Eventually—and none too soon for her—the incantation was finished and the next rough

CRIMSON SHADOW: FORBIDDEN DANCE

tug against the chains sent a powerful surge of heat into their prisoner's body, causing him to cry out in pain.

There was no chance of escaping now; not unless Dianna or Richard reversed the spell.

"Now,"—Richard's mock-friendly tone towards the vampire sent a fearful quake up through Dianna's core; if there was anything more terrifying than her brother when he was angry, it was him when he was excited—"you're going to lead us back to your clan of leeches. And for this, you will die a clean, quick"—Richard shook his head and rolled his hand at the wrist; obviously not caring about what he was saying—"and, y'know, honorable death."

"What would you know about honor?" The vampire spat, tugging harder at his shackles and getting rewarded with more pain.

"I know," the hunter cracked his knuckles and smirked wickedly, "that it'd be my honor to take your fucking head off now and drain your fading mind for the answers I want."

The vampire glared, but didn't seem surprised to hear the threat.

"And judging from your reaction," Richard went on, "you already know what we're capable of. Now would you rather do all of this on your own free will or have us tugging your strings and making you dance while we butcher you and your clan?"

The vampire stared at him for a moment, contemplating his options. Dianna could see the moment of truth as it dawned on him, his face sagging in complete and utter defeat; his clan was doomed to die no matter what he did.

He was, as Richard had been hoping, too weak to hold back.

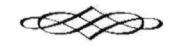

⋄≫≪⋄

Dianna barely moved a muscle as Richard rocketed about the clan's underground lair—shooting like a bullet from place to place—dispatching its members. The sight of her seemingly invisible brother was incredible—albeit terrible and horrifying— and, as he darted about, creating momentary blurs when he stopped long enough to finish off a writhing vampire, she couldn't bring herself to look away. Without the benefit of adjusting her eyes to Richard's supernatural speed, it appeared as though the vampire clan's members were suddenly and randomly losing limbs before collapsing where they'd stood.

Several were quick to try and retaliate, but soon after disappearing from sight they would reappear—singed and smoking from a magical attack—and be pinned to a wall for Richard to dismember at his leisure.

He didn't slow down.

He didn't tire.

He didn't stop.

Not until the entire vampire clan had been reduced to nothing.

Dianna knew he was having too much fun to be angry that she hadn't helped him in his rampage. He wouldn't have wanted to share in the slaughter anyway. Instead, as he finished up, she went into their bags and began unloading the C4. Richard, no doubt, would want to level the entire subterranean system, and if the explosives weren't ready when he was finished then she would be in for it.

She knew it was pointless to tell him what sort of effects doing so might have on the ground level above.

It was all part of the mission...

The last small brick of explosive putty emerged from the duffle when Richard suddenly appeared in front of her, sweaty and bright red with effort and excess body heat, but happier than she'd seen him in a long time. He looked down, taking in the sight of the explosives, and smiled happily.

"Good girl," he commended her, sheathing his swords and grabbing the detonator from her. He played with it a moment, tossing it up and down in a display that made Dianna nervous that it may be dropped and send them all to Hell earlier than planned. Nothing happened, though. Instead, he smiled, keeping his eyes on his sister while continuing his threatening game of catch. "Set the rest of them up," he ordered, "Cover each of the corners of the main hall and one in each of the dividing halls." He smiled, "Any of the little scab-eaters who were lucky enough to live will be buried."

Dianna cringed at the thought but nodded, disappearing

from Richard's sight as she sprinted at the vampiric speed around the area and set the explosives. When she was done, she returned to the spot she'd been standing before. Returning to a normal speed, she felt more tired from the whole ordeal than Richard seemed to be feeling and wondered, again, why the serum was working better for him than it was for her.

Richard smiled at her return—though she knew that, for him, she'd only been gone a second or two—and turned to leave. Quick to follow, Dianna fetched their things and scampered after her brother, not wanting him to suddenly see her as obsolete and bury her in the explosion, as well. When they were finally clear of the vampires' catacombs Richard pressed the button on the detonator and destroyed it all.

"That," he smiled, tossing the remote to the ground and destroying it under the bottom of his boots, "will *definitely* ruffle a few of the monsters' tail-feathers."

CHAPTER TWENTY-THREE
SERENITY

THE MOMENT WAS PERFECT.

The moon—a pale crescent hanging low in the night sky and accompanied by several puffs of dark, meandering clouds—illuminated the clearing. The sounds of the wilderness washed over the peaceful clearing that Xander and Estella had found themselves in, and, free from the city lights and the ever-constant burning of the therions' campfires, the stars shone brightly above them like a dark and infinite curtain.

And, though it was cold, they had ways of staying warm.

Though they'd made love before, the experience was made new with the addition of Estella's vampiric abilities as well as their combined pent-up aggressions. This and their newly sparked passion were let loose in a rolling, writhing whirlwind that they were sure rocked the very forest to its deepest roots.

Xander had passed Timothy on to Satoru for training, explaining that he needed to focus his efforts towards teaching Estella how to control her new abilities. Though the nejin hadn't said a word as he'd explained where the little vampire was in his training, he'd felt oddly comforted by the bright, cat-like eyes that shone like two green flames and the off-putting attempt at a human smile—the resulting gesture looking more like a monstrous sneer filled with needle teeth.

And Xander had thought shark-like teeth of the alv were scary...

When they were finally alone, he had gotten to work on helping her focus on jumping into—and maintaining—overdrive. After a short while of slipping in-and-out of the process, she was able to hold it long enough to get across a predetermined distance—a short stretch of clearing, free of any potentially harmful trees. Appearing over the makeshift finish line, she had seemed more surprised than Xander at the achievement and began bouncing on her heels and clapping her hands in celebration of her accomplishment. While Xander hadn't wanted to commend her too early for such a simple lesson, seeing her gleeful bouncing was enough to force a smile to his face and drive him to congratulate her with a passionate kiss.

Eager to continue and wanting to try something else, Estella asked if they could move on to vampiric jumping. Earlier that year, when she'd still been human and living in the attic of her parents' house, she'd often marveled at Xander's ability to leap onto the rooftop near her window from the ground each time he came to visit. Though it wasn't a surprise to him that she'd be interested to try what she'd admired for so long, Xander was hesitant to move on so quickly when there was still so much training left for honing her overdrive. He'd been prepared to turn her down, but was unable to say "no" when Estella's pouty face came into play.

"You manipulative witch," Xander had groaned, shaking his head.

Estella beamed and shrugged her left shoulder, "There's no better kind."

And so, after finding a tall enough tree with a series of branches that jutted out at random heights, Xander explained the process of preparing for a superhuman leap and displayed it by jumping to a branch a little over thirty feet above them.

Estella, excited to join him, tried to copy the movement, but was only able to get about seven feet into the air before crashing down to the ground. Dropping down from the branch and landing gracefully on his feet, Xander had helped her back to her feet and began to check her for any injuries only to be surprised to find her giggling at her own folly. Seeing that she was alright he, too, laughed and they went on to try again... and again... and again.

After nearly two hours of practice, Estella was able to get to a branch—clumsily landing but at least remaining upright this time—a little over fifteen feet from the base of their "training tree". Though both were excited at the accomplishment and they knew that they should continue the training, they had decided that a walk through the woods would be more enjoyable.

The walk had lasted ten minutes before they'd come to the clearing and their clothes had come off.

As they climaxed, the release of raw, throbbing energy—Estella's waves of magic coupled with Xander's thrashing aura—took its toll on their surroundings. Trees uprooted and toppled along the invisible force, and the ground beneath them trembled and burst into clumps of frozen earth and stone, leaving the two vampire lovers in a smoldering crater. Spent, they separated and lay back on their discarded clothes. Their breathing was hard and labored, the resulting clouds that issued from their mouths swirling in the night air and mingling before fading away.

"Was that a part of the training?" Estella giggled, rolling to her side and tracing a circle with her finger on Xander's chest.

He laughed and shook his head, not taking his eyes from the night sky. "I'm starting to think it should be," he took a look around at the damage that their activities had birthed—seeing that they'd cleared nearly a football field's worth of foliage around them—and chuckled, "I'm just not sure the forest could handle it."

Estella smiled, "I wouldn't mind."

Xander looked over at his lover's face and returned her smile.

It really was a perfect moment.

When the two vampires finally got back to the therion camp they found Timothy and the Nejin in a heated sparring session. Though Xander had specifically told the little vampire that he was not allowed to use overdrive when training with somebody who wasn't a vampire, he found his apprentice dodging all of his trainer's lunges with vampiric speed.

"Timothy!" Xander's stern voice startled the little vampire and he turned towards his mentor, stammering and keeping his eyes down as he poked at the ground with the toe of his shoe. After a moment of letting him sweat, Xander ruffled his hair, "How about a game of tag with me and Estella?"

"Yay!" Timothy ran forward and joined the two after turning and waving goodbye to Satoru, who returned the gesture before turning away to return to the therion camp.

After a short distance Estella looked at Timothy, "Where's Trepis?"

"He's with Osehr and the ther'on kids," he boasted, "He gets bored watching Xander 'n me train, so he *definitely* would've been bored watching you."

Estella laughed at the little vampire's answer—Xander noting a small blush that crept over her cheeks as she did—and nodded her understanding, "As long as he's happy, right?"

"Oh he is," Timothy assured her, "He likes to give piggy-back rides to the smaller kids, and the older ones are always feeding him."

"Is that so?" Xander asked playfully, "No wonder he's been getting so fat."

"Trepis isn't fat!" Timothy shot his mentor a glare, "He's happy!"

Xander smirked and ruffled the boy's hair again, "Yea. Happily fat!" He laughed and ran ahead.

"Hey!" Timothy chased after and leapt at him just as Xander jumped up-and-over his young apprentice—performing a back-flip over the lunging vampire—and landed behind him.

Xander stuck out his tongue playfully, "Still too slo—*OOF!*"

Estella roared with laughter as Timothy rocketed into

Xander and knocked him down with enough force to send them skidding across the ground. Timothy smiled up at her, clearly proud of his accomplishment, and looked down at Xander, who was already laughing, as well.

"Spoke too soon, I guess," Xander corrected himself as he stood, patting Timothy on the shoulder, "Good job. I guess that makes me 'it'."

The little vampire beamed and nodded.

When they finally reached the clearing Timothy was shaking with excitement. While he enjoyed sparring, it was clear that training with games was still number one in his heart. Xander briefly explained to be careful with Estella, because she was still learning.

Timothy smiled at her. "Don't worry," he gave her a thumbs up, "I'll help you!"

Soon they were all in overdrive, Estella proving a fast learner as well—though her control was still a bit shaky as she shimmered in and out—and they darted back and forth, tagging and dodging one another's attempts.

At one point, Estella and Timothy decided to gang up on Xander, and the vampire found himself narrowly dodging a wave of "tagging" attacks that seemed to hold more threat to his wellbeing than some of the rogues he'd taken down in the past.

Their games went on for the rest of the night, and as they progressed so did Estella's control. As Xander watched he saw that as his lover's tension faded, so did her sloppiness. By the close of the night, she looked as though she'd been training for weeks.

Their game came to an end when Estella, finally tired of being outdone, muttered a few magic words and Xander found himself pinned to a tree. Once immobilized and helpless, his two apprentices began to tag and tickle him until he begged in between bouts of laughter for them to stop.

"Hey! No fair," he coughed out between his laughter, "No magic!"

"Seems fair to me," Estella laughed as she continued. "What do you think?" She asked Timothy.

The little vampire, laughing harder than all the others,

nodded, "It's definitely fair!"

As the night drew to a close Xander admitted defeat to the two and they finally headed off to his tent for some synthetic magic-blood and some much needed rest. Estella made a face at the taste of the artificial blood, but nonetheless drank it and admired the results as she was revitalized in a few short seconds. Timothy did the same, pinching his nose and tipping his head back as he slammed down a hard slug of the stuff from a thermos lid. For a moment it appeared that he might not keep the substance down, but he finally gulped before smiling proudly as he displayed his empty mouth to the two.

When they were reenergized from the exhausting night of training, they all lay down; Timothy once again falling fast asleep first and leaving the vampire lovers to talk.

"I really appreciate all of this," Estella said after a long moment.

Xander rolled onto his side to face her, "Appreciate what?"

"You know, taking me back and training me and treating me so nicely," she frowned, "I'd have hated me after all that I did to you."

Xander smiled and shook his head. "There's nothing you could say or do to make me hate you," he promised her, "After all, you were my best friend even when I was a total douchebag."

She blushed at that, kissing his cheek. "Goodnight, Xander. I love you."

Xander looked over at her as he heard this. While her emotions towards him weren't a mystery by that point, there was something in hearing the words that warmed his heart and filled him with a serenity that he'd long since thought had been lost.

"I love you too, Estella. Sleep well."

CHAPTER TWENTY-FOUR
"WE ATTACK TONIGHT"

DIANNA'S SICKNESS HAD started to pass with the coming of the new day. Feeling the wave of nausea and dizziness subside, she saw hope on the horizon that she might actually get a few hours of decent rest. As it was, she'd not been able to get a full night's rest since they'd first started injecting the enchanted mythos blood into their bodies.

A short distance away, Richard was swooning over the Oliver-monster that they'd created. "Who's a good beasty-boy? Yes you are! Yes you are!" he cooed at their mutated abomination, "Are you ready to sniff out that nasty ol' mythos scum?"

He rubbed Oliver's head once more before turning towards Dianna, who quickly put up her psychic shields to protect her deeper thoughts and masked them with thoughts of their parents that wouldn't be construed as lies to her brother. Rather than analyzing her mind, however, Richard sat down on the air mattress that served as his bed and looked at her.

"We attack tonight," he informed her.

She looked up, surprised that he wasn't yelling or lecturing. "Tonight?" She bumbled for a moment, "Are you sure Oliver is ready?"

"Well he ain't getting any prettier," Richard joked.

Dianna faked a laugh and nodded, "Right. Would... uh, would you like me to do anything to prepare?" she asked. Questions were good; there was nothing for Richard's psychic invasions to interpret as a lie.

Her brother frowned for a moment, possibly sensing, if only for a second, something lingering deeper in her mind. He narrowed his eyes at her, but finally shook his head. "Just get some rest. I expect you to be in top form when we go in after them. I intend to do most of the work... again"—his tone was almost accusatory, but seemed too pride-filled to make her nervous—"but I *do* expect you to keep them from getting too far. I don't want them getting away again."

"How would you like me to do that?" She asked.

He growled and shrugged, "It's your fucking job to figure that out! I don't care *how* you do it. Shoot 'em in the knees; saw off your own leg and dangle it as bait! I don't care! Just do whatever it takes!"

Dianna flinched and nodded, "I understand."

"Good."

She sighed and looked down, thinking. "How are we going to get Oliver through the streets without anyone seeing?"

Where she expected Richard to get angry again he instead offered a wide smile. "I'm glad you asked. I've been working on it, actually. You see, those brain-rape vamps have that ability to control minds and make people see whatever they want them to see—real useful weapon, actually. Anyways, I've been practicing and I think I got it down."

Dianna gave a slow nod, working against letting the consideration that his thought didn't necessarily ensure success rise to the surface of her mind.

He nodded again, smiling to himself and lying back on the air mattress. "Those fucking monsters won't even see it coming."

Dianna nodded—agreeing with what he said but not happy

about a word of it—and rolled over. Knowing better than to dwell on the thoughts any longer, she pulled her blanket up to her ears, doing her best to cover the itchy slits that were her developing gills.

They really wouldn't see it coming. How could they? Nobody was prepared or equipped to take on what they had become. Richard had almost single-handedly buried an entire clan of well-trained mythos, and their targets were just a band of five misfits—four if they didn't include the child. They really didn't stand a chance. It wasn't even a hunt to go after them like that; it was a massacre.

An *inhuman* massacre.

Richard's snores started up, confirming to Dianna that she was free to think the thoughts that were itching in her mind like the gills at her neck. She wondered how much longer she could continue doing this; following under her barbaric brother's shadow. It was already becoming too much to bear. She was never interested in torturing innocent creatures that had done nothing more than be in the wrong place at the wrong time, and she couldn't constitute taking lives that didn't deserve to be taken. Early on in their careers they'd agreed that the monsters deserved to die for what they were and what it was in their nature to do, but all she'd seen these creatures do lately was try to protect their own; to try to survive. Even their parents had been killed in the middle of a hunt in self-defense.

Were they on a mission to avenge the real monsters?

Dianna's stomach lurched and she jumped to her feet and ran from the boathouse before vomiting again.

She already knew that there would be no rest for her.

Not when she knew what was coming with the setting of the sun.

CHAPTER TWENTY-FIVE
DATE NIGHT

THE VAMPIRES—Xander, Estella *and* Timothy—had all decided that they'd take a break from training and go out to a movie. Zeek had been reluctant to let the little vampire leave the sanctity of the therions' territory, but was, with a few well-placed and reassuring words from Estella, convinced that it would all be alright.

Once they had the okay to go, they quickly jumped into overdrive—both Estella and Timothy having enough control in Xander's opinion to make the trip—and headed through the woods and towards the city. With the pressure of training no longer weighing her down, Estella's command over her vampire body was far greater than the night before. Marveling at this realization, Xander watched as she weaved through the forest beside him. Ahead of them, Timothy made a show of his own abilities with a series of kicks and spins, battling imaginary foes with every step, as he went along. Finally, when the lights of civilization began to show through the trees, they slowed and finally dropped out of overdrive.

It was a good walk from the outskirts of the forest to the movie theater, and though the trek would have been enough to exhaust a human the vampire couple and their young comrade were more than up for the stroll. Nearly forty-five minutes later they were standing in front of the concession stand with their tickets as Timothy looked skeptically down at the cup of his first-ever soda.

"Does it taste like blood?" He asked, looking up at his mentor.

The young lady behind the counter stared for a moment, not sure what to make of the young boy's question. Xander, chuckling as he rolled his eyes and entered the girl's mind to erase the memory of what she'd heard, looked down at his apprentice and shook his head.

"I'm afraid not, little buddy," he tussled the little vampire's hair, "But I think you'll like it, anyway."

Estella giggled and knelt down, explaining to Timothy that he had to be careful of what he said around humans. He blushed and covered his mouth, nodding and apologizing.

"It's alright," Xander smiled, taking a box of candy as it was handed to him by the dazed clerk, "No harm; no foul."

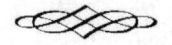

⋘⋙

The movie was a standard action flick, and Estella, halfway through the feature, leaned over to Xander and asked if he thought it might be too violent for Timothy. Startled by the question, he looked first to his lover and then to the little vampire, who, only a day earlier, had been drinking deer blood while the animal lay several feet away. After some deliberating the two of them finally decided that the gore would only serve to make the little one hungry and shared a stifled chuckle at the idea.

When it was over they left the theater amidst a wave of humans and headed to a nearby coffee shop for hot chocolate. Though they were about to close, Xander was able to convince the owner to let the three of them in with a quick auric tweak to the manager's mind. Unsure of what the treat was, Timothy was slow to take the first sip from the Styrofoam cup. The two older vampires—both of whom had once been human—laughed at his skepticism as they watched his face light up at the taste. By the time they had left, the collar of Timothy's shirt was stained with some of what his eager mouth had been unable to hold.

That's when Xander, laughing at the sight of Estella trying to clean the giddy little vampire's face, doubled over as he received the psychic call.

Osehr had always been precise and calculated with his auric messages, and as the jumbled, wordless wave of pain and emotion flooded the vampire's head he knew that something was wrong. Estella and Timothy frowned as well, sensing the psychic message but not understanding what it was or what it meant.

Xander scowled and threw away what remained of his hot chocolate in a nearby trash can; Estella soon after doing the same.

"What is that?" Timothy complained, trying to hold onto his cup while he worked to cover his ears, not knowing that the chaos he was hearing was *inside* his head.

Shaking his head, Xander took the little vampire's hand. He cried out in surprise as his cup dropped from his grip, landing on the sidewalk and spilling its steaming contents across a patch of ice. Eyes widening, he looked up with an enraged glare at Xander, who was already looking down at his apprentice. Seeing from his expression that something was wrong, the accusatory glare faded to one of worry.

"What's wrong?" Timothy's voice cracked.

"We need to get back," Xander told them, "Now!"

The two nodded as Xander looked around him, noting a few straggling humans scattered about, but nothing substantial. With the hands of his companions in his own, he threw out his aura and ensnared every potential onlooker, erasing their memories of the three of them before jumping into overdrive and rocketing back towards the forest.

Timothy, knowing that something was wrong and abandoning his previously carefree antics, darted ahead once his feet had had the opportunity to touch the ground. Xander tried to call out to him—to demand that his apprentice stay behind them—but the three of them were moving too fast for his words to mean anything. By the time he'd been able to utter a syllable they were in the forest and the sound waves had been left behind in the city streets.

Slow down and get behind me! He sent out a psychic call, desperate to keep the little vampire and Estella safe from whatever Osehr was warning him of.

Neither paid any attention to him. He scowled and sent the message out again and again, each time getting no result. They were both too caring—too concerned for the others—to fall back and protect themselves.

He pushed ahead, forcing his half-blood body to catch up with the full-blooded sang boy. The exhaustion began pulling hard at him as he caught up. He ignored it. Reaching out, he grabbed Timothy and pulled him off his feet once again, forcing him out of overdrive. The boy struggled for a moment before his mentor sent out another—far angrier—psychic message.

Timothy stopped struggling.

Xander fell back, handing him over to Estella. *Find someplace to hide!* He told her before he shot ahead alone, *Keep him safe!*

Sensing Estella's silent agreement in her auric shift, Xander felt the energy in the night dip as she dropped out of overdrive disappeared into the distance that Xander put between them as he continued on ahead. There was no time to get his weapons and he shot past the path towards his tent as he made his way towards the therions and their clearing.

Whatever it was, he'd have to face it unarmed.

He could "see" the hunters before he'd completely made it through, and as he leapt over the barricade of shrubs he released his body from the energy-draining state of being and threw his aura at the closest hunter, a young man slightly older than himself with short-cut brown hair. Before the attack was able to reach his target, however, the hunter turned and blocked the strike with his own aura.

Xander landed and scowled at the human; the warrior who'd visited them before had been right.

They were stealing mythos powers.

All around there was the mayhem of battle; the humming charge of powerful magic floating in the air. Many of the pack were already dead while those still breathing were struggling against binding spells that held them down. Most, including the newcomers, were trapped in the same way and lay in the dirt, flopping like docked fish. Even Osehr had been bound magically to his throne and, unable to rise, was forced to watch the scene unfold before him.

"Interesting," the hunter said, looking Xander up and down, "A leech amongst wolves. Although I shouldn't be surprised since they're obviously taking in strays."

Xander snarled and bared his fangs. "Leave. Now!"

"Not until I'm done with some unfinished business."

Growling, Xander struck. Though most of his energy had been diminished due to his efforts in getting there, the promise of the hunter's blood was motivation enough for his lagging system to push him forward. He ran, clenching his fists and preparing to evade his enemy's swords but found he'd sheathed them and was now glowing with the energy of a spell.

Xander dove out of the way as the ground beneath him shook and burst with the force of a dozen landmines, sending dirt and rocks raining down on the clearing. He rolled and pushed off the ground with his aura, landing on his feet once again and continued towards his opponent. Not wanting to be a clear target he ran in a serpentine pattern, evading the magical and auric attacks that came at him. As he shot past the nearby fire pit, he grabbed a still-burning branch and swung it with all his might into the chest of the hunter. Watching with a swell of satisfaction as the hunter slammed into the ground on his back, Xander cast aside his makeshift weapon and moved in for a killing blow.

The hunter scuttled away, spotting something behind his attacker and reaching out in desperation, "Dianna!"

Xander frowned at the name and turned, his eyes widening as he saw the girl from the café staring back at him. Her own eyes were wide with surprise and the gun that she had begun to level in his direction wavered.

The male hunter growled and Xander felt his auric signature

writhe; the glow of his stolen taroe tattoos casting a blue iridescence across the forest floor as he cast a spell on his own comrade and she shrieked in pain. "SHOOT HIM, YOU STUPID COW!" he roared.

Dianna shook in agony and started to lift the gun again. Xander watched, not sure what to make of this new development. His energy supply was too spent to jump into overdrive again; he knew that his vampiric system would shut down and he'd pass out if he even tried. Even then, these hunters, human or not, had gained enough auric control to see an attack coming if he had the control to muster anyway. Even now he could sense the male hunter's dark-blue aura slowly stretching out to ensnare him from behind.

But the gun—and the girl holding it—still held his attention. Exterminators...

She'd said she and her brother were *exterminators*!

How could he have been so stupid?

How did he not notice it then? Sure, her sweater had kept the taroe tattoos covered, but her mind—her *secrets*!—had been open for him to explore!

And he'd just sat there, too polite to invade the strange girl's mind for any potential threats; he'd just sat there and talked it up with one of the enemy!

Like a chump!

Like an ignorant human!

She had a clean shot lined up, and no better opportunity was going to present itself. But her eyes still shone with confusion and fear. All of it genuine. She was in shock. And Xander could see in her awestruck gaze the truth. She hadn't known at the café that he was a vampire, and seeing him now—much like himself— she was lingering on the memory of their chance encounter.

But why?

She was a hunter!

Killing his kind was what she did...

The male behind her roared and his aura lurched forward to grab Xander, who, still staring at the female hunter and her wavering hand-cannon, deflected the attack with his own aura before it could make contact with him. He needed to believe—for the time being, at least—that the female hunter wouldn't shoot him. Whether he trusted his instincts or not, he felt that there was logic and reason staying her hand, and he needed that delay to keep him and his loved ones safe while he defended himself from her brother. There was too much of a threat with him alone; too much power and potential in him to try adding a second threat to the equation. And so, with his aura clashing and colliding again and again with the male hunter's desperate strikes, he turned his back on Dianna.

Finally, irritated by the whole ordeal, the hunter withdrew his aura, using it to push himself to his feet and allowing him to rocket at Xander in overdrive. Sensing the lethal intent, Xander pushed his body to dodge the attack and, avoiding the hunter's sword, was knocked into the dying fire in the center of the clearing. The impact shifted the burning kindling and stoked the embers at the bottom of the pit, and Xander cried out as the flames wrapped around him. For a moment there was only confusion; no place to go that wasn't filled with the agony-bringing flame.

So he went up; leaping straight into the night air.

Still in midair, he wrapped his aura around him again in an oxygen-free bubble and, forced to hold his breath, waited for the flames to starve and snuff themselves before freeing himself. Still gasping for air, he came crashing to the ground...

Where the male hunter was already waiting for him.

A steel-toed boot was driven into his side with the stolen strength of all the mythos breeds he'd killed. The force was enough to push the air from Xander's lungs and he heaved, his cries of pain coming out in gasps as he fought to replenish his aching lungs.

Xander rolled to his back and focused his aura, grabbing the hunter's foot as it started to come down in an attempt to crush his skull. Yanking the foot to one side, he tossed the hunter to the ground and dragged himself to his feet. Though he'd put out the fires, his skin was still burning, and he could already feel blisters forming all over his scorched body. His clothes were singed and hole-ridden, allowing enough of the winter air through to provide a slight relief to his pain.

It wasn't enough, though.

He groaned, trying to move but finding the process too excruciating and collapsed to his knees. The male hunter, already on his feet and charging towards him, filled the forest with his enraged cries.

With no way of physically defending himself, Xander closed his eyes and shifted his mind's eye to sense the auras that were present around him. Focusing on his attacker, he pushed out his own aura, blocking the attacks again and again before ensnaring the hunter and lifting him into a magical whirlwind and hurling him into the side of a distant tree.

The sound of bones breaking brought a slight smile to the vampire's scorched face.

Immobilized, the hunter growled. "Oliver! Sic 'em!"

Xander frowned, sensing a psychic call as it was sent out into the depths of the forest.

In the distance, something roared.

The sound carried, resonating throughout the woods with enough force to still the struggling therions' efforts. Xander opened his eyes, trying to see what was coming, and watched as a large tree groaned and shook as whatever was approaching dragged against it and a nearby bush was parted and crushed in the middle under an enormous paw. Xander gaped, watching as something that looked like a massive, prehistoric wolf with golden fur stepped into the wavering light of the fire.

"No... fucking... way..." Xander groaned.

The hunter's aura swirled happily behind him and his voice was gleeful despite his broken bones.

"Kill him!"

The dog-monster let out another roar and charged, its brown-and-gold aura flaring as it drew nearer. Xander frowned, calculating whether or not he had the strength to defend himself from this monstrosity when...

Another roar emerged just outside the clearing and all heads—including the dog-monster's—turned as Trepis leapt into the clearing and snarled at the monstrosity, his lips pulled back to expose his lethal assets as the heckles rose along his mane. The tiger's tail jerked methodically as it circled the hunters' monster; its bright blue eyes narrowing as its light-blue aura swirled like a tornado around it.

"Trepis... no!" Xander called out, sending an auric call for Trepis to fall back. His tiger companion had never been in a fight, and he wasn't even sure if the animal knew how to defend itself, let alone challenge the likes of what it was up against.

His friend ignored his attempts, however, and pounced at the dog-monster. Massive, claw-filled paws impacted with the mutant dog's side and drew first blood. The dog whimpered as it side-stepped, catching itself before it toppled over, and snarled at Trepis as it jumped back to distance itself from the tiger and its claws. Trepis pounced again, his jaws opening wide and aiming for the dog's neck. Seeing the big cat's intention, the dog rotated and met tooth with tooth; both large creatures grabbing the others neck, only to get locked in by the other's bite. Animalistic shrieks and whimpers filled the night as the two beasts fought. Claws tore; teeth ripped; bodies collided. Soon the two of them were blood-soaked and limping, but neither stood down nor retreated.

Xander shook his head, tears rolling down his scorched cheeks.

He couldn't lose Trepis.

He couldn't!

With all of his strength and focus he cast out his aura and wrapped it around his friend, commanding him to run away.

But the tiger refused!

Trepis' mind was filled with the need to stay and protect both Xander and the pack that had become their family, and just like the vampire wouldn't give up for them the tiger refused to stand down.

Xander nodded slowly, understanding the need and drive...

But that didn't mean he couldn't help.

A deep instinct overtook him and he pushed his aura into his animal friend until the two of them became one sentient force and Xander could see through the tiger's eyes.

The dog began to charge at them again and Xander-Trepis roared out with new vitality, confusing the monster and stalling its advances. As their enemy stumbled with its hesitation they leapt forward, their minds synced and ready to fight. A mighty swipe with the right paw tore into the monster-dog's muzzle, blinding it and allowing them to drive their thick skull into their enemy's own; dazing the creature and allowing them to position themselves at its side. As the monster-dog shifted to get the tiger back in its sights, they lunged and landed on the mutant's middle, knocking it to the ground. Snarling, it tried to raise its head, only to have them stomped down on it, forcing it back into the blood-caked dirt.

Xander continued to feed his auric energy into the tiger as they fought as one, and with a loud growl, they bit down on their enemy's neck and yanked, dragging the monster-dog back and forth violently until...

SNAP!

The mutant's muscles slacked as the body went limp and they released its nape just as Xander released his strange psychic ties with the tiger. As his consciousness returned to his own body he was reintroduced to the pain of his burns and, though it was agonizing to do so, he stood and turned to face the male hunter.

Only to find him and his sister gone.

CHAPTER TWENTY-SIX
LAST CHANCE

RICHARD PUSHED HIMSELF further away from the clearing. He cursed—again and again and again. He cursed the pain in his body; cursed the monsters and their damned resilience. He cursed at the clusterfuck that the mission had become; a mission that was supposed to be so simple. He cursed the tiger and its interruption of Oliver's big moment; cursed the loss of one of his strongest weapons. And he cursed the vampire punk and whoever had been behind his obvious training.

But, most of all, he cursed his sister; the useless bitch who had choked and allowed everything—*everything* that had motivated his previous curses—to occur.

"... the fuck keeps a tiger, anyway?" He groaned, pushing himself further and further away from what should have been his victory, "Fucking freaks! Goddam fucking monsters! Shit," he cringed as the fractured ends of the bones in his arm scraped against one another and he drove his opposite fist into a nearby tree, howling in pain as he broke his hand. As the tree toppled over and sparked a storm of chatters from a nearby creature,

Richard glared at his mangled fist.

He cursed that, too.

And, again, he cursed his sister for being the cause of all of it.

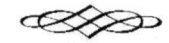

⋘⋙

Though she couldn't feel the winter chill through all her layers, Dianna couldn't stop shaking.

The boy from the café was a vampire!

She'd sat there and talked with a creature that she'd been raised her entire life to believe was the enemy; been friendly with something that she'd been taught to see as nothing more than a monster. But he wasn't...

He wasn't!

He'd jumped into the middle of the slaughter—*their* slaughter—to save the pack of therions and the ragtag bunch of mythos that had gotten away from them in the first place.

He *protected* them!

And he'd nearly *died* doing it!

How could she possibly construe *that* as evil?

How could she justify killing him?

How could she justify killing any of them?

She shook her head and sobbed.

She'd been raised to kill monsters. Creatures that invaded the peace and sanctity of others and butchered them without mercy to quench an insatiable need for death...

Monsters...

Monsters like her and her brother.

The word lost all meaning as everything she'd ever believed crumbled.

She'd seen how those mythos had panicked upon their arrival; had felt the fear and desperation roll like a collective tidal wave as they watched their packmates murdered and maimed. The same fear and desperation that her parents had accused their kind of breeding in the hearts of humans.

The same fear and desperation that Richard created.

Neither human nor mythos were spared. Not as long as her brother's insatiable need for death continued to motivate him.

Not as long as the monsters they'd become were—

Her brother's aura slammed down heavy across the back of her head and knocked her to the forest floor. Head reeling, she focused on rolling over to face him, his features blurred in her tear-filled gaze. Even without the ability to see him clearly, she held out her arm to protect her face from any further abuse. The blur shifted and she heaved as he kicked her in the stomach, allowing her to fold over on herself before he stomped down on her shoulder and twisted his heel until he'd forced a choked cry from her.

"Fucking bitch!" He roared, lifting his foot and driving it into her ribs three times, "You almost got me killed! And you cost us the damn mission!"

"No; please!" She cried curling up to protect herself, "I'm sorry! I'm... I'm so sorry! The vampire... he took hold of my mind and—"

Richard's aura lashed out and hit her across the face and took hold of her throat as he knelt down over her, spitting in her face. "Don't you dare lie to me, you worthless cunt! You think I couldn't see *everything* he did with his mind?" Another length of his aura whipped out and slapped her again as he pulled her to her feet; the auric hold around her neck tightening. As she struggled against her brother's supernatural hold, she saw that both his left arm and right hand were twisted and broken. She cringed with the realization that, even without the use of his hands, he could still beat her just the same, "I saw enough of that black-and-red shit-stain surrounding that blood-sucking punk to know it never *once* touched you," his voice hissed from between his clenched teeth as another auric slap landed and a second wave of spit caught her in the eye. The hold on her throat released then and he threw her back to the forest floor. "You hesitated! You had the shot and you *hesitated*!"

Dianna sobbed and wiped the mess from her face, "I..."—she shook her head, choking on a sob—"I'm... I'm s-sorry."

"Sorry's not good enough, you stupid piece of shit!" He kicked her again and pulled her up to her feet with his aura before high-kicking her in the face and knocking her down again. "You had a shot—a *perfect* fucking shot!—and you let that monster live!" He stepped down on her throat and held back just enough to let her speak, "What the hell were you thinking?"

Blood poured from her nose and she coughed and gagged from the pressure on her windpipe. "Please... please forgive me, Richard," she chose her words carefully so that he wouldn't see she was lying, "B-but... it *was* him! Somehow he wouldn't let me shoot!"

And he hadn't.

The compassion—the sincerity and kindness—that she'd seen in him that day at the café had forced her to stay her trigger finger at that moment. Though he hadn't been making a conscious effort to stop her, she had known what kind of person—not a monster; not a wretched, murdering creature—he really was, and *that* would not allow her to shoot him.

Richard stared down at her a moment, his eyes darting across her bloodied features as he scanned her mind. Though he now had a great deal of control over his aura, he still didn't know the extent of their powers. That she could just as easily shroud incriminating details while spotlighting those that supported her claims.

And, no matter how hard he searched, he could see no glimmer of dishonesty.

Something that the Xander-vampire had done *had* kept her from following his orders.

He growled, shaking his head in disgust and pulling his boot from her neck. "Get up," he ordered.

"W-where are we going?" She asked, groaning in pain as she rose on unsteady legs.

"Back to the damn boathouse, dumbass," he spat, "We have planning to do, and you've got *one* more chance to do this one right!" He glared back at her, "Or else you die with them!"

CHAPTER TWENTY-SEVEN
MOTIVATION

WITH THE THREAT dealt with for the time being, Osehr was quick to send one of the fastest in the pack to Xander's tent to retrieve his synthetic blood. Though Xander was insistent that he could get himself to his tent, the elder therion knew that he'd sooner pass out than successfully drag his burned body to his tent. Though he hated to feel like he was being waited on, Xander knew that he wasn't physically up to the challenge of arguing with his friend.

After downing three thermoses of the enchanted elixir, however, his body was quick to begin healing. Satisfied that his system was restored, he stretched his body, shedding a few layers of charred flesh in the process and uncovering the new, healed skin beneath it.

Though the stuff tasted rancid, it sure-as-hell did the trick.

He smirked to himself and made a mental note that he'd have to visit The Gamer—his source for the dwindling substance—to get some more of it in the near future.

By the time he was fully healed, Estella and Timothy had returned and were anxiously waiting to see him. Despite everything that had happened, seeing that they were alright brought a smile to Xander's face and he hurried to embrace Estella. Behind him, the therion children did their best to be helpful as a few of the elder pack-mates tended to Trepis' injuries. Though the wounds looked tolling, the healers assured Xander that his tiger comrade would be alright.

But there was still the issue of the dead...

Nearly a dozen bodies had been collected and piled near the scattered remains of the campfire—one of the packmates clapping a massive hand on Xander's shoulder and remarking at how well he'd faired within the flames; none of the others batted an eye when the exhausted vampire planted a fist in in the bold therion's jaw—and were being prepared for cremation. Though it wasn't Xander's first choice, his therion brothers and sisters believed that the best cleanup for *any* situation was done with fire.

Sighing in resignation as he turned away from his recently humbled packmate, Xander rolled his eyes. "Fire clean good," he muttered to himself, shuddering at the sight of the new flames as the bonfire was rebuilt.

In the end, taking in the silent process of feeding the flames the bodies of their fallen one-by-one served as a means of showing respect to those who had died protecting the pack.

Timothy, unable to watch, covered his eyes and sniffled away the beginning of a sob as he buried his face into Estella's side. Xander eyed his apprentice, admiring his strength given the circumstances, and decided that the pack could handle the rest of the ceremony without them. Sending a silent message to Osehr to inform him that he was going to take his apprentice and lover elsewhere, Xander took Estella's hand in his own and gestured for her to follow with Timothy. Rather than walking straight to the tent, the vampires meandered in a large figure eight several times in silence in an effort to calm their shaky nerves.

"It's all my fault!" The little vampire cried out.

Xander turned and looked at his apprentice with a frown, not sure what to say to console him.

Estella, however, was quick to kneel down and cupped her hands on Timothy's little shoulders, "No, sweetheart. It's not your fault at all. None of this was."

"But they followed me here," the boy pressed, "They wouldn't have come if it wasn't for me!"

Xander sighed and nodded. "That's right, Timothy," both Estella and Timothy looked up, shocked that he'd agree to such a claim, "*They* did follow you here," he sneered and looked off into the distance, "But you didn't make them! Nobody *made* them! They made that choice on their own." Xander locked his gaze on the young boy's, "If poachers showed up right now to kill Trepis and take his fur, would it be his fault for being born with such beautiful stripes?"

Timothy's eyes began to water at the thought, but he quickly shook his head.

"That's right," Xander nodded, "The world is filled with horrible people who believe that they're monstrous actions are justified simply because they feel it's their right to thrive off of the pain and suffering of others. Hell, those bastards back there would accuse *us* of being the monsters, but I've seen firsthand their willingness to tolerate *anything*."

Estella bit her lip and looked down.

Xander looked over at her and offered a reassuring smile. Seeing her mirror the gesture, he turned back to his apprentice, "You'll never be loved by everybody, Tim. If my old man's legacy taught me nothing else, it's that you can be nothing short of a saint and *still* be despised for it. What's important is to remember that it's not *your* fault that the hatred of others' can go so far. It's *their* fault that all this happened..." He growled and shook his head, "And it's *my* fault for not ending it sooner."

Estella frowned and began to stand, "Xander..."

He shook his head and smiled, "No, it *was* my fault, but it's not a mistake I'm going to make again." He looked down at Timothy, "They *are* going to pay for what they did tonight, and I'm going to make sure that they can't ever hurt you or your family again."

Timothy's eyes lit up excitedly, "You're going to fight again? Just like in your stories?"

Xander smirked, "Better than the stories, little buddy."

Estella nodded, "And I'll be there to help you."

Xander's smile faded and he turned to her, "What?"

"I'm going to fight with you," she told him, her own smile remaining.

He shook his head, "No! Absolutely not! It's way too dangerous! I'm going alone!"

Estella's smile shifted into an enraged sneer and she narrowed her eyes at him as she took a long stride that closed the distance between them. "Alone? Are you insane? They almost killed the entire pack; the *two* of them *alone*! And who knows how many others they've slaughtered! Like it or not—all your petty pride and hopeless pleading set aside—this is neither something you could hope to do on your own"—she stabbed a narrow finger into his chest—"nor is it something I'd even consider letting you try to do on your own."

Xander growled and shook his head, "I'm doing this to *protect* you and Tim and the pack! How can I do that if you're putting yourself in the crosshairs, Estella? You're not strong enough yet! You'd be a liability!"

"Then train me harder!" She growled back at him, "Give me the next few days to learn how to fight and I'll prove to you that I can do it!"

Xander, the vampire was shaking his head and about to argue further when Osehr's psychic call interrupted him. *Got an old friend here for you.*

Xander frowned and looked back at Estella, who'd clearly heard the message as well. "This conversation is over. I know you're trying to help, but I'm not going to risk losing you again." Though he knew that, despite his words, the conversation was far from over, Estella didn't press the issue any further. Xander smiled, kissing her on the forehead. He was exhausted—more mentally than physically, but the latter was quickly catching up— and in no mood to deal with whoever was waiting at the clearing for him. Silently promising himself that he'd gut the visitor if they wasted his time, he ruffled his apprentice's hair and smiled weakly to Estella. "Take him somewhere and play tag," he paused for a moment and looked down at Timothy, "Take it easy on her."

"Hey," Estella pouted, "What's that supposed to mean? I'm strong too!"

Both Xander and Timothy shifted their eyes towards her. Biting her lip, Estella sighed. "Men..."

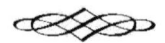

※

The still-burning therion meat reeked like skunk corpses left on a freshly paved street, and Xander nearly gagged as he stepped through the dividing line of shrubbery and into the clearing. The pile of dead bodies and the roaring fire that consumed them was nearly eight feet high, and it was a moment before the vampire could bring himself to look away from the spectacle. The others of the pack, however, paid no attention to the ritual. Once again, they'd formed a tight circle around the newcomer with Osehr and his throne in the center along with whoever had come to visit.

Xander, too tired to jump over the snarling pack, pushed his way through—ignoring the snarls of his pack-mates in his ear—and stepped into the inner portion of the circle. Standing there was the warrior from before; this time wearing street clothes and missing his weapons.

Xander sighed and shook his head, already tempted to tell his packmates to eviscerate the intruding warrior, and as he approached the vampire visitor turned to face him.

"Here to try to convince me to take care of your hunter problem again?" He narrowed his eyes.

"Would it matter if I was, Stryker?" The warrior glared at him and looked around at the thinned pack, "Besides, it appears that it's just become your problem, as well."

Xander scowled, realizing he'd been caught in his own bluff. He didn't have a retort, so he simply sighed and gave up the fight. "So what's with the getup? Almost didn't recognize you without your Kevlar."

"We were attacked," the warrior said; his voice cracking around the confession, "My clan's been completely destroyed; every one of my comrades has been slaughtered." He frowned and shook his head. "I can't even get through the wreckage to give them a proper burial."

Xander frowned, caught off guard by this, "How did you survive?"

"I was out on recon," he answered, "I'd received a call for backup back at the base, but when I got there the entire place was buried in rubble." He sighed, and for a moment Xander thought he might start crying; though he wouldn't have blamed him if he had. He knew *exactly* how it felt to discover that sort of scene. But the tears didn't come. Instead, the warrior took a deep breath and locked his gaze on Xander's, "I have nothing left but the last mission I'd been given: tracking down those butchers and seeing an end to their activities."

Xander sighed and nodded, "You at least got a place to stay?"

The warrior shook his head slowly.

There was an exasperated groan from Osehr as Xander looked back at him. Though the therion was clearly not happy with it, he nodded.

Xander nodded his thanks in return and turned back to the warrior. "You do now," he shifted his voice then as he glared at the warrior, "But you'd better remember whose turf this is. You treat my packmates with respect, or I'll kill you myself."

The warrior nodded and stood rigid as if being given an order from his leader.

Xander rolled his eyes, "What's your name, anyway?"

"Sawyer," the warrior answered.

"Well, Sawyer, I want you to stay with the pack and protect them for the next few days while I prepare."

"But we should go after them as soon as possi—"

"Protect. The. Pack!" Xander growled, baring his fangs, "You're a part of this family now, and we're going to do things the *smart* way, not *your* way! I just saw how these fuckers fight, and I'm not stepping into another round with them half-cocked, you got me?"

Sawyer frowned at the insult but gave a slight nod.

"Good," Xander sighed and turned to the outsiders, eyeing Zeek and Satoru, "You two feel up to a little revenge?"

Both nodded.

Xander nodded and turned back to Osehr, "I need you to get me three or four of the swiftest—*not* the strongest!—fighters you've got. If we're gonna beat these bastards we need speed and cunning, not muscle." Osehr grunted and bobbed his head and raised his eyes, motioning to several of those around him to step forward. Xander turned and inspected the therion leader's choices and smiled at his decision. They certainly were the four fastest in the pack. He'd seen them in battle before, and he was confident that they'd perform to his expectations. "This will not be an easy fight," he explained to them, "I want all of you to train and condition yourselves as best you can for the next few days. Osehr and I are expecting the best from you, and we won't accept anything less!"

As the therions barked and nodded, he turned away and motioned for Sawyer to follow him as he headed out.

"You're quite the leader"—Sawyer said behind him—"considering how young you still are."

Xander shrugged, "I'm just as surprised as you are, believe me," he growled and shook his head, "But these bastards have threatened the only family I have left, and I'll do and be whatever it takes to make this work." He thought for a moment and sighed, "I'm guessing that your weapons were all back at your base?"

"No," Sawyer's aura spiked behind Xander, "They're in the car."

Xander stopped and turned, "Car?"

Sawyer nodded, "Yea. How do you think I've been getting around?"

Xander smirked.

"Show me."

⋘⋙

"A black BMW," Xander mused, "Why am I not surprised." He walked the length of the car, marveling at how easily it melded with the surrounding night and running his fingertips across the sheen surface. Noticing Sawyer's aura flinch at the sight of him touching the car, Xander looked over his shoulder, "Was everyone in your clan so pretentious?"

Sawyer glared. "It was clan-issued to all warriors!"

"I bet it was," Xander scoffed. "Only the best when The Council's buying, right?"

"The Council understands the importance of being discreet!"

"Oh yea! This fucking thing is 'discreet', alright," Xander laughed and slapped the trunk, enjoying another auric flinch from his companion, "Anybody seeing it would figure that the humans' Secret Service was patrolling the streets; no suspicion of inhuman activity here!" He laughed again. "Alright, Agent Smith, show me the goods!"

Still glaring, Sawyer raised a set of keys and, with the press of a button, popped the trunk. Moving beside Xander, he lifted a panel from the inside of the trunk that concealed its contents. Xander's eyes went wide as he gawked at the extensive arsenal that was organized inside.

"I keep the swords in a compartment under the back seats," the warrior explained.

Xander nodded as he ran his fingers across an assault rifle, "God-fucking-damn! I can only imagine what sort of blades you're packing."

Sawyer smirked, "One for every occasion."

"Good to hear," Xander continued to take a mental inventory of what was laid out in front of him, "Mind if I borrow one or two?"

"Whatever it takes to beat those assholes."

Xander smirked and nodded. "Whatever it takes," he repeated.

<hr />

The two vampires found Estella and Timothy playing tag a short distance from Xander's tent. After introductions were handled, Xander explained to his apprentice that the remainder of his training would be handled by Sawyer. The boy had been nervous about this at first, his shyness returning under the looming weight of the newcomer's stern presence. However, after a game of tag with their new comrade he quickly warmed up to his new trainer.

"I'm not sure the tent's gonna be big enough for all of us," Estella said as she and Xander watched Sawyer play with Timothy.

Xander nodded, "I'll go into town in the morning and get

another one." He looked at her with a smirk, "Just for the two of us."

Estella frowned, "Are you sure we can trust him with Timothy so soon?"

"Yea," Xander studied the warrior and his movements, "If he'd planned on trying anything I'd have sensed it by now. He'll be a good combat trainer for him. And it will give me the time to train you one-on-one."

"Really?" Estella's eyes widened, "You mean it?"

Xander sighed, looking down in defeat, "I don't like the idea any more than I did before, but I also know that you won't be talked down from doing this." He looked at her and sighed, "And if they're fighting with magic I'd like to know that we had someone on our side that could counter it."

Estella squealed happily and jumped on him, wrapping her arms around him. The sudden and violent embrace knocked them both over, and they lay there for a moment, listening to the warrior and the boy continue their game as they stared at one another.

"Just promise me you'll be careful," Xander whispered.

Estella smiled and nodded, "Promise."

They kissed on it before separating and joining the game.

CHAPTER TWENTY-EIGHT
PREPARATION/KNOW THE GAME

EVERYONE AGREED THAT three days would be enough time to train. Though he was worried that they might be giving their enemies a chance to strike again while they honed their skills, Xander figured that the male had enough broken bones to keep them out of the picture for a decent stretch of time. He even held—albeit loosely—to the idea that they might be able to catch them still weakened and vulnerable.

But it was never that easy, and he knew better than to hold on too long to any strands of hope that could lead to disappointment.

The first night—after Xander had finished putting up the new tent he'd picked up that day—was dedicated to cleaning up Estella's control of her sangsuigan abilities. This proved surprisingly simple because of both her level of dedication as well as her superior sense of focus, and within a couple of hours she was performing at a strong enough level that Xander felt confident enough to move on to combat training.

This, however, proved harder than he'd expected...

"C'mon, Xander," Estella pleaded, growing more and more desperate to get things started, "I'm not gonna learn anything if you're not willing to fight me."

Xander shook his head. "I just... I can't hit you," he confessed. Estella pouted and the cuteness in her face made the idea of throwing a punch at her all the more difficult. He sighed and shook his head, looking down. "Maybe you could go punch a tree or something."

Estella stared at him, "How will that teach me anything?"

"I don't know. I just..." He shook his head, "Even when you were kicking my ass back at the train yard I couldn't fight you."

Estella blushed and smiled, though she was clearly still agitated that she wasn't getting any training done.

Several yards away, the sound of Timothy and Sawyer's sparring drew their attention, and they strained to watch as they darted about in overdrive. As the lovers looked on, one of the two would suddenly appear to catch their breath before vanishing again. At one moment, the warrior and the little vampire came crashing into sight, Timothy gripping Sawyer's neck and knocking him out of overdrive and to the ground hard enough to tear the frozen turf apart. After some struggling, Sawyer freed himself by tossing his young opponent over his head and went back into overdrive to try and catch him off guard. Timothy, twisting his body in midair like a cat, landed on his feet a split second before disappearing from sight as well and soon after crashed into Sawyer, once again throwing the two of them to the ground.

"See?" Estella pointed to the display, "He doesn't have a problem fighting a little boy!"

Xander smirked, "That 'little boy' could probably give me a run for my money!"

Estella sighed and rolled her eyes, turning away from him. "Fine, then I'll train with them."

"But—" Xander started before suddenly realizing that Estella had disappeared into overdrive to join the other two. He sighed and looked over at the seemingly empty clearing for a moment when suddenly the three appeared as they all returned to normal speed. As he watched, Estella asked if she could train with them. The two looked back at him—curious about the new turn of events—but nonetheless accepted. Xander sighed, feeling like he was the butt-end of a bad joke and, feeling ashamed and defeated, started forward to join them.

Sawyer looked up at him and smirked, "Can't hit a lady, huh?"

Xander rolled his eyes and sneered, "And I suppose it's easy for you?"

The warrior gave him a playful glare, "There's a difference between being a jerk and being a trainer."

"Well," Xander chuckled, "I guess I'm just a shitty trainer."

"Guess so," Sawyer teased.

After a moment of thinking Xander smiled, "So you've got this covered then?"

Sawyer raised a questioning eyebrow, but nodded.

"Mind if I borrow your car for a couple of hours?"

Sawyer's other eyebrow raised as his aura flared nervously, "What for?"

Xander smirked at his reaction, "I was thinking of visiting an old friend for some supplies."

"What kind of supplies?" Sawyer asked.

Xander shrugged, "The kind of supplies that put big holes in bad people."

Sawyer's car keys were flying through the air and in his hands only a second later.

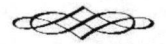

※

"Xander, my friend!" The Gamer greeted him at the back door of the videogame shop he worked in during the day, "Long time, no see! Hmm... you *could* use a haircut." He sniffed the air, "And a shower."

"And you could use a treadmill and a diet that *doesn't* include Hot Pockets dipped in gravy," Xander smirked as he gave the pudgy magician a slap on the shoulder.

"Don't knock 'em 'til you tried 'em," The Gamer chuckled and patted at his gut, "I see that your little therion-embracing camping trip hasn't changed you too much. You're still the same pouty, vindictive asshole, eh?"

Xander shrugged, "Well I wouldn't want to disappoint my adoring fans."

"Oh? Is there still a demand for damaged, grunge-metal wannabes? I thought that pleasantly plump geeks were the new flavor of the month," The Gamer laughed as he led Xander through the door, "So what can I do for you? More of that enchanted artificial blood? I thought I'd given you at least half-a-years' worth the last time you visited."

Xander shook his head, "Been sharing my supply with a few needy friends."

The Gamer chuckled, "Never pegged you as the 'sharing' type." He thought for a moment and laughed, "Or the friendly type, for that matter."

"And what did you have me pegged as?" Xander looked over at the man.

The Gamer turned bright red and stammered for a moment before turning away. "Anyway, to what do I owe the pleasure?"

They'd already, though neither had said a word about it, started to head towards the basement where The Gamer kept the weapons. Nearly a year-and-a-half ago Xander had been introduced to the overweight-yet-underestimated magician who, despite being a professional nerd during the day, spent his nights manufacturing magically-charged weapons for a mostly mythos clientele. He was also the miracle-worker responsible for the synthetic blood that had saved Xander's life after his skirmish with Lenix, which had left him looking as though he'd just dragged himself out of the world's biggest food processor.

He had also been Xander's supplier of enchanted ammunition, but his need for magical bullets had fizzled away after...

"Still no sign of Yin?" The Gamer asked.

Xander sighed and shook his head, "I'm afraid not. Though I haven't exactly had a need for any of my guns lately." He started down the staircase, "That's changed, though."

The Gamer's aura swirled excitedly behind him, "Oh? Somebody new to kill, hmm?"

"*Two* somebodies, actually," Xander corrected, "Couple of

power-hungry hunters who want to slaughter some new friends of mine"—he shook his head—"as well as every other mythos on the planet."

"Well *that* would certainly make for bad business around here," The Gamer quipped as they reached the basement. Starting towards his workbench, The Gamer rubbed his chins thoughtfully. "Those types always have been a pain in the balls. Can't just 'live and let live' and the such." He shook his head, "I can see where that could be annoying, but why would you need me? Shouldn't be a problem for you to take out a couple of humans."

Xander nodded, "And ordinarily you'd be right," he picked up a spare round sitting on a nearby table and rolled it in his fingers as he turned to face him, "But these fuckers stopped being human a while ago. They're playing with mythos blood and magic—gone to great lengths and killed a lot of innocents—and they've turned themselves into some sort of..." Xander shook his head, at a loss for words.

"Enchanting mythos blood?" The Gamer's voice sounded suddenly curious, "Never would have thought—"

"And for your sake I suggest you *don't* think about it!" Xander barked at him, "This is some seriously fucked up shit that we're dealing with, and when I cut this weed down I intend for it to *stay* cut down!"

The Gamer sighed and nodded, a disappointed ripple traveling across his aura as he averted his gaze. "Right," he moved to his work table and sat down, "So what exactly can I do for you?" He asked again, clearly more interested in what the answer might be now that he was aware of what they were up against.

Xander smirked at that, knowing that the formalities were officially finished. "What'cha got?"

The magician grinned, a familiar excitement overcoming him, and clapped his hands together, "Oh the toys I could show you!"

"Slow down there, big boy," Xander held up his hand, "First, I need ammo; lots of it."

"How much is 'lots'?" His voice was nervous.

"Anything and everything," Xander answered, "Whatever you have."

"Wha—all? Fucking hell, Xander! You've gotta be kidding me! Do you know how busy I am? I've got a lot of business orders to fill already! I can't just sell you my whole stock!"

Xander narrowed his eyes, "I'm not asking you to sell me your entire stock; I'm *telling* you! I don't think you're understanding the great picture I'm painting here. What I'm going up against is the beginning of a potential mythos *Armageddon*; the end of all non-humans—your entire fucking clientele! So if you don't suffer this minor hiccup in your business, you might as well kiss all of your clients goodbye. You're little night gig is going to take a pounding one way or the other, so the only thing on your mind should be how severely you're willing to take that pounding!" Xander made sure that his friend could see his fangs past his parted lips as he finished.

The Gamer sighed in defeat, "I hope you've got something bigger than a backpack this time around, sports fan."

"Sports fan?" Xander gave him a look.

"Damn right," The Gamer smirked, "'Cuz I'm about to stock your entire court!"

Xander sighed and shook his head, pinching the bridge of his nose, "Jesus, man, you gotta get laid." Without looking up, the vampire pointed towards the back of the house where he'd parked Sawyer's car, "I got a car out back."

The Gamer chortled, "A car? You didn't steal it, did you?"

He shook his head.

The man let out a relieved sigh, "Good. Last thing I need is the cops coming around here."

"Yea," Xander chuckled, "They might eat all your powdered donuts."

"Don't even joke about that! Telling a man his livelihood is at stake is one thing, but to speak harm of his snacks..." There was a pause as the magician wrote something down on a notepad.

"You got anything that can allow me to load Yang faster?" Xander looked over, suddenly recalling past fights when reloading the revolvers one-by-one had proved a tolling—and often dangerous—process.

The Gamer scoffed, "Reloading in overdrive not fast enough for ya?"

Xander shook his head and sighed, "Not when the assholes I'm up against can move in overdrive, too."

"They can do that too?" The Gamer's eyes went wide.

"Were you not listening, big-boy?" Xander rolled his eyes, "They've changed themselves using mythos blood. You think that a sang wouldn't be, like, one of the *first* things they'd target in that little campaign?"

The Gamer looked down to think for a moment, "Fuck me sideways..."

"I'd rather not," Xander cocked a brow, "Now, about loading Yang?"

"Uh... yea, actually," The Gamer snapped his fingers and turned to a drawer at his left and pulled out a small plastic box. "I had these ordered a while back when I first caught sight of the twins"—he reached into the box and pulled out a small, black wheel with a rubber knob on one end—"and, though they're pretty common for gun-owners, I didn't have any for an eight-chambered cylinder handy."

Xander studied the proffered object and shrugged, "What the hell is it?"

"It's a speed loader," The Gamer rolled his eyes and fetched a few scattered rounds that were lying in the drawer. As Xander watched, the man began to fasten the end of each bullet into the opposite end of the object and, once he'd attached five rounds, held it up to illustrate the setup, "See? This will hold eight rounds at once, so when you need to reload you simply pop the cylinder, fetch one of these bad boys, and then feed all eight rounds into the chambers at once. Twist the end to detach the feeder from the bullets once they're in place and you're good to go."

Xander blinked at the object for a moment before shifting an enraged glare at The Gamer, "And how fucking long have you been sitting on these?"

The Gamer shrugged, "I suppose I got 'em a few weeks after I stocked you up for your trip to Maine when you took out your ol' step-daddy."

"And you never thought to give them to me anytime between

then and now? For fuck's sake, fat man, do you know how many times I've nearly *died* trying to get the damned twins loaded in mid-fight?"

The Gamer scoffed, "More than once just goes to show that your stubborn ass didn't learn to be better prepared the first time." His soft chuckle shifted to a hearty laugh, "And besides, it's not like you ever *asked* any of the other times you came in. Usually you're orders were—like now—so batshit crazy and complicated that I never had a chance to consider them! Now, since I'm guessing you'll be wanting these"—he set the plastic box containing what looked like a dozen of the ammo feeders— "we can move on. So what else you gonna need?"

Xander sneered and shook his head, "Remind me to kill you when this is over."

"Uh huh, remind me to set an enchantment on the doors that'll melt your dick off if you come in here looking to start shit," The Gamer smirked at him. "Now what else do you need?"

Xander, unable to hide his growing smirk, shook his head and looked around the room, "Uh... couple dozen of those miniature explosives."

More writing; The Gamer smirked, "You liked those, huh?"

Xander nodded, still looking around, "Well, they certainly worked well in bringing down an entire parking garage on that murderous fuck-wad. Sort of hard to argue with *those* results," he felt a shiver of rage travel up his spine at the memory of Lenix. "You got anything small that doesn't run out of ammo?"

The Gamer stopped writing and looked up, "Like what?"

"I don't know," Xander shrugged, "Like ninja stars or some shit like that."

The Gamer smirked, "You a Batman fan?"

Xander stared at him a moment, "Uh... when I was a kid, I guess."

"Remember the exploding Batarang?"

"Yea, I think so."

The Gamer's smile was widened by the second as he stood and went to a nearby drawer, pulling it open and shuffling through it. After several moments he pulled out several small throwing stars, each with a foreign glyph engraved in the center.

"These bad boys don't explode," he explained, "Not really, anyway. They're infused with a special kind of spell that spreads along the surface it lands on—*any* surface within a fifty-foot radius—and tears it apart molecule-by-molecule."

"Isn't that a little... unstable?" Xander asked.

The Gamer shook his head, "Oh ye of little faith! Didn't I just tell you that the spell is contained! As long as you or anything else you don't want non-existent is outside of that fifty-foot radius you've got nothing to worry about."

"So what if I'm inside of that radius?" Xander asked.

The Gamer frowned and shook his head. "You don't listen too good, do you; *don't* be within the radius. It will eat through anything—and I do mean *any*-fucking-*thing*—that it comes in contact with for that allotted space. I once saw this spell cast on a rune stone that was then buried in the middle of the desert. Ten seconds after it was activated—after all the dust settled—we were treated the sight of a massive crater. Thing was *perfectly* spherical, and *everything* within that sphere was **gone**!" He shook his head, "There was this one unfortunate rattlesnake that was halfway out of its range, and it was none too pleased to discover half its noisy ass missing. Now I'll repeat myself: if you happen to be standing inside the spell's barrier, then you're going to be taken apart along with everything else. Magic doesn't know the difference between 'friend' or 'enemy'; it just follows its initial programming."

Xander nodded slowly and sighed, "Well, with that in mind I guess I'll take all of them. Oh! And I'm gonna need whatever you've got left of your synthetic blood."

"Cha-ching!" The Gamer smirked, going back to the table and writing down some more in the notebook, "This, my fanged friend, is going to cost you a fortune."

Xander rolled his eyes, "You know I'm good for it."

"If I didn't *know* you were I'd have kicked your ass out and put up a barricade spell by now."

Xander nodded, "Alright. Let's get this shit to the car."

CHAPTER TWENTY-NINE
HOPE

THE DRIVE BACK to the forest was a quiet one. Xander opted to leave the radio off, his own thoughts far too loud to entertain any hope of hearing anything else, and let his mind wander as he navigated the barren path back to the park. From time-to-time the occasional pair of headlights would appear—casting their dual beams across the murky slush and huddled snow banks before passing and returning the scene to darkness—and he found himself easily lost in the backdrop of his own thoughts.

Thoughts of Estella…

He was still hesitant about letting her go with him on the attack. No matter how fast she was learning—how quickly she seemed to be catching on—there was simply no way she'd be ready to take on the hunters in time. There was also no way she'd take "no" for an answer at this point.

Xander slapped the wheel in aggravation.

She'd sooner go down fighting than let herself sit back and

do nothing.

The lot outside the park was empty as he turned in and he returned the car to the same spot that Sawyer had taken before. Getting out, he grabbed the duffle bag that The Gamer had stuffed full of artificial blood and slung it over his shoulder. After double checking to make sure that the car was locked and the weapons were secure, he headed into the forest and followed the path back to his pack's territory. He stayed out of overdrive, seeing no need to waste the energy, and after more than an hour of stomping deeper into the woods he heard the warning growl from the trees above.

"It's just me, numb-nuts," he threw one hand in the air, giving the lookout a visual. The snarling quickly stopped and the therion guard dropped down from the trees, landing close by and transforming back to his human form. Xander frowned at his comrade and shook his head, sighing. "Speaking of 'numb nuts'... Cul, didn't you get the memo about wearing pants?"

The therion frowned and looked down at his naked body, still steaming in the cold air from the metabolic rush from the change. He sneered and looked back up at Xander. "Pants not comfortable."

Xander shook his head and averted his eyes from the naked therion and started towards Osehr's clearing, "Comfortable or not, Cul, we've got a lady with us now."

The therion frowned and followed after him, "Lady not see man-body before?" He scoffed.

Xander stopped and turned, "No, Cul. Lady doesn't *want* to see!" He shook his head at his friend's confusion, "Look: it's a vampire thing. Vampires like clothes."

Cul sighed, "Vampires strange."

"Yup. A regular gang of brain-dead, cloth-loving scab eaters; that's us in a nutshell."

"Vampires not nuts..." Cul gave him a confused look, "Are they?"

"Depends on the vampire," he rolled his eyes and continued towards the clearing, "Anything happen while I was gone?"

"No newcomers," the therion boasted, "Others train hard. Osehr say ugly humans will fall; Osehr say big feast when done."

Xander nodded, "Glad to hear it. If everyone does well I'll be sure to buy beer."

The therion perked up at the promise—his aura writhing excitedly and his breath coming in heavy—and he looked down at the bag, his voice growing hopeful, "That beer in bag?"

"No, Cul. This is vampire food."

Cul sniffed the air for a moment, "Nuts?"

Xander laughed, "No. Not nuts."

"Why no bring beer?" Cul pouted.

"Beer's to celebrate, buddy. When the hunters are dead, then I'll bring beer."

Cul huffed, "What if hunters win?"

Xander sighed, "Then we'll all be dead and there won't be any need for the beer."

Cul looked down, "Oh..."

They made it into the clearing then, and Xander heaved a sigh of relief at the excuse to end the conversation; not sure how much more of the inquisitive nude therion he could take.

Osehr, seated in his throne, watched Trepis and the kids play. Seeing Xander emerge, the therion elder sat upright and cleared his throat. As he adjusted himself in his seat he scratched the stump that was what remained of his right arm and leaned forward.

"Any news?" Xander asked, settling beside the therion leader and watching Trepis for a moment. Though the tiger still walked with a slight limp, he didn't seem bothered by it. Other than this and the few bandages that still adorned his deeper wounds he looked fine. Watching the tiger pant excitedly and roll about the snow with the kids, Xander couldn't help but smile.

"The warriors I chose are training along with the nejin and the anapriek," Osehr told him.

Xander frowned and looked up, "Zeek's training *with* them?"

Osehr nodded and smirked, "Do not worry. He will not be eaten."

"What makes you so sure?" Xander raised an eyebrow.

"Karen is watching them," he chuckled.

Xander smirked and nodded, "Fair enough."

"I would not underestimate him, either," Osehr went on, "I

saw him sparring with the nejin; he's quite strong."

"Let's hope it'll be enough." Xander sighed, "Anything else I should know?"

Osehr took a deep, calculated breath and Xander frowned. He knew the therion was about to drop a bomb on his lap. "Estella," the therion said her name quietly so that only he would hear him, "I do not believe she will be ready in time. She's strong—yes—but she still requires a great deal more training; weeks, perhaps even months." He shook his head, "It's too dangerous to put her in battle so soon"—he gave Xander a sympathetic look as he rested his remaining hand on his shoulder—"and I do not want to see you suffer from losing her again."

"You're preaching to the choir, Osehr." Xander sighed, cracking his knuckles one-by-one. Finally, he got up and hoisted the duffle bag over his shoulder—surprised to find it feeling heavier than it had before—and nodded to his friend. "I'll make sure neither of us has to suffer that fate."

<hr />

Xander found the others resting by the tents. All three looked out of breath and scuffed—clearly having done a great deal of sparring—and as he joined them he pulled a thermos out of the duffle bag and passed it to Estella. As the magical concoction made the rounds between them, Xander watched their vitality return and smirked. They made sure to leave Timothy the most, and the little vampire eagerly chugged down the rest.

Sawyer looked up at him when the little vampire had finished, "How'd it go?"

Xander nodded, "We're pretty well stocked. I'll show you how to handle the stuff I got later. Right now I need a word with Estella."

Hearing her name, Estella looked up at him with concern. Xander, motioning with his head for her to follow, put out his hand to help her to her feet. Accepting the offer, she pulled herself up and, though already standing, kept his hand in hers as they walked to their tent.

"Do you think they're gonna kiss?" Xander heard Timothy

ask Sawyer.

The warrior chuckled, "Something like that, I'm sure."

The two's laughter was silenced as Xander zipped up the tent behind them.

"What is it?" Estella asked.

Xander sighed and shook his head, "I'm just... I'm not sure that you're going to be ready for this."

"But I'm getting better," She assured him, "I really am!"

"I know you are. But you're still so new at all of this. I know you're getting stronger—I'm not saying you're not—but this is..." Xander sighed, "This is going to be big, Estella. Battle is... it's unforgiving. And these hunters are going to be a big, *big* battle; probably bigger than Lenix from what I've seen from them so far."

"I'm not going to let you go into this on your own!" Estella was beginning to turn red with anger, "Have you forgotten that I fought Lenix, too?"

"But not for very long," Xander pointed out, "You were lucky and caught him off guard—granted you saved my life when you did—but you can't compare that few seconds of instinct to what's going to be needed against these two." He took her hand in his own, "I'm certain that you'll be a strong fighter, but I just don't think you'll be ready for this fight in time."

Estella looked down sadly and Xander could tell that she knew what he said was the truth. She stared at the floor of the tent for a long, silent moment, her eyes drifting back and forth as she thought.

"What if there *was* a way?" She finally asked, "What if I could guarantee that I'd be just as strong—just as skilled and trained—as you are?"

Xander frowned. "How could you possibly guarantee something like that?"

"Don't you know me well enough to figure that out by now?" She looked up at him, her eyes bright with realization and excitement, "Magic."

CHAPTER THIRTY
FROM "WEAK" TO "WARRIOR"

ESTELLA KNEW GREAT magic. There was no question about her studies and abilities in the arts. But, even as she prepared for the spell she had planned, Xander couldn't help but be skeptical.

However, given her brief explanation of the process, that skepticism didn't make him any less eager to try.

"So how exactly is this supposed to work?" He asked, already in the process of pulling off his shirt.

Estella smirked and shook her head at his eagerness. "Magic, as you *should* already know"—she teased him, her eyes drifting across his bare chest—"is about energy and the process of harnessing those energies to get a desired effect. In almost all systems of spell casting, sex is an incredible source of building up energy, as well as being a powerful means of transferring those energies if properly harnessed." She smiled as she, too, began to pull off her shirt.

Xander smirked but tried his best not to appear too distracted during her explanation.

Estella rolled her eyes as she caught him ogling her assets. "I'm up here, stud." She waited for Xander's mismatched red-and-hazel eyes to meet her own before continuing, "Your knowledge and abilities with vampiric control and combat reside in your mind in the form of electrical energy—just like any other skill or memory." She reached back to unclasp her bra, "This spell will fuse our minds—as well as our bodies—and allow us to share those energies freely. When it's all over, I'll have 'cloned' your skills and absorbed them, making them my own." As she finished her explanation, she let her bra slip from her shoulders.

Xander, making no effort to hide his wandering eyes this time, shook his head, "So it's like magical file-sharing through intercourse?"

Estella rolled her eyes and shrugged a bare shoulder, "Something like that. Sure."

"So it's like The Matrix-meets-porn?"

Estella glared at him, "Do you wanna get lucky tonight or not?"

Laughing, Xander began to work on his pants, "Do you hear me complaining? I mean, even if this doesn't work we'll have fun trying, right?"

"Perv," Estella giggled as she began to escape from her own pants, as well.

Xander stuck out a tongue, "Hey! I've been pent up for *months* in a pack of mostly naked beast-people! Sue my ass if I'm not a little pent up!"

Estella considered this for a moment and then nodded her understanding, "Fair enough. Just try not to destroy the forest again."

"Didn't hear you complaining," Xander winked at her.

Estella blushed and shrugged, "Guess I was pent up, too."

"Guess so," Xander looked up at her, feeling a rush of blood to his cheeks as he took in the sight of Estella in all her glory. "S-so..." He cleared his throat, "Aside from—y'know—the fun part, what do I need to do?"

Estella smiled and shook her head, "You only need to keep a

clear mind." She crawled towards him—closing the distance between them inch-by-tantalizing-inch—and planted a kiss at the base of his neck. "I'll be focusing and channeling all of the energies to make this work," she whispered before kissing his throat, grazing his skin with her aroused fangs, "Just let me do all of the work."

Groaning and shivering at the contact, Xander struggled to keep a level head despite his body's growing urge to forego all thoughts and concerns, "Th-this isn't going to be dangerous for you, will it?"

Estella inched away only slightly, "All spells have some degree of danger."

Xander's hazy mind cleared and he glared at her, "Estella!"

"Well... there *is* a chance that my mind can get lost in the process," she chewed her lip, "but that's—"

"What?" Xander shook his head and backed away from her, "No! No deal! You've officially talked me out of this! I'm not taking that risk!"

"But, Xander..."

"No!" The vampire shook his head, "I'm not going to risk you becoming a vegetable for this. You'll get strong the old fashioned way: through time and training."

Estella's eyes narrowed at him, "You honestly think I'm so sloppy with my magic that I'd botch this spell?"

Xander stopped at that, suddenly seeing he was on the spot, "N-no, of course not. But what if something *did* go wrong? I couldn't live with that."

A small, soft hand touched his cheek and warm lips pressed against his own before pulling away and curling into a smile, "Trust me," she spoke softly, "This *will* work."

"But... I can't lose you. Not again."

"You won't," Estella kissed him again. "You won't ever lose me again."

Unable to fight her touch or his desires any longer, Xander surrendered control of his own lips and pushed against his lover. "You promise?"

Estella giggled at his renewed passion and nodded, "Cross my heart."

The two fell into a comfortable silence as their bodies intertwined and Estella began the spell.

Xander lost himself almost completely as his lover began to tap into his mind. Sensing Estella's auric probes against his subconscious, he let down all his defenses—both physical and mental—and allowed her to penetrate his mind as he penetrated her body. Though his eyes were closed, his mind's eye watched her aura encompass him and begin to explore for what it needed. The sensation of succumbing to his lover's psychic whim overtook him as it caressed the back of his mind, and, as he felt the two of them merge into a singular consciousness, he slammed his lips against hers; distantly aware of his body's growing tempo and vigor.

Their auras flared suddenly as the spell merged their energy signatures, and the tent went bright with a color like sunrise. Startled by the overwhelming glow, Xander's eyes went wide, only to have Estella pull him back into the serene union with a hard kiss. Pleasure and clarity consumed him, and he knew that her invasive kiss was her way of keeping his mind clear.

The crafty witch.

Once again allowing himself to fall to the whim of Estella's magic, Xander felt the energy between them grow. At that moment he could feel her aura reaching into his mind, and the dizziness grew as she continued to probe further into his mind, until, finally, when it was almost too much for him, she found what she was looking for.

The energies—and the two of them—climaxed then, and the frame of the tent rattled as his essence spilled into her.

And then it was over.

Their auras slowly slid apart and became their own again. Estella smiled and kissed him again, this time for all the right reasons, and then slowly parted.

Xander blinked several times and shook his head, "Did it work?"

"You tell me," Estella giggled.

"You know what I mean," Xander groaned, glad that she at least wasn't in a coma.

Estella smirked and began to get dressed again, "I know what you meant. Get some pants on and follow me."

For the third time in a row Estella brought Sawyer down.

As the warrior came out of overdrive, he corkscrewed through the air, a pained cry emerging from him. The ground, once again, was not a forgiving surface for the well-trained vampire warrior, and he landed hard with a grunt that made Xander and Timothy—watching on in awe and admiration—once again fall into bouts of hysteric laughter.

With Sawyer still struggling to remember which way up was, Estella appeared in front of the still-cackling vampires and took a victorious bow as they applauded her.

"Wow, 'Stella! You're real good now," Timothy got up and hurried over to her side.

Sawyer groaned and stood, shaking his head, "I don't know what you did, but is there any way you can cast some of that magic on me?"

Xander patted him on the shoulder as he walked passed and shook his head, "Believe me when I say neither of us wants that."

Sawyer frowned in confusion and shrugged. Rubbing his aching shoulder, he stepped up to the still beaming Estella, "Still, I gotta say that I'm impressed. If I had to guess I'd say you'd spent years training."

"So do you think I'm ready for the hunters then?" Estella asked.

"I'd say so," Sawyer spoke first.

Timothy, having no say in the matter, stayed quiet and shifted his eager eyes towards Xander.

Xander frowned, "I'm still no—"

"So help me, Xander! The next words out of your mouth had better be 'still not sure I ever doubted you' or you are going to be my next sparring partner!" Estella growled at him.

A smirk crept across his face, "Alright. Then I guess you *are* ready."

Estella smiled and clapped with excitement as she skipped over and gave Xander a kiss on the cheek.

Timothy made a face, "Ew!"

"Get a room!" Sawyer chuckled.

CHAPTER THIRTY-ONE
ATTACK

EVERYONE WAS IN AGREEMENT.

They would attack that night.

The four therions that Osehr had hand-picked were sized up and given street clothes that would allow them to walk through the city without stirring up a scene. Satoru retrieved his old clothes and pulled his hooded sweater over his cat-like head, tying the draw-string so tight that his face was almost entirely hidden. Xander, seeing this, stifled a laugh as he was reminded of Kenny from South Park and silently hoped that the nejin would have a better chance of survival. Zeek was almost normal-looking enough to pass on his own, and after pulling his hat on over his head and tucking his long, pointed ears under the rim everybody agreed that he could pass as human.

When they were certain that they were prepared, Xander and Osehr cast out their auras and scanned the city for the auric signature of the male hunter, finding it at the edge of the lake that bordered the outer rim of the nearby park. Xander shuddered at this finding.

They had never been very far away.

Fortunately, the location and its proximity meant a short trip as well as a secluded one; it also meant that they would have the element of surprise on the most-likely still-recovering hunters.

As they all worked their way through the woods to the parking lot where Sawyer's car was parked Xander began to go over some of the preliminary warnings. The others all listened intently, though they'd heard it all before in some form or another and were more than aware of what they were getting themselves into. The therions all tugged and scratched at the clothes they'd been forced to wear for the time being while Zeek tapped the ground with the end of his staff with each long step he took. Satoru, keeping pace with the others, handled a small hunting knife like it was a toy while he listened. Sawyer's stride was quick, and as Xander spoke the warrior took the lead and forced the others to hasten their own pace to remain in tow. Estella stayed at Xander's side, her aura bubbling with her growing nervousness. Xander studied this for a moment and found that, though she was scared, she was not without confidence.

He gave her a reassuring smile and squeezed her hand within his own.

When they reached the car, Sawyer popped the trunk and inspected the newest additions to their arsenal. As he did, Xander explained the different rounds that he'd obtained.

"Magic?" Sawyer's voice sounded skeptical as he cast a disbelieving eye in his direction.

Xander nodded, "Everything that's new here is enchanted in one way or the other. Mostly concussive spells, but these"—he held up the throwing stars—"have a very dangerous spell cast on them."

Estella's eyes widened and she grabbed the small weapon and studied it a moment, looking at the glyph in the center and her lips curled into a wicked grin. She waved it in front of her, making sure they all saw it.

"Any of you see this land in-or-on *anything*, make sure you're not near it."

Xander frowned, "You know this spell?"

She nodded, "Just never had a reason to use it." she shrugged and handed it back. "Really dangerous magic."

"Very dangerous magic," Xander nodded as well, handing it back to her, "And that's why I trust you most with them. Just be careful."

"Look at who you're telling," she taunted, "How many times have I patched you up after a fight?"

"Fair enough," Xander smirked and looked at the therions, "You boys want anything from the toy box?"

They all barked with laughter.

Xander rolled his eyes; of course they weren't interested in the weapons. They were too proud of their claws and teeth to even consider anything else.

"Suit yourselves," he turned to Satoru, "How 'bout you?"

The nejin shrugged.

Xander raised an eyebrow, "Uh huh..." Thinking for a moment, he went into the back seat and pulled a katana from the secret compartment that Sawyer had told him about. He knew that the nejins, though not all from Japan, prided themselves in much the same regard as samurai, and as he held the sword out in front of the mythos he was happy to see the slits of its eyes widen and shimmer with excitement. Slowly and methodically, he reached out and took the weapon, unsheathing it and examining the blade before nodding his thanks. When this was done, Xander turned to Zeek. "You want anything?"

The anapriek shook his head and held out his staff. "This is all I'll be needing," he assured him.

"Alright then," Xander looked around, making sure everything was ready. "There's not a lot of room in the car, so I want anything with fur to go on foot." He looked at Satoru, "You're the exception. I'll be driving, Este—"

"You're driving *my* car?" Sawyer frowned.

"Yea. I am," Xander nodded and smirked, "Or do I need to have my girlfriend kick your ass again?"

The warrior frowned, but stayed quiet.

"As I was saying: I'll drive; Estella, you're riding shotgun. The rest of you get to snuggle up in the back. We're gonna meet a quarter-mile from the lakeside and from there we'll all move in on foot and do our best to ambush them. With any luck they won't see us coming and this can be over real quick."

Everyone nodded.

"Alright," Xander took a deep breath and set a hand on the lone, white revolver—Yang—that was holstered under his left arm before moving it to the pair of pistols at his hips. It felt almost right to have them on him again, though he hated to admit it, "Let's do this."

Though the bone had mended in Richard's left leg, it still hurt like hell. He'd spent the past few days draining his sister of her life energy—bit-by-agonizing-bit, of course; punishment for her behavior at the monsters' camp—and, while she'd started to look a little on the gray side, he was doing much better.

With any luck they'd be prepared to strike again within a day or two.

He tested the leg, slowly bending it at the knee and then standing and gradually putting more and more weight on it and finding himself pleased with the results. There was still a slight ache and tightness where the break had been, but nothing unbearable.

"Dianna," he called out. His sister opened her eyes, still looking a bit groggy from being drained earlier, and turned towards him. He growled, "Get over here!"

She whimpered but rose from the floor and hobbled over, stumbling halfway and falling to her hands and knees. After a moment she pulled herself up again and closed the distance.

"What is it, Richard?"

He shook his head, "You're fucking unbelievable! You fuck me over in the middle of a fight, and now, when I need you to help me recover from *your* fuckup, you cop a 'tude with me!"

"I'm sorry..." She chewed her lower lip and looked down.

Richard shook his head again. "You'd better be," he sighed and pointed to his leg, "I need some more juice."

Dianna pouted for a moment—a gesture that was remedied with a hard slap across her face—and then nodded. Her tattoos began to glow and, as she built up the required energy, she rubbed her thumb over her opposite palm, setting an outlet. Finally, she pressed her energized hand to her brother's leg and pushed the power into the limb, mending the rest of his injuries.

He exhaled deeply as the magic filled him like a drug and sent a rush of warmth through his body. "Nothing quite like it," he mused to himself.

Dianna stayed quiet.

When it was all over he was feeling like a million bucks and his sister—ever the useless bitch—couldn't even stand.

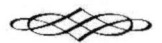

Though he couldn't see them, Xander could sense the therions' auras just behind the dark thickness of the trees that shot by as he navigated through the roads towards the lake.

Estella continued to admire one of the enchanted throwing stars beside him while the others sat in the back. Sawyer had ended up in the middle with Zeek to his right and Satoru to his left; both their weapons—being of the longer variety—crossing over his lap.

After fifteen minutes of driving along the winding path they came across a sign informing them that the beach was half-a-mile ahead. A quarter-mile later Xander pulled the BMW to the side of the road. Seeing the car stop, the therions came out of the woods and joined with them as they exited the car and began to arm themselves from the trunk.

Though he'd grown used to dealing with most situations with his guns alone, Xander took his old mentor's advice of always carrying a blade on him and took a machete from the back and strapped the sheathe to his left leg. A pack was stuffed with ammunition—both magazines for his pistols and spare rounds for Yang—as well as a few of the enchanted throwing stars and some of the miniature, marble-sized explosives.

"You're going to fight them with paintballs?" Sawyer scoffed as he armed himself as well.

Xander smirked. "These 'paintballs' took down an entire parking garage and saved my life."

Sawyer stared at him a moment and finally held out his hand

for a few of the explosives.

Xander chuckled and nodded, handing a few of the enchanted bombs to the warrior, "That's what I thought."

Estella, who, after copying Xander's abilities, now had an extensive knowledge of guns to match his own, pulled out a few of the Gamer's loaned pieces and loaded them with ease. When the weapons were ready, she holstered them and pulled out a few more spare magazines of ammunition. Before turning away, she grabbed half-a-dozen of the enchanted throwing stars.

Not surprisingly, Sawyer armed himself with the standard issue gear that he'd been armed with the first time Xander had seen him, and though it seemed a bit on the light side, he wasn't about to question his methods.

Through all of this the therions stood and stared impatiently along with Satoru and Zeek. Xander couldn't help but see the irony in the werewolves and the anapriek finally finding something worth agreeing on and chuckled to himself.

Still, their impatience was justified.

They had some killing to get done.

⸻

Something didn't feel right.

Though Richard was new to all his powers, he was in control enough to be able to sense something a short distance away.

Some swirling mass of mythos energy.

He scowled. There was something going on out there, but, with his sister barely conscious, was it worth it to try and check it out on his own?

Whatever it was, it seemed substantial.

And, amongst it all, familiar...

Curling his lip in disgust he stood and crossed the boathouse, throwing open one of the many cases and pulling out his swords. He wasn't about to let something catch him with his pants down.

⸻

Xander and the others moved quickly and silently like a group of supernatural ninjas.

Mythological assassins on a mission.

It was a beautiful thing.

Xander, Estella, and Sawyer were in the lead with the others close behind on either side in a V formation. As they got closer, Xander searched with his mind's eye for the auric signatures of the hunters and adjusted their course accordingly. Finally, after a short while of running through the darkness, a boathouse came into view; light flooding from its windows.

They'd found them!

⚜

Whatever was out there was getting closer.

And fast!

Richard sneered and drove his steel-toed boots into his sister's side.

"Wake up, bitch," he glared down at her, "We've got company."

Dianna's eyes flew open, but soon after crossed with exhaustion and dizziness; the hazy orbs beginning to roll back in her skull.

"You hear me?" He jabbed her again, then once more before ending his kindness and flat-out kicking her. "GET UP, DUMBASS!"

She was up; cringing in pain and clutching her side, but up nonetheless, "W-what...?"

"There's something coming!" Richard growled, sick of repeating himself, "Get your guns, and don't fuck me over this time!"

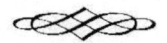

⚜

The mythos army of nine charged at the boathouse, ready to spread out and find their own, personal ways in to ambush the hunters inside when the roar of automatic gunfire started and perforated the side wall facing them.

"SCATTER!" Xander ordered.

Caught off guard for only the briefest of moments, the army began to spread out. The loud, pained whimper of an injured therion sounded—an earth-toned aura spiking in agony—and Xander looked over his shoulder briefly to make sure they hadn't already lost one of their own. The therion, Charu, clutched his hip with a growing clawed hand, but—with his pained whimpers turning into enraged snarls—obviously was still raring to fight as he sprinted for cover.

Xander smiled at him and nodded his approval.

Alright, he spoke to his army with his mind so that the hunters wouldn't overhear, *If you got a stronger form, now's the time to show it.*

All around him the sound of four simultaneous therion transformations sounded. Though he had no idea what the sensation was like, he'd come to figure that it was both incredibly painful as well as indescribably liberating. As the agonized howls stretched on, he could almost hear the joy in them at the chance to be free of their frail human disguises.

"FALL BACK!" Estella warned as she jumped forward, drawing one of the throwing stars and hurling it at the boathouse.

As the projectile stuck to the planks of the structure it began to glow, and the wood around it cracked and creased as the glowing spread into a wide orb—fifty feet in either direction, Xander guessed—and everything within it vanished in a blinding burst. With the structure's stability compromised by the magical incinerator, the rest of the boathouse started to creak under its own weight; two of the remaining walls that had neighbored the destroyed one creaking and beginning to bend.

The two hunters, now visible, ran for cover. Xander snarled and reached into his bag, snagging three of the cherry-sized explosives and hurling them. As they sailed through the opening, the vampire caught a glimpse of the gas tanks occupying the wall closest to the water.

"Oh shit... GET DOWN!" He called to his comrades, turning away and covering his own head in preparation for what was coming.

⋙⋘

Though he wasn't sure what had ripped the wall away,

Richard *did* know that standing in the middle of an exposed base filled with gasoline could be a dangerous thing.

As the vampire-punk from before threw something in his direction he grabbed his sister and fled the base; using his vampiric abilities and jumping into the next phase of movement to clear the scene.

A moment later the boathouse exploded and went up in flames.

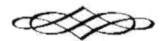

Xander sensed the auric hiccup from the hunters before the explosives went off and looked over his shoulder at Sawyer and Estella, who had knelt down and covered their heads in preparation for the blast.

"They're in overdrive!" He warned them, "Keep them away from the others!"

The two vampires nodded and vanished from sight a moment later.

Before joining them, Xander looked back at the others, "Wait here and watch yourselves."

The forest froze around him as he joined Sawyer and Estella in overdrive, and they found the hunters trying to circle around them. The vampires split up—Estella rushing to the left and Sawyer to the right while Xander cut straight ahead and pulled the machete from the sheath at his leg.

Seeing him coming, the male hunter drew his own swords and shifted towards him. Once again the female hunter's eyes locked on to him and went wide with uncertainty. Xander frowned at this.

Was she *really* so hesitant to attack him?

The twin pair of swords came down at once, barely giving Xander the chance to lift the machete over his head and block the twin blades as they dropped down on him. Metal clashed at superhuman speeds and rattled through the blades. The force and vibration proved too much and all three swords warped and fused to one another.

Both combatants—wasting no time in mourning their weapons—dropped their ends of the useless hunk of metal and lunged at one another. The two grappled; punching and tearing at each other to try and achieve dominance over the other. Out of the corner of his eye, Xander could see Sawyer striking out again and again at Dianna, who dodged each attack with stunning agility. Side-stepping a would-be uppercut, Xander caught sight of Estella over the male hunter's shoulder as she came around to attack from behind. Giving his lover a nod, he yanked the hunter towards him by the collar of his Kevlar vest, driving an elbow into his throat and shoving him into Estella's attack. As she collided into him, Estella drove her forearm into the back of his neck, slamming him to the ground.

Both vampires dropped out of overdrive, trusting Sawyer with the other hunter while they wrestled with the male. This proved harder than anticipated, however, and as Estella threw out and dodged blow after blow, Xander was forced to carry on a heated battle with the hunter's seemingly free-thinking aura. The hunter—glowing with power as his tattoos began to charge—rolled both legs around him in a vicious tornado kick that forced Xander and Estella to fall back. Seeing an opening, the hunter jumped to his feet, positioning himself between the two vampires, carried on a series of complex maneuvers to both block and attack them.

Punches and kicks flew and were deflected.

Auras struck and clashed.

Spells were cast and simultaneously reversed.

And, amidst the chaos, not a single attack landed.

Xander couldn't believe it! This one hunter—somebody who was, somewhere deep inside, still only human—was taking on the two of them at once, and, more to the point, *overpowering* them!

Sawyer and Dianna came out of overdrive nearby, caught together in a violent bear-hug. The she-hunter was clearly trying to reach for her guns, but was rendered immobile as her arms were pinned to her side. At the same time Sawyer, who was putting all his energy into avoiding being shot, was unable to retrieve his own weapons.

Momentarily distracted by this, Xander caught a side-kick to the stomach and was struck again soon after by an auric blast and finally a concussive spell that threw him back. Still dazed by the magic, he sailed out and crashed into the rocky beach, skipping like a well-tossed stone several times. Shaking the wave of dizziness, he was quick to pull himself back to his feet and sprint back towards the fray, not wanting to leave Estella on her own for long. Jumping into the air and steadying himself in midair with his aura, he drew Yang from its holster under his left arm.

Fall back!

Receiving the psychic warning, Estella blocked one last punch and kicked out—forcing the hunter to step away—and jumped away from their enemy just as Xander began to fire round-after-round at the hunter. The cylinder spun, the hammer pounding like a heartbeat and launching a combination of magically-charged explosive rounds and enchanted hollow points from the eight chambers. As the shots hit the ground around the hunter there was a series of magical flashes and powerful bursts that tore the landscape to pieces.

But none of the shots connected with their target.

Xander scowled and tossed Yang into the air as he drew the twin pistols from his waist. Moments before his feet touched down on the ground, he caught the airborne revolver in his aura and, retrieving one of the speed feeders that The Gamer had given him in another auric tendril, loaded the gun before returning it to the holster under his jacket. As he landed, the male hunter made his move; darting towards him to get in close and throwing a series of rapid punches at him. Anticipating this, Xander repeatedly spun the pistols on his trigger finger and, gripping the guns' barrels, used the grips to block and counterstrike with one as he fought to line up a shot with the other. Each time, however, the hunter had adjusted his stance to dodge his aim as well as strike out at him again.

"Xander!" Estella called out as she hurled a throwing star at the ground a short distance from their enemy.

Already seeing the weapon's magic beginning to shimmer, the vampire jumped back, landing far enough away to avoid the destructive spell. Dumbfounded by the reaction, the hunter turned, facing the small weapon as its magic began to take effect. Seeing what was taking place, the hunter's aura shifted and his stolen taroe tattoos began to glow as he cast his own spell, neutralizing the other and rendering the weapon useless.

Xander growled, "Damn!"

Sawyer and Dianna were up and firing their weapons at one another; dodging the others shots in an acrobatic display.

And barely five seconds had passed since they'd fallen out of overdrive.

Five seconds, and the vampires were already beginning to lag from all of the energy they'd spent...

We need backup NOW! Xander called out to their group.

The rest of the small mythos army, now able to actually *see* their enemies, charged forward. The therions roared and loped side-by-side while Satoru and Zeek brandished their weapons and sprinted close behind. The hunters turned at the sound of the approach and tried to jump into overdrive, only to be forced into blocking an oncoming attack from one of the vampires. Letting out another wave of howls, two of the therions shot past Xander and Estella and their enemy to aid Sawyer in his fight while the other two flanked the vampire lovers and leapt at the male hunter.

With two eight-foot beasts sailing through the air at him, the hunter smirked and put up his aura in a defensive wall that his attackers crashed into with twin whimpers of pain and surprise. At the same time Zeek swung with his staff, missing by a hair as the hunter rolled under it and surprised the anapriek with an uppercut to the jaw while, at the same time, using his aura to deflect an incoming katana-strike from Satoru.

Dianna side-stepped the first therion and leapt straight up to meet the second, doing a back-flip that brought her feet into the beast's chest and threw him over her and into the distance. Landing on her feet, she drew her gun and leveled it at the first, only to freeze with her finger on the trigger.

Xander frowned when he saw this.

She really couldn't do it!

Taking a chance he psychically connected with her.

Help us, he pleaded, *I know you're not like him.*

Dianna's eyes widened at the voice in her head and she turned to look at him, her aura whipping and writhing as she struggled with her own thoughts.

To prove he was sincere Xander opened a connection to everyone in the fight except the male hunter.

Hands off the girl; she's on our side.

He hoped...

The others all stopped and stared at him in disbelief but slowly took the message before they all turned on the male hunter and began to close in.

Dianna stood, dumbfounded, and watched as the fight left her and converged on her brother.

Xander watched for a moment, hoping he was right.

"Dianna! Shoot them!" The hunter called out.

But she didn't.

"You stupid cunt!"

She showed no movement, save for a noticeable flinch at the bite of her brother's words.

She just stood and watched.

The hunter scowled and shook his head. "Fine," his scowl faded and his aura flared as he smirked at the nine mythos closing in on him, "So be it."

He disappeared into overdrive then, and three of the four therions were suddenly without heads, their bodies dropping to the ground where they had been standing. Knowing better than to waste time mourning then and there, Xander and Sawyer both jumped into overdrive to follow after him and caught sight of him closing in on Zeek. Pushing forward and reaching the target first, Xander tackled the hunter, knocking him away from the anapriek while Estella, appearing beside him, drove her foot into the hunter's jaw as Sawyer punched him in the side and forced him to his knees.

The four burst in and out of overdrive again and again as the battle waged, each time one of the vampires knocking their enemy back to normal speed before he could kill somebody else. Growling in rage at being knocked out of overdrive yet again, and was met with Zeek's staff in the sternum. The anapriek followed through with the attack's momentum and brought the staff's opposite end around in a flash that took the hunter's feet out from under him. While falling, the lone remaining therion brought both fists down on their enemy's chest—the force of the attack driven by the rage and anguish of the recent loss—and sending him crashing even harder into the ground.

Dianna had begun to back away from the fight, and, though he kept his mind's eye on her as a precaution, Xander did nothing to stop her. As long as she wasn't a part of the problem, she would be left alone.

The hunter growled, kicking up an auric whirlwind and giving him a chance to stand and cast a spell. Satoru, the closest to him, swiped with his katana, only to have the blade disintegrate in mid-swing. Seeing his weapon rendered nothing more than the handle and a portion of the guard, the nejin cried out—the first sound Xander had ever heard him make—as he was kicked in the stomach and forced out of the circle.

"Filthy fucking creatures!" The hunter spat as his tattoos began to glow.

Before Xander could call them back, the advancing therion growled in pain as he was lifted from the ground and his leg was ripped from his body, followed soon after by an arm. As Xander watched, the creature exploded into an assortment of bloody body parts, coating all those around him in a layer of blood and innards.

"YOU GODDAM BASTARD!" Xander roared as he jumped at the sneering hunter.

The tattoos flared again and suddenly he, too, froze in midair and felt the tugging force of the hunter's magic on his limbs.

"NO!" Estella cried and tensed her muscles, casting a counter spell that released Xander from the hunter's hold.

With the pain subsiding, Xander felt himself begin to fall and caught himself with his aura; stumbling to his knees as his feet met the ground. Estella joined him at his side, looking at him with concern before he finally nodded that he was alright.

When the two looked up, their enemy was in a heated battle with Sawyer, Zeek, and Satoru, who had already drawn two small blades from his hoodie. The three lashed out again and again; throwing whatever attack they could at the hunter only to have him roll and duck and evade under and around each and every one. The two vampires growled and sprinted into the battle,

pitting four against the one.
　　But it made no difference.
　　Nothing landed.
　　And they were getting tired...

CHAPTER THIRTY-TWO
RETREAT

THEY WERE LOSING.

There was no denying it.

Xander knew that if he pushed them any further they'd lose more lives.

Probably *all* of them.

"FALL BACK!" He ordered.

The others were hesitant to obey, but one-by-one jumped back from the fight and began to run.

Estella stayed, battling furiously alongside Xander. They needed to give the others a chance to get away, and they knew that this hunter wasn't above chasing down his victims. Kicking out and swinging with a rapid set of punches, she began a low chant and cast spell after spell as Xander struck out with his aura to keep their opponent occupied.

Whatever it took.

Finally, when he was certain that the others had put enough

distance between themselves and their opponent, Xander motioned to his lover to run as well. Though she looked afraid to leave him alone—her aura lashing against her own logic in an effort to hold its ground—she understood and turned away, jumping into overdrive and disappearing.

No longer forced to worry about the wellbeing of the others, Xander unleashed the full fury of his aura. As the energy between the two escalated, their feet began to lift from the ground; the immense force of their combined powers pushing them ever-upward as they continued to pummel one another. Without the distraction of other combatants, however, the hunter was free to focus on his sole opponent, and—with the benefit of both his strength, his aura, *and* his magic—he soon got the upper hand and cast an immobilization spell on Xander before throwing a series of attacks at near-overdrive speeds into the frozen vampire.

The fight didn't last long after that...

Hitting the ground several yards away, Xander sucked in a breath of air—the intake a painful one—and tried to calculate how badly he was injured. He whimpered, struggling to get up but finding that he couldn't move his right leg. A short distance behind him, the frost-covered rocks scattered across the beach quaked and rattled as the hunter touched down and began his approach.

Xander grimaced, knowing he would only be able to hold back another onslaught for so long with all of his injuries.

Wrapping himself in his aura, he prepared for the end...

A series of shots echoed in the distance—the bullets whistling mere inches over his head like furious insects—and forced the looming hunter to fall back and seek cover. Shortly after, more gunshots followed and the storm of bullets tripled in intensity as one of the enchanted throwing stars joined the mix, followed soon after by another. As the distance between Xander and the hunter grew with his enemy's retreat, Sawyer appeared and carried him back to the others.

Estella, dual-wielding Sawyer's pistols with all the precision and fury that Xander knew, paused long enough to hurl another enchanted throwing star before joining Dianna—an agonized mixture of pain and rage twisting her tear-stained face—in shooting at the male hunter.

Xander groaned, looking at the scene with shock and awe before looking back at Sawyer.

Sawyer, not needing to be psychic to understand, simply nodded, "I know. I'm having a hard time believing it, too."

"FALL BACK!" Dianna shouted over the roar of gunfire.

Sawyer, despite the skeptical writhing of his aura, didn't hesitate in shouldering Xander's weight and following the others back to the car. Estella, throwing open the back door, helped ease him into the backseat before joining him and beginning to cast a healing spell on his broken and bloodied leg.

As the tension from Xander's injuries faded, all eyes turned towards Dianna.

Feeling the weight of the combined gaze, the girl shivered and looked down; her knees buckling beneath her and threatening to give out at any moment. "Please..." She said, her voice nearly inaudible but the desperation hanging in the chilled air like a ghost, "I... I have nowhere to go; nobody to trust." A well of fresh tears flooded the shimmering orbs of her eyes and cascaded down her cheeks, "I can never express how sorry I am for everything I've done... b-but I can begin to make amends if I can stop..."—her voice caught and she heaved; her legs finally giving way and dropping her to her knees—"He needs to be stopped!" She dared a glance at the group, extending an apologetic and pleading look at each one of them. Xander watched her aura shift and roll inward as she took in the sight of them with a new understanding—a new appreciation—before landing on him. "Please... Take me with you. Let me help."

The five frowned and thought for a moment before Xander groaned and leaned forward.

"Let her in," he ordered as he grabbed his legs and moved them, making space for a third in the back seat.

Though the rising tension was clear to his mind's eye, none questioned the decision as they went about fitting everybody into the car.

Zeek sneered as he watched Dianna slide in beside Xander, joining him and Estella in the backseat.

"I'll walk," he announced, turning away from the car.

Xander frowned, "Zeek! She saved our asses back there! Whether you like it or not she's switched sides, and, in case you hadn't noticed, we're not exactly better off without her! If we expect to—"

"I do not question the motives, Stryker!" Zeek twisted on his heels to face the car; jabbing his staff in Xander's direction, "But that *does not* mean that I can—or *should*—forget what I and mine have suffered at *both* of their hands!" Still snarling, he narrowed his eyes on the shivering girl, who whimpered under his gaze, "I won't begin to try to understand what that monster's done to you, and—while I thank you for your assistance on this night—I suggest you neither weigh your burden against your victims' nor expect your decision to wipe your slate clean."

Estella bit her lip, "Zeek, it's too far to—"

The anapriek slammed the butt of his staff into the earth, "I *will* walk!" He inhaled sharply—his eyes clenching against the pain that shone within his gaze—and shook his head, "I... I need that much."

The others stared at him a moment, coming to terms with just how much pain was dwelling within their comrade and offering their sympathetic nods. As his eyes fluttered open, struggling against the weight of their owner's grief, they fell sadly once again on Dianna. The girl, seeing in the anapriek the full extent of what had come of her and her brother's efforts, fought back a sob as she opened the door and stepped around towards him.

Xander shook his head, "Dianna, don't—"

"No," she stepped in front of Zeek and let out a jagged breath, "It's not your decision to make, Xander." Fighting to straighten her posture, Dianna reached to her side and unclasped the fastener on her holster. All eyes but Zeek's, who took in the act with a stoic curiosity, widened as she withdrew her gun and, kneeling down before the anapriek, turned the gun in her hand and offered it to him. "I should have never allowed my brother's will to become my own, and I don't expect to be easily forgiven for all the innocents that have been slain. You and your family have more right to decide my fate at this moment than any other," she bowed her head to him, "And I won't blame you if you choose to pull the trigger."

Zeek's eyes took in the gun as he took it into his hand; his index finger gliding across the trigger as his aura spiked and bubbled. As the others watched on in silence, he pressed the barrel to the top of her head and glared down at her. Seconds passed, each one an eternity, as his churning mind drove a shift in expressions on the anapriek's face—his eyes and mouth twitching as memories flooded him with emotions—and he forced his gaze to the passenger seat where Satoru sat.

"Brother...?"

The nejin whimpered and reached up, drawing back the hood and freeing his hidden face. Xander watched from the back as catlike eyes took in the female hunter—recalling every scene of horror that she represented—before falling away.

He shook his head.

Zeek watched this and sighed, nodding slowly, and dropped the gun beside its owner.

"You're now a victim of mercy, hunter; something that you'll have to remember every waking day from henceforth." He turned his back on her and began to walk away, "I suggest you learn its ways, lest it destroy you in ways your violent past could never fathom."

CHAPTER THIRTY-THREE
UNSTOPPABLE

RICHARD GROWLED, ENRAGED at the creatures as well as himself for allowing them to get away.

Especially that punk-vampire!

He knew he'd hurt the bloodsucker; bad enough to keep him off his feet.

Bad enough to make him bleed...

He'd given up on Dianna once and for all, and though she'd always been a useless bitch, she'd finally crossed the line by not only stepping out of the fight and putting all the weight on his shoulders, but *also* for daring to draw her weapon—a weapon he'd *given* her!—against him!

No matter; he was better off without her weighing him down and complaining all the time and second-guessing every little goddam thing.

Besides, he had bigger things on his mind just then.

Like finding that punk-vampire's spilled blood!

He knew the sample would be tarnished by the open air and the rest of the elements it had been exposed to, but it would—hopefully—still serve his purposes. That vampire had something special; not just his genetics—both sangsuiga *and* auric; a very rare and very powerful mythos, indeed!—but his fighting spirit; his drive.

Even Richard couldn't deny that there was something special in the creature. Something to be admired. Something powerful.

And he wanted that power.

With it, none—not even his treacherous sister—could stand in his way.

Smirking at the idea, he found a large sample splashed on a rock where the vampire had landed after his midair ass-kicking and carefully took the stone with him as he gathered what was salvageable and headed down the beach.

He'd been sick of the boathouse anyway.

CHAPTER THIRTY-FOUR
HEALING

OSEHR HAD GOTTEN Xander's psychic call for help and, by the time the BMW had pulled up near the park, there were several therions—two of the pack's strongest—waiting for them. Extracting the injured vampire proved slightly difficult due to his shattered leg and other injuries. When he was finally free of the vehicle, he was carefully hoisted onto one of the therion's back to be moved back to the clearing. He stayed quiet all during the process, having very little to say and feeling too exhausted to try.

Besides, what was there left to say anyway?

They'd been beaten, and, in the process, hadn't put a scratch in their enemy.

But they *had* earned a new ally, and, in doing so, robbed their opponent of his own.

Dianna, clearly nervous, stayed several paces back, still unsure about the whole situation. After explaining to the others that she was with them, the others left her alone—save for the occasional glare or growl—and stayed close to Xander. Everyone had seen how far their comrade had been willing to go to keep them safe. They knew that he'd be willing to die for their safety, and, whether they agreed with the decision or not, they respected his request that the female hunter be treated as an ally.

Walking alongside the therion carrying him, Estella continued her spell-casting on his injuries.

Xander turned his head towards her and smiled weakly. She'd made it out of the fight with only a few bumps, bruises, and scrapes to show for it. It had been a catastrophic battle, and she'd more than proven herself able. So much so that she had helped to save his life. He reached out, keeping his left arm hooked around the therion's neck, and took her hand.

"You did good," he assured her.

She blushed, and though he could tell she was happy to hear it, she was unable to express much joy given the situation.

"Right back at'cha, Crimson Shadow," she forced a smile.

Xander blushed at her words—recognizing his late mentor's mocking title for him—and coughed out a lame chuckle. "Don't call me that," he recited.

Osehr was already up and waiting for them by the time they reached the clearing; Trepis standing beside him and shifting about impatiently, clearly knowing something was wrong. Taking Xander in his left arm, the therion leader easily hoisted the vampire from his pack-mate's back and gently sat him in the stump throne. Xander frowned and looked up at his friend, shocked that he had given him the seat that had always been reserved for him and him alone. Nobody—*nobody*!—had *ever* been allowed to sit in it; even the youngsters were disciplined harshly if they dared to play too close to their ruler's seat.

"You've earned it," Osehr's voice rang with both pride and sadness.

Xander watched as Trepis loped over—noticing he still had a slight limp in his front left leg—and slumped down by the throne before he looked up at Osehr again. He shook his head and cringed slightly as he adjusted himself in the seat.

"I'm so sorry..."

Osehr shook his head and smirked. "All things worth doing are worth failing... at least in the beginning. You took a great chance and fought bravely, Stryker."

Xander smirked and shook his head, "The great guru Osehr..." He sighed and leaned back, groaning and clutching his side, "Ow! Dammit! That bastard really wrecked me!"

"Yes," Osehr nodded, "He most certainly did."

"Hey! Move your ass, hot-cheeks! I can't see shit over your brick-wall shoulders!"

"Sasha! Manners," Karen's voice rang out in the distance, "Excuse me, are they back?"

Seeing Xander sitting in Osehr's throne, Karen and Sasha both stopped and stared. Though the confusion the therion sisters shared at seeing the vampire plopped in the pack leader's private seat seemed unbreakable, the moment was shattered when—

"MURDERER!"

Karen's eyes fell on Dianna and a roar that shook the clearing and all those in it emerged. Before a word of protest could be uttered, her body began to twist and contort—her clothes tearing to shreds as her body exploded into its bestial form—and she rocketed towards the huntress. Spotting her sister's target, Sasha, maintaining her human form but shedding her usually playful composure, was quick to follow after.

"STOP!"

Both of the therion sister's froze in mid-lunge and looked over their shoulders.

Zeek stepped forward—the crowd of therions breaking and allowing him to pass without the slightest sign of hostility or contempt—at that moment. Offering Sasha a nod, the anapriek turned to face the heaving, fox-like form of his lover and rested his forehead against her own.

"There is much to be explained, my love," though he kept his voice low, the solidity of Zeek's words rang loud enough for Xander to hear, "But she has made the decision to join us and assist us in killing her brother, and after the night we've had I can assure you we need that assistance."

Still growling, Karen's predatory gaze shifted towards Dianna—a low, grumbling sound emanating from deep within her chest—before she offered a slight nod to Zeek and turned away to retrieve her shredded clothes. As the bulk and height of her therion form began to melt away with the reversing of the transformation, Zeek removed his duster and draped it over his lover's emerging form to hide her assets from the group. Finally, he whispered something to the therion sisters and motioned towards the tents. As they turned to leave, Sasha turned her gaze back to Xander.

"Glad to see you're still in one piece, cutie," she winked, "Feel free to visit my tent later if you need *anything*."

Rolling her eyes, Karen dragged her sister off by the ear.

Estella watched the two walk away before looking at Xander, "What was *that* about?"

Xander blushed, "She's... uh, sort of—y'know—aggressive with her flirting."

"So I noticed," she frowned; her aura writhing and tightening above her head, "Before I came back, did you—"

Xander laughed, "No. Fuck no," he shook his head and looked at his lover, "Really? I mean... *really*? Do you *honestly* think I could... I mean, look at what a bumbling idiot being with *just* you turns me into! There's no way I could—"

Estella silenced his nervous rant with a kiss to the cheek, "Just remember whose bumbling idiot you are, Prince Charming."

Xander blushed and nodded, "I won't forget."

Once satisfied that his lover and her sister were out of the clearing, Zeek turned back and approached the throne.

"Well that was fun, huh?" Xander smirked.

Zeek stared at him, puzzled, "Which part; our horrendous defeat, the tension-soaked union with a previous rival, or my personal struggle with telling the love of my life to spare the life of one of the sources of our recent tragedies?"

"I take it your people don't have sarcasm," Xander sighed. "You got back here faster than I thought you would," he shrugged a shoulder, "Not that I'm complaining."

Zeek nodded, "You'd be surprised how fast my kind can navigate through the trees when there's nobody around to slow them down."

"Makes sense," Xander smirked, "The payoff of living a life of running, I suppose. Are you feeling better?"

The anapriek offered a slight nod, "I am; as well as can be expected, at least," he sighed, looking towards Dianna for a moment before bowing his head again. "My apologies for ever having doubted you, Stryker," the anapriek spoke before rising again to his feet. He looked at the vampire's mangled leg and frowned, motioning to it, "May I?"

Narrowing his eyes, Xander looked to Osehr, who shrugged. Neither was sure what the anapriek meant.

"My people," he explained, "rarely fight. Though I *am* one of the exceptions to that, we are, first and foremost, known for our affinity for healing."

Xander smirked, "Your people fall out of trees a lot?"

Zeek chuckled and shrugged, "Not as often as you'd think. But when one is as often hunted as we are, it pays to know how to care for one another."

The smirk was wiped from Xander's face and he nodded.

Stepping forward, the anapriek began to gently run his hands over Xander's shattered leg, inspecting it. Several times the pain from the contact was too much and he cringed and inhaled sharply between clenched teeth, at which point Zeek would move away from that spot and start elsewhere, making a note of the places that it hurt the most. After several minutes he nodded and stood.

"Five breaks—two definite fractures," he informed them, "They need to be set before anything can be done."

Xander let out a heavy, burdened sigh. "Well shit, that sounds fun..." He cursed again before gritting his teeth and nodding, "Alright. Do it."

Zeek nodded and returned to the leg, finding the breaks and adjusting the bones to fit them back together. The feeling was excruciating; Xander groaning and clenching his teeth each time the broken segments were shifted, grinding against one another as they were pushed back into place.

"AH! FUCK!" His hands balled and he ground his teeth so hard he was sure they'd break.

After ten minutes of hell the leg was set and the anapriek stood and headed towards Xander's tent to retrieve his synthetic

CRIMSON SHADOW: FORBIDDEN DANCE

blood.

"Will that be enough?" Osehr asked when Zeek was gone.

Xander nodded, "It should be. I just need to be able to stand on it for now. On its own it will heal in a couple of days."

The therion frowned, "I don't think we have a couple of days."

"You're probably right," Xander sighed.

Estella stepped up and sat on the arm of the throne. When Osehr didn't protest Xander looked up at his lover and smiled.

"It'll be fine," He told her.

She nodded and kissed his forehead, "I'll stay with you all the same."

"Xander! Xander! Xander!" Timothy came sprinting into the clearing, and jumped towards him.

Every set of eyes in the clearing widened, expecting to see the little vampire crash into his lap. Instead, in a stunning display of speed and agility, Satoru caught him out of the air and held him by the shirt collar, shaking his head sternly.

Timothy frowned and looked at his mentor, studying him for a moment before realizing that there was something wrong. "Are you hurt?" He asked, his voice both concerned and shocked at the thought.

Xander shrugged, "Just a little. I'll be fine in a day."

Timothy shook free of the nejin's grasp and looked around the clearing to make sure that the others who had left to fight were alright, frowning when he didn't see the other therions. As his eyes fell on Dianna, they went wide with terror and he jumped back and hid behind Satoru.

"Xander! They're here!" He cried out, "They're..." He stopped and looked around, noticing that he was the only one surprised by this. He frowned and narrowed his eyes back at the hunter, noticing that she was making no move to hurt anyone. Satisfied that it was safe, he looked to his mentor for answers.

"It's alright." Xander explained. "She's on our side now." He looked over at Dianna again, the huntress' face twisted in an effort to contain her growing anguish at the response her presence had earned her. Seeing this and her lagged aura, Xander frowned, knowing how much she regretted her history already.

Like it or not, however, it wasn't up to him if the others chose to forgive her past.

Timothy, though still jittery, seemed satisfied by his mentor's answer. Turning back to the nejin, he tugged at Satoru's sweater and asked that they go somewhere else to spar. A pair of cat-like eyes looked over at Xander and he nodded to him, figuring it would be best if the boy was somewhere else for the time being.

Shortly after, Zeek, true to his claims, strode with a startling swiftness that Xander had yet to fully appreciate, and the pace only wavered slightly as he passed their new comrade. Spotting Dianna, the anapriek's eyes took her in—the majority of his earlier malice had passed, but there was an undeniable bitterness remaining—before looking away and returning to Xander's side with three thermoses of The Gamer's magic synthetic blood. Xander thought this was a bit excessive, but who was he to argue with "Doctor Zeek the Anapriek".

He laughed to himself.

Estella looked up at him.

"I'll tell you later." He promised with a smirk.

The first thermos was offered to him and he drank it down, letting the magic flow through him and take its course. It wasn't long after that the pain in his leg began to numb.

Moving on to the second thermos, Xander was startled to find that the pain had nearly disappeared and had been replaced by a warm itch where the bones had begun to knit.

As he drank the third, his confidence—possibly the most broken part of him at that point—began to mend, and he stood; smiling when he found that it wasn't unbearable to stand upon.

Satisfied that his injuries were, while not completely healed, at least dealt with, he turned to Zeek and nodded.

"Thank you."

The anapriek gave a slight bow, "No thanks are necessary, my friend. It was an honor."

This brought a smile to Xander's face, which was quickly wiped away again as he overheard Osehr talking to several of his pack-mates about preparing for a celebration.

"And what, exactly, are we celebrating?" Xander asked,

CRIMSON SHADOW: FORBIDDEN DANCE

limping towards the pack's leader, "We just got our asses handed to us on a bloody platter and you just lost another four of your kin! All that and you *still* want us to have a party?"

The therion elder smiled and gave the vampire a light pat on the shoulder. "It is most important to celebrate when spirits are low," he explained. "So that we can all see what's still good in life. Besides," he straightened up and turned away, "those we have lost would not want to see our festivities suffer on their account. After all, would you wish for your loved ones to suffer upon your passing?"

Xander frowned and shook his head in disbelief. "You're unbe-fucking-lievable, you know that? Only you could make a party after a night like this sound so goddam logical," he shook his head, looking over as he heard Estella giggle. Finally, he rolled his eyes and smirked, "Party on, Wayne!"

Osehr raised an eyebrow, "Who is—"

"Just get things started, Osehr," Xander pinched the bridge of his nose.

Nodding, the therion elder let out a barking laugh before turning towards his pack to begin the festivities.

⁂

It was a different kind of celebration than Xander was used to. There was no feasting and the fire that was constantly kept alive in the center of the clearing was put out, casting the clearing in complete darkness. Even the music was different; the usual upbeat rhythm and howls replaced with the ghostly hums of several of the more musically inclined therions.

It was all strangely and eerily calming.

Osehr allowed Xander to remain seated in the throne with Estella at his side, and the two vampire lovers stayed still for a long time and enjoyed the event.

Though things showed no sign of dying down as the morning approached, the two vampires started to make their way out of the clearing. Realizing that they were leaving Sawyer behind, Xander turned to call for the warrior to follow, only to notice that he and Dianna were deep in conversation. Raising an eyebrow at the sight, he watched them a moment to be sure their conversing wasn't about to lead to a fight, but found that they were actually getting along rather well. Deciding that the other vampire could handle himself, he left him behind and started towards their camp with Estella.

Halfway there, they found Timothy asleep on the ground next to Satoru, who sat cross-legged and watched the beginning of the sunrise. The two stopped and admired the scene for a moment before they approached the nejin and Xander's slumbering apprentice.

"We'll take it from here, buddy," Xander smiled at Satoru as he gently bent down to scoop up the little vampire. "Thanks for training with him."

Satoru's ears perked happily and he gave a single, appreciative nod back to him.

They skipped the rest of the sunrise that morning, their exhaustion and injuries too burdening to tolerate its rays. Instead they brought Timothy into their tent and lay down quietly, falling asleep soon after as well.

As Xander dozed off, the only thing he could think of was how bad this problem had become.

Something had to be done.

CHAPTER THIRTY-FIVE
STRANGE LOVE/SOLUTION

THE NEXT NIGHT was accompanied by snow. The flakes—if they could still be called that—were large and wet and, moreover, depressing. It was not the kind of snow, much to the disappointment of the younger therions as well as Trepis, that could be played in.

Xander, shortly after awakening and drinking another thermos of The Gamer's miracle elixir, helped the pack spread a tarp over the top of the clearing, making sure to give the quick-fix roof a coned top to be certain that it wouldn't collapse under the snow's weight and cover the pack and their recently re-lit fire in wet plastic. Once their area was protected and dry, the therions settled in and began to tell stories around the fire.

Sawyer and Dianna once again sat together and talked, much to the surprise of Xander, who would have thought that the warrior would be resentful towards the huntress. Despite this, however, they seemed to get along surprisingly well, and he opted to not interfere.

After a short time of telling a few of his more glorious tales to the pack, Xander offered the stage to Osehr and followed after the little vampire with his lover at his side. Zeek, after once again checking Xander's leg and telling him that it was almost entirely healed and offering him an herbal remedy to hasten the process, joined with Satoru and Timothy in a sparring match. The vampire was pleased with his apprentice, who, despite the depressing conditions, refused to take a day off.

As the three sparred, the two vampires sat to watch. Timothy, much to their surprise, was advancing by leaps and bounds, and though he was up against two grown and conditioned fighters he held his own startlingly well. During the show, Estella laid a hand on Xander's back and continued to cast her healing spell into him, mending the last of his more severe injuries. Soon he felt better than he had in a long time, and while he was content just sitting and watching, he and Estella were quick to join in and soon all five were in a heated match against one another.

A short time later, Xander sensed Sawyer's approach, and he was only moderately surprised to see that Dianna was with him. Separating himself from the match, he composed himself and approached the two.

"I see you're healing well," Sawyer said with a smile.

Xander smiled back, "And I see that you've made a new friend."

Sawyer smirked.

Dianna blushed.

Xander, seeing this, raised an eyebrow.

"We think we may have some information that can help us beat Richard," the warrior offered.

Xander frowned, "Richard?"

Dianna nodded, "M-my brother; the other hunter."

"Ah yes. Your brother..." Xander nodded slowly, his frown deepening, "I never stopped to consider that somebody would go to the trouble of *naming* that pile of shit."

"Y-yes, well..." Dianna pursed her lips and looked down, "I agree that he *has* taken our parents' efforts to some unforgivable heights."

"He had some help, though," Xander speculated.

Dianna blushed and gave a single nod, "I never wanted to hurt anybody," she explained. "He always made it sound like... like if I didn't do what he wanted that I was letting down our parents. After a while it became a punishable offense to not do *exactly* what he said..." She looked up at him. "But I couldn't do it anymore!" Her fists clenched and shook at her sides, "I... I can't stand what he's turned me into."

Xander nodded, noticing, for the first time, the gills on the side of her neck, "So you're certain that you're with us then? You're sure that you'll be able to kill him with your own hand if the chance arises?"

She nodded again, "I'd sooner die than go back to that life."

"Let's hope it doesn't come to that," Sawyer said.

Dianna blushed again.

Xander stayed quiet for a moment, his eyes moving between the two before finally falling on Dianna again. "You two seem awful... cozy."

Dianna's blush deepened, "Sawyer's been... um, very understanding."

"Has he?" Xander raised an eyebrow to the vampire warrior.

Sawyer frowned, "Is there something wrong with that?"

"No," Xander shrugged, "I'm not complaining. It's nice to know that we can move forward. It's just a little strange; you two getting along so easily after everything that's happened."

Sawyer shrugged, "To be fair, Stryker, I think it's safe to say that strange days have found us." He motioned towards Zeek, "An anapriek who is romantically involved with a therion—nothing short of a wolf mating with a deer. Then there's the bizarre union between you and the witch—the son following in the sins of his father—or your unusual adoption of the boy as an apprentice."

Dianna's eyes lit up and she smirked, "Strange days, you say?"

"Yup," Sawyer shrugged, "After all, people *are* strange."

Xander frowned, "Uh... about that information?"

Sawyer frowned, "Not a Morrison fan, I see?"

"Who?" Xander looked over.

"A shame..." The warrior shook his head, "Joseph is no doubt turning in his grave."

Xander glared and cleared his throat, baring a fang, "About that information..." He growled.

"Uh... Yes," Dianna nodded; her voice suddenly very serious, "I think there may be a way to beat him."

"And that would be...?" Xander pressed.

Sawyer smiled, "The serum they've been using is unstable."

"Unstable?" Xander repeated the word and looked to the huntress.

Dianna nodded. "We were trying to perfect the formula that our parents had come up with, but..." She looked down, ashamed.

Xander narrowed his eyes, "But...?"

Sawyer frowned and put a reassuring hand on Dianna's shoulder, "It's alright."

"But..."—Dianna looked up—"Richard was impatient. He... he never gave me enough time to do it right."

"So what's wrong with it?" Xander asked.

"The magic has no limit," Sawyer said.

He scowled. "So he's only going to get stronger?"

Both nodded, though this didn't seem to bother them as much as it did him.

Xander shook his head, sneering, "How exactly is that good for us?"

"Because his system was never meant to hold all that power. He has limited control," Sawyer boasted.

Dianna smiled faintly and nodded, "And a human heart."

Xander narrowed his eyes, not understanding.

"I forgot how young you still are, Stryker," Sawyer rolled his eyes and sighed, "There's a reason the human body needs to die and go through the transformation to handle the energies and strengths of a vampire."

Xander's eyes widened with realization, "Then the more power he gets..."

Dianna nodded, smiling as she saw that he was understanding, "No amount of magic could prepare the heart for all the stress he's putting on it."

"So—what?—he's just gonna keel over and die on his own?" Xander asked.

"Probably not," Dianna went on, "Though it won't prepare the system for the strain, the formula *is* still stable enough to not collapse on its own."

"Then what the hell good does all of this do us?" Xander demanded.

Dianna shivered nervously and Sawyer gave him an irritated look.

He sighed and calmed his tone. "I'm sorry, I'm just not following."

"It means we need to overwork him," Sawyer explained, "If we can force his system to flood itself, the chain reaction will trigger the collapse."

Dianna nodded, "Force him to work all his new powers at once! Rather than slowing him down or stopping him you need to focus your efforts on making him push harder and further. If you do this the magic that's bonding the mythos blood to his own will start to weaken until it breaks altogether and then—"

Xander smiled, "Then he'll become human again."

Dianna and Sawyer both nodded.

CHAPTER THIRTY-SIX
SHOWDOWN

OSEHR WAS QUICK to offer more warriors to Xander, but the vampire was even quicker to refuse them. He would not be the cause of more death within the pack if he could prevent it. What he needed was fighters who could keep the hunter—Richard, as it turned out—moving in overdrive and using as much of his stolen strength as possible.

He already knew that Estella's skills mirrored his own and that, because of this, she could be trusted for the job. Furthermore, with her he also had the added benefit of somebody who could work magic with magic; something that, along with Dianna and her taroe tattoos, could keep Richard's spell-casting in check.

Then there was Sawyer. The warrior, who had already on board for another go at the hunter responsible for destroying his clan, was motivated all the more by the mistreatment of Dianna. While Xander was still startled by the growing affections between the two, there was no denying that they were genuine and that, because of this, they would be that much more motivated in fighting side-by-side.

In either case, even Xander found it easier to forgive and forget Dianna's history since she was just as eager to volunteer in the mission to take Richard out. Her skills—both her natural skills as a fighter and a marksman as well as her new, more unnatural powers—were of great value to the cause, as well. Though it had not been her choice to do so, the injections she'd been taking were the same as their enemy and, by that account, she was practically his equal. Though she assured them that, for some reason or another, the blood hadn't fused to her system as strongly as it had her brother's, Xander was hopeful that she just hadn't reached her full potential yet.

The mythos that had died for Richard's perverted quest for power had to have died for *something*.

There was no talking Zeek out of going, but that didn't stop Karen from trying—over and over again. Though he was severely limited in what he could do in the battle against the superhuman hunter, he assured them that his skills as a fighter as well as a healer would come in handy. Satoru volunteered as well; stepping forward beside Zeek and nodding his furry head to Xander. Having seen the anapriek and the nejin in battle, Xander could not deny that they were, indeed, worthy combatants, but was still skeptical about what they could do against an enemy that would be moving faster than he could see. However, though the vampire didn't want to bring any more potential casualties into the battle, it proved too hard to argue with the two.

As they prepared for another fight, Timothy hurried to his side.

"I want to fight too!" His apprentice announced.

"No," Xander didn't even look down or bother to raise his voice to the little vampire. This was not something he was going to argue.

Timothy scowled. "But—"

"No," Xander repeated again, just as flatly.

"But—"

"No!"

This time everyone—save for Satoru, who gave the boy a

sharp glare—repeated the answer.

Timothy pouted at this, but, before having the chance to fight it any further, was interrupted by Osehr, who had come up behind him to wish the group luck.

"Come, my boy," the therion leader rested his hand on Timothy's shoulder, "Trepis will be needing a playmate while Xander's away."

Xander nodded to the therion and smiled thankfully before kneeling down in front of his apprentice. "I need you to stay here and watch over my family for me, okay?" He looked up at Osehr and a few of the lingering therions that occupied the trees around them, "They mean a lot to me, and I need you to promise me that you'll protect them if anything happens to me."

Timothy, still frowning at being denied the chance to go into battle, nodded.

Xander smirked and raised an eyebrow, "You promise?"

"Promise," the boy repeated.

Xander smiled and ruffled the boy's hair as he started to stand. Before he had the chance, however, Timothy jumped up and wrapped his arms around the vampire's neck in a tight and suffocating embrace.

"Please don't die!"

"Gah! Yer choking me!" Xander gasped and tried to pry the young vampire off from around his throat.

Timothy let go and looked up at him with serious eyes, "You promise you won't die?"

Xander sighed, rubbing his neck, and nodded, realizing he'd been trapped by the young vampire, "Yea. Yea, I promise. None of us will be dying tonight," He assured him, looking back at their small army with a reassuring nod. It was as much a promise to them as it was to his apprentice. Rising to his feet, Xander adjusted the holsters and the guns that occupied them. He smiled at his apprentice one more time. "And when I get back, I'm gonna teach you how to handle a gun."

The boy beamed, "Really? So cool!"

Xander smirked at this as Zeek glared at him, his aura bubbling and thrashing about angrily.

He'd known that the promise would piss the anapriek off.

He couldn't help but laugh as they all turned and headed out.

※

They'd developed a plan of attack on their way through the woods, and as they all piled into the BMW—Xander driving, Estella riding shotgun, and the others crushed in the backseat side-by-side with Dianna sitting on Sawyer's lap—Xander extended his aura and searched the beachfront for Richard's energy signature. Having grown familiar with the hunter's unique energy signature, he found him still staying along the beachfront. Relying on his memory of the landscape, Xander guessed that he was now occupying a lake-side cabin that, he hoped, had been empty before the hunter had taken up residence there.

"You're sure this is gonna work?" He called over his shoulder to Dianna.

She nodded. "It should," she assured him.

Xander groaned. "That 'should' isn't very encouraging."

Estella laid a hand on his shoulder and smiled warmly, "If she says it will work then we need to believe that it will." She gave his shoulder a squeeze then, "You know as well as I do that magic begins with faith."

Xander rolled his eyes.

There was that "faith" word again.

He sighed and looked in the rearview mirror, "Dianna?"

"Yes?"

"You know all that research into names and their meanings you told me about?"

"Yea," Dianna's voice mirrored her confusion in her aura.

"You ever getting around to finding out what the name 'Richard' means?"

Dianna scoffed, "It means my brother's a dick!"

Xander chuckled and nodded, "That's what I thought."

The rest of the car ride was met with silence, though Xander could see that the minds of those around him were busy contemplating what was about to come. It came as no surprise that they were all nervous, more for the safety of their comrades than themselves. Xander smiled at this; they were the perfect warriors. He switched on the radio and put it on a rock station to calm them and give them something else to focus on.

Nobody complained about the distraction.

Are you ready for this? Xander opened a psychic connection with Estella.

Estella's eyes shifted towards him for a moment, a smile beginning to grow, *Are you afraid the spell's wearing off?*

Xander frowned, *Can it wear off?*

Estella shook her head, *It doesn't work that way. Your skills are officially mine, too.* She glanced over at him, *Is that what you were afraid of?*

Not at all, Xander smirked, *If I was afraid of the skills wearing off I'd just insist on another sex-spell session.*

Estella smirked back, *Oh ye of little faith.*

Xander smirked and glanced at her.

The spell won't just wear off.

Xander's nodded slowly, *Right...didn't mean to doubt you.*

Estella shrugged, *It's okay. I'm typically right, besides I don't think we need an excuse to have another sex session—it's no less magical.*

Xander stared at her for a long moment. *You...* He shook his head and stifled a chuckle, *You manipulative little witch!*

Estella beamed, *There's no better kind.*

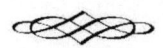

◈

As they drew closer to the cabin, Xander turned down the music and looked over at Estella.

Nodding to him, she looked over her shoulder at the others as Xander began to accelerate.

"It's time," she told them, "Brace yourselves."

The others all nodded—saving their words—and shifted in their seats, solidifying their resolves. Sawyer wrapped a protective arm tightly around Dianna as she and Zeek each gripped their neighboring door handles. Xander, tightening his grip on the steering wheel and continuing to push on the accelerator, felt the pressure on his back increase as all four pressed their knees against the back of his and Estella's seats. This was, of course, all part of their plan, and as they all readied themselves he floored the gas pedal and sent the BMW flying past the driveway and onto the front lawn of the lakeside cabin. The car pitched—catching a patch of ice and skidding before Xander regained control and steered back to course—but continued to pick up speed.

Sawyer sighed, "Goodbye, Bassie..."

Xander ignored the warrior. "Now Estella!"

Nodding, Estella began to chant under her breath and Xander watched as the car's hood began to shimmer like the hunters' stolen taroe tattoos.

Moments before the glowing hood collided with the cabin, Xander threw his aura out and lifted the car several feet off the ground, sending it through the wall and into the living room of the structure and headlong towards their target.

Richard was already waiting for them—having sensed their approach earlier on—and was already armed and poised. Despite the extent of his preparations, he had *not* anticipated the group's Kamikaze entrance, and was forced to jump straight up into the rafters of the ceiling as the jet-black BMW burst through and nearly ran him over. As their target narrowly evaded the magically-charged hood, a plush sofa fell victim to the spell and exploded into fiery bits as the car collided with it.

Sawyer gasped and shook his head, "Bassie..."

Xander glanced back, "Who the hell is 'Bassie'?"

"My car," Sawyer shrugged, "I named it Sebastian."

"You've got some major problems," Xander shook his head as he gripped the door handle. Then, "FALL OUT!"

Xander jumped out of the car and drew out his pistols. Laying down a wave of cover fire, he made sure to keep Richard occupied and at a distance, giving his comrades time to exit the vehicle. He fired in rapid succession, the enchanted rounds tearing through the wood of the ceiling and forcing Richard to evade again and again; each time vanishing from one rafter only to appear a split-second later in a neighboring one. Xander kept this up, conserving the rounds as he worked to keep their enemy in the rafters. Though he had the gift of vampiric speed, the laws of physics would not allow him to move from the ceiling to the floor any faster than gravity and his own strength would allow.

Estella and Satoru were right behind him, and as she supplied further cover fire the nejin leapt into the rafters after the hunter. As the two vampires fired into the ceiling, they were forced to keep the storm of bullets clear of their nejin comrade. Satoru swiped and kicked expertly at the hunter; the two of them swinging and jumping from rafter to rafter in a stunning display.

They were all more-than well aware that there was no chance that they'd be able to take out the hunter so easily, but were confident that it would distract him long enough for the others to situate themselves.

As long as he was up there, he was contained.

When everybody was free of the car, Sawyer pulled open the compartment in the backseat and pulled out a spare katana—the only one they had left after the first had been destroyed in the previous battle. Calling out to Satoru, he tossed the sword up to the nejin, who caught it swiftly in one hand and, with a powerful flick of the wrist, freed it from its sheath and began swinging and stabbing after the hunter with it.

As Richard retreated from the attacks, Xander and Estella continued to send round after round into the ceiling, keeping their enemy contained. When they were sure that things were going according to plan they nodded to Sawyer, who returned the nod and jumped into the rafters to help Satoru.

The first part of their plan, for the time being, was simple enough. Though Xander knew better than to invest entirely in a single tactic, they were hopeful that keeping the fight off the ground would remove the potential of using overdrive against them, leaving him vulnerable to *all* of their warriors. As Richard's evasions continued, Estella stopped long enough to draw several of the enchanted throwing stars and readied for the next step in their plan.

When the time was right, Xander made the psychic order for all of them to fall back.

Satoru and Sawyer dropped from the rafters at that moment as Estella threw the magical weapons into the ceiling, not far from their enemy, who'd barely had a chance to dodge them as they *whiz*zed past. The magic began to take effect then, and spread its ominous light over the logs that made up the rafters and roof. Richard, seeing what was happening, let himself fall from the ceiling and descended then as the mythos army prepared to box him in.

Seeing their intentions, the hunter threw out his aura and shifted his fall to the other side of the room, landing on the roof of the BMW and rolling to the opposite side of the car. Above them, the roof finished disintegrating into nothing, leaving nothing over them but the night sky.

Dianna! Xander called out.

The huntress nodded once and disappeared from where she was standing and emerged in front of her brother, ready to strike.

Richard growled, "You would betray me? Your own brother? What would Mom and Dad think?"

"They probably wouldn't recognize you as their son and take you out like the monster you've become," She growled as she swung at him with a left hook.

Richard ducked under the attack and, seething with rage, lunged at her.

Dianna jumped back to evade; doing a backward handspring over the top of a chair and putting the furniture between them.

Richard roared—his taroe tattoos shining from under his clothes—and the chair erupted into pieces.

Sawyer, calling out to the huntress, dove over the car and caught the hunter in the midsection, taking him down and throwing a punch into the back of his head.

Close in! Xander called out to everyone.

Most of the group circled the car while Xander and Estella vaulted over it side-by-side in an attempt to get to the hunter. Richard's eyes widened at the attack and threw out his aura in a wide arc to throw them all back, only to have it deflected by Xander's own as he came in from above. The hunter hissed at him; his skin beginning to glow again as he started to cast another spell. The others stepped away cautiously as the entire cabin started shaking and bending as boards were broke and strained. Estella frowned, studying the magic around them, and quickly countered with another spell that neutralized the hunter's spell. As the cabin came to rest once again, Richard's aura whipped into a frenzy as he realized that he was being overwhelmed. Knowing that he was running out of options, he tried to jump into overdrive only to have Sawyer and Dianna jump in and hold him down. Zeek, seeing an opening, hurled himself over his comrades then, using the car's warped hood like a springboard and brandishing his staff, ready to bring it down on the hunter's head.

Richard sneered and roared, his aura flaring out and throwing his sister and Sawyer off of him. Jumping to his feet, the hunter grabbed the end of Zeek's oncoming staff in his right hand and swung out, dragging the anapriek off his course. The others rushed in, trying to keep the distance between them and their enemy to a minimum, only to have Richard use Zeek's attack against them. The anapriek, still holding tightly to his weapon, crashed into the crowd, forcing them all to back away. Once again gaining the upper hand, Richard kicked out at Estella as she tried to get close and threw his aura out into Satoru, throwing the nejin back over the car, before grabbing Zeek by the wrist and dragging him into a fierce head-butt in the face. The anapriek stumbled back, dazed—blood spilling from his nostrils—and before he could react the hunter delivered a spinning kick to his sternum that sent him back and into the side of the car.

The hunter smiled as his enemies all turned to face their comrade in shock; the realization that the fight was far from over dawning on them.

"Did you think it would be *that* easy?" He taunted them. He narrowed his eyes at Xander and smirked, "Especially now that I am stronger than ever."

The vampire frowned, not knowing—or particularly caring— what the hunter meant by this. He ran forward, fooling his enemy with what appeared to be a punch aimed at his throat that, at the last moment, he shifted to an attempted side-kick to the knee. Richard evaded this, however, raising his leg and pulling it away from the attack and kicking back at Xander's ribs. Dodging this with the side of his forearm, the vampire threw out his aura like a fist to "punch" the hunter in the face; only to have the hunter's own aura counter and drive the auric blow to the side wall.

Estella appeared behind them and rotated her body to put momentum into a kick. Richard ducked under it and swept his arm to take her supporting leg out from under her. Baring her fangs at her opponent, she jumped to avoid this and flipped to a safe distance before casting a quick spell. The floor under Richard creaked and suddenly tore away.

Richard's eyes went wide as he started to fall. Before he was all the way through, however, Xander snagged him in his aura and started to crush him—an auric attack that the vampire knew well from past experience hurt like hell. A choked cry echoed down the chasm, confirming Xander's suspicions as the vampire hoisted him from the magically-created hole and slammed him hard into the roof of the car to cave it in on itself.

Sawyer shivered as he charged towards the hunter, "Poor Bassie..."

"Will you forget about the goddam car, for fuck's sake," Xander growled, bringing the hunter down harder on the BMW—more for emphasis against the warrior's complaints—"I'll"—*SLAM!*—"buy you"—*SLAM! SLAM! SLAM!*—"a new one!"

The others wasted no time in closing in again, hoping that the multiple impacts had crippled the hunter long enough to get a kill shot in. Instead, he scoffed and, throwing Xander's aura off of him with his own, lifted himself on one arm and, after kicking out at Sawyer and Satoru, landed on his feet. In a stunning display of sangsuiga strength, the hunter leapt into the air and vaulted over the now-destroyed roof of the cabin, taking the fight outside.

Xander roared in rage and tore out the nearest wall with his aura, allowing the others to flood through to the beach. As Estella passed he called to her and, at the same time, tossed Yang to her. She barely stopped to catch the bone-white revolver, nodding to him as she thumbed back the hammer.

She didn't need to be told how to use the gun.

The knowledge was already within her.

She was as intimately aware of the heirloom as Xander.

Once again Richard found himself in the center of the mythos ring; the attacks coming in from all directions. However, like before, the sheer numbers made no difference, and all were easily deflected and reversed.

Zeek swiped with his staff and nearly struck Satoru as Richard ducked under the attack.

The nejin struck out with his claws and stabbed with the katana, but only succeeding in slicing through the winter air.

Dianna kicked and her foot was caught and pulled upward, throwing her to the ground.

Xander snarled at the sight and ran alongside Estella, both jumping into the air simultaneously and aiming their descent for the middle of the crowd. Still in midair, Xander drew his guns and the two vampires began to fire at their enemy while psychically warning their comrades of the incoming shots. The army jumped back as a series of magically-charged hollow points and explosive rounds came in contact with...

Richard's auric shield.

Though the blast was an impressive sight, none of the rounds made it through, and as the smoke cleared the hunter burst through and met the two descending vampires, kicking out at Xander while he gripped Estella in his aura and threw her downward. Sawyer was quick to catch her before she hit the ground and returned her to her feet.

Xander stretched his aura to the ground and held himself aloft, hovering in the air and striking out again and again at Richard, who had done the same.

"Eerie, isn't it?" the hunter laughed, "Sort of like fighting a mirror."

The vampire narrowed his eyes and tossed one of the pistols into the air, snagging it in an auric tendril and freeing his hand so he could drive a fist into Richard's face. While the hunter was stunned from the blow, Xander raised the other pistol in his left hand, lining up a shot as he moved the other gun—still gripped in his aura—to Richard's blind side. As the hunter shifted his aura to dodge the obvious shot, Xander spun the weapon on his trigger finger and brought the handle of the gun down on the hunter's face several times before willing his aura to pull the trigger.

Though dazed, Richard held enough control and awareness

to deflect the shot with an auric shield. Using the distraction, Xander threw a superhuman kick into the hunter's groin and pistol-whipped him across the jaw again.

Richard's aura faltered under the assault and started to fall.

Dianna, seeing this, ran forward and jumped into the air, grabbing her brother in her aura and, flipping over him, used her momentum to pitch him that much harder into the jagged rocks below.

Xander felt a swell of satisfaction as he watched Richard crash down on the beach; his body bouncing and forcing a pained grunt from his lungs.

Xander let his aura retract and allowed his body to drop to the ground, landing on his feet before he started to sprint towards their fallen nemesis.

"GODDAM MONSTERS!" Richard roared as he pulled himself up.

Satoru was quick to lunge at the hunter, who used his aura to pull a large rock from the ground and into his hand. As the nejin descended on him, the hunter swung it into his skull with a sickening *thud*. As their ally's muscles slackened and he hit the ground, unconscious, a battle cry issued from Zeek, who pole-vaulted off his staff at the hunter and began a series of strikes that were a blur to even the vampires. Richard's hands flashed and darted back and forth as he deflected each and every attack before finally getting a punch of his own in on Zeek's chest, knocking the air from the anapriek and sending him stumbling back. Before the others could intervene, the hunter snatched the staff from Zeek's hands and used it to pull his legs out from under him. As he fell, the hunter swung the weapon over his head and brought it down on the falling anapriek's chest, breaking the thick wood in half along with several of his ribs. Zeek cried out as he smashed into the rocky ground and curled over on himself, clutching at his sides.

The hunter smirked and moved to break Zeek's neck then, but was stopped at the last moment as Sawyer appeared behind him and kicked him away. Rolling from the impact and using the momentum to get back to his feet, Richard growled and ran at the vampire warrior in overdrive, catching him off guard and tackling him. Once on the ground, the hunter attacked with his fists and elbows. Sawyer was knocked and battered; too startled and dazed by the attacks to counter.

"GET OFF OF HIM, YOU BASTARD!" Dianna cried out and sprinted at them.

Before reaching the scene, however, her brother had successfully immobilized Sawyer with a spell—his tattoos glowing brightly and cutting through the darkness—and tossed him aside.

"... deal with you later!" Richard promised as he turned and braced for his sister's attack.

Estella was in overdrive before Xander could decide what they should do next. Not wanting to be left out of the action, he quickly followed after, joining his lover at her side as they closed the distance in a blink of an eye and moved to strike at the hunter. Richard had seen the vampires step into overdrive, however, and as they neared they found their enemy in the same state and waiting for them.

Reverse the spell on Sawyer, Xander instructed Estella. *We won't last long without him.*

Nodding, Estella darted out of Richard's range and hooked around to join Sawyer; her aura already beginning to writhe with the start of her counter-spell. Knowing he had to keep the hunter occupied long enough for the binds on the vampire warrior to be removed, Xander snarled and hurled himself at Richard.

Their battle waged on.

Dianna was in the fight soon after, and the two took turns rotating around their enemy and striking wherever and whenever they could. Richard proved just as evasive in overdrive, though, and as they continued to try and find a weak spot in his defenses they found themselves growing more and more exhausted.

But that meant he was, too!

Refusing to step down, none of them dared to drop out; all of them too committed to the battle and afraid of what would happen if they returned to normal speed.

Xander swung with a hard right-hook that Richard ducked under before lunging at Dianna, who, not expecting the attack, made a sloppy attempt to dodge the advance and caught a powerful kick to the hip that sent her reeling out of overdrive and through one of the still-standing walls of the cabin. Enraged, Xander's aura flared and ensnared the hunter, lifting him off the ground and forcing him out of overdrive.

Xander was sick of trying to exhaust the bastard!

He was sick of continuing on like this!

Richard was going to die!

He moved to attack his trapped victim and was shocked when the hunter's aura shot out back at him, piercing through the auric bind like a blade. Xander dove to the side to avoid the attack, which continued on and smashed—full force—into Dianna as she fought to pull herself out of the cabin's debris. Caught off guard, the huntress was knocked off her feet and thrown backward into the woods as though she'd been fired from a cannon.

Estella rose to her feet with Sawyer close behind. Seeing the attack on his lover, Sawyer roared and charged towards Richard as Estella joined Xander at his side. Xander nodded to her and opened his mouth to call out a strategy but was interrupted by a loud buzzing. Turning his head, he saw that the sound was coming from the hunter's tattoos—Richard powering up as he clapped his palms against either side of Sawyer's skull and forcing the warrior to drop to his knees—as they began to shine brighter than ever.

Whatever spell he was casting, it was a strong one.

As the static whine grew more unbearable, Estella pitched back and howled in agony. Xander's eyes widened as he saw the spell for what it was...

Richard was *binding* Estella—body *and* magic—in an effort to take her out of the fight.

"DON'T"—Xander clenched his teeth and fists and charged at the hunter—"YOU"—he threw out his aura, scooping up every large rock he passed in a ray of red-and-black tendrils—"FUCKING"—he dropped down, relying on the graveled surface and his momentum to carry him between the startled hunter's legs; the wave of hurtling rocks colliding with Richard's chest—"HURT HER!"

As Richard was knocked back by the impact of Xander's assault, the vampire rose to his feet behind him and swung out with his knee. Richard howled in agony as Xander's attack connected with the base of his spine and he locked his fingers—mimicking a blade—and jabbed the hunter in his side; twisting his hand halfway through the attack and smirking as he felt one of Richard's ribs snap under the force.

Though Estella was still alive, the spell had pinned her aura—and, with it, her magic—and drained her of all her energy.

Despite his injuries the hunter smirked, "Now it's just you and me, you blood-sucking punk! And after I'm done with you I'll be free to take care of all your freaky fuckin' pals one-by-one at my leisure."

Xander frowned at this and took a stance across from the hunter, "No," he shook his head and took a deep breath, collecting his focus, "You're not going to hurt anybody else. Not ever again."

"We'll see," Richard's aura sparked and began to raise high above him.

The vampire's own aura swirled and heaved in response, building up and coiling like a serpent, ready to strike. His body heated up with rage as his energy signature grew.

For a moment they stood, staring each other down as they built up their energy. Their auras leaned, bending slowly towards one another and clashing lightly, bumping and swirling; seemingly independent from their owners.

And then they attacked...

CHAPTER THIRTY-SEVEN
THE DEATH OF XANDER...

ONE MOMENT THEY'D been standing still several yards apart and the next they were at each other's throats. As they continued kicking and punching at whatever their feet and hands could make contact with, the rocky ground shook and rattled under the assault of auric waves rolling off of the two; the stones rattling as they shifted and spread away from their fight.

The beach itself seemed to be fleeing from the chaos.

"We've been in this position before," Richard taunted, "Do you remember how *that* ended?"

Xander hissed, his fangs fully extended and snapping hungrily in the hunter's face.

Richard reared back and tried to drive a fist into the vampire's face, only to have his wrist grabbed. He struggled, trying to get his arm back, and threw his opposite hand into the mix. Xander ducked under this and wrapped his arm around it, trapping it under his armpit and rotating in an attempt to break the hunter's arm, bringing his knee up and into the hunter's broken rib three times. Richard, crying out, struggled against the force and bent his arm at the elbow to save it from snapping. With nothing left to attack with, drove his forehead into the vampire's face.

Xander howled in pain and drew back, clutching his broken nose and fighting to see past the tears that welled in his eyes and blurred his vision. As he tried to keep his focus on Richard, he saw a flash of movement and the hunter was on him, his martial arts abilities being applied in full, superhuman force.

Xander roared and grabbed his enemy, deciding to counter the hunter's formal training with some old-school dirty fighting. Trapping his arms at his side, Xander kneed the hunter in the crotch, reveling in the pained cry that issued forth, and gripped him by the shoulders as he jumped as high as he could, dragging the writhing hunter into the air with him. With the law of gravity a distant concern, Xander continued to drive his knee over and over between Richard's legs until he was certain there was nothing of substance left. Satisfied with this, he wrapped the hunter in his aura again and began the crushing maneuver in an attempt to break his spine as they began to fall then, coming down over the frozen lake.

Xander, seeing the ice coming at them, threw out an auric tendril in an effort to catch himself, only to punch through the surface below them.

The frigid blackness of the frozen lake consumed them as the two of them went under.

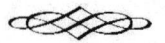

Xander had been brought to the brink of death more times than he cared to admit, and he was more than aware of how cold and lonely a process it was.

Freezing; dark; isolated.

Drowning in the icy lake, he realized, was a very appropriate way to die.

He tried to look around to see which way was up, but there was nothing in any direction but blackness.

He tried to move his body to swim to the surface but found

his muscles unresponsive.

He was already dying!

This wasn't enough for Richard, however, who was suddenly in front of the vampire with a maniacal smirk across his face. As Xander's eyes widened, he caught sight of the hunter's gills as they opened and closed rhythmically at his neck, pumping oxygen into his body.

And that stupid bitch thought these were a bad idea, Richard's musings chimed in Xander's head. *But just look at me now; I get a front-row seat to watch you drown!*

The bastard!

He wanted to watch him die? To make sure that the one, remaining threat to his mission was out of his hair so that he could swim casually from this icy hell and go back to killing?

Xander closed his eyes and focused.

He wasn't about to give up on them now!

At that moment, he saw the truth; the way it was supposed to be. He *was* a protector. Whether he had an army backing him up or not; it didn't matter. It was his destiny—not fate or some predetermined place, but his nature and his legacy—to keep his family and his friends and all the innocents in the world safe.

So many times in the past he'd failed to be there for the ones who needed him, and he'd suffered for those follies long enough!

He was not about to fail again!

The numbing cold faded as his aura expanded from his motionless form and encased him in its warming energy.

Richard, swimming just ahead of him, watched; his cocky and content aura slowly moving about in the cold water like an oily mass. Even with his eyes shut, Xander could see the son-of-a-bitch as the unnatural stain he was to the world. The vampire pushed himself, recalling what he'd done with his aura and his tiger-friend several days earlier.

So he couldn't move; couldn't breathe; couldn't see...

Who needed a body anyway?

His crimson aura was a bolt of lightning as it shot from his body and into Richard's head, lighting up the pitch-black depths and creating a blood-red lake. Once secured in the hunter's mind, he traveled through the connection, leaving his body and possessing his enemy.

Xander was a part of the hunter now.

And he fought him where it hurt the most.

There were no attacks. No kicks; no punches; no bloodshed or broken bones.

There was only the beautiful chaos of a collapsing mind!

Xander could take any form inside Richard's head, and as the hunter struggled to get control of what was happening within him the vampire traveled through his system, bringing up painful memories and playing them in an infinite loop until the cracks of insanity developed on the horizon. He dragged up fears and phobias and created nightmares that had Richard screaming inside-and-out like an infant.

As he tore his way through Richard's mind, Xander saw a more recent memory and his anger flared up again. The hunter had created a serum with *his* blood!

Like fighting a mirror, he'd said.

The bastard!

So you want to be like me? Xander thought, *Then let me show you how!*

Xander reflected on his past—drawing forth his most painful memories—and flooded Richard's mind with the encounters, trading places and letting the hunter experience every grim torture and act of abuse from his sadistic, auric stepfather. The beatings; the taunts; the harassment. Being beaten with belts and broomsticks. Being held against a coiled, red-hot stovetop. Being taunted and tortured and mocked. Then, finally, being forced to watch his mother crying out to him as she was raped by a group of men and repeatedly stabbed.

But Xander didn't stop there.

Richard hadn't seen pain.

Not yet!

Five years of anguish; of hoping against hope that his suicidal efforts might come to fruition. Finding out the truth of his kind at the expense of his grandmother. Finding joy with the Odin Clan—his rightful family—only to have them massacred while he lay underground, going through the change.

The loss of his mentor and the closest thing he had to a

brother.

The brutal kidnapping and biting of Estella; the pain of losing her.

The looming weight of total and complete failure.

All of it—every bit of agony Xander had felt in his lifetime—flooded Richard's system all at once.

Then, after tearing through and paving a path of horror and suffering—treating the murderous, abusive bastard to every moment of suffering he'd inflicted on his sister and all those innocent mythos all at once—he began taking the hunter's weakened mind apart at the seams.

Hurt his friends?

Kill his loved ones?

Destroy all the glorious races of the mythos underworld?

No!

Not while Xander was there to protect them.

Like he'd been meant to all along.

All of Richard's stolen powers flared up at once as Xander forced his body into overdrive; pushed the hunter's system harder than it had ever been pushed.

So the chemistry of his system was unstable?

Then Xander would overwork every damn part of this bastard until his entire body refused to hold itself together.

He would turn every gear—work every synapse and cylinder that fired within the core of the sadistic son of a bitch—until the machinery could operate no more.

And then it happened...

Richard's overworked heart stopped.

And everything in his mind began to go black.

Freezing; dark; isolated.

A very appropriate way to die.

Very appropriate, indeed.

Xander's aura rolled away from the vacant mind of the hunter as he fell back into his own head.

His own clouded, dimming head.

Shit!

He was still dying.

In a final attempt he threw his aura out in an ever-increasing orb, scrambling to find the ice—the surface. When it presented itself, he grabbed the hole they'd fallen through and fought to pull his body towards it. Halfway there his aura stuttered and his hold broke as his focus waned. His oxygen-starved body ached at the effort, begging him to give in and let death relieve it from the pain.

But he refused to give up.

Pushing his numbed muscles to swim, he reached the surface and began pounding with his weakened body at the frozen roof of ice above him. His frozen fists uselessly battered the barrier between him and the life-sustaining oxygen on the other side. Feeling the darkness closing in, he pushed his aura out again, but it, too, was too exhausted and weakened to free him from his icy prison.

Slowly, Xander felt the coldness of death close in around him; his entire body beginning to shut down. Futilely he threw his lame fist once more into the ceiling of ice, trying one final time to break free before he finally succumbed to the inevitable…

As Death consumed him, he uttered a silent apology to Timothy for breaking his promise and began to sink to the bottom of the lake.

CHAPTER THIRTY-EIGHT
THE BIRTH OF STRYKER...

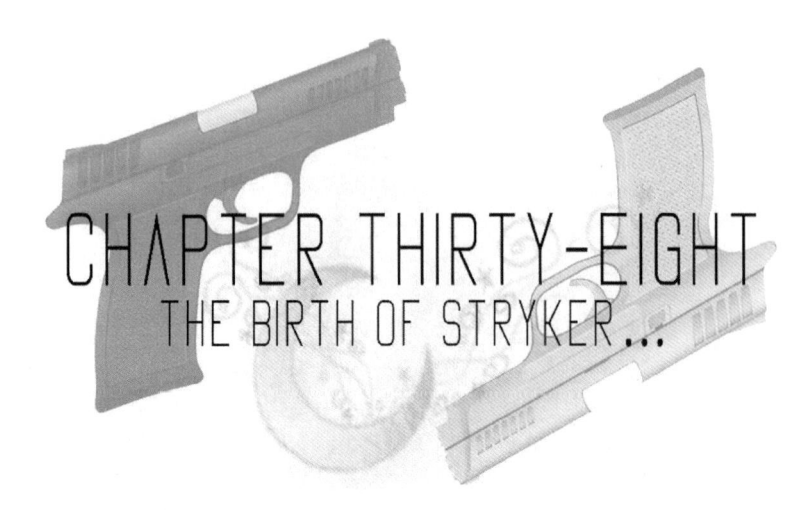

LIFE AND DEATH.
Light and dark.
Yin and Yang.
The balance of opposites...
Xander wasn't cold. Not anymore.
Though he was having a hard time remembering what cold felt like...
This was the first thing he realized as he tried to squint his eyes against a bright, blinding blood-red light that was all around him...
But there were no lids to close.
So he just stared.
Just took it all in.
Wondering what it was he was seeing.
Could this be death?
Then the light dimmed, and, as it did, so did his awareness of it...

"No! Don't die, dammit!"

"Again! Hit him with it again!"

"It's not that simp—"

The warmth and the light!
So intense!
Had he been here before?
He could've sworn...
It was all so familiar.

"Xander!"
Familiar voice...
Was it?
He focused, tried to capture it; to hold it long enough to place it.
But the light was fading...

"WAKE THE FUCK UP! PLEASE!"
A jolt.
Muscles spasm.
Pain?
Was that what that wa—
Xander's world lit up as the weight and bulk of life slammed into his chest.
Fire...

An inferno flooded his veins and he felt an icy chill fill his lungs.
Pain?
Pain...
What was...
PAIN!
He cried out as he felt his essence collapse and explode over and over and...

Light?
It was so...
"Again! You've gotta do it again! We're losing him!"

Darkness...
Lots and lots of pain.
Pain and...
Xander gasped and blinked.
It was dark... no—dim.
Trees—he could see the tops of trees—and, beyond them, he saw stars.
And then he could see her: the only star that mattered.
Estella.
Her face was red. She was crying. And suddenly she was kissing him. Over and over he felt her lips press against his face, and each time they came back for more. He blinked and moved his eyes; where was he?
What had happened?
Estella was still kissing him and he felt an ache in his chest—his lungs?—start to fade as he suddenly remembered to inhale.
Estella stopped kissing him for a moment, "That's it, Xander! That's it! Breathe!"
He took another deep breath and coughed; hard. He turned to his side and curled up as his body lurched with a coughing fit.
Water came up with it.
Lots of it.
His eyes went wide as his thoughts collected and he was suddenly aware enough to worry that he might drown all over

again. It felt like he was coughing up the whole damn lake. He grabbed his aching chest and felt the thick, dry cloth. He looked down and saw Satoru's hoody and sweatpants on him; his soaked clothes in a heap a short distance away.

The nejin was nearby in a tee-shirt and a pair of boxers, though he didn't seem to mind the December chill. As Xander dragged his eyes from the nearly naked nejin he saw the others around him, staring intently and hopefully down at him.

"Wha...?"

"It was Dianna!" Estella explained, "She saved us!"

Xander blinked, "Di-anna..."

Sawyer helped the huntress step forward, her body bloody and broken, and she took a deep, pained breath as she knelt down beside Xander, smiling weakly.

Estella smiled wider, "She released us from Richard's magic!" She pulled the hood up and over Xander's head to try and keep him warm, "When we were all free we went out on the ice to find you."

Sawyer nodded, "Your lady nearly melted the whole damn lake out from under us." He chuckled.

"But you were already d-dead!" Estella choked on the word.

Xander shook his head, confused. "Dead...?"

They all nodded.

"Dianna and I used magic to start your heart again while Zeek monitored your vitals," Estella smiled.

Xander tried to sit up, only to have the anapriek push him back down with his foot and shake his head.

"You're still too weak to move," Zeek informed him, still wearing the caked blood on his face and clutching his chest.

"Not... not like you look any better, Doctor Zeek," Xander stuttered and coughed up more of the lake.

Zeek groaned as a chuckle caused his chest to heave, "Still better than you."

"It's alright," Estella said, running her hand over his forehead, "Osehr's on the way with the artificial blood."

Sawyer nodded and Xander noticed that he was holding Dianna's hand. "You'll be up and kicking in no time," the warrior smiled.

Estella moved her hand and kissed his forehead, "You did it!" Xander smiled and shrugged his shoulders.

What else was there to say?

⁂

They didn't have to wait long for Osehr to show up with the entire cooler of The Gamer's magically-charged synthetic blood. He burst out of the woods in his bestial form, Timothy dropping down from his back as soon as he stopped a few yards away. Moments later the rest of the pack emerged, Karen and Sasha taking up the lead. Xander smirked at the mock-medics' arrival and pushed himself upright, despite Zeek's previous warnings, to accept the first of many thermoses. When she saw that Zeek was still alive, Karen howled happily and rushed in—interrupting the anapriek in mid-scold at Xander's movement—and planting a passionate kiss on him while she was still halfway through the transformation back to her human form. Still clutching his wounds, Zeek struggled with his body's pain and his obvious refusal to break the kiss.

Timothy, following Karen's example of blatant defiance of obvious injuries, charged over and hugged Xander as the vampire finished his first rejuvenating drink.

"You really did it?" The boy asked excitedly, "You killed him?"

Xander smiled and nodded, "Hell yea, little buddy. I really killed him."

"YAY!" The little vampire cheered and hugged his mentor again and then jumped to his feet and began chanting, "Xan-der ki-i-illed the hun-ter! Xan-der ki-i-illed the hun-ter..."

While Timothy celebrated, the pack all beamed down at their savior. The closest two therions stepped forward and helped him to his feet and offered him another thermos. Xander smiled, though more at the happiness around him than at the attention, and turned with a smile to Osehr.

"Well done, Xander," He congratulated. *A superb* Kriss-mas *present.*

Xander frowned. "Christmas?"

The therion elder nodded—a strange motion considering his

bestial form, *You said we had to wait.*

Estella smirked, also able to "hear" the therion leader's thought-speak, "You didn't realize?" She asked and smirked at Xander's confusion, "It's Christmas Eve."

"MERRY CHRISTMAS, XANDER!" Timothy called out suddenly, tackling his mentor.

The vampire smirked and looked around at all his friends—his *family*—as they looked over at him and he nodded, "I suppose everybody is still interested in this Christmas-thing then?"

The pack erupted with excitement.

He smiled and nodded slowly, "Well I *have* been thinking…"

"I have to say," Luther said in his thick Italian accent, a smirk spreading across his chiseled features as his aura swirled excitedly about him—a massive and powerful plume of purple with wisps of orange—"I *was* surprised to hear that you wanted to see us."

Xander smirked, raising his eyebrow, "Should I be insulted by that?" He asked coyly, taking a quick sip from a small cup of espresso. He had to admit, it was better than the stuff that he'd had at the café with Tennesen.

Luther's grin widened, "Oh not at all! It wasn't a question of your character. It's just that we didn't think that this day would come." He took a sip of his own coffee and shrugged, "That's not to say we didn't *hope* that it would."

Xander nodded and shrugged absently, "Sometimes you need a little faith."

"Amen to that," Luther chuckled and bowed his head slightly, the orange in his aura taking on a slightly golden tint before fading once again.

It was nearly a week past Christmas day, and though the therion pack had gotten to celebrate the holiday in their own way—with a great deal of deer meat and singing around a fire—Xander had promised that the real present would take a little more time…

… and *a lot* more effort.

Setting up a meeting with a member of The Council proved to be, while not exceedingly simple, not as difficult as he would have thought. Sooner than he'd expected he had found himself on a flight to Rome with Estella at his side and, within several days, sitting at a table with one of the higher-ranking officials of the international mythos government.

Luther, a powerful pure-born sang-auric hybrid—a "perfect" vampire as Xander had come to know them—turned out to be every bit as powerful a mythos politician. Despite all of his strength and powers, his abilities as a diplomat were what made him a powerful ally or a terrible enemy. And it was for this reason, more than anything else, that Xander was glad to not only be on Luther's good side, but to be in his good graces.

His was the sort of power that Xander was hoping to have on his side for what he had planned.

"So what exactly is it that you want from us?" Luther asked then, his voice growing hushed and serious.

Xander smiled at the question, feeling that it and the response were long overdue. "I'd like to rebuild what my father started," he answered.

Luther narrowed his eyes for a moment, studying him, "Rebuild? How so?"

"The old Odin mansion"—Xander frowned as he pictured the burnt-out remains of the once-proud clan headquarters—"I'd like to have The Council's permission—and, of course, their support—to reestablish it as a clan headquarters."

Luther frowned at this and, after shifting his gaze towards Estella—who sat with them and held a manila folder containing the details of Xander's plans—looked down at his own steaming espresso. "While I'm happy to hear such aspirations, I feel it necessary to remind you that, despite all of your services to us and our people, you *are* still *very* young, Stryker," he leaned forward, resting his elbows on the table, "And, though effective, your methods *are* quite unorthodox. You understand that you put us in a difficult place by asking for The Council's support in assembling and ruling over a clan that has already suffered a great deal."

"I *do* understand that," Xander mirrored Luther's posture,

"And I also understand that it's an even more difficult place to be since I don't intend to rule over The Odin clan."

Luther frowned, "My apologies, but did you not just say that—"

"I said that I'm going reestablish the old Odin mansion as the site for a clan headquarters, yes," Xander nodded, "And, make no mistake, that part isn't the request—I *will* be following through with those plans with *or* without The Council's blessing."

Luther's frown deepened into a scowl, "Then what is it, exactly, that you're requesting?"

"That The Council grant me the resources and funding to start over; to create a *new* clan—one that takes my father and Depok's original plans and builds upon them—so that we can begin to move the mythos community in the right direction. I think that it's safe to say that change is coming, and that it *needs* to come. The Odin Clan suffered at the hands of those who sensed and feared what that change represents to them; to all of us." Xander took a sip of his coffee before reaching out to Estella for the folder, "I've served The Council as little more than an errand-boy and, in doing so, I've seen just how ugly the rogue element can become, and I believe that I can do much, *much* more. I'm requesting that The Council put the same faith in me that they did my father."

"You speak of significant changes, Stryker," Luther rubbed his chin, "But I still don't feel that you're old enough to handle this sort of thing on your own."

Xander nodded, "Which is exactly why I don't intend to run it alone."

The Council member nodded slowly, looking at Estella again. "And how do you feel about all of his, my dear?"

Estella cleared her throat, "I believe that Xander was put on this world to do great things. I believe that he's suffered enough to empathize with those who need these great things to happen, and I believe that he's strong and determined enough to get them done." She smirked and reached across the table, taking Xander's hand in her own, "And I also believe that he's too stubborn to let anybody stand between him and his beliefs."

Luther smirked and shook his head, turning to face Xander

once again. "I like her, Stryker; all the wit and wonder that your mother had I see in her. I take it she'll be assisting you in these efforts?"

Xander opened his mouth to answer, only to have Estella squeeze his hand.

"You bet I am," she smiled.

Nodding, Luther took a deep breath and took another sip of his coffee as he contemplated the proposal.

"Look," Xander went on, "I know what kind of a blow it was to you and the rest of the mythos world when the Odin Clan was wiped out. There isn't a single question on anybody's mind that it happened *because* the mythos community was expecting me to do *exactly* what I'm here to do. So, while I can appreciate the formalities, I don't think it's fair to waste too much time pretending that what I'm proposing isn't something that our world has been hoping for."

Luther frowned and furrowed his brow at that, "You're quite presumptuous."

Xander grinned at that, "Am I? Even you said you'd been waiting for this day, Luther; you must've had your guesses about what it was for."

The Council member laughed, "Indeed!" He sighed, calming himself, and nodded, "I suppose there is no denying that much. And you *do* sound every bit as determined as your father did…"

Xander's eyes lit up, "Does that mean…?"

Luther smiled and nodded, "If you provide us with the details on your plans and who you intend to assist you in the process, I will see to it that you have The Council's full support to follow through with these plans."

Final entry: January 14th

Dear Journal,

It's been a while since I last wrote anything, and a part of me wonders if I'll ever feel compelled to write anything again. I'd started the process a while ago as a means of punishing myself (something that Osehr had often told me but that I refused to accept until now). For that reason, and because there's just so much damn work to be done, I've decided that I no longer need to continue doing this to myself.

Anyway...

The process of starting up this new clan (we've decided to call it the "Trepis Clan") has turned into quite the fiasco. What I originally thought would be a moderately small project with the occasional pain in the ass has become a global event for our kind. Because we are the first clan open to not just vampires, but for <u>ALL</u> mythos as well as magically inclined humans, we have been receiving a great deal of traffic from all around the world. While it seems to be pissing a lot of people off, we came to the conclusion that this was the best choice for a number of reasons, though the biggest contributors were my father's original plans to unify ourselves as well as the unity that I personally witnessed between the variety of species that have helped to establish the Trepis Clan.

After all, if a therion and an anapriek can love one another, than anything is possible for us.

This can be a dangerous thing for us, however (a thought that's keeping me awake this morning). Something this unprecedented, like my father and his efforts with the Odin Clan, is bound to get the attention of naysayers who will be willing to go to great distances to stop us.

It wouldn't be the first time something like that has happened, after all...

But this is supposed to be a happy event, I suppose.

The Council has already sent over several of its own to help me and Estella run things (not that I feel that it's needed, I DO have Osehr here to help me run things, after all). Nevertheless, I wasn't about to turn away the offer, especially when (to be honest) none of us know the first thing about running a clan.

Though I suppose the fact that they're bank rolling the entire thing has a little to do with it.

So far they're doing a decent enough job of overseeing the rebuilding process as well as finding us members and support (they're actually fantastic with the whole PR thing – go figure).

With Osehr agreeing to help me run things the remaining members of the pack were quick to join in as well. Zeek and the others were also eager to join, as well as Sawyer and Dianna— who are doing quite well and will probably be married before the end of next year—who, because of their experience, I'm appointing as head warriors (they seemed pretty honored by the title).

I'm still waiting on the responses from The Gamer and Father Tennesen. Earlier this week I sent them both invitations to join the clan—The Gamer's knowledge of weaponry and magic will be a powerful asset to us as well as his synthetic blood, which we're sure will revolutionize how songs around the world feed. While I'm confident that he'll be willing to join, I'm not so sure about Tennesen, but I wouldn't feel right not extending the offer; Tennesen is a good man and, as such, I feel he'd be a perfect candidate to help bridge the gap between us and the humans (as well as humanity). Either way, I'm sure I've pissed off plenty of mythos out there just by considering bringing humans into our world like that, but I think that this is the way that it should be...

It's how my father would've wanted it, I'm sure.

Timothy's doing well. He and I have been keeping up with his training and, in all honesty, I believe that he'll soon surpass me. He still has a little trouble with handling guns, but that's to be expected. His skills as a fighter continue to grow, and though he's eager to show off his skills, both I and the others have forbid him to go on any missions for the time being. He argued at first, but seemed satisfied when we finally agreed that he'd be ready in a few years (we're still trying to determine a safe age, but, truthfully, I think he'd pose more of a threat to rogues on the street than vice-versa).

Still haven't heard a word out of Satoru, but he's got his own way of communicating when he needs to... not sure if that's how it is with all nejins or if he's just the quiet type. Either way, he'll make a fine addition as a warrior, though I don't think he'll be one for asking questions (that'll make for some interesting negotiations, I'm sure).

Things with me and Estella are going well—terrific if you consider how miserable we both were a little more than a month ago. The therions have already begun referring to her as "Queen", though she doesn't seem thrilled by this (she was never one to think highly of herself... but, then again, neither was I). We're currently in a silent race with Sawyer and Dianna to walk the aisle.

And me...?

Well, I'm just trying to get used to all of the changes that are being made.

Either way, it'll be interesting to see where it goes from here. Though this is my last entry, this is hardly the end.

Ready or not, world...

Xander Stryker
("The Crimson Shadow")

EPILOGUE
GET THEE BEHIND ME

~One Year Later~

THE CABBY RAISED his eyebrow as the man entered his taxi. Though it was late and the air was still dank from that evening's rain storm, the man's approach seemed to bring an electric hum to the air, and the otherwise sleepy moment came alive with it; not far off, a jet took off and the roar momentarily drowned out the din other din of the comings and goings of the airport. The windshield wipers squeaked slightly against the drying windshield, leaving a greasy streak across the glass and the sound pulling the driver's attention away from his new fare long enough to feed the parched glass a dose of washing fluid. As the man took his seat he let out a relaxed sigh and the door shut behind him.

The cabby frowned and swiveled his head to see if somebody was standing outside the cab.

Had the door just closed on its own?

CRIMSON SHADOW: FORBIDDEN DANCE

Sighing and shaking his head, he snatched the nearly empty can of Rip It from the cup holder and took a sip, hoping that the dose of caffeine would clear his hazing mind. Holding back a wretch at the stale, lukewarm beverage, he forced himself to nearly empty the can and gulp the contents.

Though he appeared no different than any other fare, the passenger had a discomforting air about him. He carried with him only a single, small overnight bag that looked foreign and expensive, which he set beside him before setting a meticulously carved wooden walking stick across his lap. The driver eyed him through the cruddy rearview mirror, tilting his head irregularly in an effort to get a decent look before finally sighing and turning in his seat so he could face him.

The man was dressed in a long, black coat that wrapped around his body with such intimate tailoring that it seemed as though it were a part of him; the crisp collar hugging his neck and birthing the tanned, flawless skin of his throat. As the driver took him in a smile stretched across his chiseled features—a smile that forgot to carry over to his serious and eerily penetrating blue eyes—and he ran a gloved hand through his blond and was slicked back hair; tucking the bulk of his long hair into the black collar. The cabby frowned. Though he had been standing in the rain for some time before finally getting picked up, neither his clothes nor his hair seemed to have suffered a single blemishing drop of moisture. The cabby sniffed nervously as he took this all in with a single, passing glance and wetted his lips.

"Where to, buddy?"

The man tapped his thumb three times against his walking stick as he thought, his smile never fading and his gaze never softening. For a moment he seemed lost in his own mind before his smile broadened.

"I'd like to visit the West Ridge high school."

The cabby frowned at this and blinked in confusion, "The school?"

The man gave a single nod.

"At this hour?"

The man's smile remained as his eyes narrowed, "Is that a

problem? You *are*, after all, being paid, are you not?"

Wetting his lips again, the cabby shrugged and put the taxi into gear, "True enough. You're the boss."

"I'm certainly one of them," The man's face relaxed and he leaned back, letting out another relieved sigh that ended with a sharp, audible inhale. After an uncomfortably silent moment he chuckled and leaned forward, "I must apologize, it's been a very long day of traveling and my behavior must be unnerving, to say the least."

The cabby shrugged, "No worries here, pal. I've seen all types in this cab."

"I'm sure you have," the man nodded, "But none like me."

"Pardon?"

The cabby could feel the man's smirk growing behind him, as though the air in the car chilled with every increased curve in his lips. "You've seen many types, but you've never seen any like me, have you?"

"I'm not sure what you—"

"You know what I mean, and my question is sincere. Have you—or have you not—encountered another like me? Or have any of your colleagues recounted any like me in their recent dealings?"

"Listen, man, I only thought it was weird that you wanted visit the high school in the middle of the night. I ain't calling you a freak or nothing, and I definitely don't know what you mean by others like you. You just another fare after all, y'know."

The man nodded slowly, "Yes. Another fare," he looked out the window. "A teacher."

The cabby looked back at the mirror, "What's that?"

"You were curious about the school; I used to be a teacher there."

"You don't say," the cabby peaked over his shoulder to check for oncoming traffic before signaling and turning to the neighboring lane. He was surprised to find that getting out of the airport was easier than usual; the customary line of cars inching impatiently forward and honking at one another seeming to have taken a break at that very moment and giving him a clear path through. Settled by this, he eased back in his seat before peaking back at the man in the backseat. "So why'd you stop?"

The man didn't seem to hear him at first as he peered out through the window at the rain-slicked city. The awkward silence stretched for some time before he finally parted his lips, "Family."

"Oh yea?" The cabby smiled politely for effect, "I got a sister in Paris." He shook his head with a scoff, "She visited there a few years back and decided to marry this wine-maker she met. The folks complained about her moving out of the country, but—y'know—what're y'gonna do?"

The man acknowledged this with a soft hum and a single nod, still keeping his gaze aimed out the window.

The cabby frowned, feeling the discomfort creep up his spine like chilled spider legs.

As though the fare could sense this, he turned his head to face the rearview mirror and the cabby's eyes reflected therein, "Is she happy?"

"Huh?" The cabby suppressed the shudder he felt in his shoulders.

"Your sister," the man clarified, "Is she happy in Paris?"

"Oh, yea. Yea, she is. She whines about not being able to see us as often as she used to, but we always got Christmas."

"Yes. There's always that," the man's eyes shifted back towards the window and his face dragged after.

"So who were you visiting?" The cabby pressed, not wanting to face the silence for too long.

The man blinked, but didn't look away from the window, "I'm sorry."

The cabby gulped, "You said you were visiting family…?"

The man shook his head, "No I didn't. I said I stopped teaching because of family."

"But…" The cabby thought for a moment, "wouldn't you have been visiting if you left your teaching job?"

"Not at all," the man's tone remained calm and polite. "My family is not the type one willingly visits. I was running from them."

The cabby furrowed his brow, "Running? Why on earth would you—"

"Some families aren't as loving as others," the man interrupted, "Sometimes it's safer *not* to be around them."

"So—what?—you owe them money or something?"

The man scoffed, "If only it were that simple." He shook his head. "No. Money I've got; more than I or any beneficiaries will ever need, in fact. No, the people I'm running from are after much more than that."

"Jesus-H-Chri—are they dangerous?" The cabby asked, remembering the man's questions about others like him. As the pieces came together, he felt himself getting more and more nervous. Maybe this fare was a member of the mafia... or worse! He bit his lip and pulled a dry piece of skin free, almost instantly tasting blood.

Had he just put his own life in danger by picking up this man?

"Very dangerous," The man nodded, "But you have nothing to worry about."

"But you just said—"

The man turned his gaze towards him, "*Nothing* to worry about."

The cabby's eyes closed tightly for a moment as a sudden pain gripped his temples. His body slackened, his foot lifting from the accelerator briefly. The taxi swerved slightly in the lane as it passed a Sheriff's patrol car, but the jerked as the wheel seemed to catch itself and the cabby was distantly aware that his taxi was driving itself.

"What in the..."

"Relax and take the wheel," the man's voice was calm and steady, "You're about to be pulled over."

"What did you—"

The dark, rain-slicked road went alive with flashes of red and blue as the wail of a siren sounded behind them.

"Oh shit!" The cabby cursed.

"It's fine," the man assured him, "Just relax. You have nothing to worry about."

"Why do you keep—"

"*Nothing* to worry about."

The cabby felt his mind flutter again, but as his body fell

slack behind the wheel this time the cab seemed prepared and maintained its speed and course without him.

In the neighboring lane, a blood-red sports car honked its horn as it rocketed past the pursuing cop car; a beer bottle flying from the window and smashing against the patrol car's windshield.

"What in the world...?" The cabby watched as the sports car gunned its engine and rocketed by them.

Sure enough, the Sherriff steered into the other lane; shifting his focus on the other car and driving by the taxi.

The cabby stared for a moment and tilted his head to see the man in his mirror. How had he...?

He shook his head as another wave of pain hit him. Bad migraine; probably one of his worsts. Lucky he had medicine in the glove box.

The cabby was halfway through reaching across the seat to retrieve his pain killers before he suddenly remembered he'd never suffered a migraine before and that there was *nothing* in the glove—

As his fingers triggered the latch on the compartment and dropped it open he saw the prescription bottle.

"What the hell?"

"*Nothing* to worry about," the man repeated.

Another wave of dizziness.

The cabby nodded and popped a few of the pills and washed it down with the nearly full can of Rip It in the cup holder. As the sweet, ice-cold beverage carried the capsules down his throat, he smiled.

The man was right!

He had no reason to worry.

"So how was your—" the cabby paused. What had they been talking about again?

In the distance, the high school came into view and he let out a relieved sigh. Something about this fare was creeping him out and he would be more-than-glad to be rid of him. Pulling up to the empty building, he shifted into "park" and forced himself to face the man.

"Here we are. You want me to keep the meter running?"

"No need," the man began to gather his things to get out, "I can walk the rest of the way. What do I owe you?"

"Thirty-two forty-five," the cabby announced after a quick look at the meter.

The man smiled and nodded as he stepped out of the back, pulling his bag and walking stick along with him. Quickly and methodically he worked his way around the back of the cab and stopped at the driver's side window, reaching into his pocket. The driver, not happy about having to open his window in the rain, reluctantly pressed the switch and recoiled as the cold, wet air swept in through the opening.

"Thanks for the chat," the man said as he held out his hand and pressed a folded bill into the cabby's own. "Keep the change."

The cabby smiled and opened his palm to make sure he hadn't just been handed a twenty. As the hundred dollar bill came into view, his eyes lit up.

"Whoa! You sure?" he asked.

The man smiled and nodded, "I'm always sure."

"Hey, thanks!" The cabby smiled, feeling bad for ever having thought poorly of the man. Quickly, he tucked the bill away.

"It's no problem," the man assured him, "No problem at all."

Still beaming, the cabby nodded and rolled up his window as he slowly pulled away from the school.

The man stood in the rain for a moment as he watched the taxi grow more and more distant until it turned off onto a new street. When he was sure that the driver was out of his range he lifted the hold he'd had on his mind. It hadn't been too difficult to ease the driver's panicking mind—no more than it had been convincing him that the crumpled dollar bill was something of far greater value. Of course, by the time the poor man realized that he'd been tricked he'd be long gone.

Sighing, he turned away from the street to face the school and allowed the wave of nostalgia to crash over him. It had been a very long time since he'd last seen it, and he suddenly realized that he'd missed it a great deal more than he'd ever thought he would. For a long time he stood and stared, letting the life he'd abandoned flash in tiny bursts in his mind. He knew that any normal human being would have been hindered by the rain and cold, but the truth was he didn't feel the biting sting—hadn't felt it in so long that he'd forgotten what cold was.

He wasn't sure, in the long run, why he'd had the cab driver bring him here. After all, he hadn't come all this way just to be reminded of the past. In many ways, he supposed he was delaying what needed to happen—what he'd come back for in the first place. Unfortunately time was against him, and as the rain picked up and the wind kicked up his coattails he turned away from the school and started up the street.

"I'm coming, Xander," he whispered to himself, "And so are they..."

DARK.
GRITTY.
SURREAL.

NATHAN SQUIERS (AKA THE LITERARY DARK EMPEROR) resides in Upstate NY with his wife and fellow author, Megan J. Parker. Nathan is usually found in his writing lair where he is either typing away at his latest work or staring out the window as he plots a new idea in the subspace of his mind. His first series, Crimson Shadow, is a bestseller on Amazon in both Dark Fantasy and Horror categories. Along with that, his Death Metal novel two awards in 2013 for best paranormal thriller and best occult. Nathan Squiers was awarded 2012's best indie author of the year and has since then been rampaging the literary world with his take on vampires and the paranormal world.